THE SCENT OF COLOR

by
LANA LAFORTUNE

Published by Lana LaFortune

Copyright 2015 by Lana LaFortune

Editing by Cara Quinlan

Cover design by Rosie Lemons
Cover photograph by Lana LaFortune

All rights reserved

The main and supporting characters are entirely fictional. Any resemblance to actual events is purely coincidental. The settings, however, are real with an occasional name change. Some minor characters are based on real people.

This book is licensed for your personal enjoyment only.
Thank you for respecting the hard work of this author.

ACKNOWLEDGEMENTS

With sincere gratitude I want to thank the Marines and soldiers and airmen who, since the start of the war, have courageously shared their stories, their insights, their pain, and triumphs with me. I especially need to thank Marine Sergeants Oscar Garcia and Travis Walker for their technical military assistance.

I want to thank the soldiers at Ft. Dix for allowing me to experience the reconstructed "little Fallujah" and FOB; the reenactments and practice of securing a building, taking fire, and forming a perimeter; treating and evacuating a wounded soldier; and all the other exercises to prepare soldiers for upcoming battles. Although it wasn't the real deal, I was assured it was a close approximation.

I have to thank Susan Thompson who took me by the hand and introduced me to self-publishing. Through her patient consultation I also learned about copyright laws, cover design, and editing. She must be pleased to see the Oxford commas.

I want to thank, too, Cara Quinlan, my editor, who patiently, tenaciously, brought this book into publishable form. Thanks goes, also, to Rosie Lemons, who designed the cover, and Lucinda Campbell who made the magic happen in formatting. I can't forget Jennifer Lonack who held my hand through web designing, tutored me through Facebook, and served as my overall cheerleader.

Probably at the top of the list I should thank Col (R) Gregory Meyer for his encouragement and belief in me as a writer, and as a friend, for all these years.

Finally, I must thank our brave warriors and their families in all the branches of service, for their courage, dedication, and sacrifice. It is for you that I have written this book, so others might understand that even when it's over, it's not necessarily over for you. You are the bravest and best and I thank you from the bottom of my heart.

The Scent of Color
TABLE OF CONTENTS

CHAPTER 1 – Bloomfield Hills, Michigan	9
CHAPTER 2 – Second Thoughts	27
CHAPTER 3 – Rome	31
CHAPTER 4 – The Vatican	48
CHAPTER 5 – Cinque Terre	60
CHAPTER 6 – Nice	83
CHAPTER 7 – Les Baux	93
CHAPTER 8 – The Luberon	102
CHAPTER 9 – Arles	111
CHAPTER 10 – Egypt	119
CHAPTER 11 – The Nile	130
CHAPTER 12 – Turkey	153
CHAPTER 13 – Home	177
CHAPTER 14 – Newark	183
CHAPTER 15 – New York	191
CHAPTER 16 – Alaska	195
CHAPTER 17 – Kaktovik	207
CHAPTER 18 – Garmisch-Partenkirchen	250
CHAPTER 19 – Venice	263
CHAPTER 20 – After the Concert	275
CHAPTER 21 – More Venice	289
CHAPTER 22 – Paris	313
CHAPTER 23 – Back in Newark	339
CHAPTER 24 – Harlem	355
NOTES: Remi's Request	380
ADDITIONAL NOTES: Deidre's Request	384
ONE FINAL NOTE	384
ABOUT THE AUTHOR	385
CONNECT WITH LANA LAFORTUNE	385
BOOK CLUB DISCUSSION QUESTIONS	386

DEDICATED TO THE

MEMORY OF

HLN

THE SCENT OF COLOR

CHAPTER 1

BLOOMFIELD HILLS, MICHIGAN
April 2011

SHE WOKE SUDDENLY from the dream, sat bolt upright, eyes desperate for the clock. 4:20, the face told her. Reassured, Deidre Sinclair relaxed, though she realized the nightmare of her life was just beginning. How much time? Sixty minutes to an hour. Twenty-four hours to a day. Thirty days to a month. Six months. She mentally calculated 259,200 minutes, each slipping silently into oblivion. Time, she knew, was her enemy.

* * * * *

SUNDAY WAS FAMILY day, which her mother deemed should be honored with a formal dinner, appropriate dress, and, typically, guests. Her grandmother arrived, as she did every Sunday of Deidre's life, and insisted on speaking French, "the only truly cultured language." It was a beautiful language, but Deidre simply had no talent for it, or, for that matter, any other language. Braille. How would she ever learn Braille?

Her grandmother hugged her and whispered in her ear, "We'll get through this, be assured," as if somehow she could change the inevitable.

"Yes, Grandmama."

The Louis XIV table seated sixteen, but shouting over its expanse seemed excessive, even to the Sinclairs. The family, therefore, chose the more practical solution of sitting at the end farthest from the kitchen.

From these seats the family could see the flames of the candelabra flickering in the drawing room. The polished surface of the grand piano reproduced the yellow flames to near perfection. The prisms of the Venetian chandelier sparkling above their heads added to the opulent atmosphere.

At first the dinner conversation was general, but the elephant in the room trumpeted when Deidre announced, "I've decided not to return to college."

"I beg your pardon?" her father said.

"Deidre, isn't that a little extreme?"

Deidre wanted to laugh hearing that from her mother, Janet Sinclair, the famous over-the-top dramatist. Calmly, she answered, "I just wanted you to know."

"We've already contacted the Dean's office and they're making arrangements for you to do both semesters this summer."

"You contacted the Dean's office? No. That's not what I want." Failure to listen had been her mother's chief talent throughout Deidre's entire childhood, but now that she was no longer a child she would be heard.

Ever the diplomat, her father cleared his throat. "Yes, it will be hard work, Deidre, but it is the most practical thing to do. Once you...once you are sightless, school will be nearly impossible to finish."

"So what."

"So what! You have to graduate!" her mother declared.

"Why? Who made that rule?"

"But, Deidre, you always wanted a college degree," her grandmother said.

"I'm not opposed to a degree. I'm just not going to spend the last months of my seeing life looking at books." She raised her hand to stop them from interrupting. "I want to change the timeline. I want to take my Grand Tour early, while I can still see. I'll worry about school afterwards."

"Well, I can understand—"

"Cassie is going to start the trip with me, but then she has to go back to school."

Her parents looked at each other.

"I've decided I don't want to just see Rome and the pyramids and the Eiffel Tower. I want to really immerse myself in the culture."

"Too many sociology classes," her father said.

"I do want to see all the famous sites, of course, but I don't want to be on a tour bus and see only what the tour company thinks I should see."

"I understand, darling, but there isn't enough time for all of that," her mother said in an attempt at practicality.

"This takes planning and money," her father said.

"The money, we have," her grandmother said.

"Yes, yes, we can finance it," he said. "Of course, of course. But the plans. And you say Cassandra will leave you when you are the most…the most…vulnerable?"

"Yes, but I've worked it all out. First I want—"

"I am not going to listen to this, Deidre." Her mother raised her voice.

"Janet, let's hear what she has to say. Please." Her father nodded for Deidre to continue.

Deidre took a nervous breath. "Just before finals we had a guest lecturer come in, a photographer. He's traveled all over the world taking pictures, and, oh, Daddy, you should see where he's been! He's been on safari and climbed the Alps and seen the northern lights and the midnight sun and everything. Daddy, this is the answer! He knows where to go, and he sees what I want to see. He knows how to just hop on a plane and go. Maybe his next trip is all planned out and he'll take me along. It's perfect. Don't you see?"

James Sinclair looked into his daughter's gray eyes, eyes that soon would no longer see him. He turned away so she wouldn't see the emotion filling his own. The room was quiet. Deidre could see some calculation playing out in his mind. She looked from one face to the other. Her grandmother was clearly on her side. Her mother's face was set in stubborn opposition. Her father—he was the key. If she could convince him he might be able to convince her mother. Maybe.

Sinclair finally broke the silence. Ignoring Deidre, he gave his wife a hard look. "I think she should do it."

"Absolutely not! I will not let my only child get on an airplane and fly around the world with some strange man when she is on the verge of—"

"I think she should do it."

"Well, she isn't going to! What is the matter with you? Don't you see the danger?"

"She's growing up, Janet."

"No!"

"This is her last chance."

"Aren't you listening? No, no, no!"

He took a deep breath, set his jaw, and said, "Janet, I've held this ace for nearly twenty years. Now I'm playing it."

A look of disbelief fluttered across her lovely face.

Deidre was absorbed in the drama unfolding before her. Her mother seemed off balance, struggling to understand her husband's words. Then she re-engaged, determined to have her way.

"No! Not this time, for God's sake!" Her face, red with rage, turned ashen with fear as she looked at her husband's hardened features.

She looked stunned, disbelieving. But Sinclair didn't waver.

"It's my call." His voice was unyielding, like tempered steel.

"I'm her mother."

"My call."

She took a swallow of wine. A war was waging within her.

Deidre could see her fighting for composure. She had never seen this side of her parents' relationship. What was going on?

Finally, after several long minutes, Janet made one last hopeless effort. "Please don't do this."

"She needs this."

"You're sure?"

"I'm sure."

An understanding passed between them. Deidre's mother nodded in defeat.

Defeat. No one defeated Janet Sinclair. Deidre waited in confused anticipation.

Another minute passed, but it seemed longer. "It actually sounds plausible, doesn't it?" her mother finally said calmly, as though no one else had witnessed the battle.

Some kind of miracle had just transpired in front of Deidre, here, at her own dining room table.

Deidre leapt up from her chair and ran to her mother's side. "Yes, it is plausible. It really could work. You know it could." She almost reached out to hug her, but restrained herself and took her mother's hand instead. Could this be happening? Deidre wondered. If this was a trick, she had never before seen such a strategy. She looked over at her father, who smiled back. So it was real! She squeezed her mother's hand in gratitude.

"Always so full of ideas," James said. "Always so smart; never takes 'no' for an answer."

Deidre rushed to his side. He hugged her. "You are a spoiled girl who turned out well."

"I love you, Daddy. I love you, Mother."

Her father smiled. "Ah, baby, we love you, too. I don't want you to count on anything just yet, but let me see what our money can buy."

SPRING WAS PARTICULARLY vivid. March had been warm, but was pushed aside by an even warmer April, which soon gave way to the longer days of May. Nighttime rains turned to glistening blue mornings. The flowers bloomed early and the lawns turned emerald green. The smell of cut grass mingled with blossoming fruit trees, freshly turned gardens, and earthworms. Springtime birds swelled with song as they greeted the day, charmed their mates, and built their nests. The world seemed alive with hope.

Finding Remi Lamont didn't prove too difficult. The university kept a list of guest lecturers, along with their vitas and contact information. Sinclair hired a firm to find out about the man's character, but a search turned up nothing particularly objectionable. In fact, his major weakness—modest income—might be exploited to Sinclair's advantage. First, he needed to meet Lamont; it was the only way to know what the man was really about. Perhaps a showing here at the house…

* * * * *

REMI LAMONT HAD accepted the invitation to be the featured photographer and exhibit his work at the Whittier Mansion, now the home of the James Sinclair family. The opportunity both pleased him and made him suspicious. He was pleased because maybe he could bring in a little money. He was suspicious because invitations like this didn't happen to people like him.

He drove to the house on the morning of the exhibit to set up the boxes of framed photos that had arrived the previous day. Preparing for the show—unpacking, selecting, and placing pictures, then watching as the interior decorator Sinclair had hired rearranged them—took several hours. People dropped by throughout the afternoon to watch the set up. Mrs. Sinclair was the biggest surprise. She might have been an actress with her good looks, self-confidence, and air of entitlement. She certainly caught Remi's attention, and when she mentioned a daughter, he found himself wondering if the acorn looked as good as the tree. Well, he imagined, he'd find out soon enough.

That evening, the upper strata of Detroit society filled the gallery at the Manor. The guests, champagne flutes in hand, wandered around the large room admiring his photos.

A waiter approached Remi with a silver tray of unfamiliar edibles. "Canapés, sir?"

"What's the difference between a canapé, appetizer, hors d'oeuvre, and a snack?"

"Sir?"

"Never mind." Remi waved him away, a tinge of annoyance on his face. Pretentiousness aggravated him.

He had to admit, though, that there was quite a turn out. He'd already taken three orders, large ones. How had Sinclair gathered so many people on such short notice? What kind of power did he wield?

As if summoned by Remi's thoughts, James Sinclair suddenly appeared at his elbow. He was shorter than Remi—but most men were—and slightly stocky. A well-tailored suit concealed his extra weight. Remi, on the other hand, was well cut and even his ten-year old blazer looked good on his tall, muscular frame.

"So how is it, Mr. Sinclair, that you learned of my work?"

"I wish I could say I have been a longtime fan, but…"

"Well, then, I'd know you were flattering me. I've only had a few shows. I think Detroit is number three, in fact."

"Good publicist. You filled half a page in Sunday's *News*."

"Ah, the newspaper, then."

"No. Actually, you spoke at my daughter's school last month. You impressed her, and your photography impresses me. You do have an interesting way of seeing things, Remi." Sinclair raised his hand to stop the younger man's protest. "And this isn't empty flattery."

"Good, because I haven't much use for it," Remi said.

"I'm curious—how do you fund your adventures?" Sinclair gestured to the scene of a mountain lion taking down an antelope.

"The best I can."

"I take it you are not independently wealthy, have no benefactor, no recent lottery winnings…"

Remi laughed. "None that have appeared lately."

"And, so far, you haven't sold enough to enjoy the luxury of traveling around the world and taking more pictures."

Remi looked down to hide a bit of a smile. "No, I can't say I've reached that level yet."

"I think that's the problem with so much of our artistic talent. They spend the first half of their career fighting for exposure, when those are the very years they should be exploring the world and perfecting their craft, not running around waiting tables just to scratch a few dollars together so they can—"

"I don't wait tables." Remi looked the older man squarely in the eye.

"Well, that was just a figure of speech," Sinclair said brusquely. Then, in a more conciliatory tone, he asked, "What do you do when you are not taking pictures?"

"Speaking at colleges, mostly. An occasional sale here or there."

"And before you became a photographer?"

"Marine Corps."

"Infantry?"

"Yeah." He took a swallow of his drink. "And after that I took a contract job."

"In the Middle East?"

Remi nodded. "Blackwater." He used the term most civilians were familiar with.

Sinclair raised an eyebrow. "A mercenary?"

"Perhaps. Interesting perspective over there in Afghanistan and Iraq."

"I can imagine. And do you still supplement your income with that kind of work?"

"Not if I can help it."

"Dangerous?"

"Yeah, but for me, the danger was the attraction, not the problem." He smiled and paused for a moment to find the right words. "That interesting perspective isn't one I liked very much. It poisons you after a while. And that poison is cumulative. You leave a little bit of yourself on the battlefield every time. The better parts. Pretty soon there isn't much left."

"Is there anything good about going to war? Or that danger you speak of?"

"The chance to serve your country. A chance to do something more than you thought you could do. Those are good things. But the fun part is the adrenaline rush, until you get addicted to it. Then *that* becomes your new normal."

"I can certainly understand the lure of adrenaline." Sinclair chuckled. "Are you a religious man, Remi?"

Remi gazed at his host. *What the devil is the man up to?*

"Not much. Raised Catholic, but once I grew up it didn't fit."

"Before or after the war?"

"I grew up in Iraq."

"So during."

Remi shrugged to cover his increasing discomfort.

"Religion is a very strange thing," Sinclair said. "In my experience, there are four kinds of people. First are the truly religious people who live by their church credo, the kind you want to do business with. Next are those who have no creed and no morals at all. Too many in the city at the moment. Then there are people who wear their religion like a banner but don't have an ounce of morality. Look at half of our politicians, or maybe all of them. And the last are those who are moral but have no use for religion. How would you rate yourself?"

Curiouser and curiouser. What rabbit hole have I fallen into?

"Well, I'm not a businessman, I don't live in Detroit, and I'm not a politician. Let's say that I'm spiritual but with my own individual code, or 'morality' if you prefer."

"So how do you feel about rules?"

Was this some kind of interview? For what?

"I guess I believe that rules were made to serve man. Man wasn't made to serve rules. Break 'em when they stop being useful, or get in the way."

"And sometimes suffer the consequences?"

"And sometimes suffer the consequences," Remi agreed.

Sinclair slapped him on the back. "A man after my own heart."

They each took a swallow of champagne.

"I have a proposition for you," Sinclair said.

Here it comes.

"What if I offered you patronage for the next six months or so?

Paid expenses to travel throughout the world. The locations would be negotiable, but you would also have some free rein to choose."

"Negotiable, huh? Such as…?"

"Well, some of the tourist sights, Paris, the Riviera, Rome—"

"That's not what I shoot." Remi swept his arm around the room to indicate his photos. "I'm more into nature. Not a city guy."

"But I see portraits. Surely you could find interesting people in the cities."

Remi ran his hand through his hair. "What's your gig, Mr. Sinclair? I don't take you for a smuggler. And for some reason, patron of the arts just doesn't suit you either."

Sinclair laughed. "Ah, insightful as well as talented."

"So why would you pay me to 'perfect my craft,' as you put it, while dictating my itinerary—"

"*Some* of your itinerary," Sinclair interrupted.

"—dictating *some* of my itinerary, and not benefit from it in the long run? Because, Mr. Sinclair, the one thing I'm sure of," Remi said looking the older man in the eye as he took a swallow from his glass, "you're no fool."

"No, Remi, I am not a fool. I am a father." The older man smiled.

Remi took another swallow of wine. "Not the answer I expected."

"I am the father of a young woman, and I want to give her the trip of a lifetime. Her mother and I cannot accompany her. Her friend, well, she is no more experienced than Deidre. And they need—"

"Whoa, whoa, whoa, whoa, whoa. You want me to chaperone two girls on some round-the-world trip? Are you serious? I am truly sorry, Mr. Sinclair, that you are somehow under the impression that I would have any time, interest, or aptitude to babysit—"

"Mr. Lamont! Please!" Heads turned in their direction. Sinclair lowered his voice. "The girls, Deidre and Cassandra, are not children. They are young adults, but they have led, shall we say, sheltered lives."

Remi caught the scene of several guests seated across the room, lounging in plush chairs, as waiters bent to serve them. Nearby, someone spilled his drink and walked away, but one of the servers had it sopped up within seconds. A group of teen boys were trying to impress a girl and he saw the sparkle of diamonds as one lad pulled up his sleeve to look at his watch.

"Sheltered lives?" Remi said. "I can believe it."

Sinclair continued. "There are many people I could ask—"

"Good. Ask them."

"But I want someone who can provide protection, who is wise to the ways of the world, and who can show my daughter…" His voice broke and it took a moment to compose himself and start again. "Who sees the world, really *sees* the world, and can share that gift with her."

"Mr. Sinclair—"

Sinclair held up his hand. "And in exchange, after covering the highlights on my daughter's list, you will have at least half the time to go where you want, take her—"

"Take her. Now you see that's the problem," he said in annoyance.

"Take her with you and show her things she doesn't even know to ask for."

"Mr. Sinclair, thank you for your offer and for this evening, but quite frankly, sir, I respectfully decline." Setting his glass down, Remi turned away and headed toward the other end of the gallery.

He passed an attractive young woman with chestnut hair walking toward him, but he was too ticked off to respond, though, as an afterthought, he noticed the scent of citrus and vanilla.

Looking over her shoulder at the back of the tall man, Deidre continued on to her father's side.

"Daddy? That's Mr. Lamont, isn't it? What do you think?"

"Yes. Yes," he said thoughtfully. "I think he might be suitable. I like him. He's a bit stubborn, but…Why don't you go be charming, Deidre? I think a woman's touch is what's needed now."

She squeezed her father's arm with a smile.

Deidre crossed the thickly carpeted room eager to meet her future travel guide.

"Mr. Lamont?"

He turned toward the voice, with a stiff smile, until he actually saw her, looked at her. Then his face relaxed and a natural appreciation filled his eyes.

Her dark wavy hair fell softly down her back. Her intelligent eyes were captivating. Her skin was smooth and flawless, fair like porcelain poured over fine bones.

She held out her hand. He took it.

"I go by Remi."

"I'm Deidre Sinclair." She smiled.

The muscles around his eyes tightened when she said her name. "Nice to make your acquaintance."

She pulled her hair over one shoulder, her gray eyes searching his brown ones. They stood there—he appraised her, she appraised him, each one fully aware of what the other was doing.

"I understand you are planning a trip around the world."

"Oh, so that's what you and Father were talking about. I thought perhaps it was photography."

"Well, it was that, too."

"I can tell you have been everywhere," she said.

"Not everywhere, just these places." Remi indicated his photos.

"But certainly a family of your means has traveled, too."

She peered at one of the photos.

"No, not much."

"That surprises me."

"It's Mother. She's terrified of planes."

"Really?"

"She used to fly, when she was young. But there was a crash. Pilot error, they say."

"Small plane?"

Deidre looked up at him. "Yes, but her phobia extends to all forms of flying, for her and for us. Even Daddy tries to limit his trips, to spare her. But I've finally gotten her to agree to let me go on a world tour."

He noticed how she held his gaze steadily, in a curious way, not challenging, and her lips were that natural red color that no lipstick could enhance. Still, the gloss she spread on them and the way her mouth moved…

"—it's so impressive."

"I'm sorry, what were you saying?"

"Just you've been to so many places, and seen so many things."

He followed Deidre as she walked over to one of his photos, looked at it closely, and then raised her eyes to his.

"Where was this taken?"

"Australia. Primary habitat of kangaroos," he teased under the gaze of a curious joey looking straight into the camera lens.

"Yes, of course," she said, a blush spreading across her face.

She moved to the next photo that showed a lioness defending her kill.

"This was taken in Kenya."

She paused longer at the next one, where a penguin family clustered protectively over their young.

"These cute little guys posed for me near the South Pole."

"I like it."

They were nearing the end of the display.

"And this one?"

"Hmm, oh, yeah, Scotland, the Isle of Mull. I was trying to find a waterfall, but took a wrong turn. I ended up face-to-face with these two rams at the sea." He smiled at the memory. "They didn't much fancy me pointing my camera at them. Three frames were all I got before they charged. Well, one of them charged."

He guided her to the next picture.

"Charged? So what happened?"

He turned back to her pretending he'd forgotten what they'd been talking about. Then he let a smile touch the corner of his mouth. "Oh, well, I grabbed a rock, about yay big…" He formed his hand into a fist the size of a large grapefruit. "And threw it hard. I nicked the first one and grabbed another rock, hollering and waving my arms as I pitched it at the second guy."

He turned back to another picture.

"And?"

Remi smiled down at her.

"I guess they decided I wasn't worth the trouble, and so with great dignity, they slowly turned their backs on me so I could see just how big their balls were." Seeing her blush again, he corrected, "Excuse me, their testicles."

"That's worse," she murmured, her cheeks flaming as she concentrated on the carpet nap. "Does that happen often?"

"You mean being upstaged by a ram?"

"No." She laughed. "The rest of it. The charging and all that."

"Yeah. Sometimes. Photography, the kind I do, isn't for distracted fools. You have to pay attention all the time."

"But you do have to take some risks."

"Calculated risks. You have to know what's going on around you. I've seen photographers get so caught up in their work they forget where they are."

"Such as?"

Remi found her easy to talk to. She smelled good, too. A little too much makeup, maybe. Her lips were good. He wished she'd stop flipping her hair, though.

"One guy, from South America, I think, stood still for so long waiting for the perfect shot that he didn't notice the rattlesnake that had decided to sun himself on the toe of his boot." He reached for a glass from a passing waiter. "Now *that* was a tricky situation. He couldn't shoot it or he'd lose a toe. He couldn't shake it off or it might strike." He smiled and started to walk away, but she grabbed his arm and held it a few seconds longer than he would have expected. It caught his attention on a different plane.

"So what happened? You are the worst storyteller, by the way!"

He grinned. "Somebody went for a mongoose, but I left before that fun began."

"Oh." Deidre turned to inspect the last photo, then turned back suddenly. "Wait a minute. Don't mongooses attack cobras?"

Remi laughed and ran his hand through his hair. "I think you might be right."

After leaving the photo exhibit, they walked to the far side of the gallery and looked at the paintings hanging on the damasked wall. He recognized the work of Renoir, but had never seen that particular painting in any art book. He peered closely at water lilies in a pond, looking for Monet's signature. It was there. Throughout this wing of the gallery, the walls were dotted with well-executed paintings, many created by famous artists.

They stopped to stare at the portrait of a lovely aristocratic woman wearing a silver-gray gown and powdered wig, her hands gracefully folded in her lap. She wore a chain of pearls loose around her throat and a large ring on one long, graceful finger.

"A relative?"

"No, just a—This was the first painting I studied in my humanities class."

"Because?"

"I was lazy, and we owned it."

Remi laughed. Hearing her own words, Deidre laughed, too.

"That sounds fairly pretentious, doesn't it? I didn't mean it to be." She looked back at the portrait. "When I was young, I thought I wanted to be a grand lady just like her. I insisted on having my portrait done for graduation—high school graduation," she clarified.

"You had your portrait done?" It was an incredible concept to Remi.

"Yes." She gave him a thoughtful smile, her brow wrinkling slightly. "While he was painting, the artist had described—either me or the portrait, I don't know which—as 'Seductive vulnerability underlying the strength and beauty.' I wish the portrait lived up to the description."

"You don't like it?"

"It's not her," Deidre said, pointing to the massive painting.

"She's a statue," Remi added. "There's no personality, no depth to her. She's all show in her jewels and satins and velvet chair."

"You're probably right," Deidre said. "Still, someone thought enough about her to have her portrait done. She'll be admired forever."

"As a marble statue."

They continued walking around the room.

"You're not very patient, are you?" he said.

"No. Not my strong suit."

"Me neither. So what is your strong suit?"

"Curiosity. But it killed the cat, you know."

Remi smiled. "So what would you like to see in your travels?" Perhaps, he thought, she wouldn't be a total pain in the ass. Maybe he could stand babysitting her, for a while, maybe a few months. He could try to work it out so they went to his places first. And then, if she turned into a headache, he could take her back to her father and let him take her to see Paris and Rome and the pyramids.

CHAPTER 2

SECOND THOUGHTS

REMI PARKED HIS car in the double-wide circular drive and got out. The guard at the gate had probably announced him by now.

Walking up to the house Remi thought, I must be out of my mind.

He was more convinced of it as he waited in the foyer.

"You're early," Deidre called down to him over the banister.

"Your mother said you're always late," he called back to her.

"She exaggerates. I'm not *always* late."

It was the first of June, and she looked as fresh as the spring.

That, he thought, wasn't helping. He was determined to be in a foul mood.

"I want to see what you're packing. I don't have much experience traveling with women, but one thing I know for sure is they always take too much."

Deidre frowned. "How much is too much?"

"I'm limiting you to one suitcase. A carry-on would be better." He gave her a defiant look, hoping she would challenge him.

"You must be kidding!"

"Nope. That's why I'm here, to make sure what you think you *need* fits into one bag." His sarcasm was thick.

"That, Remi Lamont, is impossible!"

"Then this trip, Ms. Sinclair, is equally impossible!"

At that, she stomped out of sight.

James Sinclair came out of his study. "Ah, the women-and-their-luggage war. Good luck, young man."

"Not negotiable," he muttered crossly.

"You're the boss." Sinclair chuckled. "But may I suggest you pick your battles carefully?"

Remi scowled. "Meaning?"

"My daughter is fairly confident that she doesn't make mistakes, which is reinforced by the fact that she rarely does."

"Because everyone gives in to her and she never discovers there might be a better way."

Sinclair shrugged. "Could be. I'm just saying, sometimes it's okay to yield to her preference. Experience has a way of teaching some interesting lessons." Seeing the set of Remi's jaw, Sinclair took him by the elbow. "Now let's go into the library and finalize the terms of the arrangement. I'm making hotel reservations, so I want to nail down this itinerary."

UPSTAIRS, DEIDRE muttered with angry restraint, "'One suitcase,' he says. One bloody suitcase!"

She brushed by Cassie, who had heard the exchange on the stairs.

"No one can exist with one suitcase," Deidre said. "We'll be in frigid Alaska, sweltering Egypt, and everything in between! Impossible! Who does he think he is, dictating what I can pack? 'A carry on would be better!'" she mocked. "Pure insanity!"

Cassie sighed. "I don't like it much, either, but I suppose he doesn't see himself as our porter."

"Of course not. We'll hire people. And when we can't, he can help out sometimes." Deidre jerked out a pair of silver high heels. "He's got muscles, right?"

"He's our tour guide, not our servant. What's gotten into you?"

Deidre slumped onto the bed. "I don't know. This trip was supposed to be fun, but our *tour guide* just seems bent on making me as miserable as he can."

Cassie sat down next to her. "He seems okay to me. Why do you think that?"

Deidre picked up a silk scarf and fingered the edges.

"While we were setting up the itinerary, he wanted to do all of *his* things first. You'd be back in school before we even got to Europe. I wouldn't have it. I insisted we start in Rome and see Italy first. All he would agree to was Rome, Milan, and the Italian Riviera."

"The Italian Riviera?" Cassie asked.

"Cinque Terre. He said we can do Florence and Venice afterwards, but I think you'll be home by then."

"Why not all together? It doesn't make sense to leave Italy only to return later. Did he have a reason?"

"Something to do with the lavender blooming in France at the end of June."

"Ah, so he actually wants to work on this trip. Amazing concept."

Deidre glared at her friend.

"Listen, I don't care, really. Just traveling and having fun with you for the summer is enough. It doesn't matter where we are."

Deidre sighed.

"So what else has he done?" Cassie asked.

Deidre got up and started pacing. "He calls me 'dear child,' for one thing."

"Oh," Cassie said. "I see."

"I am not a child."

"And he's a hunk."

Turning around, she snapped, "What's that supposed to mean?"

"Oh, nothing. Just boy-girl stuff."

"What are you talking about 'boy-girl stuff'? He's old enough to be my father! Well, nearly."

"So what? That is one sexy man. I don't care if he's forty, fifty, even. So he's pulling your pigtail, Deidre. Go with it." Cassie went to her suitcases and began taking things out. "I just wish he'd pull mine."

"I'll see if I can arrange that."

Deidre looked at the suitcases, an idea forming. She slowly took out a wrinkle resistant top and rolled it tightly, condensing it small enough to fit into a loafer. The toes of her high heels would hold nylons and silk panties. Lacy bras would fit into their arches.

She began to rearrange the clothes, rolling, squeezing, and tucking things into smaller and denser bundles. Soon the base level of one suitcase was carefully finished.

The two girls worked in silence. Cassie's side of the bed was littered with clothes she had to leave at home, while Deidre industriously moved items from one suitcase to the other, until the larger one was packed. She had to remove a few extravagant things, like her favorite gold-tipped high heels and a flattering beaded dress, but overall she had managed to pack the contents of both suitcases into one.

"Cassie, come sit on this."

"What are you doing?" Cassandra asked, looking up for the first time.

"Taking only one suitcase," she said triumphantly as Cassie sat on the luggage. The zipper caught on the fur of a vest, but Deidre forced it forward. Finally, it was secure.

Cassie tried to lift it. "What have you done, Dee? This must weigh a hundred pounds!"

"I'm doing what I'm told, taking only one suitcase," she said in an innocent voice as she hung up the sacrificed dress. "I'm sure Monsieur Lamont will be quite pleased."

CHAPTER 3

ROME

AT THE ROME AIRPORT, Remi retrieved their luggage from the carousel. When he lifted Deidre's suitcase, he knew exactly what she had done. His suspicions were confirmed when the yellow tag with the black letters flipped up and the word, "HEAVY," stated the obvious. He let the bag fall and looked up to find her watching him, a look of triumph shone in her eyes despite the sweet smile of her lips. He hadn't taken her for a game player.

All he said as he walked by was, "Your decision. Live with the consequences." He'd be damned if he was going to lift her bag again.

When they had checked into the hotel, Deidre had been right. Bellhops were waiting to handle the luggage. Remi opted to carry his own, anyway. His irritation intensified, though, knowing she had been rescued.

His sour mood continued as he sat in his room. He had chaffed at Sinclair's need to plan every detail of the itinerary. He demanded to have the flexibility to cancel or change plans based on weather, a newly discovered event, or simply on a whim. In the back of his mind, Remi knew he was rebelling like an adolescent. In fact, he actually did like to have a somewhat detailed plan, though flexible enough to change. The thing was, Sinclair didn't need to know that. The concept of unplanned travel was totally alien for the older man. Despite a great deal of argument on Remi's part, Sinclair had booked the hotels anyway, based on the existing itinerary, while conceding that Remi could change any and all reservations.

As Remi looked around the large suite of rooms with baskets of flowers, fruit, and wine, the message was clear: Remi was expected to be the leashed dog, and he would enjoy it. But gilded collar or not, he wasn't having it. He had to get out of there, now. He'd unpack later.

Photo bag slung over his shoulder, he made his way through the lobby, taking note of the dark lounge and well stocked bar. How long would they be in Rome? Long enough to know the bartender? He hoped not.

Rome was exciting, noisy, crowded, and hot, with just a tinge of grittiness. He stepped out of the hotel, and there it was. For no reason, and out of nowhere, it materialized. Like a thick, damp fog, he felt the familiar anxiety of impending danger envelop him. He had to keep moving. To stand still increased his vulnerability. The street was too busy.

Move, his brain directed. He had grabbed a map on his way out of the hotel, but had yet to look at it. He made his way through a crowd of newly arriving tourists descending from a bus. Their carefree chatter enraged him. The closeness of their bodies suffocated him. Their smell sickened him. Mostly, their ignorance of the danger all around them infuriated him.

His destination was uncertain. He just needed air. Once free of the tourists, he crossed the street, keeping the stone wall to his right. Most Marines preferred the opposite, but he was left-handed and wanted free range on that side. Carrying his camera bag over his right shoulder kept it shielded and more secure, too.

He focused on slowing his breathing. He needed a distraction, some way to calm his anxiety. Women tended to be the most effective, the quickest diversion. He looked around, observing as he walked. What did he see? The stereotypes. Yes, the big-hearted, pasta-eating, big-assed mama types were there, along with the reed-thin models in mini-skirts and stilettos. Definitely a distraction.

There was a third type, not mentioned in the guidebooks: the students, lots of students, wearing jeans and backpacking their way through Europe, he supposed. Or else out on summer break. He saw children out playing, too. That was good. A sign of safety. Otherwise, their parents would keep them inside. The tension in his neck and shoulders hovered near the edges, but started to ease as he walked.

The tourists thinned out as he wandered through the *calles* of the less populated places. On one hand, he felt he could breathe easier without the crowds pressing in on him; but on the other, he couldn't shake the sense of being watched. Buildings did that to him. Or walls. They didn't need to have roofs. Tall ones were the worst. His skin crawled and his lower organs contracted. His grip tightened around the barrel of his camera, wishing it was his weapon instead. The instinct wasn't something he could control. He needed to focus on something else, anything else.

He saw a man in profile, backlit, a policeman. He was standing with his hands clasped behind his back in front of a shop window. The sign above read 'Armani.' Along the narrow street, cobblestones still glistened from an early morning rain. The tall, dark buildings on either side of the narrow street rose beyond his viewfinder. A perfect frame. He took the picture.

He walked past the policeman—no, he wasn't a local *Polizia*, he was a *Carabinieri*, the much respected state police. Remi should have recognized the red stripe down the pant leg, like the Marine blood stripe, and the cut of the man's jacket. He slowed and looked through the window that captivated the Roman. Men's suits. Okay, Armani. So what? The government supposedly hired the famous designer to make the *Carabinieri* uniform. He looked at the reflection of the man. Grudgingly, he had to admit it was stylish. The officer met his eyes in the reflection, nodded, and each man headed off in opposite directions.

Eventually, Remi reached the Coliseum. He liked the open area better. He should have come with the girls, he realized. Well, they could take a tour, he thought, either tomorrow or whenever it was scheduled.

Cars and motorbikes zipped around the perimeter of the famous ruin. He didn't expect the cars or pedestrians. Of course, it was a tourist site, so by definition there would be people, but some of them were Romans. The big asses and stilettos gave them away, and the Armani suits. Okay, the bicycles were a clue, too. And the horns. What the hell was up with the horns? Like owning a car with a horn was a status symbol?

How the hell was he going to get a shot? He walked in both directions, knelt down, then considered a shot from a second floor window. Nothing, it seemed, blocked the humanity circling the ancient structure. Obviously, he wasn't getting a picture during the day. Maybe at sunrise. It was June. He could try again at 0500 hours.

Putting his camera away, he went to a nearby vendor selling tourist kitsch. He thumbed through the postcards, cheap quality, and vintage. "Probably before they invented cars," he muttered. Nothing there.

He could go into the Coliseum, get a bit of history. The line was short. A pang of guilt nudged him again. He should do that with the girls. It was definitely on the itinerary. He planned to do as little as possible with his wards, but Deidre's father was expecting something from him.

"Show her the world through a photographer's eye," Sinclair had said. "Give her anything she wants. I'll pay. Don't even consider the cost. And keep her safe."

Two girls walking around Rome without him was probably not Sinclair's definition of safety. Even before Operation Enduring

Freedom, Rome would have set his antennae twitching. Crowds. Tall buildings. Too much opportunity for mischief.

The thing was, he knew—in his rational mind, he *knew*—there were no enemy combatants or sniper rifle pointed at his head, but he couldn't convince his body. He couldn't stop his eyes from scanning the rooftops. Or slow his heart rate when a couple of teens started shoving one another playfully. Or react to the dozens of unexpected things crowds did. He stood for a while with his back against the wall, taking it all in, willing his body to unwind.

"Fuck it," he finally said to himself, and headed toward the Forum.

DEIDRE WALKED back into their hotel room. Cassie looked up expectantly.

"He isn't there. I knocked."

"Could he be in the lobby?"

"How do I know? The man simply has no manners. When he gets back we will definitely have a sit down and go over the rules for comings and goings."

Cassie looked at her skeptically. "I'm thinking that may not be such a good idea. It will probably work for us, but Remi? Not so much."

"I don't give a rat's ass," Deidre glowered. "It is common courtesy to let your traveling companions know where you are and when you will be back."

Recognizing the look, Cassie said nothing.

So here she was, Deidre thought, her first and only exciting trip to Europe, and she was stuck in a hotel room for some indeterminate amount of time, waiting. For what? An inconsiderate guide.

"Want to get something to eat?"

"Yes!" Deidre said. "Let's get out of here."

"So what are we missing today?" Cassie asked. "We can head there and eat along the way."

"Today was supposed to be the Spanish Steps after a nap. What's it called in Italy, a *siesta*? No, that's not right. That's Spanish. *Riposo*, I think."

"Jetlag, I call it," Cassie said, stretching. "When do we see the Vatican?"

Deidre opened her laptop and found the file Remi had loaded. "Wednesday: St. Peter's Basilica and the Vatican Museums."

Cassie looked over her shoulder at the file. "Does Remi know this afternoon was the Spanish Steps?"

"Certainly. It's his itinerary!"

"Maybe he forgot."

"Maybe we grab a cab and let him wonder what happened to *us*!"

REMI STOPPED by the bar on his way back to the room. He needed some fortification. The bartender would be hospitable. The hotel attracted the kind of customer who made it profitable to be friendly.

"What kind of Scotch do you have? Islay."

The man listed the various whiskeys they carried. A good selection.

"Lagavulin—ten year. Ah, do you have a fifteen?"

"I have a twenty if you prefer." The bartender's English was excellent. British accent though.

Remi nodded. While he waited, he looked through the pictures he had taken. The one at the Forum would be good. Nice composition with the color of the flowers in the foreground and the arch in the background. All nicely focused. The single arch and the broken stone roofline of the Coliseum was the only one worth saving in that group. He continued scrolling through his pictures. The

Carabinieri was good. Good backlighting.

It occurred to him that he had no other people in his photos. He had often been accused of disliking people, to which he argued that he liked people well enough, just not in his pictures, unless it was a character shot or portraiture. He should take one of Deidre and Cassandra, though, in case they got lost or abducted. Then he'd have a picture to post on the Amber Alert or whatever they had for missing children in Europe. His face lightened at this thought. They weren't children, of course. Still, he liked to tease them.

The bartender served his drink in a brandy snifter. Remi rolled the liquid around in the plump fullness of the glass, letting the whiskey aerate. He put his nose in the snifter and inhaled. Then he slowly tipped it on its side, resting the foot and bowl of the glass on the table. He watched the amber liquid fill the generous bowl of the snifter and stop exactly at the rim. Not a drop too much. Or too little. It was a perfect shot, and not premeasured. He gently rolled the bowl of the glass back and forth on the table with the palm of his hand. He looked over at the bartender, who had been watching. He held the glass up in an informal salute. The bartender acknowledged it with a slight nod. The guy knew his business.

He took a small sip, letting the liquid fill his mouth, savoring it before he swallowed. It was old and smooth, the harshness aged out in the barrels. He'd put it on Sinclair's tab. This part, he might enjoy.

Remi looked around the room as he savored his whiskey. Once he'd been a heavy drinker, but not now. Alcohol no longer made him open up and become the life of the party. Nor did he become quarrelsome. Now, it made him quiet. He'd learned the hard way that before he reached the stage of forgetfulness, he had to first pass through the reflective remembering stage, distorted though it was. He wanted to obliterate the reflecting, not amplify it. The "cure" had proven to be worse than the "disease." Now he limited his drinking to a pre-dinner cocktail, sometimes two, a couple of glasses of wine at dinner, sometimes three, and sometimes a nightcap. This afternoon, with the surprisingly good whiskey he was enjoying, the dinner wine could be easily sacrificed. The important thing was to live in the moment, he reminded himself.

Clearly the bar had been designed for the upper class. From the corner table, he could take in the whole room: the deep, rich leather seats, the heavy brass foot railing at the bar, the gold-trimmed ornate mirror, the plush Chinese rugs, the crystal chandeliers dimmed to an intimate glow. Yes, money flowed here.

He was surprised by how few single women were in the lounge; in fact, as he looked closer, he saw *no* single women in the room. Only a few wives or "girlfriends," from what he could gather. He wondered what that was about.

The whiskey didn't relax him. Not even the second one. All day he had felt like his skin was crawling, and his muscles had ached with anticipatory tension. But this was different. Was he feeling guilty about his wards? Wards. Once he thought up the word, he used it often when thinking about the girls. They were the wards. He was the warden. He wanted to make sure things stayed in proper perspective.

He had a stiff neck. The thought of Deidre and Cassandra only made it worse. How the hell did he sell his soul so cheap? All expenses were paid up front, but his salary would come at the end. Sinclair was no fool; he'd been right about that. The travel would be tolerable, more than tolerable. If he wanted to, he could make it downright fun. But the girls—what was he supposed to do with them? And the hyper vigilance. Maybe once they got out of the city…

He took out his phone, found the top name in his favorites, and called the familiar number. "You'll never guess where I'm at."

The voice guessed.

"No, Rome." He smiled at the laugh from the other end and, finally, felt the tension begin to ease.

After the call, Remi made his way through the lobby to the front desk. The clerk handed him his key and a note that read, "Gone to see the sites. Be back before dinner. D and C."

More like the DMZ, he thought. He was North Korea, they were South, or maybe the other way around. Whichever, the land between was hotly contested; a battle of wills he had no intention of losing.

Dinner in Europe didn't start until 7:30, later in the bigger cities. He looked at his watch. It was nearly 5:00, 11:00 back home, but he'd been up for most of the night. He was bushed. Jetlagged. He'd grab a quick nap before dinner and hope he could sleep tonight.

"Gone to see the sites." Damn.

* * * * *

HE LATHERED HIS face and reached for the razor. He had survived day one only slightly bruised. Beginning with the attempted scolding by Deidre at dinner, the evening had gone downhill from there. Remi had to admire the way Cassandra stayed out of the fray. Practice, probably. Deidre couldn't be easy to be around. She had a tongue on her, that one. All refined and made-up when she wanted to be, but nasty as tacks under a saddle the rest of the time. Still, once back in the quiet of his bed, he grudgingly admitted that from now on he should probably let the girls know where he was going and know where they would be. God forbid if something happened. He was just so use to dealing with men... or being on his own, he sighed, rinsing the shaving cream from his face.

They had agreed to meet for breakfast, but he'd been up since 4:00. That nap had interfered. He'd gotten some good shots of the

Coliseum at 5:00 and was back by 6:00. He'd called for room service by 6:30. He had already downloaded, viewed, and adjusted yesterday's pictures.

What was today? The Trevi Fountain, the Catacombs and some collection of churches. His head began to throb.

DEIDRE LOOKED at her watch for the fourth time. She stirred a sugar cube into her cappuccino, disturbing the pretty heart design of cream floating on top. Though it wasn't even 8:00, she felt annoyed. He had been explicit that he expected punctuality from them. They showed up, now where was he?

Lifting her head, she saw him standing under the arch, searching for their table. He saw Cassandra waving and walked toward them. She felt her heart pumping a little harder. He had shaved, and looked far too attractive for this hour of the morning.

He passed a table where a woman gaped boldly after him. So did her husband. It was then that she noticed others calling attention to the tall American walking through the dining room. The women's appreciative stares—and some of the men's—were uncomfortable, yet exciting, too. As he approached their table, the eyes in the room continued following him and locked on the two young women waiting for him.

Cassie saw it, too. "They're all *staring* at him," she whispered. "Of course, with eye candy like that…"

"Shh," Deidre said. "He'll hear you."

Like the others, she wanted to absorb every last detail of him: the width of his shoulders, the tight waist, the lock of dark hair falling on his forehead, his brown eyes, his strong jaw, the bluish-black of a beard already threatening to push through the smooth skin, and his swagger. Yes, his swagger—that arrogance that made her tingle all over.

Remi seemed oblivious to the stares. "*Ciao, raggazze.*"

"Translation?"

"Hi, kids."

"Well, that certainly dampened the tingle," Deidre muttered under her breath.

Pretending not to notice the obvious offense she had taken to his words, Remi mentally scored one for his side. He didn't know why he wanted to needle her, but the heavy suitcase was somehow involved. Cassandra laughed, so he focused his charms on her. "So it's the catacombs, is it?" Remi looked up at the waiter now waiting to attend him. "Ah, no thanks, I've already eaten. But yeah, I'll have an espresso."

The waiter bowed an exit.

"You've already eaten?"

"And good morning to you, Miss Deidre."

"Good morning. When did you eat?"

"In my room a couple of hours ago."

"Oh. Jetlag." She sounded rather reasonable this morning.

He looked at her and smiled. "Yeah, it'll go away in a few days."

"The books say we can expect to suffer at least a week or two," Cassandra volunteered.

"Yeah, well, I started changing my sleep schedule a couple of weeks ago, so nearly there."

"That was smart. You could have shared your trick with us," Deidre said.

"I assumed you would have read up on it," he said dismissively, nodding at the travel guidebook on the table. "So, it's the Trevi Fountain, the Catacombs, and what else?"

Deidre looked like she wanted to smack him.

* * * * *

BEFORE HE FELL asleep at night, Remi had developed the habit of looking back over the day and deciding whether or not it had been good, or if he had lived as fully as he could have. In the beginning the answer was always no. After Fallujah, there were no good days, only a crushing burden that tomorrow he would have to wake up and do it all over again. Especially after the deployments, after the Marine Corps, when he had to return to civilian life.

Then, a few years ago, some of the guys had stumbled onto the trick of the nightly assessment. It helped.

He was in a better place now. Those black years that had haunted him were mostly shades of gray, with the rare patch of blue sky or ray of actual light. When that speck of light broke through the thick clouds, no matter how briefly, it always caught him by surprise. Hope. Normality. The lifting of the oppressive weight. It did exist then, somewhere beyond the gray. Like diving too deep and swimming urgently toward the surface, he was desperate to see the sky again. He would then try to reconstruct everything preceding the magical moment: his thoughts, what he was doing, what he heard or smelled, anything to capture the light and bring it back again.

But there never seemed to be any pattern. He couldn't call up the small patch of blue at will. He just needed to wait, hoping it would appear again—someday.

The blackness, however, was always there, just out of sight beyond the gray, hovering, waiting for any excuse to consume him. Images of his men, his friends, dead or maimed, drifted in and out of the darkness. And the bodies—insurgents or civilians, who could tell? Except he was pretty sure the children, the babies, the women huddling to protect them, were just ordinary people caught up in this damn war. White phosphorus. They weren't allowed to talk about it.

But they knew—the Marines, the soldiers. Thank God most of the civilians had left before it started.

So much death, gruesome death, seared into his brain. He was supposed to bring them back in one piece. He had promised their wives, their families. He was the Platoon Sergeant. That was his job. But he had failed. And the mistakes, the mistakes he'd made during battle. Jerry. Oh, God, Jerry. He relived it over and over and the guilt nearly consumed him. It never lessened.

In the quiet of the night, that was the worst. For years he couldn't sleep, didn't want to sleep, for fear of the nightmares. But in the dark of pre-sleep, the memories came, nearly as bad as the reality. In those first years only the drinking helped. It numbed him, gave him a few hours when life would disappear into a haze devoid of meaning, yet all the while he knew this was just a drug-induced illusion from which he must eventually emerge. Some of the guys got addicted. He just got huge hangovers. When his hands started to shake, he knew something had to change. He gave it up for a while. Then started drinking again. Then got tired of being sick all the time.

Now he drank in moderation, and because he liked to, not because he had to. He substituted distraction for drinking, living in the moment of now to obliterate the before. Photography intensified his focus on the immediate, while he got his adrenaline fix from the hunt and the danger. He had lied to her about the rattlesnake. As he had waited for the lioness to emerge with her cubs, it had been *his* boot that had attracted the snake. The warm leather, apparently, seemed the ideal spot for a nap. There was nothing to be done. He just had to wait the damn thing out. Eventually, one of them would have to move, and he had just prayed it would be the snake. He knew it would be gone by sunset, if he could remain still for that long. He hadn't thought about Iraq once during that whole long day.

Six years into the healing, the razor edge of the memories was beginning to dull: the nightmares were less frequent, less terrifying. He had learned to calm his mind at night, assess the day and plan how tomorrow could be better. He was living, or at least he pretended to be. He owed it to his brothers, who were not, to keep on living and do it the best way he knew how.

Sometimes, he envied those who had made the ultimate sacrifice. They were at peace, at rest, unfettered by conscience or remorse. When those thoughts intruded, he had to shake himself. He was past the point of suicide, so why even go there? Their lives were over, but his wasn't. He had to keep moving, and do it the best way he could. For them. He owed it to them. His brothers had died so he could live, and so he had better goddamn get on with it.

In reflection, the day hadn't been bad. In fact, the hair on the back of his neck only rose a few times. His wards had seemed agreeable. No major incidents. The catacombs he could have skipped. Pretty macabre. The attraction there was beyond him. The Trevi Fountain was trite, just a couple of horses and naked men above a waterfall. Cassandra told him he needed to develop a taste for fine art. The crowds really bothered him. Out of the corner of his eye, he had glimpsed someone drawing a gun, and after the first step of a three-step lunge realized it was just a camera with a long lens. And then there was the backfire of a jalopy, and he nearly dropped to the ground. Well, he did actually, but when the girls had looked at him he pretended to be searching for a fallen lens cap. God, he'd been home for three years. He should be over the worst of it by now, but the muscle memory wouldn't let go.

If only he could just get out of this damn city.

He was sitting at his desk in his pajama bottoms when she knocked. He opened the door to Deidre's worried face.

"It's Cassie. She's sick."

He hurried through their room to the bathroom and found

Cassandra clinging to the toilet bowl, the smell of vomit pungent in the air.

Remi bent down and pulled back the long red hair from her face, gathered it in his hand, and expertly made a loose knot at the base of her neck.

"Where did you learn to do that?" Deidre asked.

Remi ignored her.

"I'm okay," Cassie gasped. "Just some bad mushrooms."

"I am so sorry," Deidre said.

He could smell the alcohol behind the vomit, and looked over to the counter where the vodka bottle stood half empty. A carton of orange juice was tipped over on its side.

Turning to Deidre, he asked, "You've been drinking?"

"It's not Dee's fault," Cassandra said. "It was my idea."

"No, it wasn't." Deidre frowned at her best friend, then glaring at Remi she said, "There's no age limit in Italy."

"Does your father let you drink hard liquor at home?" He already knew they drank wine with dinner.

She hesitated. "No."

"Kids," he muttered as he turned back to Cassandra. He reached out his hand to hold her forehead.

"Don't call me that!"

"Then don't act like it!" he snapped back.

Cassandra retched.

"Vomiting is good. The room should stop spinning soon. When it does, start sipping on water to dilute the alcohol and rehydrate yourself. Not too much, just sips."

Cassandra tried to answer, then just nodded, which caused the retching to begin again. Her skin felt hot to his hand, but more like excursion than fever.

"You're going to feel like hell tomorrow, but we're going to the

Vatican whether you do or not. And I don't want to hear any whining."

"I'll be ready," she gagged.

He stood up, looked down at Deidre, and shook his head in disapproval.

"We have a schedule to keep, after all," she smarted up at him.

Remi's face hardened as he walked out of the room.

Deidre followed him into the hall and grabbed his arm. There was no softness under her fingers.

"What are you doing here?"

"What?"

"Why are you here?"

"I'm your escort."

"Really? Then why did we hire a photographer?"

"Let go of my arm."

Surprised that she still held it, she released him. "You're stalling."

He was.

"What were your instructions?" she demanded.

The hair bristled on the back of his neck as he gazed down at her. He'd have to control his temper before he spoke or else it could get real nasty real fast. He took a deep breath. Thank God she didn't say anything. She just stood there.

"Your father asked me to show you the world through a photographer's eye."

"Well, so far you're doing a crappy job."

"That's not all I'm supposed to do, Miss Sinclair. I'm supposed to keep you and your girlfriend out of trouble, and I can see I've got to up my game in that department, too." He glared at her.

Deidre returned the look. He never backed down, but neither did she. An older couple stepped out of the elevator at the end of the hall and turned their way. She pivoted back toward the room and closed the door behind her. At least she didn't slam it, at least not too loudly.

CASSANDRA DID manage to pull herself together, though she was clearly miserable at breakfast. Deidre looked like she had eaten bad mushrooms, too, but neither girl complained.

"Vatican City is a crown jewel embedded in the heart of Rome," Remi said.

"You're mixing your metaphors," Deidre said, though she wasn't trying to start an argument. The fight seemed to have gone out of her. Remi was glad of it. He was tired of the game, too. But their parting words the night before had stung him. He didn't fail at things. If his commander told him to take the hill, then by God he'd take the hill. Even though this trip was something different, he had agreed to it, so he'd better man up and do what needed to be done. He began by thinking about what he could do for all of them. If they had to endure one another for five months, perhaps he could make it more palatable. He could try, at least.

"There is one thing I want you to pay attention to. Well, two things. While you're all caught up with the big things, make sure you notice the little things. They're more important. Tourists only see what they're told to see, but I'd like you to look further, deeper. The value is on the small details, the inconspicuous places, the subtlety of what is before you. And the history. If you can, try to understand the context, the reason it developed that way. Then you'll know what to look for, the underlying meaning."

The women nodded. Professor to student—a familiar role, and acceptable. And perhaps a page had turned.

CHAPTER 4

THE VATICAN

A LIGHT FOG HAD settled over the city during the night and early morning. The dampness was a relief from yesterday's heat. Deidre even felt a slight chill in the air. As they turned the corner onto Via della Conciliazione, all three sets of eyes were drawn to the end of the street as if by magnetic attraction. Standing majestically before them was the Basilica of St. Peter, the most celebrated architectural wonder of the High Renaissance.

Priests, nuns, locals, and chattering tourists hurried past, but the trio stopped to take in the grandeur of the architecture before them. The fog threw a diaphanous veil that softened the outer edges of the Basilica while emphasizing the misty white of the façade. The enormity of the great church became apparent when, at this distance, the people at its door seemed to resemble small bugs.

They walked down the street past the apartments and shops, the parked cars, and the moving ones. Each had a sense that within minutes they would leave this world of noisy automation and step back into some ancient time when, perhaps, the world was less complex.

The street ended at a semi-circle of short white pillars embedded in the concrete, marking the end of vehicular traffic. In the center of the *piazza* was an Egyptian obelisk with an oxidized copper cross on top. The elliptical space was defined on its right and left by giant marble columns like curved arms about to give a hug. Beyond this was an equally large trapezoidal area, a second *piazza*, creating a grand welcome to the Basilica.

They turned to the right and entered the curved portico

supported by the colonnade of mammoth stone pillars. The Doric columns were four deep and formed three aisles.

Remi stopped, took a step backwards, and then another. He moved a little to the left. He peered through his viewfinder at the overlapping vertical lines of stone with their horizontal veining. He positioned a hanging wrought iron lamp with white frosted glass toward the descending line of columns. He waited for a pedestrian to move out of the frame before snapping the picture. Sometimes a shot just jumped out from nowhere.

Cassandra stood behind Remi with her own camera. He noticed Deidre left hers slung over her shoulder. She stopped and studied the scene, but made no record of it. He wasn't sure why that bothered him, but it did.

They emerged from the colonnade and crossed over to stand at the base of the stairs leading up to the grand church. On either side were the statues of St. Peter and St. Paul. Other statues adorned the top of the Basilica: Jesus in the center with St. John the Baptist and eleven apostles flanking him. Additional statues, perhaps of popes or saints, lined the roofs of the columns.

Although some called it a cathedral, it was not. Earlier, in the hotel, Deidre had read that a cathedral was defined as the seat of a bishop. Although the Pope was the Bishop of Rome, his actual seat was in the smaller but older Archbasilica of St. John Lateran, just outside the boundary of Vatican City.

As she was explaining it now, Cassandra asked, "How many people actually know this, and does it really matter? I mean," she added seeing Deidre's frown, "not that the distinction isn't interesting, but is it relevant to Catholics?"

"Enough for people to kill one another over," Remi said quietly.

Two pair of eyebrows raised.

"Maybe not this particular issue, but some not much more

significant than this. It doesn't take much for intolerant people to take offense while maintaining they're motivated by their love of God." He pulled the bag off his shoulder and dropped his camera into it. "Religion has been the basis for a lot of bloodshed over the centuries. Religion, greed, and power: three reasons to go to war."

"By war and religion, you're referring to the Crusades," Cassandra said.

"Actually, religion may have been merely the cover-up for greed during the Crusades."

"But the intolerance—you're talking about the Middle East then, aren't you?" Deidre said. "Don't the Sunnis and the Shiites practice nearly identical forms of Islam, only they differ in pronouncing a few sacred words, or how to hold their hands in prayer? Something like that? Really insignificant stuff, I thought."

Remi nodded as he held the door open for them. "And one group has tried to dominate the other for generations all in the name of Allah."

"That's crazy," Cassandra said.

"That about sums it up."

THOUGH THEY entered the Basilica from an overcast day, it took Deidre's eyes several minutes to adjust to the dim interior. The first thing she noticed was the drop in temperature. The shelter of the stone kept the heat out, like a cave, she thought, or a tomb. She shivered as much from the image as from the cold.

Inside the cathedral, as their eyes sought light, they found themselves looking up at the apex of Michelangelo's magnificent dome. Even in fog, the windows around the perimeter of the dome lit the interior of the massive space.

"It's wonderful," Deidre breathed.

"Fabulous," Cassandra agreed.

"A hundred and twenty years to complete," Remi said. "Michelangelo was the architect for twenty of those. He died before it was finished."

"How old was he when he started?" asked Cassandra. "I think he died when he was ninety, or something like that."

"That would make him seventy when he began. That can't be right," Deidre said.

"He was an optimist." Remi grinned.

They began their exploration of the interior. A small crowd was quietly admiring Michelangelo's famous Pietà. The beautiful sculpture depicted the Madonna with the dead Christ stretched across her lap.

Though somber, the brilliance of the work couldn't escape even the most novice observer.

"Mary is so young compared to Christ," Cassandra said.

"Michelangelo's idealized woman," Remi said. "In the sixteenth century, they believed if a woman stayed pure and virginal, she stayed young."

Deidre grinned at her friend. "Do you think it's worth it?"

"Virginity and perpetual youth versus fun and wrinkles. Ugh! What a choice." The girls giggled.

Remi rolled his eyes, then moved forward to get a better look.

"It says here that this is the only piece he ever signed." Deidre struggled to read from the guidebook in the dim light. She blinked to clear her vision, but it didn't help. What was the matter? She read just fine in the church yesterday.

Like the hand of a malevolent ghost, a shiver ran across her shoulders. Was it real, then? Was this really happening? Everything, well, almost everything, had seemed so normal until now. Maybe it took a little longer for her eyes to adjust to a dim room, but she could live with that. But, now, what if she couldn't read? In the abstract she understood, of course, that eventually she would be unable to read, but theory and reality had no relationship until that very minute. She might actually go blind. Not might, she told herself. Here was hard proof that the blindness was winning over her denial. She had tried telling herself that it was going to happen, but she didn't quite believe it. She was young and strong and healthy, attractive and educated and had a good family. And she was stubborn. Nothing bad would happen to her. There were just too many layers of protection. Bad things happened to other people. Blindness happened, but not to people like her. It was all some kind of mistake. She squinted at the guidebook again. The letters faded from the page in a pale blur. She closed the book. It was just too dark in here to read. Everything was going to be all right.

She turned her attention to Cassandra.

"Do you know why he signed it?" her friend asked.

Deidre and Remi shook their heads.

"The way the story goes is that Michelangelo and his assistants brought the statue into the Basilica one night after it was closed. This was his first masterpiece in Rome, and he was curious to hear what people had to say about it. So in the morning, he disguised himself and sat near a pillar to listen. The piece was hugely admired, but no one was able to guess who had made it. Another local sculptor, Solari, was getting the credit."

"Who?" Deidre asked.

"Exactly. Cristoforo Solari. Not a great talent, apparently. The thing is, Michelangelo wasn't really known, not in Rome. He was only twenty-two, and from Florence. He wasn't even considered an artist here. That night, angered by the lack of recognition, he chiseled his name across the Madonna's sash so there would be no question who the artist was."

"Good for him," Deidre said. Then, seeing Remi's look of

surprise, she nodded toward Cassandra. "Art major."

"Ah."

"It's more than just his name, though. Look." Cassandra pointed to the string of letters after "Michealaglus."

"'Michelangelo Buonarroti, Florentine, made this'." Remi translated.

Now it was Deidre and Cassandra's turn to be surprised.

"You read Latin?"

Remi shrugged. "Jesuit high school."

He looked closer at the statue.

"Why is it encased in glass?" Deidre asked.

"Vandalized," Remi said. "See the nose? The guy attacked her with a hammer, fifteen whacks. Knocked off her arm here and her nose."

"That makes me sick."

"Fragments of marble flew everywhere and people, tourists, rather than stopping him, just started pushing one another to get pieces of the statue. Some of it came back, but whoever took the nose kept it."

"The nose of the Pietà," Deidre said. "A priceless artifact that you can never claim. How stupid. How selfish."

"But the restoration is incredible," Cassandra said. "How did they get the color to match? I mean, she's five hundred years old."

Remi moved to another angle. "They took a plug of marble out of her back." There was a glare on the glass, so he knelt down for a better look. "Really excellent restoration. He got her left eyelid, too. See? You have to know where to look, and then because of the veining in the marble the seam could just be grain. Really impressive."

The young women took turns looking at the Pietà restoration from various angles.

"Which do you like better, in general: sculpture or painting?" Cassandra asked.

Together, they said, "Sculpture."

"Why?"

Remi motioned for Deidre to answer first.

"Because you can feel the form. You can understand the piece even with your eyes closed." She was careful not to look at her friend.

Cassandra nodded, then turned to Remi.

"Because it's harder," he said. "Painting is adding to, while sculpture is taking away from. If you paint something wrong, you can paint over it and correct it. But if you chisel away too much, it's ruined. How about you, which do you like better?"

"What works for me?" She swung her long straight red hair. "Any medium where I can look at male models in the nude." Her candor shocked them both into silence, then laughter. Another English-speaker nearby looked up at her and grinned, too.

Remi and Cassandra started to walk away.

"Do you mind if I just stay and looked at her for a while?" Deidre asked.

"As long as you like." Remi's voice was soft. "For most of us it's a once in a lifetime chance to stand before greatness."

Deidre gazed at the beautiful statue. Mary's face reflected a peaceful acceptance of the tragedy upon her.

She's still in shock. But when the shock wears off...

She studied the love on the young mother's face and the lifeless body of her son draped across her lap. The statue evoked a sense of helplessness and waste. As she stared into the Madonna's face she felt tears welling in her eyes as her own grief surfaced. Her denial was crumbling, and reality threatened to overcome her. She would never gaze down into the eyes of her own child. She would never know if he was beautiful or in need of a confidence boost. She would never see bruises from a fight at school, or whether he needed a haircut, or if he wore stripes with plaids. And a daughter—how would she braid her hair, or paint her nails, or teach her about style? What color eyes would she have? Even if someone told her blue, would it be deep blue, or pale blue, or gray-blue like her own? Would they be almond-shaped, or round, or cat-like? She would never know, never, no matter how much she wanted it. The Virgin Mary had thirty-three years of looking and loving. Deidre would never see her future child.

Those thoughts had been tickling the edges of her conscious mind, but until now she had been able to keep them out. Now the grief seeped through her. She wished she were alone to sob audibly. Still, it was a strange comfort to feel like this mother would have understood.

The tourists around her took no notice of her wet cheeks. They were focused on the Pietà. But when she turned, Remi, who had come back for her, saw the tears. She quickly pulled her fingers across her cheeks as he smiled softly at her.

"Quite a genius to create something that moving," he said.

She nodded, understanding the miscommunication. He didn't know, wouldn't know. What other conclusion could he draw? And he was right, too. The statue did evoke tremendous emotion. And Michelangelo was a genius. But Remi's understandable lack of understanding left her feeling empty and alone. She wanted him to know, to understand. But he didn't, and couldn't. She wanted to reach out to him, wanted him to reach out to her, to comfort her, to tell her everything would be all right. But wouldn't that be pity, the very thing she dreaded? She wondered if she had ever felt so absolutely alone.

She took a deep breath. "Really moving."

They wandered down the right side of the Basilica, commenting on the artwork on the tombs.

"It looks like the popes were more interested in building monuments to themselves than spending money on the people," Cassandra commented.

"Shrines to themselves," agreed Deidre.

"This one was fairly full of himself. Look at the marble angels all over the lid."

They pointed out the most ostentatious tombs.

"Look here, Clementine XI. I like this one." Cassandra and Remi turned to see the simple slab embedded in the Basilica's pavement. "I could respect a pope like this."

Remi looked up. He had a curious expression, like a question mark, on his brow. But the girls were already moving on to the next big thing.

The Basilica, like all ancient churches, was shaped in the form of a cross with the altar at the east end. The three walked toward it.

Cassandra read through the pages of the guidebook that Deidre had handed her. "This is the high altar of St. Peter, the Apostle. Apparently, he is buried under it." She looked up at the bronze statue. "Gian Lorenzo Bernini built this *Baldacchino* over it. The four pillars are supposedly taken from the Temple of Solomon. See that cross on top of the globe, way up at the top? That is supposed to represent Christianity saving the world."

"Let's see." Cassandra paused to read further. "Wow. It says that this is literally the center of Catholicism. When you think of it that way, I mean, it could also be said it is the center of Christianity. That blows my mind!"

"Do you think this is really St. Peter's tomb?" Deidre hadn't considered that the two-thousand-year-old saint might actually be beneath her. In her mind he had been, for the most part, merely the apostle who betrayed Christ three times and the author of a small book in her Bible. And something about keys. Suddenly, she was in awe.

"I think Peter, the fisherman, is probably here," Remi said.

"Isn't that amazing!"

"It gives me chills."

Remi was ready to move on.

A brilliant stain glass window hung at the far end. Its central image was a six-foot dove, and the round yellow stained glass radiating from it suspended over the Throne of St. Peter like a benevolent Holy Spirit blessing the observers.

Remi was tempted to take a picture without a flash.

"Why don't you?" Deidre asked.

"Not enough light, and I don't have my tripod. This is just one of those things we have to photograph with our eyes and file away in our brain."

Deidre turned away. *I've got a lot of those. Hope my memory card doesn't fill up and I can download when I need them.*

Stained glass windows in brilliant hues of red and blue, green and yellow, allowed the sunlight to dance on the sheen of the mosaic tile floor throughout the space.

"The sun's out," Remi said, nodding to the rays streaming through the high dome windows.

"I saw that a few minutes ago. No matter where I stand my eyes keep going back to the light." Deidre craned her neck back to get a better look.

"It's the tallest in the world."

"Look over here," Cassandra called out to them. They walked over to the monument to Pope Alexander VII. A collection of statues connected by a large marble-colored stone drape made up the doorframe.

"All of these have some kind of symbolism, clues to the message the artist was trying to tell. Maybe because I like mysteries I like figuring out the story," said Cassandra.

"Are you Catholic?" Remi asked.

"No."

"It helps if you know the saints and what they supposedly did. Then you can figure out who it is and go from there."

Remi studied the sculpture, then smiled. "Of course, knowing a bit about history helps, too."

"What are you smiling at? You discovered something, didn't you?" Deidre said.

He chuckled. "Details, ladies, details. Look here. This one's supposed to represent Truth or Faith, and look at her foot."

"It's on a globe."

"Yep, but *where* on the globe?"

The girls looked closer. "Great Britain?"

"Yep. And not by accident."

"I don't get it," Deidre said.

"Neither do I," said Cassandra.

"I see a brief course on the history of Catholicism is in order."

"Jesuit school." Deidre nodded knowingly to Cassandra.

"Exactly. I knew it would pay off someday. So pay attention. You have been exceedingly good students, so as a reward you have earned the extremely abbreviated version."

He cleared his throat as if to present a substantial lecture. Instead, he summed it up in two sentences.

"The reigning king, or queen, determined whether England was aligned with the Anglican Church or the Roman Catholic Church. Some decades you were on the right side, and some decades you were not."

"Oh, terrific. So you might have to change your religion at the coronation?" Deidre groaned.

"Or lose your head." Remi chuckled. "When Alexander VII was Pope, apparently England," he nodded to the globe, "was not Catholic."

CHAPTER 5

CINQUE TERRE

THEY SPENT TWO more days in Rome before flying to Milan. They got a car, though driving in the city was impossible. Like Rome, walking or taking the cab was the only reasonable way to get through the crazy traffic.

The major sites on their itinerary, the Duomo and Leonardo Di Vinci's "Last Supper," were interesting, but Deidre and Cassandra were more impressed with the fashion show, an event Remi happily bowed out of.

"This is her thing," Cassandra explained to Remi when they were alone. "She was going to be a fashion designer."

Remi caught the slip-up. "Was?" He saw the blood rising in Cassandra's cheeks.

"Is, I mean," she stammered. "She's thinking about something else, though."

Remi considered that for a minute. He didn't peg Deidre as flighty. She seemed pretty clearheaded to him. And stubborn. But, on any account, it wasn't his concern.

The fashion show was important enough to force Remi to rearrange the schedule. It made much more sense to fly into Milan, take a train to Rome, and rent a car there for the rest of the trip. But now, constrained by the date of that silly show, they would have to backtrack. Somewhere in the quiet of his mind, though, a small voice forced him to admit that he might have done the same thing if an event was important enough to him. But he wasn't ready to be charitable just now. This plan seemed like a waste of time and money, even if it wasn't his.

Finally, he checked off Milan. Another thorn disposed of. Milano was just one more big, ugly city to leave as fast as he could.

"*Arrivaderci Roma*," Cassandra sang.

"*Arrivaderci Milano*," Deidre chimed in.

"What's next, boss?" Cassandra asked from the backseat. Both girls sitting in the back made him feel like a goddamn chauffeur. But if he was being honest, he preferred the solitude. Still, intended or not, the implied class distinction irritated him.

"Pisa."

He could hear them laughing as they flipped through their guidebook.

"Tourists call it a must see, a big thing," he grumbled.

They were getting used to Remi labeling things big or small. Rome, Milan, Florence, the French Riviera—all the exciting places they were interested in, those he lumped into the "big" category. His tone conveyed his opinion about people impressed with "tourist big." They were shallow, gullible, and uninspiring—the places, and the people. Small things were anything he was interested in, like the nun in Rome who crossed a busy street simply by holding up her hand against traffic. She proceeded without looking at the drivers; her outstretched arm was her only shield. Impressive. Or the sun's rays that streamed through St. Peter's dome once the fog had burned off. It produced an almost ethereal light. Or nearly anything off the beaten path—things worth noticing, not things thrust in your face.

"You won't find much there," he informed them. "Just a tower that leans. A quick stop, climb to the top, take a few pictures, and we're outta there."

"I thought you said there was always something to see," Deidre said coquettishly. "You just have to find the right angle."

He looked at her face in the mirror, the smugness seeping

through the innocent round eyes. He'd ignore that. Besides, he couldn't think of a good response.

"After Pisa we go to Cinque Terre."

"Cinque Terrrrrrre," Cassandra said letting her tongue roll. "It sounds romantic."

"The five lands," Remi translated.

"Have you been there?" Deidre asked.

"Once, a long time ago."

"Should we read about it or will you fill us in?"

There was a story. Riomaggiore. He didn't like thinking about it, but the memory, like a poisoned dart, shot through him.

It was a bright, cloudless day, warm but windy. The sun rose behind the town, casting it in shadow during the morning. Nonetheless, the colors of the houses behind him, like a patch of mixed-colored pansies shaded by the boughs of a tree, insisted on being noticed. The town, modestly aware it was breathtakingly beautiful, went about its quiet morning routine. An anxious sea rose in front of him. Spectacular waves exploded against the rock face supporting the town—one hundred and fifty feet, at least. Monstrous waves, the best he'd ever seen. Across the inlet and above the rock formation, above most of the village roofs, people were standing at the railing to watch. The size of paperclips fastened to a sheet of slate gray paper, they stood and taunted the angry waves. The sea crashed hard as though frustrated by the humans who eluded it.

He wanted to get a better picture, so he had followed the others out to a point. His foot had slipped on wet algae covering the steps, and he nearly fell. A warning tremor flashed through him. It was too far, too dangerous. The others went ahead. He held back. As he stood still, contemplating if he should ignore the warning, the wave hit. The long white fingers at the leading edge of the curl grabbed the man in the lead and dragged him down as fast as Neptune heading for Hades. It was over in a blink. The man was there, and then he was gone. Remi tasted the salt, felt the spray, heard the shouts, then shuddered with an overwhelming wash of helplessness, as strong as the waves crashing against the mountain.

It was in the papers the next day: a German tourist, traveling with his family, lost. It hit Remi hard. At least in war you knew it was possible, had some preparation, even signed up for the possibility. There was some purpose in dying on the battlefield. This poor sap simply woke up that morning on vacation and wanted to take a picture.

Not PTSD. Just a sad memory, though it triggered other memories of that same helpless feeling. Talon's death. The battle of Fallujah. The battle of Ramadi. Life.

He shook his head to dislodge the scene.

Deidre had been watching his face in the mirror.

"Tell us," she urged.

Remi looked back at her. Her eyes penetrated his, exposing him a fraction of a second before he could veil them.

"Well, there are five villages strung out on the coast. 'Pearls on a necklace,' the poets have said. Some sit at sea level and some are perched higher up. There are two ways to get to the villages, and a car isn't one of them. You either take a local train or you hike between the towns. Except for the northern town of Monterosso, which is the only one big enough to have a hotel…"

Deidre sat back. So the man had secrets. How interesting to have secrets. Her own life had been uncomplicated and transparent. Her parents knew everything, except the one. Cassie knew, of course. That secret wasn't interesting. It was embarrassing. And her blindness—that was a secret. The family had agreed that Remi didn't need to know. It was all too new, and she didn't know how to deal with pity yet. In case he had any.

That other one, the embarrassing secret… Mostly she forgot about it. She had been a dumb kid. How could such an insignificant—what would she call it? Rape, well, not exactly. Event—still embarrass her? A pimply-faced kid of fifteen took her when she was fourteen. He'd surprised her, pulled her panties down, and made her bend over the couch in the basement. It was over in five minutes, maybe three. Had she been damaged? She didn't think so. She started her period a few days later, so she didn't even have to worry about a pregnancy. Still, her cheeks burned when she thought about it. Shame? Maybe. She probably shouldn't have been down there with him. The fact that she wasn't a virgin didn't bother her. Neither did, the fact that her "first" wasn't much of anything. Or that he was the extent of her experience so far.

What was his name? Could she pick him out of a lineup? No. It was really nothing. Only her first big secret.

REMI HAD BEEN right about Pisa. It was a tower. That leaned. Of course he had been right. Could one possibly imagine that the man might even for one second be wrong?

"It leaned more when I was here before."

"That's impossible. Towers don't just straighten themselves up." The words popped out of her mouth before she could stop them.

He stood there, hands on his hips, and shook his head. "Dee, sometimes I question your parents' choice of educational institutions." He turned and walked away.

Later, she read about the decade-long project to prop up the foundation and, yes, the tower was straighter.

"You were right," she said, "about the tower."

He looked up from the gas pump. "Yeah, I know."

She wanted to throttle the arrogance right out of him.

"It isn't arrogance when a man knows what he knows," he said, reading her thoughts.

They stared at each other. Could he—no, no one was that right all the time.

"Do you bluff sometimes?"

His lips twisted into a crooked smile. "Yeah, sometimes I do."

She smiled back. "Me, too. Sometimes." So far, though, he'd caught her every time.

THE TRIP TO Cinque Terre was lovely. The countryside was ablaze with patches of dancing red poppies and brilliant yellow rapeseed. Remi pointed out things to see and stopped to snap pictures of the scenes, like the field of blazing poppies into which a single yellow flower had flourished. The field was on a slight slope. Remi stooped down to use the blue sky as contrast, but filled the rest of the frame with red flowers, each bending its lovely head to look down at him, while the yellow flower stood stately and defiant.

They stopped again for a lazy herd of sheep meandering down the road, munching the grass and weeds they found along the cracks. Interspersed among them were five or six donkeys and three or four dark-skinned shepherds. Gypsies, they thought.

"Why the donkeys?"

Probably pack mules, they guessed. When the guidebooks didn't comment on something, best guessing became the new pastime.

As they passed through a small village, Remi pointed out and stopped to photograph a widow in draping black clothes—a truly ancient, tiny, wrinkled thing—getting on her bicycle. When she looked up and saw the camera, she glared, and they hurried on.

Definitely out of "Hansel and Gretel," the girls agreed.

They drove through Carrera.

"Isn't Carrera where the famous marble comes from?"

"Where Michelangelo got the blocks for the Pietà and the

David?"

Remi smiled. They were getting it now, the small places. "And other quarries, but Carrera was his favorite. It has the whitest and best marble."

"My parents have Carrera marble in the kitchen."

Remi shook his head. "Probably just the name of some white marble mined in the States or Mexico. Too expensive to get it from here."

But then he wondered if maybe he was wrong.

They got back on the main highway at La Spezia and headed north. Finally, he saw the sign for Riomaggiore, the southernmost of the five villages. He didn't want to stop there: too many ghosts. They might hike to it another day.

The next village was easier to see. They parked their car above Manarola and walked out to the edge of the cutaway to look down on the village. The afternoon sun lit up the town, and a brisk wind whipped their hair. The stucco buildings below, like a collection of brightly printed postage stamps, stood fast against the wind that threatened to blow their color into the sea. Only the orange tile roofs appeared to keep things under control.

Cassandra, and even Deidre, took out their cameras to catch the contrast of the brilliant water that formed the backdrop against the colorful town's perch.

"What color is the sea?" Remi asked. "Look with your heart, not your brain."

They all looked out beyond the village.

"It's not the peacock blue of the Caribbean," Cassandra said.

"It's certainly not the brown-green of the Detroit River!" They laughed.

He could see the wrinkles between Deidre's eyebrows as she concentrated on the challenge.

"Sapphire," she said. "It's sapphire blue."

She looked up at Remi and felt the warmth of his approving smile.

"Yeah, that would be what I'd call it: sapphire blue."

"And the spots of reflected sunlight, like a sprinkle of tiny stars on the water. Star sapphire, then."

He gave her shoulder an affectionate hug. It was the first time he had touched her. He felt her lean into him.

THEY CONTINUED past Corniglia and finally stopped at Vernazza. The parking lot above the town looked full, but Remi maneuvered the car into a small space.

"Better consolidate to a carry-on. It's a long way down. And even longer back up."

Cassandra, compliant as ever, began sorting through what she would need for the four days they would spend in the town, while Deidre, true to form, balked. In Milan, she had sent home a big box of shoes and dresses she would never wear, but her struggle to lift the suitcase into the trunk gave proof that it was still far too heavy. Now, he watched as she removed a few more things, but the suitcase, he guessed, still weighed over fifty pounds. He was inclined to let her have her own way: lug the blasted suitcase down to the square, then heave it up to their room, then back down to the square, and finally back up to the car, only—yeah, why not? Teach the stubborn minx a lesson, he thought with a grim smile.

They began the trek down to the village. Remi took the lead so he wouldn't have to witness her struggle and be a gentleman. He carried a half-empty backpack with hiking boots dangling from the strap, slung his camera case over his shoulder, and held a tripod in his hand. Directly behind him, Cassandra walked with her full but manageable backpack. That was good. Deidre brought up the rear.

They took the underpass stairs beneath the train trestles, and still he wouldn't look around to see if she was keeping up or not.

They continued on through the wide but only thoroughfare of the town. The rounded cobblestones, though worn, were uneven beneath their feet. They passed shops, houses, and an occasional hotel, all seemingly connected, as if one house provided a nice wall for the next to be built upon. The preparation from the afternoon meal still lingered in the air, reminding them that dinner was hours away despite the growling of their stomachs. Lunch, a small pizza eaten at an inconspicuous café, was already a forgotten memory.

Benches for the locals dotted the street. Sometimes a chair would be added to a cluster of men, or a younger woman would stand to gossip with the older seated women. Generally the clusters were segregated by sex, which seemed odd to the girls, but perfectly understandable to Remi.

He finally stopped in the square. On the far side were outdoor tables with open yellow umbrellas claiming their share of the *piazza*. He headed for the restaurant to ask for directions.

Yes, the proprietor nodded. He knew the apartment.

Remi's eyes followed the hand pointing to a set of steep steps across the *piazza* they had just crossed. He cranked his head back to look at their designated rooms and counted six stacks of windows. Deidre was just catching up. He was going to enjoy this.

Smiling, he pointed to the windows above the clothesline. "There. See the ones with the orange awning?"

The girls looked up. These were not standard eight-foot stories. They were more like twelve feet.

"Two above that. This way." He wanted so much to look at Deidre's face, but he knew if he did he'd be tempted to rescue her.

He had to give her credit, though. She did end up hauling that bloody suitcase up ninety-seven steps to their rooms. She was slow, stopping to rest, and showed up about ten minutes after he and Cassandra did. But she never once complained.

He took the room at the back of the two-room apartment. The girls took the larger front room. The window with the view of the sea was open, and the young women hung out, enthralled.

"The view! Simply look at the view. Come over here, Remi, we'll make room."

He walked over, already envisioning what they were seeing.

Below, tiny circles of color covered three edges of the *piazza* as the bright umbrellas shaded the diners from the glaring afternoon sun. Older children played a game of soccer, but the younger ones ran through the stone square. A break wall was built on the left, and beyond it they could see the beach, the boats, and the sapphire sea. The sunbathers were topless, for the most part, but too far away to see. Still, Remi enjoyed the anticipation of a closer look.

The girls wondered if rules might be broken in favor of an early snack to tame their growing appetite.

"It's a tourist town, so probably," Remi said.

"Are those rowboats?" Cassie asked.

"Fishing boats."

"Can we rent one?"

"Well, probably not these. But there's a small cruiser in Monterosso that takes tourists out along the coast and back."

"Did you ever notice that you say 'tourists' like you have dirt in your mouth?" Deidre asked.

"Yeah, well..."

They walked down to the yellow umbrellas. Though it was only late afternoon, they were able to persuade the proprietor to prepare *Insalata Caprese*: a salad of slices of tomato and buffalo mozzarella drizzled with olive oil and basil. They promised the proprietor they would return the next evening for the full meal.

Italians in general were blessed with an easy nature. They were creative and full of fun and not particularly punctual or dependable. They tended to break or avoid most rules. Speed limits "were a suggestion," as one Italian pointed out. No, they explained, rules were for the Germans.

Except when it came to food. Food rules were right up there with holy water, genuflecting, and worshipping your mother. There was only one right way to prepare a dish, though that varied according to region. Bolognese or Milanese or Florentine—each proudly defined the region where a dish originated, and was rarely made outside of that region. If a diner requested something from the local region that wasn't on the menu, the chef most often would oblige. But if that same diner dared to request something made famous from another region, he would be promptly reminded where he was and told that such inferior meals would not be served in his establishment.

"It's rather amusing how proud they are of their cooking," Cassie remarked. "But they're not very eclectic. We don't have that at home."

"You mean regional cooking?" Remi asked.

Deidre thought for a minute. "I think we do. When we say 'southern cooking' certain foods come to mind, or 'creole cooking' from New Orleans. And we have New England clam chowder. That's pretty specific. Think of some more."

"Boston baked beans," Cassie said. "And Idaho potatoes."

"That's not a dish, it's an ingredient."

"Okay, how about Maryland crab cakes, then."

"Texas toast."

"Alaskan king crab?"

"Item. But how about a Philly cheesesteak."

"Boston cream pie."

"Coney Island."

"Chicago deep dish pizza."

"Kentucky bourbon," Remi chimed in.

"California rolls?"

"Or Hawaiian pig roast."

Remi found the girls' word games to be surprisingly fun. Throughout the drive, they'd created little contests for themselves, some silly, some stimulating. Sometimes they quarreled over a response and asked him to referee. He even liked that. This was outside his realm of experience. He was used to petty gossip and "mean girl" put-downs, except for his sister, but she didn't count. It struck him that his initial resistance to the trip, though he hadn't consciously addressed it, was based on the assumption that two teenage girls would spend their time being nasty. He had been looking for it, expecting it, and sometimes even tried to provoke it. But instead, he lucked out with two girls who seemed to thrive above the mundane, or, at least, they had so far.

The girls went on for a while until Remi asked, "What other Italian food rules?"

As nimble as young deer, they mentally switched direction.

"Lunch between 12:00 and 2:00, dinner after 7:30, and no snacking in between," Cassandra said.

"Salad at the end of the meal. *Antipasta, primo, secundo* and then the side dishes," Deidre said. "But who can eat all that food?"

"Cappuccino is only served at breakfast or for children later in the day. And for Deidre," Cassie said with a grin. "Any time after that it's some form of espresso."

"Desserts aren't very sweet," said Deidre, who, Remi noticed, suffered from a particularly acute sweet tooth.

"They don't bring you a check unless you ask for it."

"Because?" Remi encouraged.

"Because the table is yours for the night, and to present you with a check would be like ushering you out of their restaurant before you were ready to leave," Cassie recited.

"Very rude." Deidre nodded seriously, making the others smile.

"A *digestivo* at the end of the meal to help with digestion," Remi said.

"Have you found one that isn't bitter yet?" Deidre asked, wrinkling up her nose.

Remi laughed. "When we get to Venice I'll introduce you to a *scropino* which you'll think is the best dessert on the peninsula. Also known as a *digestivo*."

"Made of?"

"Lemon sorbet, Prosecco, and vodka, I think."

"I'm in!" they both said in one voice.

ON THE FIRST night in their new quarters, the girls left the window open to let in the cool sea breeze and sounds of the villagers below. Although it was well past midnight, the sounds of small children chasing in the *piazza* drifted up to the apartments above. To the weary women it was music, happiness unbound.

To keep the bugs out, they pulled a large mosquito net over their bed.

Remi's room was smaller and had a window off the back. There was a bathroom between the two bedrooms, and all three doors opened to a small foyer. The fourth wall of the foyer had a door leading to the staircase.

They had one major adjustment to make.

"What's with this bathroom?" Cassandra asked. "It's broke. There's no toilet."

Remi poked his head into the room and looked over her shoulder. "You put your feet on those ridged tiles, squat, and poop or pee into the hole. Pull the chain up there to flush."

Deidre, who couldn't believe what she was hearing, crowded into the small space with the others.

"What?"

Remi made room so she could see.

"There's no commode? Are you out of your mind?"

"Look, plumbing is plumbing. There's a hole that flushes everything away. Some cultures just don't see the need to put a chair over the hole."

Both young women looked at him through new eyes. Now they knew he was insane.

THAT NIGHT, IN the quiet of her bed, snug beneath the mosquito net, Deidre thought about this morning as they gazed out over Manarola. There are moments in life, insignificant on the surface, but incidents that endure. Deidre had the unwavering sense that this was one of them. She would remember the sun on her skin, and the sea with its glorious color, and the faint taste of salt in the air. She could still feel the wind whipping her hair, her blouse clinging to her sweaty body, the seagulls calling far off, and the sea grass swaying on the ridge. She would remember, too, the raw smell of him, the shine of sweat on his brow, and the strength of his fingers around her arm pulling her toward him. The touch was the fixative of the picture, the thing that would make it stick when other memories faded. This was the snapshot she would remember, exciting all of her senses.

Because of her impending blindness, she only took pictures for others to see. But for herself, those few rare mental snapshots would be what she held closest to her, to be called up out of the encroaching blackness.

THE NEXT MORNING Deidre reminded Cassie to make sure she had everything, though Deidre was the one who had a tendency to make two or three trips back to retrieve forgotten items. Remi judiciously made no comment.

As they followed him to the *piazza,* they passed an open window with a large wooden board. Mosquito netting was tented over it to keep the flies out. Through the sun-bleached mesh, the women saw flaccid ribbons of pale yellow pasta, freshly made, drying on the table.

"Isn't that ingenious."

"Small things," Deidre murmured to herself.

It was early morning. The sea air smelled fresh, with just a trace of fish amid the floral perfume. Flower-filled window boxes sprinkled the façade of the colorful backdrop of apartments. Solid earthenware urns guarding each end of the stone break wall were filled with a riot of happy bobbing flowers. In tiny hidden places, one could find a vase or barrel or trough filled with flowers, their perfume wafting through the air.

From a distance, the horseshoe of buildings around the *piazza* looked like one solid mass of irregular rectangles. But Deidre knew, from the trek to their room last night and their initial exploration of the heart of the village, that narrow strands of stairs and alleyways penetrated the mass of stucco and broke the density into manageable parts. Like a block of wood infested with termite tunnels, the interior teemed with activity. Last night the dinner smells from homes and restaurants had teased them and had drawn them deeper into the interior. At first, the girls were afraid they might get lost in the lamp-lit maze, but Remi's presence and sense of direction reassured them. Not only had he found them a terrific *osteria,* but after three glasses of wine he had even led them back to their apartment with only one missed turn.

Today, they were eating beneath the same yellow umbrella in front of their new favorite restaurant. They were enjoying brioche filled with hot apricot jam, and cappuccino, except for Remi, who just wanted *café corretto*.

"*Corretto?*"

"A little *grappa* to start the day," the waiter said helpfully.

Remi shrugged.

"Alcohol? At 8:00 a.m.?" Deidre said, arching an eyebrow.

"Those who can't hold their liquor shouldn't judge those who can."

Cassandra blushed, but Deidre dropped her head and held up her hand in mock defeat. "Okay, okay."

The day was perfect for sunning. "This is the last sandy beach you'll see for a while."

"We'll be in Nice all next week."

"All rocks."

"Rocks?" the girls said together.

"But I've seen pictures of people lying out in the sun," said Deidre.

"On the ground?"

Deidre frowned in thought. "In lounge chairs. On a rock beach. But they cleverly don't show the beach."

Remi smiled. "Enjoy what you've got today. Tomorrow may be a bust."

He saw a shadow cross her face. He turned to look at Cassandra. She saw it, too, but turned away when she caught Remi observing her. Something's going on, he realized.

"Ready to go?" he asked as another couple sat down. "I like to hike early. It's cooler." As an afterthought he added, "And less people."

"Which way?"

Remi pointed toward a break in the row of buildings to the right of the church. "Those stairs, there. See the red arrow?"

Remi took the lead; Deidre followed behind him. When she wasn't watching her step, she could look at him as he walked in front of her. This was a first, putting herself in a position where she could actively admire a man's physique. Of course, she noticed great bodies: on the beach, in movies, just in everyday life. But seek it out? That seemed a bit naughty somehow. She decided that she liked both sensations: being naughty, and the feeling she got as she looked at his body.

Camera gear in hand, they started up toward Monterosso, the steepest and most difficult of the village hikes. Remi's long, muscular legs took the steps two at a time. The women, though younger, worked to keep up. Soon they were looking down at Vernazza. Just twenty minutes earlier, as they sat in the shade of the umbrella, the village had started to stretch in morning wakefulness. Now it was abuzz with activity. But as they climbed higher and the path snaked forward, then back in on itself, the village grew smaller and tranquil once again.

They stopped often to appreciate the serenity of their surroundings and record it in their cameras. Each climbing curve seemed to introduce them to a better photo than the last.

Remi had spent considerable time showing them various angles for best capturing the town's beauty. Light and the angle of the sun were important, so dawn and evening light were valuable. "Noon is the worst," he taught them. "The light is too harsh and the shadows it casts are too sharp. Always look behind you, too. It gives you a totally different perspective that's just as valid and sometimes more striking than what's in front of you." They were learning, and Remi was surprised at how much pleasure he took from that fact.

Finally, they were away from that small hub of civilization.

They walked past brush and grapevines and small trees trying to live on the hillside. The path was well worn, narrow in spots with steps inserted here and there, and, rarer still, the occasional hand railing. They had walked through small vineyards clinging precariously to the sides of steep hills, enjoyed views of the sea, and noted the berry patches already ravaged by earlier hikers. Deidre had expected to see vibrant greens so close to the water, but the countryside here was closer to a dusty sage. She reached over and plucked a narrow leaf, crushed it, and smelled it. Bitter. Not at all like sage. Just dusty bushes, she decided.

They had been hiking for about three hours, silent much of the way, each absorbed in his or her own thoughts, when they heard voices approaching. Morning hikers from Monterosso were heading toward Vernazza, chattering like squirrels, breaking the solitude.

Squirrels, Deidre thought. She hadn't seen any. In fact, she had seen no wildlife at all in Italy other than birds and fish. She'd have to ask Remi if he noticed that. He'd probably know why. Or maybe they'd make a "best guess."

As they neared Monterosso the hikers grew in both number and volume. Many were American. "Especially the loud ones," Remi muttered. "Ugly Americans."

"But you're American," Cassandra said.

"Sometimes I say I'm Canadian."

"Really?"

"So lying is okay?" Deidre frowned.

"Surviving is always okay," he quipped.

If nothing else, he gave her plenty to think about.

ON THE SECOND night, after the *piazza* had grown quiet, Deidre was awakened by a sudden sound. She didn't move as she tried to identify its source. She realized it was coming from inside the apartment, from the next room. There was an urgent calling out, a tussle, a sob. Remi. A nightmare. Cassie continued sleeping beside her. There was no one else in the apartment. She crept out of bed, aware that she had to use the bathroom. His door, like theirs, was open to let the breeze flow through the apartment.

Had she imagined it? No. The sound resumed. As she squatted over the hole, she wondered what to do. Should she wake him? When she had nightmares as a child, one or both of her parents would come in, wake her, hold her, and say soothing things to help her go back to sleep. It helped. As she washed her hands, it occurred to her that this wasn't his first nightmare. And he wasn't a child. She paused in the foyer. Entering his room uninvited was a breach of etiquette. She should just go to her own bed and hope it would pass. He seemed to have quieted already.

THE FLUSH OF the toilet awakened him. The nightmare was fresh, brutal, and painful. His heart was racing and his muscles ached from the imaginary fight. He slept naked, and his body was wet with sweat, from both the heat and exertion. He wiped his eyes on the sheet. He must have cried out. His throat burned. It seemed fairly standard for him. He heard someone washing her hands. As she stepped out of the bathroom he could tell from her step that it was Deidre. He knew she must have heard him—probably the reason she was up. She paused in the foyer, and he willed her to turn into her own room. When she did just that, he realized he'd been holding his breath. Whether he had planted the idea in her head or if she came up with it on her own, he was grateful that she stayed out.

Slowly, he found his way back to forgetfulness, but not before crossing through the last remnants of hell.

THEY SPENT THE next three days sunning, hiking, eating, and

taking photographs. Shopping, for the most part, was non-existent, except for a few cheap souvenirs.

"Lightweight," Deidre said, waving a feathery trophy over her head to demonstrate as the others laughed. No one said a word about the suitcase.

"Which hike did you like best?" Cassandra asked.

"Vernazza to Monterosso," Deidre said without hesitation.

"Why that one?" Remi asked. They had come to the end of the meal, and as the last bite of the *semifreddo* melted on his tongue he considered ordering another.

"Well, I liked it because…" Deidre paused. "First, because it was the hardest."

"What's so good about hard?"

"Challenging, I mean. After you've done it, you feel like you've accomplished something."

"Okay. I get that. What else?"

"The scenery, of course."

"The pictures of Vernazza look like they came right out of *National Geographic*. Even mine," said Cassandra.

"You've got a particularly good eye," he said with sincerity.

Cassandra beamed. "Yeah, that view was pretty spectacular."

Remi's compliments were rare and never given lightly. The women valued his approval and slowly adapted their behavior to win it. This was new for Deidre, who was constantly praised for everything she did, whether from her father or her teachers or the family chef. On the one hand, she felt she could do no wrong. But on the other, she secretly questioned if she was just being patronized. With Remi, though, she knew the answer. She either earned his praise legitimately, or he gave none. Clean communication, she thought. Clear, direct, no manipulation. It suited him, and she realized that it suited her, too.

"Anything else?" Remi asked, deciding in favor of the second dessert.

"And the story."

"The story?" Cassandra and Remi looked at each other.

"Yeah, the one I made up."

Remi raised an eyebrow.

"I mean, the characters don't have names or anything. But the story is about a girl in Monterosso and a boy in Vernazza who are in love."

Cassandra nodded encouragingly.

"You know, with only five hundred people in your village, how many are both eligible and attractive? Three? So if there's a girl in the next town over, you go for it, don't you? In my story, I thought about how hard it would be for him to court her. After working all day he has to hike hours to Monterosso to spend time with her and then hike back. Or wait until Sunday. But because he really loves her, he'll do it. That's how she knows it's real, that she's special."

"Because your story can't just have ordinary love, like finding a girl from your own village." Remi sighed.

"Not if she's special enough. If it's real love, he has to climb mountains to reach her. It can't be easy. He has to deserve her."

"Deidre won't settle for anything less than epic love, Remi, in case you haven't noticed."

Remi looked from Cassandra to Deidre incredulously. "Is that how girls think? They want gladiators? Supermen? Mountain climbers? For real?"

Cassandra and Deidre giggled and nodded. "Yep."

THE TWO-ROOM apartment had worked out fine. As always, Remi was the perfect gentleman, though Cassie confided that his proper behavior was a bit disappointing. Deidre didn't laugh. In fact, she didn't say anything.

Deidre ignored Cassie's knowing smile.

On the fifth day they hiked back to the car. After dropping off his bag, Remi went back to snatch Deidre's. She protested weakly, but the point had been made.

"One day, you'll learn to trust me," was all he said.

They headed north past Portofino then turned west to follow the coastline. They stopped for lunch at St. Remo. From the high road, the town below looked beautiful, but they had little time for exploration.

"We might have to change the schedule," Remi said. "Normally I don't like schedules at all, but—"

"That's a bit of an exaggeration," Deidre said. "As I recall, you had a pretty rigid schedule when we started to plan this trip."

Remi shot her a look. Today, she was seated next to him.

"Okay, I like a general outline of where I'm going, but it's not set in stone."

Deidre looked skeptical.

"It's not," he said defensively. "When the situation calls for it, you've got to be willing to adapt. That's all I'm saying."

"And the new plan is?"

"We may have to cut the Riviera short by a few days and get to the Luberon earlier."

"The Luberon? What's the Luberon? That's a new one."

Remi switched on the headlights as they approached a tunnel.

"At the end of June or beginning of July, it's the most incredible place on this planet."

"So what is it?"

"Lavender. Rows upon rows, fields upon fields, acres upon acres of lavender."

As they emerged from the tunnel Deidre saw him close his eyes, kiss the tips of his fingers, and send it to the gods. In the mirror Cassandra saw it, too. The girls looked at each other and burst out laughing.

"Like lavender and old lace?" Why, Deidre wondered, was this very macho man so taken with lavender? "This doesn't fit with the Remi I know," she said.

"Probably not," he replied good-naturedly. He looked over at her. "Because you only see what you want to see. At some point, you're going to figure out that your head distorts things. Sometimes you've got to turn off your brain and see with your other senses, see with your heart."

Was he speaking of the lavender, Deidre thought, or of himself?

"Who kidnapped our tour guide and left this romantic behind?" Deidre asked.

Remi laughed, too.

CHAPTER 6

NICE

THE BEACH AT Nice had met all their expectations: long and beautiful, hugging the bluest sea she had ever seen. And, yes, Remi was correct, it was covered with rounded rocks. Deidre and Cassie had spent their first afternoon sunning and dozing in lounge chairs, soaking up the heat and glamour of the French Riviera.

"What color is the sea?" Cassie asked, reminiscent of Remi's question in Cinque Terre.

They spent the next hour thinking up brilliant descriptions of the sight before them. They were pleased with their final descriptors and were eager to share them with Remi when they would all meet for dinner.

DEIDRE CHECKED her watch. They weren't late, but, of course, Remi was early. He was already seated with his back to the stone wall of the outdoor terrace and cell phone to his ear. He hadn't noticed them yet. He was smiling and relaxed and exuded a genuine but rare contentment.

He had changed from blue jeans to black slacks. Brown leather loafers replaced his hiking boots. The top three buttons of his white shirt were open to reveal a gold chain, and he had rolled the sleeves to just below his elbows. He had recently shaved, she noticed, but the blue black of his heavy beard was already threatening to darken his tanned face. A lock of hair fluttered in the evening breeze before drifting to the middle of his forehead giving him an utterly charming look. It occurred to her then that if sex appeal had a single definition it would be Remi Lamont. In this café. At this very moment.

As they approached, Deidre realized she wasn't the only one admiring the handsome man. When she looked in the direction of his raised glass and inviting smile, she saw a woman about his own age, a stunning, sun-streaked blond in a white cotton sundress—very French, very sophisticated, very beautiful. The woman was returning Remi's smile with her own champagne salute.

Deidre felt her insides contract in a wave of—of what? Jealousy? Could she actually be jealous? How ridiculous, she thought. This woman was no threat. Deidre knew that if she wanted to be charming, she could have any man she wanted, including Remi Lamont. But her quivering stomach wasn't quite as convinced.

Remi motioned them over with his cell phone when he saw them. Deidre wondered whom he was talking to, but the phone disappeared by the time they reached the table. The blond woman, she noticed, had tactfully turned away.

The outdoor café on the Promenade des Anglais, just down from their hotel, the Le Negresco, was lit for the diners. As they sat on the terrace looking out at the Cote d'Azur, Deidre forgot both the phone call and the pretty woman. The sun had set twenty minutes earlier. They had sat watching the golden disk seep slowly into the sea and the sky turn from creamy orange, to bright orange streaked with navy, to darker blue, and now to nearly black. Remi had set the camera on a tripod and had focused on a sailboat in the foreground, then had snapped a photo every two minutes as the scene changed. Fourteen frames later he had captured the dramatic sky in all its various forms.

The strip of grass down the center of the boulevard was sprinkled with palm trees, each lit from its base with a green light that illuminated the underside of its clustered leaves. The effect was a green band decorated with glowing neon trees. A boardwalk situated between the boulevard and the sea was shared by lovers strolling hand in hand, in-line skaters swirling around to the music from their earbuds, children scampering away from their parents' grasps, and hopeful seagulls who really ought to have been looking for a roost.

Out at sea, spots of white and red lights emanated from the boats. Here and there, the triangles of sails were outlined in white. Yachts anchored for the night, sparkled, perhaps with a party on board. To the left, the multi-colored lights of the city hugged the mountain, twinkling as the thermos of the day gave way to the cooler night. And to the right, Cannes's peaceful glow hid the intrigues of power and wealth.

"This is where my parents honeymooned," Deidre said.

"I thought your mother was afraid to fly," Remi said as he cracked a crayfish.

"Oh, she is. They took the Queen Mary over. Or was it the Queen Elizabeth? One of the big ships."

Remi nodded and frowned; his crayfish was clearly winning.

"So the sea—what descriptors did you two ladies come up with?"

He had stopped calling them kids, thank goodness. Deidre wasn't sure how much more of that little jab she could have taken, especially since she was about to officially step into adulthood.

"I'm going to be twenty-one next month."

That caught him by surprise. He looked up. "I assumed you were a freshman."

"You only see what you want to see," she tossed back at him before adding, "Senior, in September, if I went back."

"Taking a semester off?"

College students. He sat back and looked from one to the other. Just like that, a snap of the finger, they had changed from teenagers to adults. He squinted, peering carefully at each girl. They even appeared different to him now—prettier, more poised, more confident. Or maybe this was the first time he had given himself permission to look.

"What? What are you thinking?" Deidre's gray eyes laughed at his expression.

He looked at her, then shook his head to clear it.

"Does that change things?" Deidre asked.

He gazed at her thoughtfully, then turned back to his fish before finally yanking the head off.

"Maybe."

BOTH HOTEL ROOMS had a sea view. Deidre stretched as she walked out to the balcony to watch the glow from behind the point push brighter in advance of the sun. What a glorious day.

She saw movement on the next balcony.

"Remi?"

"Yeah. You up, too?"

"My favorite time of day."

"Mine, too."

"I'm going to go for a walk. Will you tell Cassie?"

"Sure. Walk along the boardwalk?" He wasn't worried if she stayed on the main boulevard.

"The beach. I'll be back in an hour."

"Have fun."

She dressed quickly and slipped outside. She crossed the boulevard and stepped down to the boardwalk wondering if his eyes were on her. She smiled hoping they were. *Leading lady, Audrey Hepburn, dashing through traffic somewhere in Manhattan. All eyes turned...*

Instead of heading toward the town, she turned west toward Cannes. There was less chance of seeing anyone. Morning solitude was best for recharging her spirit.

The first rays of dawn: so full of hope and promise. All her life she embraced the morning. Days like today, full of early warmth and golden glow, when she had her health, her youth, and her strength, these were the moments that demanded her presence. She closed her eyes. *When I'm blind I will still love mornings. I will smell the sun. I will hear the dawn. I will hold this moment in memory.* She opened her eyes again. *If there is an idealized woman, then this will be my idealized morning.*

She found the thought thoroughly comforting.

Behind her, the sun was fully visible now. The waves lapped gently on the rocks. She would buy a conch in Nice so she could listen to the sea murmur whenever it called to her.

She stopped to watch a head bobbing in the waves. She must have caught the swimmer at the end of her exercise, because the woman climbed out just then, and shook back her long hair. Water flew and glistened in the sunlight. The woman, possibly in her late thirties or early forties, was thin and graceful. She shook out her towel and dried herself, then wrapped it around her bosom and tucked the ends in tightly. Deidre watched as she reached beneath the towel to unhook the top of her bathing suit. It dropped at her feet. She bent to pick up a bra from her bag and expertly worked the hooks beneath the towel. Next came the bottom: suit falling, panties and skirt rising. The woman wore no stockings. Finally, she slipped a blouse over the top of the towel, worked a few strategic buttons, released the towel, and let it drop to the sand. She finished with the buttons and ran a comb through her hair to straighten it, then scrunched it with her hand—and *voilà*! All was right in her world. In less than five minutes, the French woman had achieved practical elegance and was ready for work. Deidre wished her mother were here to see it.

She hadn't thought about her mother in a while. Compared to the space her father took up in her thoughts, her mother occupied very little. Janet Sinclair was beautiful. Deidre had inherited her fine bones, thick tresses of chestnut hair, clear skin and straight, white teeth. Though pale in winter, they both tanned fiercely in summer. She had yet to know a sunburn. She could eat anything, and did, and never gain an unwanted ounce, all traits she shared with her mother. While the older woman had penetrating blue eyes, hers were a softer gray, sometimes pale blue in certain light. But there, the similarities ended.

Janet Sinclair was afraid of everything. She had developed a whole set of phobias after it happened. The family spoke little of it. The plane crash, the skeleton in the closet, and the reason Deidre was suspicious of secrets. It had taken years for Deidre to piece together the story.

Janet's brother had been the pilot. They had been arguing. No one said it outright, but Deidre believed her uncle had deliberately sent the plane into a spin to frighten his sister, but didn't pull out in time. He died. She should have. A merciful God spared her face, but beneath her elegant clothes she wore the scars of the day that had changed everything.

After that, she became afraid of so many things: heights, food poisoning, germs, falling, being alone. It was Janet's fear, Deidre knew, that drove her into screaming fits, demanding that those around her do as she ordered. Her mother imagined that this conveyed strength. But Deidre had learned early on that her mother was one of the weakest people she knew.

Her father had been the buffer. When his wife tried to impose her phobias onto Deidre, he was often, though not always, there to shield her. If left unchecked, her mother would suffocate her with fear. Her father provided her air to grow. When he couldn't be there, she learned to be her own buffer to withstand the onslaught of the dangerous world her mother had invented. Deidre theorized she was an only child because of her mother's fears.

She rebelled against her mother. She wanted to be everything Janet Sinclair was not. They fought constantly; stubbornness was their only common personality trait.

Now, faced with her impending handicap, Deidre was scared for the first time, truly scared. She was even developing a small bud of understanding for her mother. Through this pinhole of empathy, she was able to glimpse the hell of Janet Sinclair's life. And that scared her even more than going blind. She would not become her mother. She refused.

THE RIVIERA WAS and wasn't like big cities everywhere. The roads were certainly too small for modern cars and heavy traffic, but, many of the interesting sites were within walking distance of their hotel. Each morning, they walked east down the Promenade des Anglais to the center of the historic district. Mornings in the *piazza* constantly surprised them. On different days they found a fruit and spice market, a flower market, and a flea market. By afternoon, the vendors packed up their carts and tables and disappeared, leaving a cleanly swept square that quickly filled with lunch tables and patrons.

They found copious photo opportunities wherever they turned. Cassandra was a natural, but Remi was especially pleased to watch Deidre's developing awareness. She seemed almost pressured to see everything. She was using her camera more and anything with color beckoned her lens. Her pictures of the spice table spilled with bright oranges, reds, yellows, and contrasting browns, all encompassed by baskets of green and blue. Not to be ignored, the pastel bars of soap in pale pink, gentle violet, creamy white, and soft yellow quietly caught her attention. She captured precisely the moment when the yellow petals of squash blossoms, those delicate trumpeters of summer, bent to the breeze. Pails of floral bouquets had her camera tipping to the happy faces of carnations, roses, mums, and hollyhocks. A tray of sweets, a cart of peppers, a wagon of wine bottles, all came alive in her camera.

Early on, she noted that in France, even the most humble display was arranged with careful thought, good taste, and artistic reverence. Remi was glad she appreciated this land of his ancestors.

Remi was able to relax on the Riviera, and there were even moments when he felt he had found himself again. Despite the confines in the heart of the old town, tall building and all, the sense of danger seemed more remote. He couldn't quite figure out why, and he didn't want to overthink it. The grays in his mind often gave way to lesser grays, and almost the blues of hopeful skies.

One day, the group left the market and went up the cobblestones into the heart of old Nice, toward the art district. Among the many unique shops one in particular stood out. Shadowboxes covered the walls, each depicting a three dimensional theme: a picnic, a road trip, a ship, a golf theme. Using pieces of everyday life the artist had assembled, not a decoupage but a suggestion: a corner of a wicker basket, a portion of a map, a crumpled napkin.

As Deidre looked at the sliced wine glass, the thistle, the open bottle of perfume, something occurred to her. "It involves more than just the visual, doesn't it?" she said. If she had closed her eyes and touched the picture, she would have understood the composition, the theme, and the art.

Cassie squeezed her hand.

Remi searched their faces, but they just smiled at him.

Later, they meandered three blocks north of the Promenade to find good prices on sandwich baguettes, the precursors to the

American submarine. They found lively outdoor cafes near the beach where they grabbed a spritzer or glass of very good wine, for practically nothing. Although Sinclair was paying, once the initial novelty wore off, along with his resentment, Remi found it impossible to waste the man's money. In time, it almost became a game, to see who could be the best bargain hunter. Not only did Deidre not object, but Remi was also pleased to hear that she was "enchanted" with the way the other half lived.

That wasn't fair, Remi chided himself. She wasn't that much of a snob. Yes, her life was different from his, but she didn't live in Marie-Antoinette's "let them eat cake" world either. He was pretty hard on her, and he wondered why. He, of all people, had no right to judge anyone.

The next day, Cassandra and Deidre left to get French braids and nails, allowing him time to work on the itinerary. And to recharge. He still wasn't used to having someone around all day, everyday, and welcomed these little reprieves.

The women—yes, he had allowed them to grow from girls to wards to young women, but sometimes he dropped the "young"— wanted to see Cannes badly.

He had planned to take them to see both Cannes and St. Paul de Vence, and maybe Eze, but while the women were shopping—and Nice was the perfect place for shopping, they assured him—he was getting the scoop on the situation in the Luberon. It had been a particularly hot spring, and the lavender was blooming earlier than usual. That meant they would have to leave Nice early. Would the Chateau have room, though?

While he let Sinclair book the hotels in the major cities, Remi chose the minor ones. The Mas Derrierre le Chateau was clean, cheap, and best of all, charming. Different from what she was used to, a new experience. No, *they*, he caught himself. Different from what *they*—yes, Cassandra, too—were used to.

Since the revelation about their ages, only thoughts of Deidre had wormed their way into his head, invading his thoughts at unexpected moments. But this wouldn't be a problem. He'd just have to toss her back out. What did she think she was doing in there, anyway? The whole thing was ridiculous. He was fourteen years older. And certainly not rich. She wanted a gladiator, or someone to climb mountains for her, and he couldn't find his way over a mogul. This was a waste of time. Like now, this conversation he was having with himself. Stupid.

He shrugged it off and headed back to the Le Negresco.

He couldn't figure out why he was suddenly angry.

Dammit.

There would only be time for one more town, and it wouldn't be Cannes.

He needed to make a call, or two.

CHAPTER 7

LES BAUX

THEY ARRIVED AT the Mas Derriere le Chateau by mid-afternoon. The reports were right: it was hot. Remi hadn't been there for years, not since before Iraq. Marie-Laure and—what was his name? Fred. Fredrick. No, that wasn't quite right. Frederick! Yes, that was it. And a little girl named Daniella. He had brought her a stuffed horse. She had been very shy, but after receiving the toy, she watched him with those big brown eyes. Not out of fear, but out of curiosity. She'd be grown by now, at least a teenager, and the horse was surely long-buried with the trash. She might even be a mother herself by now. Time was racing by. He felt old.

The chateau was really just a large stone farmhouse, left to Marie-Laure by an aunt. The windows were tall, but not particularly wide. The red paint on the wooden door and shutters was faded and peeling. A chicken coop had been new the last time he was here, but now the fencing around it looked tired and the tiled roof was chipped in a couple of spots. The farmhouse was a large, stable structure, though, with no special architectural features other than the stone. But from all angles, the vistas were wonderful.

Remi smiled inwardly as he watched the women standing in the driveway and looking in awe from the picturesque olive orchard, to the mountains beyond, to the town perched high above, and back to the fruit orchard in front.

He unloaded the car and greeted his hosts, pleased that they remembered him. Marie-Laure hustled the women inside, making them feel welcome and warm, as she invited them to pick the rooms they liked best. For most of the week, they were her only guests.

Deidre and Cassandra parted at the head of the stairs. They had separate bedrooms this time.

Deidre stood in the middle of the green-painted room and simply looked, taking it all in. The walls were exposed stone, cream and tan, soft edged, and woven together with wide gray mortar. The exposed beams on the ceiling were substantial, dark, and comforting. A bar of lavender soap dimpled her pillow, and on the nightstand stood a miniature bottle. She picked it up and examined the label, translating the simple words. *Olive oil produced by the Chateau Derriere.* A bunch of lavender sprang from a white vase, its sweet scent permeating the room. Other than these little flourishes, the room had just enough of everything. The Provençale floor tile, a curtain pulled to one side at the framed window, and the simple country furniture—all of it spoke of an uncomplicated but complete life. Somehow it felt balanced and familiar. A déjà vu moment. Like this had been her life once before.

She hummed a remembered tune from her parents' old album. She wondered what life in quiet Provence, hosting a bed and breakfast, might be like. Would it bore her? Would it work if she were blind? Would she welcome the solitude, the simplicity, or would it give her too much time to think about the unfairness of it all? What did her future hold? What might it have been? She was not yet willing to relinquish the dreams of the last four years, and wondered how she could still make it as a fashion designer in New York. How could she change things so her life would work out?

If she wanted it badly enough, couldn't she change the outcome? Or would the best course be to simply give up? But that wasn't who she was. Giving up would be a betrayal of everything she believed about life, about herself. How could she accept a future of darkness? Forever. It just seemed unfathomable. But did she have a choice? Wouldn't the medical community come up with a cure?

It must, it simply must.

Why did she torment herself thinking about it? Couldn't she just accept Remi's advice and enjoy the moment? So easily said, so impossible to achieve. Maybe tomorrow...

BREAKFAST WAS served on a large stone table under an ancient tree. The branches had been pruned high enough that even Remi could stand and reach above his head before touching one. He was already seated, absentmindedly polishing his camera lenses as he looked out at the orchard. Frederick was picking apricots. He put them gently in a basket hung at his waist. Suspended over his shoulder was a well-washed cloth strap attached to the wicker. The color of the fruit, the basket, the strap, and his shirt created a harmony of soft pastels that appealed to his photographer's eye. He fit a lens on the camera and adjusted the depth of field so only Frederick and the fruit were in focus before pressing the shutter. He took a few more pictures, bracketing the aperture, knowing at least one would turn out.

"We're here!" the girls called out in rested enthusiasm.

"Good sleep?"

"The best!" Deidre said. "What did Marie-Laure put in my tea last night? I haven't slept like this since childhood, I swear."

"It's the lavender."

Frederick had moved to produce a three quarter profile. Remi continued watching the scene unfold through his viewfinder, snapping a shot every so often.

Both girls were eating and laughing and discussing the best way to get the lavender home.

"Customs frowns on smuggling activities. You may have to forego this indulgence," Remi said from behind the camera.

"Party pooper," they teased.

He took a few more shots and put the camera down. He looked at the scene in front of him, narrowed his eyes, and set his jaw.

"What?" Deidre said to the gathering storm cloud of his face.

"Did we do something wrong?" Cassandra asked.

"He didn't get any lavender last night," Deidre said in a stage whisper.

Cassandra squeezed her knee in warning.

His frown deepened.

"It's called mindlessness," he said quietly.

The girls looked at each other, then back at Remi, and then back at each other again.

"Can you elaborate, perhaps?" Deidre suggested.

He shook his head, tamping down his irritation. "Did you even look at the table? Did you see the care Marie-Laure put into making everything just right?"

They looked at the table, now covered with crumbs, shells of eggs, a dollop of jam threatening to fall, and the general disarray of a finished meal.

"We're not supposed to eat? We're just supposed to look?"

"You're supposed to enjoy the meal with all your senses." He hadn't meant to lecture, but he was into it now. "Take that egg. I'll wager in your entire life you've never had a fresher egg, because just an hour ago your gracious hostess plucked it out of the chicken coop." He pointed to the chickens as he spoke. "Did you even taste it?"

"Not really. I mean it was good, but…"

Well, he thought, at least she had the decency to be honest.

"And those Kaiser rolls," he continued, "At oh dark thirty, while you were enjoying your dreams, Frederick was dressing for his trip to the baker, to be the first in line to bring you hot rolls right out of the oven."

"Oh."

"And you didn't even look at the jams."

They did now. Spread before them was an array of honey and strawberry, apricot, and raspberry jams, all in tiny glass dishes, each with a delicate spoon for dripping the sweetness onto the rolls. They saw, too, the porcelain pot of hot water decorated in Provincial blue flowers, the dish of yogurt, its white cream contained in a wide red bowl, the fresh berries, the mound of butter, and the tray of sliced meats.

"She personally made every one of those jams for your enjoyment. And the honey came from a local beekeeper, not from some cheesy plastic bear at the supermarket."

"You're mixing your metaphors again, but we get the point," Deidre said.

"Well, we are enjoying them," Cassandra volunteered diplomatically.

Remi sighed. "You didn't even taste them. You live so much in the future you miss the moment happening right now, and all the pleasure *that* can bring. Would you please just stop and look around you?"

"You're right. We missed it. *I* missed it," Deidre said looking at her friend, who nodded in agreement. "We'll do better tomorrow." It was delivered with just enough chagrin to make Remi almost forgive them.

THEY LEFT LES BAUX and headed north along the winding road toward St. Remy. Remi nodded to a building on their right. "The mental hospital where Van Gogh spent his last days."

"Really," Cassandra said, impressed.

"Checked himself out so he could kill himself."

"Not very effective treatment," Deidre said.

"Did he paint much here?" Cassandra asked. "In this area, I mean?"

"Yeah. You like Van Gogh?"

"Very much. The Impressionists next semester."

"Then we'll go to Arles later in the week," Remi said.

"What's there?"

"Later in the week. Right now, lavender."

In St. Remy, while waiting at a red light, he turned to Deidre seated next to him. "Navigator," he said leaning over to look at the map, his shoulder pressing hers, "I want you to get us . . . right about here."

Deidre looked at the red and black squiggles, like veins on a drunken man's nose, and the spot where his fingertip ended.

"Okay. Keep going straight." She laughed at her own joke. There wasn't a straight road in all of the Luberon.

Concentrating on her role as navigator, she studied the map.

"None of these road numbers make sense."

"Nope, they don't."

Cassie unhooked her seatbelt and hung over Deidre's shoulder to look.

"Well, look. Most of these roads are D roads, though some are N, but there's no rhyme or reason to the numbering system. It's not like north and south roads are odd and east and west are even. And it's not like east roads are higher numbered than those to their west, or even the reverse. It's like, like—"

"Like eight hundred years ago some peasant just called out a number, and over the centuries whatever numbers were left were used to identify new roads." Remi smiled.

"Exactly!"

Cassie looked at the map. "Does the D or N mean anything? It looks like the A and E roads are major highways at least."

"Just a guess, maybe the A is the European designation, but the French being French, a bit stuck in their ways and proud of it—"

"Like you," Deidre interjected.

Ignoring that, he continued, "—wanted to keep their E system."

"That kinda makes sense, though. What is the French word for expressway?"

No one knew.

"Turn up here, to the left, and head for Apt," Deidre pointed.

"You're pointing to the right," Remi said slowing the car.

"I mean right."

He made the turn. "The lavender grows on the hillside and at higher elevations, so it might be a while before we see any, but keep an eye out, anyway."

They drove for nearly an hour, never in a straight line.

"These are the craziest roads!"

"Lucky I don't get carsick," Cassandra said, clutching the seat back at a sudden turn.

"Wait, wait! This should be D32, but somehow we got on D5. Back up. I don't know where I went wrong, but we have to get back to N67 and figure it out."

"You know, there are about a hundred combinations that will get us there," Remi said. "Let's just keep going and take another route. As long we head north and up—"

"No, I want to find out what we did wrong."

Remi sighed and turned the car around. Once back at N67, they reversed direction again and started back the way they had just come.

Deidre stared at the map. "This isn't right. It shows that N67 dead ends into D32."

Remi pulled over and took the map.

"Right here. See?" She pointed.

99

He looked at the map, then up at the road sign.

"Well, I'll be… Circle this. You've just found the mapmaker's signature."

"Signature?" Cassie said.

"What signature? It's a mistake," Deidre said.

"Exactly. Every mapmaker inserts a minor mistake on his maps. It's his signature and acts as a copyright, in a way." He paused for a moment. "Head up here," he said pointing to a new spot on the map. He turned the car in the new direction and started driving again.

"I don't understand this signature stuff," said Deidre. "What do you mean, a copyright? Maps can be copyrighted?"

"If a mapmaker thinks someone has copied his map, how can he prove it? The roads are static. Anyone can say he did the work of creating his own map when all he would have to do is copy someone else's work. Changing the color, the font size, or the proportions is nothing compared to surveying the area. That's where the cost mounts up. But if the new guy really did do his own work—"

"He wouldn't have the mistake on his map," Deidre said triumphantly.

"Exactly. It's always small, something the locals would never look at a map for. It's their neighborhood, after all. And it doesn't have much of an impact on people like us, unless we think our address is actually on D32."

"The mapmaker's signature. I never even heard of such a thing."

"I've only found one myself. It's pretty rare. Keep that map. You found it."

Deidre studied it a moment more, then got back to her duties.

The landscape was changing as they headed to higher elevations. The roads grew smaller and sometimes the asphalt gave way to dirt roads. Vineyards lined the tilting landscape to catch the full benefit of the southern sun. Farmhouses sprang up in the midst of fields. They seldom saw any livestock, and even fewer people.

"Turn right."

"You're pointing left."

"She's dyslexic," Cassie called helpfully from the backseat, "Follow the finger."

Deidre scowled. "I am not dyslexic, but follow the finger."

"Really?"

"Well, you only have a fifty-fifty chance of getting it right if you listen to me, but I always point in the right direction."

"How are you with compass points?"

"Oh, I've got that down like pointing."

"Good, let's do compass direction, but keep using your finger, just in case."

"Stop laughing back there!"

CHAPTER 8

THE LUBERON

THE GIRLS WERE disappointed when they reached the lavender.

"It just looks like gray streaks. Not purple at all," Deidre complained. "All this effort for gray streaks?"

"That's not lavender, that's lavendra."

"Come again, Professor?"

"Lavender, the real stuff, is really really deep purple. That's what the French use for their perfumes. But this pale flower, lavendra, sometimes called lavandin, is used for everything else, like soaps or those little bags—"

"Potpourri," inserted Deidre.

"Yeah. It's easier to grow, but it's inferior quality."

"It looks like what's in our garden back home," said Cassandra.

"Probably is. Most Americans don't know the difference."

Deidre sighed. "So we haven't found the lavender yet."

"No whining," he said reprovingly.

He took the map from her lap and studied it. "We head north."

It was hot. The sun was blinding. He looked over at Deidre and in the mirror at Cassandra. Both girls looked wilted. They hadn't found any lavender yet, but they would.

They were traveling down a very small dirt road shouldered on each side by tall rows of grapevines with young fruit hanging from the branches. He saw a cut-through for a tractor and pulled in, then stopped the car.

"And we're stopping because?" Deidre asked.

"Because we live in the moment, and the moment says we are hot and tired and hungry. And this seems like a good place for a picnic."

He got out of the car and opened the trunk. The two women, suddenly energized, scampered after him. They pulled out two blankets and a food box prepared by Marie-Laure.

Cassandra spread the blankets under the shade of the grapevines, far enough off the road so they wouldn't be seen.

"Not that any cars ever actually drive down this road," Deidre said.

She took the food and began unpacking baguettes, cheese, fruit, and olives. Remi worked the corkscrew to get at the wine.

Like flowers in a desert rain. He smiled to himself. *They blossom.*

"Oh, this is absolute ambrosia," Deidre purred biting into the bread topped with a wedge of cheese.

"Drink the wine with the cheese," Cassandra advised, wrinkling her nose, "not the olives."

That made him laugh.

Hidden in the bottom of the box they discovered the raspberry tart.

"I died and went to heaven," Deidre said as she threw herself on the blanket, cake in hand.

"Me, too," her best friend said, joining her.

They spent the next hour whispering together, nibbling on the delicious food, and drifting in and out of sleep. Remi listened to their soft soothing voices as he, too, reclined with his arms underneath his head and looked at the blue sky just above the clusters of green grapes. The lavender grew somewhere nearby. He could smell it, as he, too, drifted to some old familiar place.

This is good. This is very good.

The sky was blue, and it stayed for a very long while.

* * * * *

THEY HAD BEEN driving for forty minutes when he first smelled it. He stuck his head out the window to be sure. Following his lead, Deidre did the same.

"Lavender?" she asked, pulling her head back in.

He nodded as the smile spread across his face.

He smiles with his eyes, Deidre thought. She hadn't noticed that before.

"Look!" Cassie shouted, pointing excitedly through the windshield.

There, just below the horizon, perched a hill bathed in color. Lavender! They had found it.

The field first appeared as a single deep purple mass, but as they drove closer the purple individualized into softly mounded rows. The rows were planted perfectly straight, but like corduroy cloth under a microscope, they took the distorted shape of the hill beneath their roots. The individual plants were four to five feet in diameter and about thirty inches high. Each plant had been tenderly shaped into half balls, but they'd been planted together so densely that the stems of one plant grew amid the stems of its neighbor to form unbroken rows.

Their timing was perfect. The lavender was bursting with flowers. Each fragile stem sprung straight out from the plant's heart, its tip ablaze with delicate purple petals half as big as a newborn's fingernail. Bees and butterflies, intoxicated by the aroma, danced from one delightful stem to the next. The bounty was beyond belief.

"So these are the lavender fields of the Luberon," she breathed. "What did you call it? The most incredible place on the planet."

"You see it, don't you?" He smiled down at her.

She met his eyes, and neither looked away.

"I see it. I smell it. It will be with me always." She reached for his hand and, as she squeezed it, said, "Thank you so very, *very* much."

A crow screeched overhead and they both looked up. The sky was radiant.

"BUTTERFLY MAGNETS, that's what they are," she said.

Cassie had gone up to bed. Deidre and Remi sat at the stone table with Remi's laptop. It exploded with the color of lavender fields.

They sat quietly, comfortably, as they looked through the pictures.

Remi captured one butterfly hovering above a flower, its gold wings folded up to make a V, the brown of its eye motionless, its delicate legs faintly touching the purple stalk of blossoms.

"That shot may be the shot of the day," Remi said in the voice of a man satisfied.

"How do you know which pictures are the special ones?"

"Hmm, not sure," he answered truthfully. "I guess after I delete the ones that are out of focus, or where someone's ear pops into the frame, or whatever, I look at the best ones and then close down my brain and listen to which of them speak to me. That's the trick, I guess. I let my heart decide."

Remi could sense she was thinking not only about his answer, but about something else, too.

Finally, she said, "The lavender is the big thing, but the butterfly is the small thing, isn't it?"

Remi paused. "Most people would think Paris is the big thing and the lavender is the small thing. But I'd say you're probably more accurate."

"Once they've seen the lavender, they could never call it a small thing?"

He reached over and ran his hand up and down her arm. "I think you're getting it," he said with a smile.

He felt a small shiver and withdrew his hand, but the warmth of her skin lingered.

Deidre looked at him with deep gray eyes. They were brighter in the sunlight, darker in the moonlight. She had a certain expression on her face. What was it? Not flirty, not longing. What, he wondered? Finally, she pushed back her seat and stood up.

"Thank you for this. For all of it, I mean." She spread her arms toward the orchard, and the house, and the town perched on the mountain.

He thought that her eyes were shining with tears, but she turned away before he could be sure. She hurried into the house, and Remi was left alone, to reflect whether or not today had been a good one.

THE EARLY HOURS were cool. A thick haze hovered close to the ground. As pre-dawn surrendered to morning's light, the pale green olive leaves possessed a haunting look. As the minutes passed, the fog slowly lifted and thinned like a diaphanous veil around each tree, to form a singular work of art in a gallery full of singular works of art. Remi was there to capture each changing moment as he waited for the girls to join him. They were getting better, but they were still late.

Although the trio got up early, Marie-Laure had set the table for them. Other guests had arrived the day before but were still sleeping. Remi had alerted his hostess of their early morning departure never imagining she would prune her own sleep to provide breakfast for them. But here it was, the stone table covered with Provencal delicacies.

They were in a hurry and had a long way to go before they

reached the Abbey of Senanque. They made meat and cheese sandwiches on Kaiser rolls, wrapping them in paper napkins to save for later. They drank down coffee, tea, and cocoa, stuffed apricots into their backpacks, and hastily buttered and jellied the last Kaiser roll for breakfast. Waving their thanks to an amused Marie-Laure, they loaded lunch, cameras, maps, and themselves into the car and headed north.

Deidre sat in the front seat with the map on her lap. She was the navigator while Cassandra slept. The conversation was minimal, both Remi and Deidre content to muse about the landscape before them. The elevation climbed as they passed carefully balanced villages on overhanging cliffs. Deidre, born in Michigan, a peninsula of lakes and beaches, forests, and lush farmland, found the surrounding landscape to be barren, almost desert in appearance. The yellow of the ground, the rocks, and village stone grew wearisome after several hours.

Remi found the scenery invigorating. The roads were good and had few travelers. The villages were architecturally brilliant, considering the time in which they were built and their enduring vibrancy. Even the landscape reminded him of Montana in an odd sort of way. The abundance of sand supporting sparse plant life, the heat even early in the day, the distant house accessible by a long dirt road, and the solitude eased his mind and relaxed him.

They were heading for Gordes on the map, but Remi passed the sign identifying the final turn.

"We can catch it on the way back," was his only comment to Deidre's turned head.

Soon the road hugged the mountainside and climbed gently, before leveling out. As Remi looked out of his window, he said with quiet pleasure, "The lavender is peaking."

Deidre leaned over his shoulder and excitedly called to the

backseat, "We're here, Cassie, wake up."

"I'm awake. I'm awake. Where? Oh," she breathed. "It's beautiful."

"It is," Remi said.

As the road descended, it curved sharply to the left. Soon they saw purple fields on both sides, but their destination, the Abbey with its perfectly manicured lavender, spread before them.

They were the first to pull in to the dirt parking lot and chose a place beneath an old tree with low hanging thick branches. Remi knew the day's heat would exceed one hundred, and this was the only possibility of relief.

He unpacked the camera equipment, slung the tripod over one shoulder, and backpack with the camera over the other.

"How about if we pack our lunch," he suggested.

"Let's eat here later on," Deidre countered. "This is such a pretty place to tailgate."

Remi nodded. He was used to the practical use of time and energy. Ambience had never played much of a role in his life. But he didn't object.

"Got everything?" he asked before closing the trunk. He didn't wait for an answer.

"Head out," he said striding off toward the Abbey. As he walked he heard the girls laughing behind him.

"What's so funny?" he asked, turning back.

"Just wondering if we were supposed to salute or something," Cassandra said.

"Or march," Deidre added.

He smiled and slowed his pace. "Old habits."

At the end of the parking lot he stopped, waiting for the girls to catch up the last few steps. His anticipation energized him, making a slower pace difficult. But he wanted to capture their reaction. It matched his the first time he had come to the Abbey.

"I have never seen anything so beautiful; I swear I haven't," said Cassandra.

"I can smell the color," breathed Deidre.

"Come on," Remi urged, satisfied he'd hit the mark.

The timing of their arrival couldn't have been better. No tourists had arrived yet, and the sun was still low enough in the morning sky to capture the brilliance of the color. The butterflies were thick on the stalks of purple, their little yellow and white wings fluttering in ecstasy as their legs worked the magic of eating, fertilizing, and reveling in the glory of the day.

Remi moved his tripod according to the changing light. He anticipated when the sun would elevate the features of the Abbey's façade to the best advantage, and the angle where the color of the lavender would be the most intense. He set up above the field to get a picture shooting down on the color. Rather than highlighting the straight rows of lavender, this angle cut across and blended the color like a painter swiping a freshly dipped brush across his canvas.

He widened his shot to capture layers of color: the background of the dark leafy trees on the hillside, the gray whites of the Abbey in the middle, the vivid purple of the flowers edged by a lush green hedge, the white pebble path, and another strand of lavender in the foreground. He looked through his viewfinder. This, he decided, would be the shot of the day.

When the sun grew high above them they packed away their equipment and entered the much cooler stone Abbey.

They opted out of the tour, but enjoyed the bookstore. Deidre's selection of historical material was always the condensed version. "Lighter to carry," she explained.

Because the Abbey provided relief from the heat, the day seemed blisteringly hot when they exited. The group headed back to the car and found a forgotten bottle of sparkling water. It was so hot it hurt the hands to open. When Remi finally wrestled off the plastic cap, a robust spray of water fanned out for five feet.

"Hot shower anyone?"

They opened the car doors to release the heat, then started the engine and set the air conditioner to high. While the car cooled off, they sat at the base of the tree and ate their sandwiches. Cassandra put two teabags in the hot water, which soon darkened to a rich brown. When it cooled enough, they passed around the bottle.

Cassandra tested the brew and wrinkled her nose.

"Sun tea, I have now discovered, should never be made with carbonated water."

She wiped the mouth of the bottle and handed it to Deidre, who, rather than drinking from it, passed it on to Remi. Though tea wasn't his first choice, in a pinch like today, he welcomed it.

He, too, made a face after taking an appreciative drink. "Salty tea," was all he said.

He handed the bottle back to Deidre. She looked at him with a sly smile. There was something essentially erotic about drinking from the same bottle as Remi Lamont. Her imagination swam with the desire to know the lips that had just caressed the same plastic she was about to drink from. As she brought the bottle to her mouth, her heart beat a little faster. She watched him laughing with Cassie as she ran her tongue around the rim, then took a swallow.

Mere seconds had passed, but she felt herself soaring to new dimensions on the tail of those fleeting thoughts. It was like a secret, passionate kiss between them, but it was her secret alone, a secret she could embrace.

CHAPTER 9

ARLES

ARLES WAS a surprise.

"Is this still France? Or have we crossed over into Spain?" Deidre asked.

"Arles is definitely Provence. Oh," Remi said, realizing her confusion. "The arena."

"Bullfights? Matadors?" Cassandra asked.

Billboards blanketed the arena walls. "Built by the Roman Empire, these walls have hosted quite a variety of shows. I guess bullfights are the entertainment of our time." He thought for a moment. "Did you want to see one?"

"No!" they declared in unison.

He acted nonchalant, but felt relief. He'd seen enough blood and human cruelty. There was nothing for them here.

Last night had been hard for him. He had his first nightmare in a long time, but it felt as if they had been storing up to dump on him all at once. How much sleep did he get? An hour? Two? Maybe. He'd functioned on less, but he was younger then. They'd make an early night of it.

The trio walked through the curved streets as Cassandra read from the guidebook.

"It says here that Van Gogh painted over a hundred and eighty paintings during his time in Arles. He used them to pay for rent, or meals, or gave them as gifts. But after all those opportunities the town doesn't have one single Van Gogh!"

"Not one?" Deidre said.

"Apparently his landlords or whoever fed him saw him as a

charity case. They only took the pictures to save his pride. But for them, let's see…" She read silently. "The paintings ended up with whatever passing tinker or gypsy came along, sold for a franc or two. They were seen as children's drawings. Isn't that sad?"

"Sad for Arles, letting a fortune slip away," he said.

The three walked on, all inside their own heads.

Cassandra stopped to look at a shop window, waving for the others to continue their slow stroll.

"What an incredibly sad man," Deidre said at last. "And such a tragic life."

Remi began singing softly.

"What is that from?" Deidre asked.

"Ah, an old song. It's called 'Vincent'."

"How does it go?"

He thought for a minute. "I don't remember all the words. It was a long time ago. Don McLean. Do you know him?"

She shook her head, reminding him of their age difference.

"Let's see." He hummed the melody to find the start of it.

He began singing and reached the end of the first verse when his voice caught.

The words startled him. Was his soul as dark as the artist's? Van Gogh killed himself at thirty-seven. They were close in age. Remi shook the thought away and pushed on.

He hummed the next line or two before picking up the words again.

"*How you suffered for your sanity, and how you tried to set them free. They would not listen, they did not know how.*"

Suddenly the words stuck in his throat and took on new meaning, and a flash of insight flooded him.

He had to stop. He turned away.

Clearing his throat, he said, "I forget the rest, but that's how it goes."

Deidre looked at Remi. Obvious the song struck a nerve. He couldn't hide it.

"What is it?"

Remi felt the thin ice crackle beneath him. This was not territory he wanted to tread.

"I'm not afraid to hear it, you know."

Well you should be.

"It's not Van Gogh, is it," she pressed.

"No."

She stood there looking up at him.

He wavered.

Should he tell her a little of it? She was so young, but there was a solid maturity there, too. Or did he just imagine it, wanting it to be there? Could he trust her to keep it private? Could he trust her to understand? No one could understand except the men who had been there.

He swallowed hard. "We tried to set them free," he paraphrased softly in explanation.

He saw confusion cross her face. *All right a few words.*

"We went over there and gave them everything."

"Where? Iraq? The war, you mean?"

From this small pinprick in an overfilled balloon, something in his brain snapped, detonated, exploded, and from the force of that explosion, the memories came out in a rush.

"Everything. We gave them everything: our best and bravest men, our blood, our lives, our youth, our faith in God. We left it all there. We stood between them and death, dying in their place. And you know how they've repaid us? When we killed Bin Laden last month? They're grieving the man. They're fucking grieving him! And where are they now? Right back to how it was before we ever showed up. What was it for? Nothing. All the limbs, all the spilled brains, all our widows and orphans—it meant nothing. We tried to set them free, but they're not listening. They're fucking not listening!"

As he spoke, Deidre's expression moved from compassion to dismay to alarm. She didn't know what to say.

"It's not your fault. You weren't there," Remi said. He knew better than to talk about it. Damn it! Why had he started? What just happened? Sometimes it just needed to come out. But not here. Not to her, of all people. Her face—God, he was so stupid sometimes.

He reached out to stroke her cheek with the back of his fingers, but stopped. Then he turned abruptly and walked away.

AS SHE STARED after him, Deidre had the awful sense she had just looked inside him for the first time. And what she saw was frightening. A soul tortured, raging, dangerous. She was quivering from the sheer intensity of his need to purge himself. The words would take a while to digest, to untangle, but the passion behind those words, the ferocity, *that* understanding, was immediate.

Who was this man? What had happened over there? He was as hard as steel on the outside, a pseudo covering of his humanity, perhaps, with a core forged in something terrible. But no, more like a molten center, on the verge of eruption. Volcanic, red-metal liquefied, simmering, waiting to burst through a thinning crust. She shuddered, not out of fear for herself, but out of fear for him.

Too many emotions filled the air here. Was it there for sensitive people to experience? Had Van Gogh felt it? Arles. Provence. Something about the lighting brought the Impressionists. That's what they said. But could it be the air, something that brought out emotions from the depth of a soul?

Her thoughts were both confusing and enlightening, and

thoroughly overwhelming.

IT TOOK A WHILE for the girls to catch up with him. Deidre, deliberately hanging back, didn't want to crowd him. Instinctively, she knew she couldn't force him to reveal whatever he needed to say. You can't change the past, and sometimes you can't change the future. Maybe all one can do is make it bearable. She wanted to try. She wanted to rescue him.

She shared an abbreviated version of the incident with Cassie.

"He's a quiet man, and angry sometimes," Cassie said. "Maybe because things hurt too much to put into words."

"Yes, I think so." But he had tried; that was something. It was a start.

They reached Remi just as he put the phone in his pocket.

Deidre was relieved to find he'd returned to himself, but she noticed, once again, that subtle, prickly stab around the edges of her thoughts. His revelation still worried her, but much like the sensation in Nice, she felt something else. The jealous was back. Who was this mystery woman he turned to, drew comfort from? He had said it plainly: Deidre just didn't get it, or at least in *his* mind she didn't.

What did he see when he looked at her? Still only a girl? She wasn't. She was older than he knew. She could handle whatever it was, if only he would take a risk on her.

But why should he? He had someone else, perhaps an equal. He had everything. He was older, worldly, experienced. With his good looks, his attraction was palpable. He moved with the pure grace of the great cats that he was so fond of shooting. Muscles rippled under his shirt. Women stared when he entered the room. Men, too. That certain je ne sais quoi surrounded him like a magnetic field that drew eyes to observe him. That cocky confidence that declared he was the real deal and everyone else were just actors on a stage—that was the man before her. It wasn't an act he put on. It was who he was.

And Deidre? In certain circles, she was notable. Considered to be pretty, refined, well dressed, and financially secure. What else? Smart but naïve, probably silly in his eyes, young, inexperienced. He had never suggested she was more than what she was, the person who paid the bills in exchange for his company. The arrangement, put in that light, suddenly seemed sordid. What was the name for a male "call girl"? A gigolo?

Other than a paycheck, what else could she be to him? She had nothing to offer him but herself, her heart. Oh, and one more thing—a white cane tapping its way through her life. Even though he didn't know that small detail, there was still little to recommend her for the role of his confidante, and maybe, in time, his life's partner.

She wanted to be angry with him.

Why? Because I don't measure up? Is that his fault?

Not only that, but Deidre had come on the scene late. He hadn't just met this other woman. Or had he? No, he couldn't have. When? In Rome? While they were shopping in Milan? That woman at the café in Nice? No, he was on the phone while he was flirting with the blond. She had been with him the rest of the time, or most of it.

She was angry that he kept this other woman hidden from her. She was angry that he didn't do a better job of it. Why did she even have to know the woman existed?

Damn, damn, damn!

Her father's reproving voice reverberated. *Nice girls don't talk like that.*

Put it aside, Deidre, she reprimanded herself, louder even than her father's words. *You have this moment. There won't be many more, so don't spoil what you have.*

She forced a smile and relaxed her neck and shoulders as they approached him.

He was standing in what had once been a street but was now a table-filled plaza. He waved them over. Next to him stood a tripod with a picture propped on the crossbar.

"That's *Café Terrace at Night*," Deidre said. She was determined to impress him, not just with her knowledge, but with her maturity as well.

Cassie raised an impressed eyebrow.

"Well, even *I* know that one!" Deidre said.

"So now, look right over there," Remi said as he bent down and pointed to a café beyond the picture.

They looked, and took in a sharp breath.

"It's the café," Cassandra said. "But, my God, look at those colors!"

A brightly lettered sign painted on the building, read, "Van Gogh's Café."

The blue was too bright, the red too vivid, and the yellow simply garish. The building absolutely shrieked, "Look at me."

"That couldn't really be what he saw, could it?" Deidre sounded distressed, as she looked from the picture to the café.

"This is a case of reality imitating art I'm afraid," Remi said. "Knowing the French, and knowing Van Gogh, it's pretty obvious who came up with those colors."

"But the French painted that!" Cassandra said, pointing to the obvious tourist trap.

"Probably some foreign enterprise relying on the undiscerning taste of tourists."

"There you go, trashing the tourists again," Cassandra said.

"Of course," Deidre said, "a Frenchman could never come up with anything so, so—"

"In your face?" Remi suggested. "I agree with you completely, Miss Sinclair."

"But what's this, then?" Cassandra asked as she walked to the tripod.

"Maybe the only thing of value," Remi replied. "This is the spot where he actually painted his famous picture."

"Really!"

They looked at the picture, then up at the café. Someone had it right. This was the exact spot. Both young women were impressed.

"Now take that back to your Impressionism class, Cassie," Deidre said, as pleased as if she had discovered it herself. "Wow." She looked up at Remi. "Lavender is better, but this small thing is still outstanding."

"Ladies," he said, offering each an arm, "let's see what poison this fine establishment is serving to the tourists tonight."

THAT NIGHT, AS he reflected on the highlights and blunders of the day Remi asked himself why he had spoken of the war. He never did that, not to a civilian. He didn't want to poison her brain. Or did he?

What did she know of adversity? Her world was so insulated, so perfect. Was he jealous? Did he want her to know about real life, to break her perfect little bubble just a little bit? No, that wasn't it. He had just gone weak at the wrong moment.

He suddenly felt protective of her. He didn't want her to leave her perfect world, a world possible because of the family's fortune. Everything good should be hers. And that would come from her father, until a wealthy husband could be found. What could he give her? Only more grief like today. He had hurt her, exposed her to another world, his world, and he was sorry for it. It wouldn't happen again.

CHAPTER 10

EGYPT

IT WAS THE second week of July when they said *au revoir* to France. They failed to figure out a way to get the lavender through customs, so they gifted the armfuls they bought on the side of the road to Marie-Laure.

The flight from Nice to Cairo, by way of Venice, was long "and uneventful," Deidre wrote to her parents, "until we crash-landed on the runway in Egypt."

"You can't write that," Remi said, reading over her shoulder. "Your father will have my hide and I won't get paid."

Deidre thought for a moment. "Okay," she said, then inserted the word "nearly" before "crash-landed."

Remi frowned.

"Well, we did."

"We porpoised down the runway," he clarified.

Cassandra giggled. "Up we go, down we crash, up we go, down we crash." She mimicked the landing with her hands.

"We hit so hard I have a lump on my head. Here, feel." As he felt around for the lump, Deidre continued, "The entire ceiling fell on us and I was smothered in oxygen masks!"

"You have to admit all those wires hanging everywhere was a pretty scary sight," Cassandra added.

"Well, it's Cairo Air. What do you want, Delta?"

"Yes!" the girls said in unison.

THEY PICKED up the rest of the American tour in Venice: seven soldiers, their spouses, and friends from Vicenza. Fifteen altogether.

Remi hated tours in general, but in Egypt he saw no way around it. He thought it would be safer, but, then again, maybe not. He'd heard horror stories both ways. Still, having a plane, a bus, a ship, and a hotel full of American soldiers had to be worth something. Unless they were being targeted.

God! Just turn off your brain, Lamont!

He stayed in the background at the gate as Deidre and Cassandra introduced themselves, chatted, and made friends with an ease born of good breeding. They smiled and laughed and looked intensely interested in their new traveling companions. Once he had that ease with strangers, but since Iraq, he'd changed. Now, small talk irritated him like flies in his ears or a pebble in his shoe. He had no interest in the trivia of life. He wanted something with meaning, though he wasn't exactly sure what that meant. He was searching for something, but it eluded him.

He felt a mix of emotions: happy to see the girls enjoying the new faces, annoyed that he could be so easily replaced. Instead of seeing the newcomers as the long-desired respite, he felt resentful, and a bit proprietorial.

As they walked up the aisle of the plane, he said, "Well, the soldiers sure like you."

"I like them."

She looked at her ticket and frowned. "Window? Trade with me. I have recently discovered the advantages of the aisle from our flight over."

"No. Not on planes. Not on my watch," he said tersely. Lifting her carry-on with one hand, he gave her a gentle shove with the other. "Window."

"Really?"

He was stone serious. She moved over, allowing him to settle into the roomy first class seat next to her. He looked across the aisle to be sure there was no mutiny from Cassandra, who was seated at the other window.

He took out his cell phone to turn it off. She eyed it suspiciously, then turned off her own.

Still pouting, she said, "Well, when I wake you up to go pee, no whining."

He closed his eyes and stretched out his legs. "No whining."

AFTER COMING up to first class to tease Deidre about her seat and to introduce themselves to whom, they assumed to be, her wealthy boyfriend, or husband, or brother, the Americans settled down for the trip to Cairo.

Remi had been vague during the introductions. They seemed nice enough. About his age. A few young ones. Some were officers, obviously. They were interested in his combat experience. Deidre pretended not to listen, but he knew she caught every word. He didn't talk about it with her, and said little to the soldiers. He had seen some bad shit. It was bad enough that it was seared into his brain: the images, the smells, the sounds, the fear. He didn't need to scar someone else by sharing it, especially not someone young and sensitive, someone he cared about. No, scratch that last bit.

Actually scratch it all. 'Cared about.' Crap. Where did that come from? He didn't stand a chance with her. She was young and beautiful and rich. Poised. Smart. Strong. She could have any guy she wanted. He just saw proof of that, here, on the plane and at the terminal. What would she see in an old, broke Marine who had just enough money to keep his head above water? If he didn't get a hold of himself, like right now, he was done for, lost, finished. He had enough issues without the complication of falling for a girl nearly half his age, one he couldn't properly support, even if his feelings were reciprocated.

God, I'm so screwed up! I'm so fucking screwed up.
He'd think about something else. Yes, he would, damn it.

* * * * *

THE AMERICAN group was assigned to tour guide Ali, a small, dark-skinned man with darting eyes. A fringe of gray hair horseshoed around his head, highlighting a shiny bald scalp. When he spoke, each word was clipped and punched. Remi wondered if the man was Indian or Pakistani, and not Egyptian at all.

The group politely listened to a list of rules, nothing particularly objectionable, but irritating, nevertheless. No one but Remi seemed to notice, though.

He climbed into the bus with the others. The sun-blackened porters handled the luggage, except for Remi's camera equipment. That went under his seat.

They made their way down the aisle. Deidre tucked into a seat, sliding toward the window, when Remi grabbed her arm. He reached for Cassandra, too, to get her attention, and pointed to an aisle seat. Under his breath, he muttered to Deidre, "Aisle seat."

"What?" Deidre asked as he pulled her back into a seat across from Cassandra.

Remi sat behind her. "I'll explain later."

A large woman, whose belly must certainly be carrying twins, took the seat next to her.

Deidre wished she had kept her window seat. It was nearly impossible to look around the rotund woman to catch her first views of Egypt.

The bus skirted Cairo, taking a well-developed highway instead. The desert sand shimmered in the heat, and distant hills seemed to undulate in the background. The trip felt long, perhaps because they were tired. They passed a peasant herding goats, another riding a bicycle while carrying a huge tray of rounded breads on his head, and several small groups of children with black, imploring eyes and hands extended toward the speeding bus, begging for a loose coin or two.

As Remi looked out at the dark faces and white turbans, he felt a sudden, sinking revelation. He'd find no peace here.

Deidre didn't notice the hotel at first. It seemed like any four star hotel she might have stayed at in Miami. The heat, the palm trees, and the white shaded portico were familiar. But that was about to change.

As the porters hustled to unload the luggage, the group moved as one into the reception area. Suddenly, her eyes couldn't take it all in, but darted from one spectacular scene to another. The impressive marble edifice rose three stories above them. Cream-colored columns held up the inlaid marble ceiling. A mosaic of color covered both the gleaming floors and bowl above. Light bounced off of every polished surface, brightening the interior nearly as much as the exterior. It was breathtaking.

Teams of servants approached the travelers with shallow bowls of water and cool, wet terry towels so they could wipe their hands, faces, and necks. A third man accepted the used cloths in exchange for drying towels, while a fourth passed out cups of sweet tea.

"For your refreshment, Madam. Sir," they said as they bowed their heads politely.

Murmurs of delight washed through the group at this unique and welcoming reception. Even Remi admitted, "Quite a show. Not bad at all."

Rooms were assigned and keys passed out. Luggage would soon follow. They were directed through the enormous reception room that ended in a wall of arches opening to an enormous covered veranda. More arches supported by columns held up the outer edge of the veranda roof. Beyond the porch, they could see the enclosed estate, though the gardens were so expansive they couldn't see a defining wall.

"An oasis," breathed Deidre.

Before them lay acres of lush grass peppered with well-maintained palm trees, a riot of colorful flowers springing from carefully maintained urns, and two aqua pools, the larger for swimming and the smaller for meditating. Stone benches and delightful statuary decorated well-groomed lawns, all knit together with white stone pathways.

For once, Remi was genuinely impressed as he marveled at man's inventive conquest of the environment.

"The pyramids are a big thing, but for a small thing this is pretty grand, too, don't you think?" Deidre said.

He continued to take in the spectacle before him. "Pretty grand about sums it up."

That evening, the Americas met Ali in the Nefertari room for dinner.

"Apparently, your court awaits you," Remi said to Deidre, barely able to suppress his annoyance at the attention she drew.

Deidre beamed up at him. "They are really lovely people. You should give them a chance."

"I'll pass. Go play." He gave her a light nudge ignoring the frown that replaced her smile.

As they mingled with their new friends, Deidre and Cassie decided they couldn't let poor Remi stand in the corner all alone. So they launched a plan. One by one, they brought individuals or couples over to meet and chat with Remi. While Cassie made introductions, Deidre was off laughing with someone else. When Cassie had finished, Deidre insisted the new couple meet her escort.

Not knowing what to call Remi had been tricky. "Escort" seemed the best descriptor, as sordid as that sounded. It took three or four introductions before Remi caught on. He tried shooting her a look, but Deidre carefully avoided his eyes.

"Brad, Mary, this is my escort, Remi Lamont. Brad is a dentist in Vicenza."

"Nice to meet you." They all shook hands. Dental officer, Remi thought. Not much use in a standoff. Good after a fist fight, though, especially for facial injuries. He laughed inwardly at his own sick humor, softening his exterior frown.

"So Deidre tells me you're a former Marine."

"Well, actually, once a Marine, always a Marine."

"Oh yeah, I heard that once about you guys. Well, I have to say you still stay in great shape," Brad said, noticing his wife's appreciative appraisal of Remi.

What, Remi wondered, suddenly tongue-tied, does a person say to a comment like that? You, too, even though it's a gross exaggeration? *Deidre Sinclair, I'd like to lay you over my lap and throttle you.*

"So what do you do now?" Mary asked.

"Photography. I take a lot of pictures."

"And is that lucrative?" Brad asked, his voice tinged with skepticism.

So are you asking how much money I make? The first class seats really confused you, didn't they, asshole.

"Not so much yet. I sell enough to keep me independent, but mostly I do it for job satisfaction. How do you like looking in people's mouths?"

They laughed nervously.

"Mary, I don't think I know what you do," Deidre interjected with a sweet smile while the men did whatever men do when they're sizing each other up.

"Oh, I'm an aerobics instructor."

Both Deidre and Remi took another look at the pretty woman. Deidre realized too late what a cute package Mary Lawrence made, and calling attention to it was stupid. She looked at Remi, who certainly seemed impressed.

Brad casually put an arm over his wife's shoulder. Smiling at her husband, she said, "Brad, you wouldn't mind if I had Remi take some portrait shots of me, would you?"

"That's not what he shoots," Brad said, while at the same time Remi said, "That's not what I shoot." They both laughed, embarrassed, and Remi, put his arm around Deidre's waist. She leaned into him. Clearly, the action said, he was more than just an escort.

* * * * *

TWO NIGHTS AT the Imperial Hotel bracketed their day trip to Giza.

"Giza, home of the pyramids," Cassandra said, climbing into the bus.

"And the Sphinx. You can't forget about him? Or is it a her?"

They were looking for seats together on the bus when Remi's long reach tapped Deidre on the shoulder and tipped his head toward the seat he wanted her to take, then pointing to another for Cassandra.

"What's with this aisle seat business?" Cassie whispered to Deidre.

"Have no idea," Deidre shrugged. "He can't make up his mind. Window. Aisle. Isn't he kinda young for dementia?"

Cassie laughed. "He doesn't strike me as indecisive."

"Hardly!"

"So let's just ask him."

"Be my guest."

"Chicken."

Deidre just grinned.

By the time they got to Giza, they forgot about Remi's capricious whims amid the flurry of activity.

The beggars swarmed them "like flies on shit," Remi colorfully declared. They were mainly children who looked up at them through round, beseeching brown eyes.

"Don't go for your wallet or they'll take it all," he warned.

Ali was telling the others the same thing.

They followed Ali through a small impromptu market selling harem costumes, veils, baskets, scarves, all kinds of food, small toys, camel blankets, and miscellaneous kitsch.

"We can shop when we have finished," Ali instructed. "Come along now," his clipped words commanded.

They came out on a great plain, and there, in the distance, they saw them—three great pyramids, growing out of the desert sand. Leading to and from the great tombs were strings of camels like fine beads on a necklace, swaying across the expanse, taking and returning those who came to pay homage to this ancient world wonder. Remi dug out his camera. There was a story to be told by this picture, but already the others were mounting their camels and Remi was being pushed along.

"Pictures when you get there," Ali said.

Damn this tour group. Still, he was able to take three shots before the camel driver grabbed his arm.

Later that afternoon, he found Deidre and Cassie sitting by the meditation pool. As he walked up, he heard Deidre reading.

"*—until we stand next to one of the stones of the Great Pyramid, seeing the incredible bulk of just one massive rock, cut square, feeling the perspiration run down our back in the blistering heat, though it is still early morning, wondering how long our water will last—only then, in the blinding sun bouncing off blinding sand, can we understand that there was a civilization five millennium ago that envisioned and accomplished something so outrageously impossible that we are humbled by their superior determination and abilities.*"

"That's so good," Cassie gushed.

"Really? You're not just saying that?"

"No!"

"Did you write that?" Remi asked.

Surprised, Deidre turned to see him standing behind her. "Oh, you heard it?"

Even through her suntan he could see the blush.

"Yes. Daddy found someone at the paper to do a bit on our travels. The reporter wanted something from my journal, but since I'm not keeping one I decided to just write articles."

"You're a good writer."

The blush deepened. "Thank you."

"Can I read the whole thing when you're done?"

"Ah, sure. Well, if it's any good," she amended.

"So you don't keep a journal. Do you, Cassandra?"

"No, neither of us do."

"Hmm," he said. "I guess my photos are my journal. I thumb through them and they take me back." He looked off into the distance. "I can remember what I felt, what I was thinking. It's good." Looking back at them, he said, "This is good, too. Keep it up. I look forward to reading it through. Don't forget."

"I won't."

"Promise?"

She smiled. "I promise."

THE PYRAMIDS of Egypt earned the right to be listed among the Wonders of the World. That night, Remi scrolled through his pictures. To get a perspective of the size of the blocks of stone, he had had Deidre and Cassandra climb onto the first tier of the pyramid. In order to encompass the entirety of the Great Pyramid of Khufu he had walked a long way back. Even from that distance, though, he was able to zoom in and get just a head shot of each, for the record.

She was right. It had been hot, and water was precious. He knew what to expect, but was surprised at how well the girls had adapted to the heat. While others in the group complained vehemently, neither Deidre nor Cassandra said one word. Instead, they had played a word game to distract themselves during the hot bus ride to the hotel. What do you call that? Remi wondered. Resilience? That was a good word. She was resilient, resourceful, and resilient.

He fell asleep still thinking about Deidre, forgetting entirely to assess whether this had been a good day.

CHAPTER 11

THE NILE

THE NEXT LEG of the tour was the cruise ship up the Nile. The second stop was the Valley of the Kings.

"It's funny saying you're going upstream when you're heading south. And it's getting cooler going south."

"How can you tell?" asked Cassandra. "A 103 isn't much different from 104."

Remi laughed. "No whining." They were good, though. The warning had become an inside joke.

Cassandra groaned.

"It will be cooler because we'll be on the water," he explained.

Actually, it was. Much cooler. But that was all that could be said for the ship. As splendid as the Imperial Hotel was, the cruise ship the tour company had booked was not. It was tired and old. The towels were frayed from too many washings, the carpet was darkened by a thousand footsteps, the pillow feathers were crushed by too many heads, and a general sigh of exhaustion emanated from the poor old gal.

"We are not impressed," Deidre confided to her friend. "But no whining."

What the ship lacked in luxury the crew made up for in service, attention, and enthusiasm. Each night, the napkins were folded into some exotic cloth origami. Hand towels in the form of swans would appear in the center of their beds. Melons were carved into humorous faces. The staff flirted with and cajoled the women, and more than one proposal of marriage was discussed with high hilarity.

The food presentation was especially magnificent. So many

delights!

Remi had schooled them on what they could and could not eat.

"Nothing raw unless the peel can be removed and you do it yourself. No fruit except bananas, oranges, or lemons. Nothing washed in water. No salads. Cooked meats and cooked vegetables only. Bread and desserts are okay as long as there is no fresh fruit on the plate. Ice cream is fine. Nuts, too."

He watched to make sure they followed the rules. They got the knack of it fairly quickly and hoped to stay healthy for the duration of the trip.

Not everyone was so vigilant.

Early one morning, Remi stepped out of his cabin to find the worried face of a pleasant Filipino. Always ready with a boyish grin, this morning he was somber.

"Not such a good morning?" Remi asked.

"Not a good morning. Much sickness here." He gestured down the hall. "You no sick?"

Remi shot a look at the closed door across the hall and heard a faint laugh. The girls were fine, so far.

"No, I'm good. What's the problem?"

"Much fever, vomiting."

"Where? Show me."

The small man led the large one to the next room and tapped lightly. A voice called them in.

"Did you bring ice?" Carrie, one of the soldiers' wives he'd met, asked the porter as she sat on the bed next to her prone husband.

"Not yet. I go now." Then pointing down the hall, he said to Remi, "All these." And hurried off for the ice.

Remi crossed the small cabin in two strides. "What's happened?" he asked, kneeling next to Carrie's husband.

"I don't know. We must have gotten food poisoning or

something. During the night we started with diarrhea and vomiting, then came the fever."

Remi put his hand on the man's forehead. He was burning up. He worked to remember the man's name. "How bad is it, Earl?"

"Bad. I don't think I've ever been so sick."

"It came on so fast," Carrie said weakly.

"The cabin boy said there are others. Let me go and see. How are you doing?" he asked Carrie, putting his hand to her brow. "You'd best get to bed, too. Can you drink anything?"

They shook their heads. "Everything comes right up."

"You'll get dehydrated. Try to crush the ice and let it melt between your cheek and gums. It will absorb that way. You'll get some liquid; not enough, but some, at least, until we can find another way."

"We need the ice to cool down," Carrie said, wobbling to the other side of the bed, nearly falling at the corner.

Seeing how weak she was, Remi realized they wouldn't be crushing ice or anything else.

"You need it more to hydrate yourselves. Look, I'll be back."

Remi went to the next room. After the fourth he headed back to find Deidre and Cassandra to make sure they were fine.

"I don't know if it's food poisoning or a virus, but all the passengers are sick. Stay in your room. Don't go out."

"Where are you going?"

"To help bring the ice." And he was gone.

He was back in ten minutes with a roasting pan full of ice. Two other crewmembers with heaping soup pots followed him down the hall. Ahead, he saw Cassandra exit one room and enter another. He dumped half of the ice into the sink, and assured Earl and Carrie he'd be back to crush it, then hurried off to find Deidre. If Cassandra was scurrying around, she was following Deidre's lead, he was certain of it.

He poked his head into five rooms before he found Cassandra. Deidre was in the sixth. The crewmen with the soup pots hadn't gotten down this far, so when Deidre saw the roasting pan still half full of ice she jumped up from the chair and went to him.

"She's really sick," Deidre said in a low voice, nodding toward the bed where Mary and Brad lay shivering from fever.

"I told you to stay in your room," he snarled, drawing her into the hall. "It could be anything. It could be contagious."

"But you're not sick. Cassie and I aren't sick. Why? Because it must have been in the food. We're okay," she said, trying to reason with him.

"So far. But maybe it's a virus that hasn't reached us yet. You should have listened to me and stayed in your room until we knew for sure."

"No. They are so sick. Some of the fevers are 104 already. I have to get back. Thanks for the ice." She turned back toward the room.

"So you're not going to listen to me," he growled.

At the door, she turned to face him. "Not this time. They need us."

Remi ran his hand through his hair in exasperation.

Then grabbing her arm, he whispered, "Ration the ice carefully. This is all there is for now. I'll triage the worst cases. There's not enough for everyone. I don't think they can even make more. Maybe. But it will take a while."

She smiled gratefully.

"If you insist on doing this, we'll have to coordinate our efforts. First, I'm sorry, but we can only take care of the Americans. The others will have to rely on the crew."

She nodded. Three people for fifteen patients. That meant five each—three rooms each for the women, and two for Remi, she explained.

"Better take four rooms for each of you and let me fight for the ice and try to get a doctor, get what food I can, that kind of thing. I think there's an easier way to crush the ice in the kitchen, too. I'll work on that. Anything else you can think of?"

"We may need more wastebaskets," she said, indicating the vomiting Mary on one side of the bed, while Brad was trying to make his way to the bathroom. "And more towels if they have them."

Remi nodded.

The plan made sense, though he hated the idea that she was involved in direct patient care. Yes, it might be food poisoning, but maybe it wasn't.

"Wash your hands regularly. Tell Cassandra. I'll be back."

The Americans were the best cared for on the ship, with the sickest among them getting the bulk of the ice. For some couples, one spouse was in better shape than the other. With Remi running interference and the young women lending a hand where they could, it seemed they might get through it. But when the fevers continued to spike through the second day, taking down even the strongest among them, something obviously needed to be done.

Remi called a meeting in the hall. Anyone who could get out of bed needed to attend. There wasn't anything left in their stomachs to vomit, but the soldiers and their wives leaned against the walls in their nightclothes holding buckets to the ready.

"We're pulling into port in a couple of hours. They have a doctor coming on board. He'll see whoever is sick, but his fee is $160 a person. He'll only take cash."

The dazed Americans looked confused. They began talking at once.

"All I've got are credit cards. No cash."

"Cash? I don't carry that much cash."

"Who uses cash anymore?"

"He'll take a credit card; he has to. You've got it wrong."

One young wife began crying. "But he has to see us."

"Actually, he doesn't, and he won't," Remi said flatly.

"But why won't he take a credit card?" another asked.

Remi felt compassion for the naïve group. He would have thought the soldiers, at least, would have come better prepared. He sighed, trying to hide his exasperation. "This is a third world country. They deal in cash. He's coming on board because there are Americans here. $160 is a steal for a house call, but he's expecting the American dollar."

He ran his hand through his hair. "Look, tell me what you have. I can front some of you. Depending on how much cash you can pool together, maybe all of you. But the really sick folks we can take care of for sure."

Their relief was palatable. "We can write you a check," said one man.

"Yes, I've got my checkbook, too," said another. "And I can write for most of us. We all see one another around the post."

Checkbooks and credit cards, but no cash. Remi just shook his head. He would have to find some way to cash the checks before long, since all of his cash would be gone. How much did he have left? A couple of thousand dollars, maybe? It should cover the group, and if they coughed up cash, too, it might be all right.

He walked to his own room while the others tallied their resources. He didn't need to show them where he hid his stash. Deidre followed him, her eyes glowing. For a moment he was afraid she had caught the virus, too. Then she spoke.

"I have never felt so safe in my life, and never so proud to know someone. And I really need to be hugged by this hero right now."

Without waiting, she was in his arms.

And without thinking, he hugged her back, smelled the shampoo in her hair, heard the beat of her heart, felt the heat of her body, and, for just a moment, he let himself get lost. He had gone so long without being touched that the effect overwhelmed him. Long after she left, the feel of her against him haunted him.

The doctor, with amazing efficiency, checked each patient and distributed the medication. Within three hours the ship was heading back down the Nile.

The fevers passed in a day and strength was slowly returning to those afflicted. The Americans were effusive in their gratitude, but Remi felt embarrassed by the attention. There was a time in his life when he enjoyed the limelight—dancing in bars, singing karaoke, and being the brunt of his platoon's jokes. But that was a lifetime ago. Now, he preferred to be behind the curtain, not on center stage. Still, being a hero was in his blood, and who could resist the allure of it?

* * * * *

THE CRUISE SHIP continued down the Nile through the night, but in the morning pulled into another dock. Ali instructed the Americans to follow him to a waiting bus. Other tours were assigned to other buses, and soon a small caravan had been assembled. While the ship continued down the river with a couple of people still too weak to travel by land, the others rode into the interior. They would return to the Nile and rendezvous with the ship later that night.

Remi and the young women were comfortably seated on the aisle, if one could be comfortable in one hundred degree heat.

"It's only 7:00 a.m. How can it be so hot already?" Cassandra asked.

Deidre whispered, "No whining," which made Remi grin.

The forty-minute ride delivered the buses to the Valley of the Kings. The passengers disembarked and headed to the main gate, where Ali picked up the waiting tickets.

"I don't know what I expected," Deidre said to Remi, "but it certainly wasn't this."

Groups of people moved down a wide gravel road defined by the obligatory shade trees. Under the trees, stone benches provided a little relief to the overheated tourists. The road was less of a road and more of an open area where large groups could convene and listen to a history lesson. Concession stands with long lines dotted the edges of the road with more frequency than the benches.

"This looks more like a rural America fairgrounds than the ancient Valley of the Kings," she said.

The tour group followed Ali to the first tomb on his list.

Upon entering the tomb they walked into a well-lit area that served as a gathering point to learn about the pharaoh who had been buried there. They looked at pictures of treasures that had been removed and listened to the history of the grave robbers and what might have been taken. The first tomb was made up of several chambers, each deeper than the one before it.

One of the soldiers, a twenty-something AFN weatherman named Glenn, said, "It's 108 frickin' degrees down here." He had brought a thermometer on the tour and had given the Americans regular reports throughout the week.

"We're underground and it's only 8:00 a.m.," grumbled Al, the only paratrooper in the group. "How the hell do these people stand it? I'm ready to quit right here and now."

Remi gave the girls a warning look. No whining, it said. Yes, it was miserable, but talking about it just made it worse. Hell, he had known heat this bad before, only then he'd been carrying a ninety pound pack and his weapon, and been wearing his thirty pound MTV as he sprinted across a street between sniper rounds. And not one single Marine had threatened to quit. God, can you imagine it? "Too hot. Not going to work today." The image made him smile.

His chest swelled with pride. He was proud of them, every last one of them. They were scared; they were all scared. They were going to be the first into Fallujah, the second time. Who wouldn't be scared? But the adrenaline was pumping, and they still held that innocent belief that since they were Marines, they were invincible, bulletproof.

They heard the ping of sniper fire hitting the corner of the wall where they stood, saw the chunks of cinderblock shatter, and practically smelled the gunpowder. And then it was time to go, and they ran, ran like their life depended on it, because it did. The shots rang out—

"Remi," Deidre called, urging him to catch up.

Like releasing a stretched rubber band, he was back in the present, in a hot tomb with a bunch of stupid people who didn't know anything. Why did that make him so fucking angry?

Shake it off, Lamont, shake it off.

The group moved from one tomb to the other in orderly fashion. They seldom had to wait for the group ahead to clear out. "For a third world country, they sure have figured some things out," Cassandra said.

Deidre caught Ali at the back of the group as they continued to the last tomb.

"Ali, you said we would see King Tut's tomb. But—"

"No, that's extra. You have to buy a separate ticket."

"But you said it was—"

"You have to buy a separate ticket."

"It's really the only one I want to see."

"There's nothing there. It has been emptied. You have to buy a—"

"I know, a separate ticket. Okay. Where?"

A smug looked crossed the tour guide's face. "Back at the entrance."

"But when I asked, you said—"

"Front gate. It is too late."

Remi watched the exchange, aware that Deidre knew this little weasel had deliberately lied. He could see her set her jaw and squint her eyes at the man.

"Where is Tut's tomb?"

"Back there." Ali pointed to where they had just come from. They were at least a mile and a half from the front gate, and somewhere between here and there lay Tutankhamun's famous tomb. His insincere apologetic shrug sealed it for her.

"We have one more tomb, you said. On the way back, pick me up." She turned and, with a determined stride, headed toward the gate.

Remi smiled, then called out, "Get three tickets. We'll meet you there. Come on, Cassandra." He shot a look at Ali, daring him to try to stop them, but the little tour guide just glared back and turned around to join the others.

"That's our girl," Cassandra said with a wide grin.

"I guess it is."

"I THINK WHAT really made him mad was when the others got tickets, too," Deidre said, still high from the mini mutiny.

Heading back to the park entrance, the Americans had stopped to sit on stone benches outside of Tutankhamun's tomb to wait for their three companions to come out. When they heard the enthusiastic reports, the others also decided they wanted to see the famous site.

"Probably threw his whole schedule off." Cassandra laughed.

They were once again sitting on the bus. Ali and the bus driver had stopped at a roadside stand to get cold bottles of water and were now distributing them, collecting money as they went. Remi had followed them, intending to help, though the two men tried to dissuade him. Remi prevailed, of course.

"Quite a little racket he's got going here," he said from his seat behind Deidre.

"What do you mean?"

"He buys the water for a dime and sells it for two bucks."

"What a slime bag."

Remi laughed. "Why, Miss Sinclair, I didn't know you knew such language."

"That, and a lot more. I just keep it under wraps," she said with a smile.

Deidre took the cold bottle and pressed it to the back of her neck. A drop of condensation ran down the back of her shirt. She moved the bottle to the inside of her elbows, feeling the blood cool. The contrast between her overheated body and the cold water made her shiver gratefully. She cooled her underarms and back of her knees. By now the contents were absorbing some of her body heat, but was still deliciously cold. She slipped it under her top and pressed it against her stomach, up her sides, and between her breasts. She repeated the process until she had brought her temperature down to a comfortable level. The water, now refreshingly cool rather than shockingly cold, filled her mouth. Slowly she enjoyed the simple pleasure of drinking water.

The first time he saw her using the cold bottle to cool herself, Remi asked, "Where did you learn that?"

Deidre thought for a moment. "I didn't, exactly. I'm hot, so I thought I'd try it. It's like standing in a cold shower."

"I do the same thing." He smiled.

"Did you learn that in Afghanistan?"

"Used it more in Iraq. Different season. Hotter weather."

"So great minds think alike," she said, settling back in the bus seat. Great minds think alike...

The line of buses from the cruise ship drove on for an hour. The scenery was monotonous. Sand. Sand-covered hills. A camel with rider. Shimmering heat waves over flat plains of sand. A hot air balloon floating above the heat. Bleached sand. More sand.

The early morning start, the rocking of the bus, and the heat were the perfect combination to induce sleep, almost as if the bus had been infused with nitrous oxide. Remi soon found himself drifting into a gentle sleep, almost hypnotically, by the swaying of the vehicle.

When the bus stopped, Remi woke with a start. They were in the middle of nowhere. Something felt off. He touched Deidre's shoulder and reached over to nudge Cassandra. Both girls woke up, stretched, and smiled.

The bus driver opened the door, although the still air outside was no cooler than the air inside the bus. Only now no moving air came through the windows. The driver quietly spoke to someone standing on the lower step. Remi watched the exchange and then saw a well-built Egyptian in a dark suit climb the stairs. He stopped in the middle of the aisle and surveyed the sleeping tourists.

In less than a heartbeat, goose bumps prickled the base of Remi's spine, racing up his back and shoulders and down across his butt and thighs. His heart rate increased but the rest of his organs slowed down as he focused on the danger. He forced his body to relax and controlled his breathing as he reached for the knife he kept strapped to his calf.

The Egyptian wore a white shirt, narrow tie, and black, three-button suit, unbuttoned. The stark contrast of the alert, heavily-clothed intruder to the lolling Americans was striking. None of the soldiers seemed to notice the man, which increased his alarm. If there was to be a showdown, he preferred the men around him to be a little less comatose.

Suddenly, and for no goddamn reason that he could tell, Deidre called the man over to her. Fuck!

"You look dreadfully hot in that suit. Aren't you about to die?"

Poor choice of words.

Like the night of his nightmare in Vernazza, he willed Deidre to shut up.

Do not call attention to yourself, damn it.

The man indulged her. "This is Egypt. You adapt," he answered, unsmiling. "And I'm on duty."

"It's really okay to take your jacket off." Deidre smiled. "No one here would mind."

His face remained impassive, but his eyes moved alertly.

"What do you do?" she asked.

Deidre Sinclair, please just shut up!

The man slowly pulled back the edge of his coat to reveal a shoulder holster with sidearm. Remi's right hand rolled up into a hard fist while the other tightened on the handle of his knife. The sweat running down his face and body wasn't from the heat. He was tensed to spring at the slightest provocation.

Deidre didn't seem the least bit alarmed.

"Ohhh. Why do you carry that?"

"I'm your security guard. I'm here to protect the bus in case there is an incident."

"An incident?" she repeated.

Ali joined the conversation. "We go by caravan, and we have armed guards because of the kidnapping of a tour bus many years ago."

"What happened?" asked the woman seated at the window.

The guard said nothing. Ali said nothing.

"Depends on which kidnapping you're referring to. Or was it the one in Cairo where the two women opened fire on a bus? When was that, three years ago?" Remi didn't take his eyes off the guard. If something was going to happen, he'd provoke it now, while the playing field was even. He didn't know who else might join the "guard" on the bus.

"Or are you talking about the slaughter at Luxor ten, twelve years ago? How many died? Sixty, wasn't it? Well, sixty tourists and the gunmen."

The guard remained unresponsive but looked sharply at Remi. They held each other's gaze for longer than necessary. He watched, and he'd keep watching, developing a strategy in case the guy wasn't what he claimed.

He chanced a quick look behind him. The soldiers, still sluggish from the heat, were totally unaware of the potential danger. Was he the only sane person on this bus? Or the only deranged one?

An hour passed while the big man continued blocking the aisle. Finally, the bus began to move. Ali announced that the other buses had caught up and they could go across the desert now. He apologized for the delay, explaining it was unavoidable.

Ali certainly looked the part of unconcerned tour guide, Remi thought, although he could be part of it.

Were they driving into a trap?

It took two more hours to cross the desert, without incident.

In the end, the big Egyptian did his duty and got off the bus with the tourists. Even with the danger behind them, Remi couldn't relax.

Exhausted from the fading adrenaline, his muscles were still tense and his mind continued to race from scenario to scenario. It was a familiar pattern.

A drink would go down nicely right about now, he thought. Too bad it was a Muslim country, or mostly. Okay, deep breathing. Distraction. Think of something good.

Lavender.

Deidre in his arms.

No, not good. Something else.

The Pietà.

The Madonna's face.

How small she felt.

The smell of her shampoo.

Dammit.

The picnic in the vineyard.

The blue sky, both in his mind and in reality.

How sweet she looked when she slept.

How he'd wanted to kiss her. Imagined it, even.

Jesus Christ! Out of one danger and into another.

Maybe this one wouldn't kill him, though. And it smelled better. His mind smiled, though his mouth remained unchanged.

"REMI, WE REALLY do need to know why one minute you have us at the window and the next we have to be on the aisle. Can you explain it, please?"

The question surprised him a little. "It's simple—it's knowing when to be in the center of the herd and when to avoid the flock."

"Oh, that explains everything, of course," Deidre said.

Remi laughed.

"It depends if the enemy is a lion or a shotgun." Their expressions amused him. "If you're in a highjack situation on a plane, for example, the hijackers will start shooting or taking hostages from the aisle, so window seats are safer."

"But that applies on buses, too, no?" Cassandra asked.

"You'd think so, but there are far fewer hijacked buses than shots fired at buses from the outside. You're safer farther in, not at a window where your head could be a target."

Except in Egypt, he thought ruefully, when armed men enter the bus.

"Wow. That makes a lot of sense. Did you figure that out all by yourself?"

He shook his head. "I thought it was common knowledge."

"Not in our world," Deidre said looking at Cassandra. "If everyone knew that, planes would be two-thirds empty—which, of course, would defeat the whole strategy."

He gave a smiling snort at that.

"And one more thing," he said, "don't draw attention to yourself."

"I don't think Deidre has any control over that," her friend said with a laugh.

"No seriously, that dude with the pistol—"

"Omar?" Yes, she had gotten him to talk a bit. If nothing else, she was persistent.

"Yeah, *Omar*. That could have gone down way different. Did you even think he might have been a terrorist?"

"Not for one minute. He had nice eyes."

Remi groaned. "Just don't be so damn trusting, will you."

She thought for a minute. "So I have one question. How do you feel about the poor person that sits at the window and gets shot?"

Momentarily confused, he asked, "On the bus?"

She nodded.

"Well, first I wouldn't think about him at all. I'd be heading for the floor. Then—I really don't have a good answer for that."

He reflected. How would he feel?

"I wouldn't feel guilty. I didn't pull the trigger. I guess I'd just feel glad it wasn't someone I cared about—or me. And then I'd see if I could save him."

THAT NIGHT, HE had one of the really bad nightmares, an old familiar one with only a slight variation. It always started in the middle. The high-pitched whistle of rockets, their sound widening and deepening as they reached the ground. The tracers spilling down from the darkness, and then the shooting flames as houses blew up. White phosphorus dropping from the sky like a sprinkle of stars, and grenades exploding from men's pockets, trailing the poison behind them. The stink, the grit, the dark, the heat. Stay covered, from enemy fire and from the white poison. Go inside; retrieve the bodies. Melting flesh, always the horror of bodies sliding off in his hands, between his fingers, so only the skeleton remained to be carried away. He wanted to gag, but he had a duty to do. He didn't pull the trigger. He didn't send the flames. But Christ, the guilt.

He was wringing wet. The sheets were wet. So were his eyes. His heart was pounding in his chest. He willed his breathing to slow. The grotesque images wouldn't fade so easily. He thought his head would explode with the horror inside it. He wiped his hands on the sheets, as though some of the dream still stuck to his skin. He looked at the clock and threw himself back on the pillow. Three o'clock. His night was over, but the nightmare wasn't. He reached for his phone and hit the speed dial. A voice answered.

"Kiss, it's Remi. I'm having a bad time of it. Can you talk me down?"

THE FINAL NIGHT on the Nile coincided with Deidre's birthday.

Cassandra decided to orchestrate a party. Along with a small band of Army wives, she started in the kitchen.

"Chocolate cake with marshmallow cream frosting. No, not butter cream, marshmallow. I have no idea how to make it. Isn't it just marshmallow cream out of a jar?"

No one in the kitchen had ever heard of it. Fortunately, one of the wives had the answer.

"Whip the egg whites until they're stiff. Good. Now add the sugar…"

Cassandra left her to it.

Next, she found the ship's captain and asked for music. Since there were no musicians on board, he sent the group and a crewman off to find an old collection of CDs and speakers. The crewman offered to be the DJ.

"Let's start off with a tribute to everyone's country."

Together they selected music to celebrate each nationality represented on board.

Decorations were challenging. While Remi kept Deidre occupied, Cassandra and the others turned the dining room into a romantic dance hall. In the storage room they found miles of white Christmas lights. They strung the twinkle lights on the artificial trees around the room. Soon, the trees sparkled with glamour. They discovered a discarded mirrored disco ball from the 70s and hung it from the ceiling, though it didn't spin. They set candles on tables to be lit later. The staff, already planning for the closing night dinner, outdid themselves with a buffet table beaming with happy carved faces on melons, pineapple, and squash. The effect was better than Cassandra had hoped.

Someone struck the dinner gong. Remi heard the girls across the hall leave their room and stuck out his head.

"Deidre? Need some help."

Cassandra nodded with a smile and kept walking toward the dining room. Remi fussed with his tie as Deidre looked on helplessly.

"In the movies the heroine always knows how to tie the tie, but—" She threw up her hands. "I just never had a reason to learn. I am no help at all."

"I can show you a Windsor knot." He began making the knot. "See? And down through here. Now grab this part and slide it up. Easy."

"Sure, easy," she said dubiously.

"All I need is for you to make sure it's straight," he lied.

"Well, that I can do!"

"Wait. I need to retie it," he stalled. Finally, enough time had passed, and he let her straighten his deliberately off-center tie.

She stepped back to admire her work. "You, Mr. Lamont, look ridiculously handsome. How did you manage to hide a sport jacket in that small bag of yours?"

"They call me Mario Poppins," he said, making her laugh. "And you, by the way, look stunning." His voice was sincere as his eyes swept over her. He saw a shiver of delight run through her as he returned his gaze to her face. The look they exchanged was brief but intense, and both turned away quickly.

Remi took a deep breath and held out his arm, smiling. "I think I'm ready."

Not quite trusting her voice, she merely nodded and returned his smile as she slipped her hand under his elbow.

As they walked into the dining room, all eyes turned to see the striking couple: Deidre, delicate features, flowing dark hair, light eyes, petite, sophisticated, and Remi, tall, commanding, dark, confident.

Since no one could find a recording of "Happy Birthday," the

DJ did the next best thing—he started to sing. Everyone in the room chimed in to sing the universally familiar tune. A multitude of languages wished her happiness. Deidre blushed and smiled appreciatively at her best friend. Then the cake was brought out with twenty-one glowing candles.

"Make a wish, sweetheart." Cassie laughed.

"Only one?"

"Make it count."

Deidre closed her eyes, made the wish, and blew out the candles to the applause of the entire room. She looked up and smiled. It has been the best of years, and it would be the worst of years, she paraphrased in her head before she could banish the thought.

The servers took the cake to serve for dessert as the guests proceeded through the buffet line.

As dinner ended, Remi excused himself, returning a few moments later with a small present. The thin package was wrapped with yellow tissue paper and secured by a string that was threaded through thin slices of dried oranges and lemons. Surprised, Deidre took the gift. She untied the string and drew back the paper to reveal a map of Provence, a new copy of the one they had used to find the lavender fields. She unfolded it. On the map a perfect gold circle identified the spot of the mapmaker's signature, and smaller silver circles marked the lavender fields.

"You are so thoughtful," she said quietly, genuinely moved by the gift.

He was embarrassed. "It had to be something that packed well and lightweight."

She laughed, and he grinned back. "So you like it?"

"I love it. It's perfect. Thank you so very, very much." She held it to her chest. "I'll cherish it always."

The tables were pulled away as Deidre took the gift back to her cabin. When she returned, the dancing had already begun. The selection of CDs was good. The "Viennese Waltz" was playing, but only one older couple was on the dance floor, though there were many Austrians on board.

As Deidre sat down, Cassie whispered, "Not many takers on that one." Then a young man Cassie had been flirting with held out his hand and she floated off with him.

"Not only art major, but ballroom dancing, too," Deidre explained to Remi.

"Ah. And you?"

"Nothing practical. Ballet. When I try square dancing I always turn the wrong way. You know, my 'left-right' challenge."

He laughed.

"And Father says I dance to the beat of some unknown alien drummer." Looking up at him, she added, "But I like dancing."

Remi and Deidre watched as Cassie whirled around on the arm of the gallant Austrian. As the waltz faded, he heard what he thought were the first bars of "America." A chill ran up his back. It *was* "America." Neil Diamond's version.

A surge of energy and excitement propelled through him. He knew the song well. In Fallujah, "Hells Bells" by ACDC brought back those memories, but back at firm camp, this was one of their victory songs. Good ole Korvinsky with his boom box and CDs. He loved playing, "We Will We Will Rock You," or the "Theme from Rocky" or "America," or anything to energize the platoon. It only took a few bars, and he was back with his guys, shirt off, shaking off the tension of the fight, a bottle of Beck in one hand, and the other arm raised in triumph, dancing around an imaginary bonfire and shouting "Today" with Neil Diamond. They stomped to the beat, and felt victorious. Ten or fifteen minutes of acting like idiots, and the exertion of dancing after weeks of fierce fighting, made them feel invincible again.

Since his days in Iraq, those songs had meant something special to him, though as the years passed he heard them less and less. They meant victory, validation, love of country, and "Thank God I live to see another day." The music washed over him like a spring shower.

"Come on," he said taking Deidre's hand, pulling her to her feet. It wasn't an invitation; it was a directive.

"I'm not very good." She laughed.

"Don't worry, I am."

Neil Diamond began belting out the words as they made their way out to the center of the dance floor.

He liked swing dancing and the song was good for it. The beat was strong, so he hoped that would help her. Three bars into the music, he found he didn't need to worry. She picked up on the moves immediately.

"You're great!" He smiled at her.

He swung her out, pulled her in, spun her in a circle with his arm around her waist, then swung her back out again. She picked up on all his cues.

The words and music inspired him. Immigrants coming to America, looking for a new life, a better life. Wasn't everybody?

They were getting bolder with their moves and taking up more of the dance floor. Before long they were the only ones dancing as the others fell back to watch. He was a strong lead, remarkably graceful with movements that were controlled and precise, but smooth and erotic.

Diamond crooned about home and longing, hope and freedom.

Freedom. Dancing was such a freeing experience. It was the one thing he would still do that cast him in the limelight. When he danced, he just didn't care who was watching or who wasn't. He looked down at Deidre and saw his own happiness reflected on her rosy cheeks and upturned mouth.

It's like foreplay or making love in public, he thought, then threw his head back and laughed at himself. No, it's just dancing.

He let her out, pulled her in. He liked putting his arm around her waist, taking her hand, and spinning her out. He didn't need to think when he danced. He just instinctively knew what to do. It warmed him that she picked up on every nuance. They fit together.

My country 'tis of thee, Diamond sang.

He slowed the pace, seductively pulling her in to him.

"Today," the Americans called out with the recording.

Sweet land of liberty.

They stepped back, eyes locked.

"Today," the room sang louder as others joined in.

Of thee I sing.

She twirled slowly under his uplifted arm.

"Today." Now everyone caught on.

Of thee I sing!

He pulled her sharply, strength rippling through him.

"Today!" the room shouted.

Today. Today. Today. As the singer's voice faded, Remi picked her up and swung her around in triumph as the circle of onlookers cheered him. He felt like Paris with Helen. The hero and his lady.

CHAPTER 12

TURKEY

DURING THE DAY, in the bright sunshine with the light reflecting off the sand, Deidre could pretend that it was all a big mistake. She had become proficient at pushing the diagnosis back behind a door marked "Not Gonna Happen." Her sight was good, really good. Maybe she wouldn't go blind. Maybe she'd just be like everyone else and have to wear glasses. There was a time when her vanity shrank at that thought, but now she welcomed it. Glasses. Maybe only glasses.

But at night, when her defenses were down and her vision diminished, the demons of reality came bursting out in full force. She found it harder and harder to see when she moved from bright light to low light, or back. She was nearly blind until her eyes adjusted, which took longer and longer to do as the days passed. She and Cassie had worked out a system of hand-holding. Cassie would lead and reach back her hand, and Deidre would grasp it like the two good friends they were. Entering the tombs had been tricky because of the steps, but it had worked. In her anger, she had forgotten her handicap when she headed off for Tut's tomb, but her friends had been waiting for her, so it had turned out all right.

Dr. Abbott said she was luckier than some. Her form of blindness progressed from the outer edges inward. She'd be able to see straight ahead until the end.

Inherited, Doc Abbott insisted. Yet no one in the family claimed responsibility, she thought ruefully. Perhaps her uncle. But he had died young. Stupid idiot. Killing himself like that.

Or could failing vision explain the plane crash? Maybe he

hadn't done it on purpose. What difference did it make? Uncle Robbie didn't matter. What mattered today was that Deidre needed to see as much as she could and remember as much as she could before time ran out. How much time did she have left? She had stopped counting minutes at the start of the trip. It hadn't helped. Rather it scared her and in her fear, she would physically shake when she let herself go there.

Don't travel to the future, she told herself. Stay in the present moment. Wasn't that Remi's mantra? She could see now. The color was still vivid. Take it in. Grieve later when it's gone. Be strong.

And yet, in the solitude of her bed, the tears stung her dying eyes and rolled into her hair.

* * * * *

"ISTANBUL, CAN you believe we're in Istanbul?" Cassandra exclaimed.

"I thought Egypt was different, but this is really another world." Remi smiled.

"Listen to the loudspeaker," Deidre said.

"It's a call to prayers. Didn't you notice it in Cairo?" he asked.

"A what?"

"Call to prayers. From the minarets." He pointed to thin, tall towers jetting high above the rooftops. Each was pure white with a tall conical gray roof that was often topped with a long and elaborately ornate gold rod. Around the upper third of the towers hung two or sometimes three balconies. The effect was that of knobs on a delicate stem. The horizon of Istanbul was littered with minarets.

"The Muslims pray five times a day," he said.

"That must play havoc with their work schedules," Deidre said under her breath, not wanting to offend anyone.

The women stared at the people hurrying to the nearest church.

"Not churches, mosques."

"What do they have under their arms?"

"Prayer rugs. To kneel on. Well, it's a bit more than kneeling. They bend down with their foreheads to the ground."

"Sounds pretty pious," Cassandra said.

"Too bad it doesn't stick for long." Deidre added quietly.

Remi shot her a disapproving look. "I've known a lot of Muslims. Most are really sincere, good people. They believe what the Koran teaches. It's just these radicals who hide behind the good guys. And you can't tell one from the other. There could be one insurgent in that mosque right now, but you wouldn't be able to pick him out. So the whole lot of them suffer suspicion. It's not fair, but that's how it is. Just don't think they're mostly bad. They aren't. They're just men and women like you and me, trying to get on with the problem of living."

Deidre nodded at the gentle admonishment.

"Do you think the Muslims of Turkey are grieving Bin Laden's death?" she asked.

The look he shot her was piercing, as was his terse answer. "No."

THE WOMEN WERE in awe of everything they saw. Even Remi found Istanbul interesting, though his "danger" antennae were on maximum alert. ForceCon Charlie. He tried to tamp down his unease, but the smell of the food, the burka-covered women, the turban-crowned men, the call to prayers, the whole Middle Eastern feel of the city, kept him on edge. Flashbacks, not in the form of images, but in sensations, disrupted any illusions he had that this might be just an ordinary tourist town. Rome was a Lego castle compared to Istanbul. But he was determined to hang in there.

As they walked through the ancient city, Deidre and Cassie stopped constantly to examine some new idea or marvel at an inventive solution to a problem.

Along one crowded street, they saw a small booth no more than five feet wide and six feet deep. The grinning merchant repaired shoes. One wall of the booth was lined with new leather to be cut into soles. Another held two shallow shelves: one for spools of heavy thread, buckles, and shoelaces, and a wider upper shelf for shoes repaired and those waiting to be repaired. Across the back was a treadle sewing machine. A naked bulb hung from the ceiling to brighten the dim space, and a worn oriental rug covered the dirt floor.

"It's so small," Deidre said, "but quite functional."

As they turned back down the street, they came across a young man with a fat gray and white snake curled up his arm and over his neck.

"Boa constrictor?" Deidre asked Remi, who nodded.

"Look at that," Cassandra said, pointing to a man leading a tame bear on a leash with a red print neckerchief tied playfully around its thick neck. Deidre felt rather sorry for the bear. It made him look absurd.

It bothered Remi, too, who remembered a pet deer he once had named Fawntine.

Remi stopped at a butcher shop to buy a small bag of meat scraps. The women's curiosity was satisfied as they walked through the crowded streets. To each skinny stray dog that staggered between the legs of pedestrians, Remi tossed a bit of meat. Soon, however, he became the Pied Piper of Istanbul with a trail of canine tongues licking lips in anticipation. He was glad when the bag was empty and the animals slowly peeled off in disappointment. Maybe it wasn't the best idea he'd had on this trip.

"They're worse than beggars."

"What is that divine smell?" Deidre asked.

Cassandra pointed in the direction of a cluster of men sitting on sidewalk stools. In the center of the group, a small grill held a boiling pot of delicious-smelling meat. They stopped to look.

Deidre smiled at the men. "What are you cooking?" She hoped they spoke English though chances were good they could figure out the question.

A toothless man with mischief in his eyes grinned and pointed to the pot in question. The others stopped in mid-sentence to watch.

Deidre nodded enthusiastically and stepped closer to inspect its contents. Although the food smelled wonderful, she found the scent of the men to be overwhelmingly unpleasant. Still, her curiosity kept her bending over the pot as a second man fished out the delicacy with a fork. She was uncomfortably aware that she had become the center of attention.

Her delight turned to horror when she realized what she was seeing. Dripping from the skewer was a large penis with a sac of testicles. The men, watching closely for her reaction, burst out in laughter. One slapped his knee while another stomped his foot in glee.

Her face flamed with embarrassment as she turned away in disgust. Then she got angry and turned back to the men. She had done nothing to these people except show an interest in their lives.

"How dare you. How dare you!" She glared at them. They might not know the words, but they certainly understood their meaning.

Remi took her arm and led her away. It was useless. No lessons to be taught or learned here. His temptation to kick over the pot was acute. If he had been on his own he might have laughed with the men, but you just don't do that to impressionable young American women. They certainly wouldn't have done it to one of *their* women. Well, of course, he conceded, Muslim women wouldn't have stopped to talk to the men. Deidre must have been quite a treat for them. Damn. He should have seen it coming and stepped in before it got that far.

"That was pretty intense for a small thing," Cassandra said.

"Ick! *That* was not a small anything."

"Do you think it was a cow?"

"I don't want to think about it at all! I just hope it wasn't human!" Deidre's stomach lurched.

"It wasn't. Come on," Remi urged, taking her elbow with one hand and Cassandra's with the other. They needed a distraction. They needed to get a different smell up their noses.

"I'm not going to easily forget that," Deidre said. "That was so disgusting."

"You sound just like Remi when he says 'tourist'," Cassie said with a laugh, significantly lightening the mood.

They crossed the street toward a shop filled with women. Women. Safe. A good environment.

Inside they found vast glass jars, each filled with a beautiful translucent-colored liquid and stoppered with a cork. A thin rubber tube was inserted through the cork and fell limply down the side of the glass. The tubes were primed with the liquid but held in place by a clamp. It reminded the girls of giant flasks from their chemistry classes.

Local women, some with headscarves, carried small, colored bottles of thin glass. The Americans watched as the women took each hose to their nose and breathed in deeply. Once they made a selection, the clerks would hold the glass bottle under the hose tip, release the clamp, and fill the bottle. At the check out, many young women had chaperones who took care of the actual purchase and carried out the small but precious parcel. The only man in the shop, presumably the owner, handled the transactions. Even Remi watched from the sidewalk.

"It's a perfume store! And the women are bringing their own bottles to fill," Deidre exclaimed in delight.

The bottles fit in the palm of a hand and were blown more delicately than an eggshell. Patterns were etched onto the colored glass and the stoppers ascended to lovely peaks that flattened into twisted pads for easy handling.

"I got some of these as gifts once, but I never knew they were anything other than pretty dust catchers," Cassie said. "Let's smell some."

She headed for a nearby counter and lifted the tips of rubber tubes to inhale the different fragrances.

"Delightful!" she announced.

Deidre followed her friend, but drifted to half-drained bottles, the most popular, she surmised.

"Which do you like best?" Cassie asked.

She couldn't decide. She loved the Fath de Fath. The bottle was a brilliant orange. The Samsara, the color of pale yellow with just a touch of green, had a sweeter smell. The younger girls her age were buying that one. The Venezia bottle was sunflower yellow and had the scent of vanilla and cherries. Ysatis, a pale yellow, had a sophisticated smell.

One lovely woman, perhaps in her mid-thirties, wearing an array of gold bangles on her arms and a brightly colored silk hijab, obviously had expensive tastes. Deidre was curious which fragrance she would choose, and tried to be inconspicuous as she watched the elegant woman. She wasn't surprised when the bangled wrist motioned toward the Ysatis. She, too, liked that perfume very much, but her nose kept taking her back to the Fath de Fath.

"This one," she said, pointing to the orange bottle. Since she had no bottle of her own, she bought a clear, etched one of heavier glass with a screw top so she could transport her purchase securely.

The clerk carefully filled the small vial and handed it to her with a smile. Remi joined her at the cash register. When Deidre produced the payment, the clerk's pleasant manner changed to one of disapproval as she looked at Remi. Of course, she didn't dare say anything, except with her eyes. The overseer was more conspicuous as he glared first at Deidre, then at Remi. He accepted the money from Deidre, but pushed the change toward Remi.

Deidre looked from one to the other.

"Outside," Remi whispered.

After Cassandra made her selection, the group gathered in front of the shop.

"What was that about?"

"I forgot. Women don't handle money here, at least not when there's a man to do it for them."

Oh, so that was it, she thought. What a backward country.

"Just a different way of doing things," he responded to her unspoken comment.

Several stores down was the equally colorful, but less populated spice shop. Basket upon basket were heaped in rounded cones of brightly colored spices. Oranges and reds and yellows bursting with pungent and savory fragrances reminded them of the market in Nice.

Down the street they came to a local shop with fruit and vegetables. The lemons, cut in half to show their freshness, were arranged on a bed of olive leaves. A basket that came up to the waist was filled with purplish-brown eggplants.

"I think the color is called aubergine," Deidre said.

At that precise moment, the sun fell on the basket and Remi took a picture.

Black olives filled another shallow box, their shiny skins lightly covered in olive oil.

Another store sold sweets, and Remi bought the young women a box of Turkish Delights, nugget with pistachio bits.

At one shop, brown eggs in a basket were carefully stacked alongside a much smaller basket of white ones.

"I guess their chickens lay more brown eggs than white," Cassandra said.

As the girls continued exploring, Remi went to find the shopkeeper. The men returned to the egg display. The girls watched curiously as the owner took the top brown egg off the mounded pile and replaced it with a white one. With a minor adjustment to the scene, Remi took the funny picture.

"I could title it, 'white supremacy,' or 'odd man out'. Either way, there's a message."

Remi bought the single white egg, herded the girls back to the shop with the eggplants, and duplicated the concept by setting the egg in the center of the vegetables. No one got the humor except Deidre, Cassandra, and a British couple walking by, but that made it all the more amusing.

Away from the crowded market area, they found other fascinating attractions. Under the shade of an old tree, a man sat in front of a typewriter.

"A scribe," Remi said.

"A what?" Cassandra asked.

"A scribe. He writes letters for people who cannot write, or if someone needs something formally typed up he can do it. And he also reads letters sent to people in Istanbul from other villages."

"It's funny to think a rural Turk can write a letter but an urban Turk can't read it," Deidre said.

Remi shook his head. "Remember the leaning tower? Think

about what you just said." He sounded slightly put out.

Deidre's face darkened in a blush and she turned away. She didn't understand the reprimand.

Cassie saw her embarrassment, then pointed to a cab. "Look at that car. It says Taksi. Isn't that cute?"

The rescue was effective giving Deidre the momentary break she needed to work out Remi's words.

"So they have scribes in villages, too, so they can send mail out," she said quietly.

"You got it," he said.

Remi had taken the reprieve to work out his own thoughts. She was more sensitive than she looked. He'd have to remember that.

A few minutes later, he told a story. "Once, I was sitting with a couple who had just sailed across the Atlantic. During their trip, a terrific storm had blown up and lasted for days. They had to take turns through the day and night to keep the boat on course and upright, with neither getting much sleep. As they told the story, I asked, what seemed to me to be a reasonable question. Why didn't they just drop the anchor and wait out the storm? They both looked at me like I was nuts."

Deidre's face showed both interest and confusion.

"You're making the same mistake I did," he said. "You see, a chain long enough to reach the bottom of the ocean would be so heavy it would have sunk the ship."

He watched recognition register in her eyes.

"So you're not the only one to have brain farts."

The gratitude on her face was so genuine that he reached out and pulled her tightly to his chest. Holding her with one arm he scratched her back with the other. "Now stop being such a pain in the ass," he said affectionately, laying his cheek on top of her head.

At dinner that evening, Remi noticed the perfume. He had appreciated her own scent, probably from the shampoo, citrus, and vanilla—a strange fresh combination. But beyond that, Deidre simply smelled good. When he commented on the perfume, she said, "When I get back home, this will be my new fragrance, to remind me of this trip."

He didn't mind the concept; he just preferred women to smell like women, not flowers or fruit created in a chemistry lab.

That night, before falling asleep, he thought about hugging Deidre. She felt small, fragile, but his impression of her was strength. He liked the feel of her. Her hug in Egypt had disturbed the fine balance he fought to hold. His hug today—well, it wasn't as brotherly as he had pretended. It had been a long time since he had touched anyone like that, too long. Having a woman in his arms again—the smell, the soft skin, the hair against his cheek—he missed it, he realized. He needed to be touched. Men didn't acknowledge that much, he thought. Maybe that's why they played rough, punched one another, or wrestled, to touch and be touched. Of course, that didn't compare to touching a woman, but maybe it provided some quasi-satisfaction.

The problem, he realized, was that she had opened up a longing in him. It wasn't like that hug would last another year or so. Instead, it was more like pulling off a scab so the need became acute again. What a hell of a mess he was getting himself into.

"IT'S EQUIVALENT to thirty-five *blocks* of stores!" Deidre said.

"Where do we even begin?" Cassandra asked.

"I am so in the moment!" Deidre grinned to a smiling Remi.

"Why don't you pick a product—say, rugs or gold jewelry or copper pots or Meerschaum pipes, just something—and see if you can get through all the stores selling that." Seeing their blank looks

Remi explained, "The products are clustered together. Look," he said guiding them to a jewelry shop. "The gold starts here."

As far as they could see down the long row of stores, gold glistened in every window. In addition to that, between every six to eight stores another pathway was also lined with gold shops. And off those were others. The maze of stores was "amazing," they giggled.

"The Grand Bazaar. And it's all under one roof," Deidre said, truly awed by the immensity of the space.

"It's the greatest shopping mall in the world, I think," Cassie said.

Like honeybees in a spring garden, they spent that day and the next gathering every exotic delight they saw. Remi, in keeping with his new role as pack mule, kept his thoughts to himself. After the fifth rug was laid over his arms, however, he felt it was time for another strategy. They found a copper pot merchant with a toothless grin, smiling black eyes, and space behind his stall to stash their purchases. While the girls continued shopping, Remi left to find a way to ship all their stuff back to the States.

HE GUESSED the American Embassy was in Istanbul, but guessed wrong. It was in Ankara, the country's capitol. But Istanbul did have a Consulate. Just as good, Remi thought.

As he approached the large building, he craned his neck to look for the American flag. It was up there somewhere, just not in view.

He patted his breast pocket to be sure the medals were where he had dropped them. He took one out and held it in his right palm. He didn't know if this would work, but it was worth a try as long as he didn't get caught. He showed his US passport to the Turkish security guard and passed on to the grounds. At the entrance to the Consulate, he found his target: a young Marine, Dress Blues. It made him proud to see that uniform on the fit Marine. No other Corps could hold a candle to it—that midnight blue jacket, sky blue trousers with the blood stripe down the leg, the white belt, white cover. But why was he in Blues? Shouldn't he be in his Service Uniform? Well, there was only one way to find out.

"Good afternoon, Sergeant," he saluted, recognizing his rank. Because Remi was not in uniform, he knew the young man would not salute back. "Blue Dress usually means a dignitary on deck. I won't ask you—I don't need to know—but I would like to buy you a beer after your duty ends. I'm sorry, I should introduce myself. I'm former Gunnery Sergeant Remi Lamont."

He stuck out his hand and hoped the young guard would shake it. He did, and Remi felt the object pass from his palm to the younger man's gloved hand.

The Marine looked down at the medal: a Bronze Star, a Combat V device attached to the suspension ribbon from which it hung. He looked up, smiled, and said, "Nice to meet you, Gunny. I'm Sergeant Erickson. Who were you attached to?"

"One eight Marines, Fallujah."

"First or second?"

"Second."

The young guard nodded. The most famous battle, most say the worst, in the war. Though Ramadi was bad, too. Both produced several opportunities for heroism, but few that resulted in a medal like this.

Handing it back, he said, "Don't see one of these everyday." He was clearly impressed. Remi guessed he might be the most decorated Marine the younger man had ever met. That was the hope anyway.

"A beer sounds good." Sgt. Erickson smiled. "Just bring your Purple Heart along tonight. You probably have one of those, too."

Remi reached into his pocket and pulled it out, making the Marine laugh. "So you're the real deal," he said.

Remi smiled. "Time and place, Sergeant. Time and place."

The arrangements were made and Remi hurried back to the Grand Bazaar. He just hoped he could get all their purchases into the car for a single delivery.

* * * * *

THEY WERE DRIVING south now, heading for the sea. The road wasn't too bad, though top speed was about forty. They saw few cars on the road and only an occasional bus.

"Remi, how did you do it?" Deidre asked. "How did you get everything mailed home?"

"You said the mail in Turkey was—what was the word, unreliable?" Cassandra said.

"No, he called them a bunch of thieves and said our boxes would be picked clean."

"Now hold on, I'm sure I didn't say thieves."

The shipping wasn't complicated once he got Sergeant Erickson on board. And that hadn't taken much convincing. He knew the medals were his credentials.

"Okay, first, a life lesson—what you see isn't always the whole story." He looked in the rearview mirror to make sure they were listening. "There are usually parallel maneuvers happening behind the scenes."

"Like in shopping malls," Cassandra said.

"You lost me."

"Me, too," Deidre said.

"I dated a boy in high school once who was a delivery driver."

"You dated a delivery driver? Who?"

"Jimmy."

"Jimmy was a delivery driver?"

"Ladies, are we getting a bit sidetracked?"

"We are. We were." Cassandra giggled before resuming her explanation. "He explained that in shopping malls there are a whole set of halls that the shoppers never see, as many as in the middle of the store, with doors to take the merchandise in. He called it a parallel universe."

Good to know in case of a fire, Remi thought, filing the tidbit away.

"That's actually a good example, Cassandra. Thanks."

"But it doesn't get my rugs mailed," Deidre said.

"No, but it does illustrate the principle. We usually only see the final product and don't consider that something completely outside our knowledge is happening, too."

"Such as?"

"So, the US military overseas has something called the APO mailing system. I think it stands for American Post Office. When troops are stationed overseas, they have an APO address. Within theater, the mail is free."

"Within theater?"

"Sorry. In Europe or in the Pacific, or wherever, I can send packages free to another APO address. We can also send things home to the States and the cost is the same as New York to wherever. New York to Detroit."

"Is New York the clearing house for all overseas mail?"

"From Europe. Not sure from the Pacific."

"We have American bases in Turkey?" Cassandra asked.

"Yes, three. Well, there used to be Izmir, Adana, and Incirlik, but Adana might be closed now."

"I don't hear Istanbul on that list."

"Will you let me finish, please?" He glared back at them. "So the embassies and consulates use the APO, too. When you were

167

shopping, I met with a Marine who offered to send your boxes to Sigonella for me. We packed them; he mailed them. And it was free."

It really was that simple. He insisted that Frank look through the boxes to ensure there was no contraband, no drugs, no weapons, nothing that would get him in trouble. Then once the boxes were taped shut, the young Marine only had to put his return address on them and haul them to the mailroom. Remi's only cost was a meal and conversation about his experiences in Fallujah and Ramadi.

"Okay, so our stuff is on its way to where?"

"Sigonella, Italy. The southern part."

"So why Italy? That's a bit of a swim to Detroit."

"I've got a buddy stationed there who will take care of the last leg."

"Is this legal?"

"No." Remi brushed off the reply as too insignificant to think about. "So from there, my buddy will ship it to your home and send me a bill for postage. It will take longer, but it will be a lot cheaper and, more importantly, it will get there."

"Another parallel universe," Cassandra said.

"Another act of heroism to add to the list," Deidre said. "An *illegal* act of heroism, but—"

"Picky, picky, picky," he said to the mirror as their eyes met.

AFTER THE HIGHLY stimulating Grand Bazaar, they were relieved to leave the city and head into the desert. Although he had tried to enjoy Istanbul, Remi's eyes had been in constant motion, scanning roofs, windows, a truck stopping for no reason, a car taking a corner too fast… His mind had been working in overdrive. The old cars driven in the city and the strange gas they used produced more backfires than a Charlie Chaplin movie. Or the Keystone Cops. It was surprising how many lens caps fell off.

They had been driving in silence for about two hours. The landscape was remarkable in its lack of variety.

Finally, Remi said, "Ladies, I am offering free driving lessons."

Deidre and Cassandra looked at each other. "We already know how to drive."

"A stick?"

"No. But no one drives a stick."

"I am, right now."

"Okay, here in Turkey, or Europe, but not back at home," Deidre said.

"Do they even sell cars with stick shifts back home?" Cassandra asked.

"They do. Especially fast cars. If you really want to impress a boyfriend, you should learn. Did you see Julia Roberts in *Pretty Woman* driving that Lotus Esprit?" He looked in the mirror. Finally, a reference they knew. "Now, who wants the first lesson?"

From the back seat came a resounding silence. He saw Deidre mouthing something to her friend, who nodded.

"I do," Cassandra said, just as he looked away.

There's a secret going on back there, he thought, not for the first time.

Cassandra climbed into the driver's seat.

It was a good lesson, and within two hours the car hardly jerked at all. At first, Deidre rolled with laughter, even more so when Cassie glared at her over her shoulder, but she was equally generous with her praise. The lesson also broke up the long drive for Remi, who was thoroughly enjoying it.

Finally, he had Cassandra pull over and told her to change places with Deidre. Her response surprised him.

"I'm going to pass," she said.

What the hell. Deidre Sinclair did not strike him as someone who was much afraid of anything. He knew she had spunk. Would he ever understand women? Probably not.

Half an hour later, they stopped to get gas, water, and pit stop. When the women returned to the car, Deidre told Remi she had changed her mind and wondered if he was still offering driving lessons.

Remi restrained his grin.

At first, she wasn't much better than Cassandra, who made ample use of "pay back," with hoots and hollers. But Deidre caught on quickly, and soon they were making their way smoothly toward Anamur.

He felt good teaching her. She was smart, really smart, but different than his kind of smart. His knowledge was practical, about life, street smart. Hers was book smart and people smart. When he told her something, she would remember it and apply it, sometimes in ways he would never think of. She wasn't too young for him, he decided. But was he too old for her? Her f-ing father probably thought so. What surprised him most, however, was why he was even having this ridiculous conversation with himself.

They spent the night sleeping in the car on the side of the road. Earlier in the evening, they had stopped at the only village large enough to boast a hotel. At first it was a welcomed sight. But when they pulled back the sheets and discovered bugs, both women adamantly refused to sleep there. After promising not to whine, and with no other options in sight, they decided on the car, though Remi opted for the warm sand. He was rather impressed at how well they adapted. At the start of the trip, he would never have imagined it.

THE DESERT WAS hot and barren with no visible life. Though Remi was out of the city and all its opportunity for ambush, the déjà vu sense of doom still hovered at the periphery. This was too much like Iraq and Afghanistan, too much sand, too much sun, too much desolation. Sometimes he found himself scouting the horizon for movement. He could bring himself back to reality with the obvious argument that no right-minded insurgent would plant an IED in the middle of a desert in Turkey with no one around to find it, but before long he would find he was scanning the desert again.

The company of the girl was a good distraction.

"Where did you get the name Remi? Does it have a meaning?" Deidre asked.

"I was named after a French saint, St. Remigius."

"Ooh, a saint."

"Remember St. Remy? San Remo? That was the guy."

"What did he do to earn sainthood?" Cassandra asked.

"I don't think you earn it. It's not like becoming a Knight of the Round Table." He paused. "Well, maybe comparisons can be drawn.

"So," he continued, "the three things that made him a saint were the conversion of the French King and, subsequently, the rest of the country, the baptism of a pagan for which he had no oil, but miraculously two empty vases put on the altar filled themselves with the needed oil so the baptism could take place, and, let's see, number three was when they dug him up four hundred years later there were two vases filled with sweet-smelling liquid buried with him."

"That's all?"

"Hey," he said feigning effrontery, "he converted the entire population of France to Catholicism!"

"Guess the Pope liked that," Deidre said.

"Undoubtedly." Remi grinned.

Finally, they saw a café all by itself in the middle of nowhere halfway between Alanya and Anamur on the southern coast of Turkey. Remi planned to find coastal routes along the Mediterranean to Izmir with stops at Ephesus to see the Roman ruins and some of the lesser-known Christian holy sites, maybe even the burial place of the Apostle John. Though he no longer believed in God, he wasn't totally opposed to the idea that the Bible might have some historic value, and even moral value when it came to Jesus. In any case, it would interest the women. Deidre did seem moved by the Pietà, so maybe she'd like to see the legendary home of the Virgin Mary.

Though small and a bit rundown the café looked like an oasis to the hot and hungry travelers. It was constructed in adobe with a corrugated tin roof that extended over a large porch providing shade for outside diners. Great troughs of colorful potted plants skirted the porch's edge and defined it in sharp contract from the desert around them.

They were the only patrons at the café. The proprietor insisted they sit outside and seated them next to a particularly lovely row of bright flowers. He took their orders, but instead of going inside he disappeared around the side of the building. Remi stretched his neck to see what he was doing.

"Hope he isn't killing the chicken for us."

Suddenly, a soft sound came from the tin roof above, and from its edge, a cascade of water fell, forming a fine mist to blow on their hot skin. It ran evenly, like a veil of water, into the flowers.

"Wow. Is this wonderful or what?" Cassandra said.

"How did he do that?" Deidre asked.

Cassandra put her hand in the water and cooled her neck.

"Don't drink it," Remi cautioned. "Better rinse your hand off with water in the car before you eat. We don't know the source."

"Well, that was dumb," Cassandra said, as she pushed back her chair.

While she went to the car, Remi and Deidre stepped out from under the porch and stood far enough away from the building to see the invention.

"Look, see that bar that runs along the peak?" He pointed.

Deidre stepped back farther to see. Realizing she was so much shorter than Remi, a good eight to nine inches, he grasped her around the waist and lifted her. One hundred and fifteen pounds, he estimated with a smile.

"I see it. There are holes all through it, each placed where the ruffle of the tin dips down."

He put her down and walked over to the side of the building.

"Ah, look. He's hooked up a hose to the end of the pipe. Open the valve, and instant cool," Remi said appreciatively. "Quite the inventor, this one."

"And water for the flowers."

"So the water does double duty."

"Speaking of cool, let's get back to our table and cool off," she said, seeing Cassandra seated back at the table and fanning the mist toward her.

It turned out the proprietor had not killed the chicken, but did make an excellent meal of lamb and sautéed onions wrapped in soft, sweetened pita bread.

"Like a gyro," Deidre said. He served it with honey-sweetened yogurt, a cherry tomato for color, and Turkish tea. They also enjoyed a wedge of spinach pie and baklava for dessert.

"I thought that was Greek," Cassie said.

"Whatever it is, it's wonderful!" Deidre said.

They relaxed with their tea in the refreshing mist. As they chatted amicably, Remi's phone rang, startling them all.

This was the first time the phone had rung in front of the young women since the beginning of the trip. He had programmed the ring tone to the *Theme from Jaws* which amused them.

Remi knew who it was, but checked the name to be certain.

Sinclair. He pushed back the chair and walked, toward the car.

"Who do you think it is?" Cassandra asked.

Deidre shrugged.

Remi listened to the voice on the other end. He was skeptical, but kept silent.

"We're in the middle of nowhere right now. I don't think we can get to an airport for a couple of days, then one more day of travel. Plan for Monday at the earliest. I'll keep you informed as things unfold here."

The voice continued.

"Sure, I'll put her right on. Talk with you soon."

He walked over to the table where the two women were chatting. "Deidre, let me have your phone."

She took it from her pocket and handed it to him, a question in her eyes.

"Your father wants to talk with you. Cassandra, come with me."

He strode off to explain the latest developments and to see what he could do with the Turkish airlines. The fastest way to Istanbul was the way they had just come.

Deidre listened attentively as her father explained the situation. Her mother was going in for major surgery, a brain tumor, and wanted Deidre back home. Very coincidental, she thought. It felt like a ploy to end the trip prematurely, but she certainly couldn't take the chance. Her father assured her she could resume her Grand Tour, as they all had begun to call it, within a week or so of the surgery, if everything went well.

Deidre sat thoughtfully. This was extreme, even for her mother. And her father did sound deeply concerned. As she tapped the phone on the table, she looked out to see Cassie scouting through the luggage in the trunk and Remi deep in conversation on her phone. *Her phone*. It struck her suddenly that she had his phone. She looked over again to make sure they both were busy, then turned her back to shield her actions from prying eyes. She looked at the call registry. Who was the person, or persons—though her instincts told her it was person, singular—he called all the time?

"Kiss."

It wasn't just a number; the name was logged in his favorites. Suddenly, her stomach sank. She continued to scroll down—Kiss, Kiss, Kiss. It went on and on, with only a few other names mixed in. Deidre had no idea Remi had called this Kiss woman several times a week, or had received calls from her. Deidre wondered what her real name was. Why would he put her in the phone as Kiss? To hide her identity? Obviously she wasn't a sister or cousin. She had to be his girlfriend. He had a girlfriend.

There were no text messages. She remembered he had told her once he didn't like texting. Not only were his fingers too big, but he preferred the old fashioned pleasure of hearing a human voice.

Deidre felt sick, like she had just been hit in the stomach with a soccer ball. She wanted to wretch. How could she be such a fool? She checked the call dates. He had even called his girlfriend on her birthday! The day they'd had that wonderful time on the cruise, and he had given her the map, and they'd danced, and he seemed like someone new. He had gone straight to his cabin, apparently, and called his girlfriend. Guilt probably.

The sense of betrayal was overwhelming. How could she ever face him again? No, how dare he face her.

"What the *hell* are you doing?" From over her shoulder, the voice fell low and ice cold.

Instantly, she flew into panic mode. She froze as a shiver went down her back. She truly felt like she was going to throw up and didn't dare open her mouth.

"You're going through my phone?" The quiet condemnation in

his voice was like sulfuric acid burning through her back and stomach, dissolving her organs, liquefying her bones.

She couldn't look at him.

He threw her phone hard on the table so it bounced. "Give it to me."

Her courage had left her. She had no defense, no excuse. She could hardly breathe. She didn't even turn off his phone; just lifted it over her head, where he snatched it. She heard him storm off toward the open door of the café. She made her escape, shoving her phone in her pocket and hurrying to the car. Her legs felt like rubber bands. She could hardly swallow. This was the worst thing she had ever done. She wanted to pull a blanket over her head so he wouldn't see her when he looked in the mirror. Her cheeks blazed with the shame of her violation. She couldn't even tell Cassie. She couldn't confess to anyone. The only thought that kept her together was that, yes, she had been terribly wrong, but now she knew he had betrayed her. That tiny bit of righteous indignation smoldered just enough to keep her blood warm and flowing as they turned and headed for Istanbul, a long and silent two days away.

CHAPTER 13

HOME

JAMES SINCLAIR pulled into the circular drive with his daughter. Grabbing just her handbag, she ran into the house.

"Mother?"

Janet had dozed off while waiting for her, but woke up instantly and hurried to the foyer.

"I'm here, darling."

On the trip from the airport, Sinclair had made it clear that, rather than exaggerating her mother's condition, he had in fact minimized it so Deidre wouldn't worry during the helpless trip home. Now a strange fear began to form. Her mother, the indomitable one, stricken by an unseen force. It seemed preposterous. If it could happen to Janet Sinclair, then it could happen to anyone. Was the cosmos really this out of control?

"Oh, Mom! I'm home. I'm home," she murmured in her mother's embrace.

"Yes you are, my little girl. Yes, you are." She hugged her, hard and long. "I have missed you so much."

"Oh, Mom, I should have been here. When did you find out?"

Her mother led her to the sofa. "No, no, no, dear. We knew before you left. We just didn't know the extent. It was better you were gone without carrying this burden, too. You already had too much luggage, from what I gather." She smiled.

Deidre swatted away the comment and the memories it brought back. "Don't joke about this. Please." She looked at her mother's face and turned her head to examine it.

"There's no bulge. It's all inside," Janet said.

"Does it hurt?"

"Headaches, but not all the time. And they're not like my migraines. Heavens, maybe I should have them do something about those silly things while they're in there." She laughed.

Deidre looked at her mother. Why wasn't she shaking with fear?

"They have me on tranquilizers," she answered the unspoken question. "Some days they work better than others. I wanted your homecoming to be special."

"How can this be special? You're dying." Deidre leaned into her mother for comfort.

Startled, Janet gently straightened her. "Darling, where did you get that idea?"

"Well, you have a brain tumor, don't you? And you sent for me."

"Yes, but they think it's benign. I mean, there may be some complications…what do you mean I sent for you?"

She looked closely at her mother, wondering if she could believe her. She seemed so different.

"When I left in June, Daddy said at the airport that unless someone was dying he didn't expect to see me until the fall, so I should enjoy myself and not worry. And then he called."

"Oh. If he told you that, he should have told you I am definitely not dying."

"But what complications?"

Janet considered the answer before she spoke. "It's the position of the tumor. Some of the tentacles seem to be twined around the speech center and perhaps the area involving my motor coordination. It may come out in one piece, but if they have to probe around it could damage things. They just don't know."

"Why did you wait so long to tell me?"

"We talked about it. We wanted you to finish your trip. And you will, by the way, just with this small interruption."

Deidre's cheeks flushed. "No, I don't think so."

"Yes, you will. We scheduled the surgery for tomorrow, and I should be home in a week. With plenty of help if—if things go badly."

"No."

"Yes."

"We'll talk about it," she conceded.

Mother and daughter sat until dusk talking, really talking, they realized, for the first time in their lives. Some of it was light and airy, some about Deidre's travels, some gossip. Tentatively, Janet touched on tender life lessons. The relationship they were trying to fashion was so fragile, so important, but couldn't be done in a day.

Her mother spoke of her first love affair and how it ended.

"Although I deeply love your father and he is absolutely the right man for me, you never really get over the first one," she said wistfully.

Janet explained about the plane crash and answered each of her daughter's questions.

She spoke for the first time of her own childhood, and the loneliness she had felt as an only child, and how she hadn't wanted that for Deidre.

She listened as her daughter talked about the wonders of Europe and the man who opened her eyes to a new world. She could see the tenderness when she spoke his name, but something unsettling lay beneath. Having kept secrets all of her life she could see intuitively that Deidre was holding something back. Perhaps with time, she might earn her daughter's trust and learn the secrets. She just hoped they weren't lovers, and that, Deidre wasn't hiding a broken heart.

Finally, Janet said, "There is something I want to tell you, while I know I can, and something I want you to do for me."

Deidre nodded solemnly. Her mother had clearly changed. Maybe it was the tranquillizers, maybe the tumor itself. Would the surgery undo it?

What a terrible thought, Deidre! Shame on you.
But I like this new mother…

Janet reached for something on the end table.

"When your father and I married," she began, settling herself comfortably, and reaching for her daughter's hand, "he loved me very much. He still does," she quickly assured her daughter after seeing her eyes widen. "But relationships change as marriage bumps along. People change, so the love changes, too."

"Mom?"

"It's all right, little girl," she said, patting her hand. "This has a happy ending."

She resumed her story. "On our wedding night, your father gave me a very special gift. It was this deck of playing cards." She opened her hand to show her daughter the near pristine box. "He told me he understood that, where our home and family were concerned, that I needed to have things my own way. And this was his gift to me. I held all the cards."

Deidre reached for the box and took out the cards, reverently fanning them.

"He only asked for one thing. That I give him the four aces."

Deidre saw them on top.

"Why the four aces?"

"During our marriage, your father wanted to be allowed to make four major decisions, and his aces would trump any opinion I might have. It seemed like a very generous offer. I pulled out the power cards and handed them to him."

"Did he use them? I see them here." She glanced at the top cards.

"Yes. The first one he used before our first anniversary. An old beau was flirting with me. 'Sniffing around,' your father called it. He didn't like it. I saw no harm in it. Maybe I was flattered. I was young. We fought, and he thrust the ace in my face. It was innocent flirting, but not to your father. I sent the man away, though, and took his ace. The second time—do you know, I can't actually remember what the second ace was for. Something silly. The third..." Janet stared off into the distance. "I remember that one. It was three years after you were born. I wanted another child. He adamantly refused. He claimed it was for my own good. He was wrong. He had no right to take that from me." She sighed. "His trump card beat the rest of my deck, so I lost."

Deidre felt a surprising wave of tenderness come over her as she saw a face full of regret and lost babies.

"You see, you were his. You filled his whole heart. He didn't need another child. But I wanted one of my own. One that would adore me the way you adored your father."

Janet spent a moment more in the memory of young motherhood.

"I tried to keep you close to me. You would be the only daughter I would ever have. But you'd have no part of it. You fought me every inch of the way. The more you ran away, the harder I'd run to catch you and capture you. Your father would lecture me. 'If you love someone, let them go.' I'd try, but you didn't come back to me. You'd just fly farther away." She smiled at her daughter. "I've never been known for my patience."

Deidre hugged her close. "So at dinner, when I explained my plan for my Grand Tour, the fourth ace..."

"Yes. He played his last one. For you."

Deidre's eyes smarted with tears.

"I always thought it would be for you. He and I, we've found our peace. We are happy most of the time. I thought he would save it for something having to do with your condition, say some treatment facility. He didn't know it, but I was prepared to let him make those decisions if that was important to him. But he shocked me when he said you could go on this trip."

Deidre looked through the cards again. "Mother, there are only three here," she said as she looked at the aces.

Janet took the deck from her daughter and continued. "He was wrong about the first three. But the fourth ace," she said, reaching into her pocket to pull out the ace of hearts, "he was right. I should have realized it right away. But you see, I've had my way for so many years, nearly two decades, that I've forgotten what it was like to compromise, to hear the other side. Marriage can't be just one way. Both people have to give. It's taken me a while to learn that again. This ace, he should have it back." She returned the card to her pocket. "Maybe I was too young to understand the importance of it before, but in these two months that you've been gone your father and I have reconnected again. It's been so very good. I wanted you to know we are happy. And if I do lose my speech, or some motor control, I know your father will take care of me. He'll be as strong as ever. But I may need him more than I have in the past."

"Mother, you'll have me, too."

"Yes, darling," she said, smoothing back her daughter's hair. "Only not here. I want time alone with your father. I'm asking that you finish your Grand Tour, and when you get home in November I promise I will do better."

Janet saw her daughter's eyes darken as she shook her head.

"I think I'm pretty much done with traveling," she said, looking at her hands resting in her lap. "I think I'd rather be home."

CHAPTER 14

NEWARK

REMI ENTERED Jerry's apartment. The sparse furnishings were a result of the need to maneuver as much as anything. He had a bedroom and bathroom in the back, and a living room and kitchen in the front. A small TV on a stand, a lumpy couch, a table, one chair for the rare guest, and a small bookcase with a stack of old newspapers, and three books: a dictionary, *Baseball's All Time Bloopers*, and an Atlas, furnished the rooms. The wheelchair was the main thing.

"You're looking good, buddy," Remi said, bending down to hug the muscular shoulders of his friend. They pounded each other on the back. "So how you doing?" Remi asked, pulling out the vacant kitchen chair.

"Me, I'm great, but you look like hell," Jerry said.

Remi ran his hand through his hair. He felt exhausted, but all of his nerves were hyper-agitated, making rest impossible. "Jetlag's a bitch."

"Yeah? And which bitch are we talking about?"

Remi looked up and smiled. "Let's not go there, all right?"

His friend chuckled. "Sure. Want a beer?" He nodded toward the refrigerator. "Grab one for me, too."

Remi opened the refrigerator and looked at the meager offerings. Other than a few condiments and the beer, the only edible food was an open package of old bologna, drying on one edge. Remi screwed open his beer and handed the other to Jerry.

"So, who've you heard from?"

Jerry accepted the bottle and took a long swallow. "Barnes got married on the fourth."

"Of July?"

"Yeah. He said the fireworks would help him remember his anniversary."

They laughed.

"He would have invited you, but I told him you were globe-trotting."

"I didn't miss the fireworks, that's for sure. Maybe I should spend July out of the country every year." He rolled the bottle between his palms. "I did hit the ground once in Rome, did I tell you?"

Jerry shook his head.

"Backfire." He laughed. "Embarrassing as hell."

"That problem, I don't have," Jerry said without malice.

Remi looked at the stubs above what should have been knees. The mangled skin no longer had the red, angry look of freshly healed scars, but it was grotesque enough to make most people look away. Jerry never felt the need to cover them. He wore his battle wounds like the Purple Heart he kept in the drawer.

Remi had stopped apologizing years ago, but the guilt, the memory, never left him. It flashed in front of him even now—the heat, the smell, the metallic taste of fear, the adrenaline, the confusion, the smoke, the screams of a woman in the distance. Gunshots pinging and ricocheting off the cinderblock, chips of stucco flying from the bullet-riddled walls, a bomb exploding somewhere nearby, shouts, warnings, the stinging sweat falling into his eyes, the beat of his heart pounding in his ears, muffling the sounds around him. They needed cover, to secure the building.

He took point, Jerry was next, the others stacked behind them. They had to get inside quick; the insurgents were pinning them down. They had guys on the roof, but they were still taking fire.

The front door smashed open with the first kick. No explosives needed, thank God. There was a door to the left. But he had gone straight, had seen a flash at the door to the right, maybe, though maybe not. He slammed the door to the room open, ready to shoot anything that moved. The room was empty. Rags in one corner? Danger there? No, a dog left behind, cowering. Behind him, taking his place, Jerry button-hooked to the left. The Marines, his Marines, followed them into the building. When did he hear the click of the trip wire? Before he saw the dog? After? Did he actually hear it? Or did his imagination fill it in later? Before it registered, the room behind him exploded. Jerry! Jerry had gone in. Remi and the others raced to him.

"CORPSMAN!!"

It was bad. Remi could see the legs were gone, and part of his abdomen was hanging out. The blood was pumping out of his legs fast. Sweeney started working on Jerry's right thigh. Polansky was doing the same around the left. He took the abdomen, holding the guts in. It was Talon all over again. The floor was slippery with blood. His hands were sticky with it. He wiped them on his legs. Jerry was in shock, knowing it was bad, but not knowing how bad. He wasn't screaming. The others were working feverishly, but mostly in silence. He had heard somewhere that limbs could be reattached, but the bits of flesh and bone scattered around were no longer limbs. Some of the pieces stuck to the door and oozed down the wall. Remi fought to keep the nausea down. The other men formed a perimeter of protection around them. Everyone knew his role. He didn't have to say a thing.

"What happened?" Jerry asked, still dazed.

Trying to form a sensible answer, Remi began, "You—, I—" And then it struck him. He was supposed to turn left. He was point. He was supposed to take the door to the left. Why did he turn in the wrong direction? *Oh, my God*, his brain whispered in horror. Why? Why did he take the door to the right? Because he fucking forgot he was on point? Or because he thought he saw something that wasn't there? What the fuck did it matter! It should have been him in that room, blasted by the booby trap, not Jerry, not his best friend, not a Marine he was responsible for.

Mere seconds had passed. The beer was cold in his hand. The old memory was as real as the event. He was ashen, hot, cold, nauseous, shaking. He ran his hand through his hair and felt the sweat on his brow.

"Remi," Jerry said.

He looked up.

"I told you, I'm good, man. Shake it off."

BEING WITH JERRY was always good once he got past the inevitable memory of the "Event." Jerry understood everything. And he jabbed Remi just enough to keep him honest. He was also the heart of the platoon. The others mostly kept in touch through Jerry. If they didn't check in with him, he was all over their sorry asses.

It was good to know Jerry still watched over the men. He knew what to say, what to do. He was the best friend Remi would ever have.

They headed for the store a few blocks away. People greeted the man in the wheelchair as they made their way down the street. Even the punk kids gave him a salute, and he saluted smartly back.

"You got friends here," Remi said.

"Better friends than enemies."

They got a couple of porterhouse steaks to grill, potatoes to throw on the coals, a ready-made salad, and a case of beer. Mostly, they talked.

They were waiting for the potatoes to cook, but had already

started digging into the steaks and salad when Jerry called him out—he was good at that—for sidestepping the whole Deidre drama.

"This girl got to you, didn't she?"

Remi had been updating his pal throughout the trip, but never came out and said precisely how he felt. He probably didn't need to. Since he'd been in that wheelchair, Jerry had developed a sixth sense that drove every guy in their unit crazy. "Eerie," Jacobs called it. But eerie in the kind of way that you trusted him, like a priest.

"So what gives?"

Remi snorted. "Well, you see, I have this little problem. She's like twelve years old and I'm like sixty-five."

Jerry laughed. "Really?"

"Fuck," he said, taking a gulp of beer.

"No, really? So she's younger than you? What's the big deal? Unless she's a kid…"

"Naw. I thought so at first, treated her like she was. But she grew up on this trip. She's pretty damn grown up. More than me sometimes."

"'Course, that don't take much."

Remi threw a fork at him.

Realizing he had nothing to eat with, he went to retrieve it, but Jerry was into a game of keep-away. They often wrestled. Remi didn't hold back. He was always impressed by Jerry's strength. It matched his own. Finally, he just took Jerry's fork and sat back down.

"She's smart, too. And beautiful," he said, cutting into the steak.

"And that's a problem because?"

What could he say? Hell, this was his oldest friend. He could say anything. "Because I'm broke."

Jerry reached into his pocket. "I know you don't have much cash. Look," he said, "I have a buck I could lend you." He grinned.

This time, Remi threw a spoon. "You fuck—not *broke* broke. Broken. Messed up. You know what I mean."

His friend looked at him for a long moment. "How long have we been friends? Fifteen, twenty years?"

"Boot camp."

"Yeah, boot camp. Okay, sixteen years." He quickly calculated. "I knew you when you were one arrogant little fuck, when every girl in town threw herself at you, when none of the rest of us could score if you were in the bar. I knew you through Sadie and the divorce. I knew you through all the ones since, but man, I've never seen you like this. This one's different. She really got to you. And I can't see you just throwing it away because you were born too soon."

"Yeah, well."

"And about this 'broke' shit. Give it up, man. You've been using that excuse to hide behind since we got back."

Remi gave him a sharp look, but said nothing. This was Jerry. He'd hear him out.

"This trip with two gals—God, I nearly jumped for joy, but no legs, see." He laughed at himself.

A shadow passed across Remi's face.

"Stop it!" Jerry flared up in anger. "Get that look off your goddamn face. Get those fucking thoughts out of your head. What the fuck's the matter with you? No one's doing anything to you. You're doing it to yourself. God, I get so disgusted with you sometimes!" Jerry threw up his arms.

The accusation startled Remi.

They sat in silence, eating with their eyes downcast. Finally Jerry said, "I just want you to get over it. I have. Why is it so hard for you?"

Remi looked up, then away. He was deadly quiet, then said, "Because I took your life from you. I fucking took your life."

"You turned the wrong way. Would you have turned right if you knew the left was rigged?"

"No. Never!"

"No. Never. You weren't a coward. You just forgot you were point. Or maybe you did see something. A simple crap-ass mistake. Nothing more. Remi, that's the risk of war." Jerry reached across the table and grasped his hand. "Look at me. I said look at me."

Remi turned back.

"You weren't a coward then. But you've become one since."

"God, just turn the knife an inch deeper, will you, and add more salt."

"If that's what it takes, I will." Jerry squeezed his hand hard now. "Stop hiding. Stop all this macho Marine crap and be vulnerable. That takes real courage. That's living. The world is not your personal war zone anymore. And your guilt, your goddamn guilt—you've got to get a handle on that, Marine. No one is holding you responsible but you. No one can turn it around but you. I don't forgive you, because there's nothing to forgive. It was just a goddamn mistake, you hear me?"

He felt tears slipping down his cheeks. He'd always stopped them before, but couldn't, not tonight. He was too exhausted. "Jer, I'd do anything to give you your legs back."

"I know you would. I know. But what you're doing is all wrong. This constant self-flagellation, how is that helping me? You know what helps me? It's seeing you happy. It's seeing you live your life. When you call and tell me all the places you've been—God! I just want to hug you! The pictures you send, the stories—I live for those, man. And when I hear that light in your voice when you talk about your girl—don't kill me, brother, but I get a hard on."

Remi laughed at that.

He rolled his chair to get behind Remi.

"I do. It's like I'm making love to her through you. I live my whole life through all you guys: Jacobs, Barnes, Sweeney. But you, bro, you're my pointman, I'm your Wingman. We fight back to back. And you've just got to pull it together, Remi."

He felt Jerry's strong fingers massage his shoulders until the tension in them eased. Finally, Remi sighed and said, "You're mixing your metaphors, you dumbass." And, for an instant, he could almost see a little patch of blue sky through the window.

CHAPTER 15

NEW YORK

WHEN SINCLAIR called, Remi was tempted to ignore him. Of course, that was totally impractical. The sly fox had only given him ten percent of his "salary" up front. And it wasn't his fault the trip had to be cut short. Was he calling to negotiate new terms?

Only one way to find out, he thought, fortifying himself before answering the phone.

Sinclair wanted a meeting. Interestingly, he chose neutral ground, not his own turf. He made it convenient for Remi. The Marriott in Times Square.

Remi took the train to Penn Station and a cab from there. He looked up at the sunlight bouncing off the skyscrapers' mirrored windows, a thousand suns shining down on the "canyons" speckling the pedestrians with light.

It was summer, and the streets were crowded. The fountains around Rockefeller Center were crowded. The sidewalks on Broadway were crowded. Times Square, well, when was Times Square *not* crowded? Even at three o'clock in the morning, Times Square was crowded.

Before September 11, he loved the city, and in abstract still loved her. But the collapse of the twin towers had changed his entire confidence in the world. No one, anywhere, was safe. Not even in New York City. In some obscure corner of his mind, he blamed her. She was supposed to be the rosy big apple, the Statue's beacon of hope, the place where nations united to keep us all safe. Instead, all she turned out to be was nothing more than brick, and mortar, and flashing lights. A façade. A vulnerable, fake façade. And because of that vulnerability, they went to war, were still at war, and men kept dying. Because she didn't keep up her end of the bargain.

He took the elevator to the 48th floor. The outer ring of the lounge moved slowly, offering spectacular views of the city.

Sinclair was waiting for him at a window table. He didn't get up when Remi approached, instead motioning toward a chair across from him.

Sinclair caught the eye of the waiter and signaled for a refill and a round for Remi. "A twenty-year Lagavulin, right?" It wasn't actually a question.

How the hell did the man know that? Remi fumed. The credit card would have shown the charge, not the specific item, unless Sinclair was having him watched, or tracked.

God, the whole family was insufferable!

With effort, he pushed down his anger.

"How's Mrs. Sinclair? Surgery successful?"

"Yes, better than we expected. She'll be back to her old self in three or four months, possibly less."

"Glad to hear it." He would not ask about Deidre, though he guessed she would have to come up at some point.

Remi looked around at the unusual décor. "This room is rather pink, isn't it?" The color of the leather on the chairs was strangely unsettling. He pictured Sinclair in deep brown leather wingbacks with brass nailhead trim, mahogany paneled walls lined with books, and white clad waiters silently knowing the preferred drink of every gentleman in the club. Anything but pink.

"I think they call it mauve."

After the necessary small talk, Sinclair got down to business.

"So, all in all, how do you think the first part of the trip went?"

First part and only part, Remi thought, but said, "I think pretty well. The girls saw a lot, learned a lot, and had fun I think."

"I agree. The phone calls and emails from Deidre were very positive. I could actually see her grow. She was happy." He sipped his Manhattan, but his eyes were on Remi. "But something happened at the end, didn't it?"

Remi held the older man's gaze. What did he know? Why was it his business, anyway?

"Yeah, your wife got sick and we had to cut the trip short."

"Something else."

"Ask Deidre."

"I did. She denied it."

"Then take her word for it. Nothing happened."

Sinclair grew thoughtful. "Have you ever been married. Remi?"

Warily, he answered, "Yeah, once."

"Children?"

"No time. We married. I deployed. We divorced."

"Then you don't know what it's like. On the day your child is born, it's like having your heart pulled out of your chest and it's now walking around in this little person, getting bruised and broken, sometimes trembling with delight. But either way, it isn't in your control anymore. You'd do anything to protect your child."

Remi nodded.

"She's hurting. I don't know what you did to her—"

"What *I* did!"

"That's what I said."

"Because your perfect little girl couldn't possibly have done anything to bring grief on herself—"

"That's what I said. It's never her fault, and it's never going to be her fault. Is that clear?"

"Can you really be that much of a fool?" Be careful, he still holds the purse strings, Remi's rational voice warned.

"I told you once before: I am a father. I am that before anything else, as long as she needs me."

Remi just shook his head and took a healthy swig from his glass, squeezing it far too tightly.

"She changed on this trip. She grew up. I entrusted a girl just out of her teens to your care. She returned a much more mature young woman. I'm pleased, but suspicious about how such a transformation could have taken place in that amount of time.

"So, moving forward, I want you to finish the trip. I want you to fix it with Deidre, whatever the problem is, and I want to be sure you maintain a purely professional relationship with my daughter."

The audacity of the man! He felt like throwing the scotch in his face. Instead, he said, "I think the trip is over for Deidre. Or maybe you should hire someone else."

"In other words, you're not man enough to fix it."

Remi pushed the chair back hard and stood over Sinclair. "Have her call me if she's interested."

"She won't. You're the man. You've got to do it."

"Just have her call me. And send the check for what you owe me so far. You know the address." He walked away. This conversation was over. Then he stopped and turned back around. "Sinclair, where did you get your kitchen counter?"

Confused, the man said, "Italy. Why?"

Shit, Remi thought as he left the hotel.

CHAPTER 16

ALASKA

WHEN REMI called, Deidre was cautious. Their last meeting had ended badly. Once he had seen her safely to her gate in Munich, he had turned away without speaking and headed for his own. Except for flight and transfer information, they hadn't spoken during the flight from Istanbul to Athens, and not from Athens to Munich, either. Deidre was always at the window, Cassie in the middle, and Remi on the aisle. But she hadn't felt particularly protected. In fact, she'd had the distinct impression that what he had really wanted to do was throw her out of said window.

She wasn't sure how she felt, either. Admittedly, she had crossed a very clearly marked line of etiquette. She had absolutely no right to look through his phone log. Absolutely no right at all. Even if they had been lovers, or married, that level of privacy should be respected. How did it differ from reading a diary? She had been enraged when her mother once did exactly that. She understood the violation.

It had been a childish lapse into temptation. A foolish, foolish mistake.

But still—how could she un-know what she now knew? He had a girlfriend, someone he identified as Kiss. How crude. Someone he called several times a week, even when he was having a wonderful time with her. *Especially*, it seemed, when they were really close, like on her birthday. How was that not a betrayal, too?

But yet here he was, calling her. She didn't want to answer, but at the same time it was the one thing in the world she did want. Finally, it stopped. She panicked, found his name—she didn't have the courage to remove it from her contacts yet—and pressed the button to return his call.

"Remi?"

"Hi, I was just leaving you a message."

"Sorry, I couldn't get to the phone." Forgetting to breathe her voice was half an octave higher.

"I called to ask about your mother. How did the surgery go?"

"Oh, really well. They got everything. She's doing really well. It was a success. She's doing great." *Why don't you work a little harder at sounding like an utter moron?*

She took a breath. He was not that important. He was just a stupid man. This, she could handle.

"At first, her words were a little hard to understand, but speech therapy is doing wonders. Everyone says in a couple of months she'll be nearly one hundred percent."

"I'm glad. Give her my best, will you?"

So this really was good-bye. Stall, she thought. Keep him talking. Memorize the tenor of his voice. Anything.

"What have you been doing since you've been back?" she asked casually.

"Visited some of the guys from my old platoon."

"Good visits?" She really didn't want to hear about Kiss, but needed to give him a chance to confess, if he wanted to.

Smiling at the memory of his steak dinner, he said, "Yeah, good visits. Have you heard from Cassandra?"

"Every day. She's fine. Getting ready for school."

"And you? Going back?"

"Ah, no."

Remi had a sinking feeling. *Maybe she already has someone else lined up.* He should just say good-bye and hang up.

"Daddy said he's going to pay you for the rest of the trip."

"Yeah, he told me. Generous of him. I'll probably decline—"

He doesn't want to be with me, she thought miserably.

"Don't do that—,"

"—unless you were interested in resuming your Grand Tour," they spoke over each other.

"I—," she hesitated.

Damn. He should have left it alone.

"I think I would, actually."

"Yeah?"

"Yeah. What do you think?" she asked.

"I think that's what we should do, then."

* * * * *

DEIDRE MET HIM in Alaska. It was late August. Remi picked her up at the Fairbanks Airport. The awkwardness still lingered between them as they headed for the hotel. The catching-up polite small talk out of the way, Remi reached into his pocket and pulled out his phone. He placed it on the console between them.

"So what do you want to know?" he asked.

She knew exactly what he meant, but feigned ignorance.

"Deidre, what do you want to know?"

"I'm fine. Really. It's okay…"

"No, it's not okay. So let's get this settled. Ask your questions."

She hesitated. Here was the opportunity she wanted, but—

"It's really none of my business."

"No, it's not. But when I offer it, you should accept."

She picked up the phone, handled it. She knew what she wanted to ask. So did he.

"Turn it on," Remi directed. "Go on."

She did. There was no password. She went to his call list. There she was Kiss, Kiss, Kiss—a long list of calls. Once in a while a different name—a Barnes, a Jacobs, a Longton—but mainly Kiss seemed to be his preference. She looked at the dates. During the time they were apart, wherever he was, the Kiss calls nearly stopped. He must have been to see her, then.

"No, I'm good," she said definitively, turning off the phone and placing it back on the console.

"What do you want to know, Deidre?" His voice was very quiet.

"I want to know who Kiss is!" she blurted out.

Remi picked up the phone, went to his favorites list, pressed Kiss, and then the send button. Handing it to her, he said, "Talk."

She held the phone to her ear, her heart thundering so loud she wondered if it would reverberate through the phone. How was she going to explain this? What was she going to say? Hi, I was wondering if you are Remi Lamont's long-time lover?

The phone rang two more times. "No one's answering."

"Just hold on."

Then, a man's voice answered. So Kiss was married. She'd gone this far. She was resolved to go all the way. Yes, let's settle it. "Is Kiss there?"

"This is Jerry Kiss."

She looked at Remi, confused. He kept his eyes on the road, but he didn't look as though he wanted to kill her. In fact, he looked rather amused.

"Who's this?" the man named Jerry Kiss asked.

"I'm a friend of Remi Lamont. I'm Deidre Sinclair."

"Deidre Sinclair. Well, well, well. I wondered when you'd call. Is that SOB sitting next to you?"

"As a matter of fact—"

"I didn't think he'd let me talk to you without adult supervision."

Remi heard the remark and laughed. "Not with a horny bastard like you on the other end," he called out.

"Just ignore him, sweetheart. He's got no sense of humor. You should know you're with the wrong Marine."

Remi rolled his eyes.

AFTER SHE HUNG up, Deidre couldn't find the words she wanted. "You're really good friends," she said at last.

"Yeah, like brothers."

"And he's a Marine."

Remi nodded.

"And you've spoken to him about me."

Remi snorted. "Yeah, a few times."

She thought some more.

"Did you say nice things?"

He laughed at that. "Mostly."

The tension in her shoulders was gone.

"He made it sound like you like me."

He turned toward her, and they locked eyes. "Don't you know that?"

"You've never said."

He was quiet for a moment. Maybe he never had.

"I told you, you've got to learn to turn off your brain and see with your heart. I don't need to say it. You know it, don't you?"

She sighed contentedly and settled deeper into the seat.

"Perhaps. But it might be nice to hear it sometimes."

Remi let a full minute pass before saying, "I'll try to do better."

* * * * *

THE HOTEL NORTH Pole was just off the Richardson Highway. A

sleepy little town, North Pole, Alaska, attempted to live up to its famous name.

"Look, Remi—my gosh, it's a Christmas town!"

Sometimes she was a siren, he thought, and sometimes a stubborn minx. Other times, like now, she was a joyous child. Then, she made him see the world through innocent eyes. It felt different. It felt good. Once upon a time it had made him feel old, the difference simply too great. But he had gotten used to her and could go with it now, enjoy it, and appreciate the simple faith she had in the world. It touched long forgotten chords, soothing him.

"Even the lampposts are striped like candy canes. And look," she said, pointing, "curved at the top. Oh, look, the fire hydrants, too."

"Pretty cool, eh."

The day was drifting toward evening, and white twinkle lights edging the roof of the hotel and twining through trees became more visible.

"I can only imagine what this place looks like when it snows."

"Like next week?" Remi teased.

They parked the car in the near-empty lot. Tourist season was over.

"The guidebook says end of September."

"It does, eh. How about we do this trip without a guidebook? Let's just enjoy whatever comes our way."

"Well that's an original concept," she said, zipping the guidebook back into her bag.

"For you, not me," he said, taking the suitcase from her. "Let's drop these off and head out before we lose all the light. If we're lucky, we might see a moose along the road."

"The guidebook says—"

"—that dusk and dawn are the best times," he finished. "I

know."

"Maybe you could write a book?"

He growled.

"Not buying it, eh?" She laughed.

"Perceptive, Miss Sinclair, very perceptive." He grinned. "Catch the door."

* * * * *

ALASKA WAS A nature photographer's paradise. In three days, they had seen twenty-eight moose. Chena Hot Springs Road was known for its moose population. One day they had counted fifteen. In the evenings, the usually deserted road was populated with slow-moving cars, binoculars hanging out of passenger windows, and hazard lights blinking red. The road was over forty miles long and ended at Chena Hot Springs. The local resort, with a working hot spring for which it was named, was once a haven for the first exhausted explorers. It evolved into the present tourist destination, and a break for winter-weary locals. It also served as a place for Japanese newlyweds to make love under the Northern Lights, ensuring many children.

They watched the woods, riverbeds, and fields for moose, and the creeping cars that stopped suddenly, a guarantee of a moose sighting. When they came upon a car on the wrong side of the road stopped on a bridge, they inched up past him to see what he was looking at. There, in the river, they saw the thrashing of water as the majestic antlers and head of a bull moose surfaced in a swirl of spray and algae.

"God, isn't he grand." Remi whistled with sincere admiration.

Remi looked ahead and saw a small dirt road running parallel to the riverbank. He pulled in, parked the car as far as he could along the edge of the road without falling into the river, and set up his tripod. The shots were fantastic. He had pictures of the dive down, the exciting lift of the head, the shake of the massive rack, the spray of water, nostrils flared, mouth dripping with algae, fur wet, eyes rimmed in red. Magnificent pictures.

Mostly, the moose ignored them, but once in a while he would stand and look directly at the camera.

They left both the driver and back doors open. "If he charges, just drop everything and get in."

"What about your camera, the tripod?"

"A broken camera or a crushed ribcage. Which do you want to travel with?"

"I see your point."

They watched the moose for the better part of an hour. Finally, he drifted so far downstream he was not much more than a brown dash floating on a slow-moving river.

Later that night, as they uploaded the pictures to his laptop, Deidre had him stop the slideshow to look at one in particular. "This one. I want this one."

Remi had to laugh. This massive, hulking bull moose with a six-foot rack had resurfaced with a silly strand of algae across his nose. He stood perfectly still, looking directly into the lens. Bullwinkle at his finest. It was a great shot.

Remi pushed the button. "It's on its way."

* * * * *

DENALI NATIONAL PARK sat between Fairbanks and Anchorage off the Parks Highway. On the eastern end of the park loomed Mount Denali, the name the locals gave it, Mt. McKinley in the lower forty-eight.

"It's the tallest mountain in North America. President McKinley never came to Alaska," Remi said, "so why should he get the honor?"

Since most Alaskans agreed, few called the mountain McKinley. Denali suited them just fine.

They entered the park, saw a quick movie, and climbed onto their bus. They had left Fairbanks long before dawn to catch the 6:00 a.m. bus, departing from the visitor center. After the first nine miles, the only vehicles allowed on the two-lane road were those going to or from their campsites. Once past the Savage checkpoint, the park could only be seen by bus, or on foot.

They decided to ride the bus to the end. The trip there and back would take eleven hours. They had packed water and food. There would be none along the way.

"The size of Connecticut! Can you believe that?" Deidre said as they bounced down the dirt road.

She was glad Remi said okay to window seats. "Not much of a terrorist threat up here, I guess," she said. Out of the corner of her eye, she caught his crooked smile.

The day was clear and bright. There had been frost in the park during the night. "That will bring out the color," he said. "And it should start driving the animals down from the high country. Let's cross our fingers."

The road before Savage, the stretch that was open to everyone, held the park's best autumn colors. First, they stopped at the edge of a vast ravine cut by some ancient river many millennia ago. On the far side, the ridge was dressed in the iridescent yellows of aspen and birch, with a sprinkle of orange. The leaves not yet turned added pale wisps of green. Punctuating this colorful canvas, slim, deep green spears of pine trees with black trunks boldly shot up into the sky.

Deidre looked at the beauty before her. *I am seeing this. I am* here, right now, in this enchanting place, seeing something totally magical.*

No sooner had the thought entered than its counterpoint pushed through in a menacing whisper. *And you will never see it again.*

Fighting off the wave of self-pity, she pushed back. *Maybe not, but most people will never see it at all.*

She picked up her camera and, in defiance of fate, she took shot after shot after shot.

They drove on to the flatter tundra with its backdrop of painted mountains and snowy peaks. The landscape was ablaze with the bearberries and blueberries in brilliant reds and burgundies, and flaming tundra grass. Yellow dwarf willows modulated the intensity of all that red, while young evergreens rose timidly above the willows, expecting someday to grow majestic like the dark pines towering high above the autumn landscape.

"There," Remi said, pointing to movement in the brush.

A moose and her calf glided through the shoulder-high foliage, dark shadows ducking in and out between the skinny trees until finally coming to rest. They remained so still they seemed to disappear in the color of the landscape.

At a rest stop, they wandered up the road and saw a ptarmigan changing to winter plumage, his feathered legs and back already white.

"Alaska state bird," he said. "And that red on his head says he's a male."

"Are they always speckled like that?" She could hardly find him in the underbrush.

"He'll be pure white by the time the snow arrives, and all brown in the summer. Nature's camouflage."

Overhead, a raven's throaty call, announcing his presence, hung in the air. From a distance, another bird answered. A wild freedom echoed between them. He spread his wings and rose on the air currents, his feathers illuminating, smooth, and black as a mirror. Then he tipped upward and the sun fell just so, reflecting its own white light, and the illusion turned the raven into a dove.

Even Mount Denali bestowed a rare showing. Covered in virgin snow, the mountain rose solid and benign. Impervious to the boasts of climbers who claimed to have "conquered Mt. Denali," she was unconquerable. Some might climb her, reach her summit, plant their flags, but they were mere fleas on the back of a dog, not worthy of even a shake.

A gray timber wolf trotted through the woods, parallel to the road they traveled. He was focused on some destination, totally oblivious to the tourists fighting to take his picture through bus windows.

A Dall sheep was gingerly picking his way over the steep, colored face of Polychrome Pass.

A mother grizzly sauntered down the dirt road with her two cubs, each the size of a child's teddy bear. Their short, fat legs scampered to keep up.

Everywhere, nature blessed them with one delight after another. It had been a wonderful day.

Deidre looked over at a peaceful Remi as they drove back to Fairbanks. These moments of contentment on his face were coming more and more frequently. They softened his features. The eruption in Arles, was that an exaggeration in her memory? Did she have it wrong back then? Did it matter, when the man seated next to her was now at peace?

How could she tell him what this meant to her, this trip, this Grand Tour that he made happen?

"You've given me a wonderful gift, and I don't know how to repay you."

He continued driving, but she saw a small smile creep to the corner of his mouth.

"I like you, too," he finally said.

CHAPTER 17

KAKTOVIK

THE FLIGHT FROM Fairbanks was long. They welcomed the stop at Prudhoe Bay, but they were anxious to press on. Finally, they left on the last leg to Barter Island.

The plane was small and only held twelve people. All had come to see polar bear. Remi looked past Deidre and pointed out the window. "Look right over there. I think there's a whale."

Looking down, Deidre couldn't distinguish the splash of a tail from the breaking waves.

The passengers could see the strands of land as the plane descended. The pilot announced he spotted a polar bear on the point of the largest strand. He flew a figure eight so people on both the left and right sides of the plane had a chance to see, but Deidre couldn't find him.

The landing at the small airstrip on Barter Island was smooth; the air outside was crisp. Though only the first of September, the ground was covered with six inches of snow. The excited travelers disembarked and waited for their luggage, one carry-on each, to be loaded into the waiting vans. By now, Deidre was an experienced traveler. She easily reduced her clothing to just the bare necessities. She practically lived in blue jeans, which would shock her friends back home.

The new arrivals put their hats and gloves to good use, but the locals who met the plane left jackets unbuttoned and heads uncovered. Two vans were sent. While their future guides greeted them, others loaded the bags into the warm vehicles. In the distance, the small fishing village of Kaktovik looked more like a large mining camp than a town.

Their guide, an Inupiat named Marvin, pointed out the simple geography of Kaktovik and what the travelers might expect.

"The airfield was built about fifty years ago. That meant a dependable way to get supplies, so the villagers stayed year round." He pointed to the sea. "Today begins the start of the whaling season. But the wind is too strong, so the boats won't go out. Maybe tomorrow." At the distant shoreline, in the opposite direction of the town, Marvin explained, was the boneyard. "That's where we drag the whale carcass. We will take you there tonight. The carcasses feed the polar bear and keep them out of the village. They can feed off one carcass for five years. In the spring, when the bear migrate north, the villagers come and harvest the cleaned bones for jewelry and buttons and things."

They drove down a wide, snow-covered road, plowed and lined with widely spaced one-story houses. The yards were littered with all manner of motor vehicles, collections of rusty tools now covered in snow, inverted boats, caribou and moose antlers, and other unidentifiable treasures. Closely planted electrical poles lined the road, boasting the ugly evidence of modern conveniences. Deidre was disappointed by the stark disconnect from charming fishing village to roof antennas and satellite dishes.

The village was quiet. They saw an occasional pedestrian walking and a moving car or two across the flat, white fields, but otherwise this sleepy village was waiting within, waiting for the whales.

They parked at the Marsh Creek Inn. There was no marsh, no creek, and this was far from any inn Deidre had ever seen. Looking every bit like a string of mobile homes shoved together with one end opening into the next, the inn was dreary. The building itself sat on cinderblocks, perhaps giving it that mobile home feel. A large parking lot was in front. Few cars were parked, so the vans were able to pull up to the door for easy unloading. Remi, Deidre, and the others waited for their small bags. They had left the rest of their luggage in Fairbanks. Remi, as always, kept his camera equipment with him. He noticed the other photographers doing the same.

The door to the Marsh Creek Inn was built into the side of an important addition. Though small, the anteroom served two functions: a place to stomp off snow and a means to keep the colder air out of the main part of the inn. A door on an adjacent wall opened to the inn itself.

"Boots off here," Marvin said, pointing to benches just inside the second door. "Coats here." He pointed to the wood pegs above the benches.

Deidre looked at the wet floor where boot-clad patrons had gone before and chose a seat as far into the room as possible. "Wet wool socks are not my idea of a fun-filled night," she said to Remi's inquisitive look.

He nodded as he chose a seat by the door and stepped through the water. His natural body heat would dry his socks quickly. There were far worse discomforts than a couple of hours of damp feet.

Rooms had not been assigned. The travelers were invited to take any they found unoccupied. Remi and Deidre found a room near the front. The tour was set up as double occupancy and, rather than each finding an unknown partner, they agreed they'd room together, as long as James Sinclair remained uninformed.

"I need to warn you about something," Remi said. "I get nightmares."

"I know."

"I figured you did," he said. "And I move around a lot."

"Sleepwalking?"

"No, just—Apparently, I have been known to punch a pillow or two. And they tell me I get loud."

He saw a small smile curve her lips.

"You do."

Well, he'd warned her. That was the best he could do.

The room was narrow with a twin bed on either side of a narrow aisle. At the end of the aisle, below a curtained window, was a single nightstand with a lamp. At the foot of each bed was a bench to put their bags. A rag rug ran down the middle.

"Not much to look at, but functional," Remi said. "Left or right?"

"Left." She dropped her bag on the bench. "Where's the bathroom?"

"Down the hall."

Deidre groaned.

"No whining. We're here to see polar bear, not the Taj Mahal."

"Right. No whining."

While she used the bathroom, Remi opened the window. The room was definitely in need of a good airing. Besides nightmares, Remi slept best in a cool room. He forgot to tell her that.

They explored the rest of the inn. The benches and coat pegs were at the entrance of a lounge area containing comfortable black vinyl couches and chairs, a television, and pressed board side tables. The restaurant—a cross between a school cafeteria and a fast food joint—was at the far end. Meal prices were posted behind the servers.

"Prices with a capital P," Remi noted.

"If they have to fly everything in, they've got to pass on the cost, I guess," she said.

Surprisingly, the menu was extensive. They certainly wouldn't starve. From the number of tables, the restaurant appeared to be open to the entire village, not just the inn's guests.

They headed back to their room to organize themselves. As they passed through the lobby, Deidre noticed an interesting art piece over the couch and stopped to study it, intrigued. A black blade about six feet long formed an elongated triangle, wide at the left, tapering to the right. Fine waves of hair-like fibers curved down from the lower edge.

"Do you know what it is?" she asked.

"No clue."

"Best guess?"

"It looks organic. Not much up here that big except for whales. Not something imported, so probably from a whale."

Harold, the other driver who they met at the airstrip, came up behind them, stopping when he overheard their conversation. "Baleen," he said.

"Baleen," Deidre repeated, memorizing the word.

"From a whale's mouth. See those fibers there? Baleen hair. They filter out what the whale don't eat."

"It's lovely," Deidre said. "Do you get a lot of whales here?"

"It's a whaling village, miss. When a whale comes in, it's like harvesting a garden down in the States."

"What do you mean?"

"It's what we eat, and has to last us through the winter. In the spring, we get another whale or two. Three a year, that's the limit. The season started today, but the wind's too strong. But there is plenty of time."

"So we might see a whale brought in?" Remi asked. "I'd like that."

"Maybe. Depends on luck and how long you stay."

"Any chance you could use an extra hand on the hunt?" he asked hopefully.

Harold looked over the rugged man, then shook his head with

regret. "No, only Inupiat are allowed to hunt the whales. But you can help with the butchering," he grinned.

"Then if I'm here, count on an extra pair of hands." He looked over at Deidre with raised eyebrows. She shrugged in acceptance, though not nearly as enthused. "Count on two sets of hands," he said, smiling at her.

SOON AFTER THE group had settled in, the call went out that the boat was ready. Half of the group would go out to the strand to see the polar bear. The other half would go by van to the boneyard. An hour before dark, the groups would switch vehicle for vessel.

Deidre and Remi were assigned to the boat. A van drove them to the water's edge where sea captain Joseph was waiting. They climbed aboard and, like the others, staked out their claim at the railing. But as they all quickly learned, wherever polar bear were sighted, the entire group flowed like water to that rail, tipping the boat a bit precariously.

Although the sea surrounded the strips of land, the wind kept the early snow from sticking. Instead of pure white polar bear found on Christmas cards and calendars, the group was met with animals in the wild: dingy fur, dirty muzzles, and bleak background. Yet no one complained. The sightseers would have been thrilled by these magnificent animals if they had only been sleeping bumps on the sand, but to see them interacting was a once in a lifetime experience.

"Look up there." Remi bent down to Deidre's ear and pointed to a low ridge.

Deidre looked to see a mother leave her cubs and charge toward a large menacing male. The sound of their roars reached them even out at sea. The male tried to skirt around the female, but she was having none of it. She knew the male would kill her cubs for the opportunity to mate with her. The male, not easily discouraged, continued to maneuver closer to the cubs who were backing slowly down the ridge and away from the conflict. The mother took a swipe at the male, probably making contact, since he kept more distance between them after that. He continued to weave, first one way, then the other, but the mother kept the higher ground. Finally discouraged, they watched the solitary male turn in defeat and leave the ridge. The sound of his disappointing farewell echoed across the water.

While the group was enthralled with the excitement on the ridge, the captain watched a curious polar bear enter the water.

"We've got to move on," Joseph announced. "Danger on the starboard side."

The group gravitated to the right side of the craft just as the last of the bear's body eased into the icy water. Now only his head was visible as it bobbed in their direction.

Danger hardly seemed the accurate description. The small black eyes and cute nose on that white furry face looked like something a child would take to bed.

It was astonishing how quickly the bear was closing the gap, though. His strong legs and wide paws, unseen beneath the water, propelled him toward the intruders.

"If he grabs the edge of the boat he could capsize her," Joseph said, already putting the little vessel in reverse. "Then we'd be in a dandy fix."

As they pulled away, the head grew smaller and smaller, but still the bear paddled.

"Determined little bugger," someone said, with agreement all around.

THE BONEYARD WAS located on a spit of land on the eastern outskirts of town. The van crept close to the piles of whale carcasses where a dozen polar bear were feeding. For the spouses, the scene was exciting; for the photographers, slightly less so. The dirty windows of the van were hinged at the top, allowing only a three-inch gap at the bottom. Only the front passenger window rolled down, making it the single opening from which to take pictures. Hearing the grumbling from the back, the front passenger eventually agreed to give up this prime piece of real estate. The entire vanload of passengers were engaged in the transfer process by moving out of the way, climbing over one another, and passing equipment to the front. After a few clumsy tries, they got the routine down. With the exception of one particularly difficult photographer, they adhered to the new arrangement fairly democratically.

While the human animals engaged in social justice, the four-legged animals, too, cooperated at the feeding ground.

"There's no hierarchy," Remi said thoughtfully.

Perhaps because there were so many bones to choose from, the polar bear seemed content to scavenge both in groups or alone. No threatening roar nor growl was heard between neighboring feeders. Cubs feasted as well as the adults, though their mothers were never far away.

The jagged skeleton of one leviathan was picked clean and warranted only a cursory walk around. The sensitive noses of the bear sniffed out where the richest pockets of food lay hidden. There was plenty for all.

For the observers, the ripping away of bloody flesh seemed gruesome. For the polar bear, it meant survival. Securely positioned at the top of the food chain, they had no natural predators other than the harsh, frozen world they inhabited.

It was impossible to count the number of whales that had been dumped there. Not that the number of bones was so extensive, though it was, but because the carcasses had been pulled apart and the bones dragged and scattered everywhere. Far from the danger of a polar bear attack, scientists could put together the skeletons and count the bones, but the tourists in the van could only look in awe at the tangle of bones piled high and strewn about.

"Uh oh," said Marvin. "Got us a little problem. Out the back window."

The backseat passengers turned around. A great male bear had found the warm sand under the tailpipe of the van to be particularly pleasing. Settling down for a nap, he remained quiet and content at the rear bumper.

"He sleeping, I think," someone called to the front.

"For now. But how's he gonna act once we start moving?"

"He'll go before we leave," one of the men assured the group.

"He's not the only problem," Marvin said. He pointed out the windshield toward the sea. "We've got us some swimmers, and they think we might make a better dinner than the whale."

Sure enough, three polar bear were making a beeline for the van.

"Close up the windows," he directed.

"I've got my camera mounted on the roof," another passenger reminded Marvin.

"Hope it's still there after we get out of this situation."

Deidre and Remi grinned at each other.

"I love this!" she whispered.

He hugged her shoulder." Me, too."

Slowly, Marvin put the van in gear and crept forward. "Folks in back, check that guy under the bumper."

"He's still there."

"Hasn't moved."

"Still sleeping."

Marvin slowly inched forward until he was clear enough to turn back toward the village. The three swimmers were just reaching the shore. They hesitated. Perhaps experienced in chasing moving vehicles, they decide in unison to try their luck with the whale instead and turned toward the bones.

The passengers looked back at the great old bear from the bumper, who continued to sleep, and half a mile up the road an arm reached up to the roof to find its camera still in place.

At dinner that night, the restaurant was abuzz with polar bear stories.

"… polar bear patrol…"

"… rubber bullets…"

"… mating with grizzlies…"

"… fur on their feet…"

"… used to be black bear…"

"… weak die off during the swim…"

"… black skin under that white fur…"

The discussions echoed throughout the room.

"Good day?" Remi asked.

"Great day!" she said.

"I was talking with some of the locals. They don't usually get this many bears. We're really lucky. Van or boat tomorrow? Or both?"

"Van."

Remi smiled. "I like that you make decisions. It saves a lot of guessing on my part. My ex-wife wasn't quite so obliging. Unless she could see a clear benefit to herself, she couldn't, or, more accurately, wouldn't, decide. But I sure paid for it later." His voice trailed off into the memory.

This was the first time he had mentioned Sadie. Deidre knew from her father's report that he had been married, but since Remi hadn't brought it up neither did she. She was dying to learn more, but maybe this wasn't the time.

"I'm going out later if the clouds move off. The aurora is supposed to be viewable from here. Want to come?"

She thought for a moment. She knew she couldn't see the lights, though she'd like to keep Remi company. He would make it exciting. But she couldn't pretend to see what she couldn't.

The edges were closing in, slowly, steadily, like the hour hand of a clock. If she looked closely, she saw no movement; but if she looked away for a while, the hand slipped forward like a thief stealing her sight. She knew time was her enemy, and time, in all its forms, exuded an ominous aura.

"Not tonight. It's been a full, perfect day. I'll load my pictures. Then, if you get back in time, a game of cribbage?"

When they discovered they both knew the game and were fairly evenly matched, they often spent their evenings playing cards. Now it was nearly a nightly ritual.

"Sure, but it will be a shame ending your perfect day with a loss." He grinned. He was far better at trash talk than Deidre, but she was catching on.

"I am so going to bury you, it will be spring before they find you," she tossed back.

Remi laughed. "Ah, such a pretty little optimist."

REMI WAS STOMPING the snow off his boots while Deidre sat on the bench pulling hers on.

"See anything?" she asked.

"Either they're very faint, or not out yet, or the village lights are interfering. I didn't want to go too far out with our fuzzy white night prowlers wandering around."

The aurora borealis was famously frequent and bright in Fairbanks, but this close to the North Pole tended to be less so.

"Going out?" he asked.

"Lost my polarizer. Thought I'd check the van."

"It's cold, really cold," he said, looking at her vest.

"I'll just be a minute. Still up for that game of cribbage?"

"Sure."

"Set it up," she called back over her shoulder as she pulled the door closed behind her.

Remi took off his coat and started to pull off his boots, when for no particular reason he changed his mind and followed her out the door.

What he saw froze his blood.

The van was parked at the far end of the lot, fifty feet away, pointing toward the road and parallel to the inn. Bending down, licking the warm headlight, was the white mass of a male polar bear. Deidre, walking to that very van, was already halfway across the lot.

His reaction was immediate. He took two steps back, shoved open the door to the inn, and raced to the coatroom door as he shouted to the men from the village. "Bear! Get a gun! He's got her!"

In his mind's eye, the bear must indeed be on her, and they needed live ammo. Rubber bullets wouldn't prevent the disaster.

He heard the rapid shuffling of chairs as he swiveled around and shot out the door. He paused to bend for his knife, and in less than four seconds was racing toward what certainly must be a slaughter. By now, he knew, the bear must have her. He listened, but heard no sound of struggle or attack.

Once outside, he couldn't believe what he was seeing. Deidre was still walking toward the bear! And the bear kept licking the headlight! His mind, calculating his next move, raced as fast as his legs. Should he shout and attract the bear? But Deidre was between them. Should he run obliquely and draw the bear to himself? Would his knife be any use in one-on-one combat? How long before the guns would fire?

Either the wind changed or the crunch of snow alerted him, or maybe he caught movement out of the corner of his eye, but all of a sudden the polar bear turned to face her, stood up on his massive hind legs, and, with a towering menace, roared.

Remi had almost reached her as she screamed.

He started shouting and waving his arms to draw the bear's attention.

"Drop and roll under the van!" he shouted, then bellowed at the bear, "Here, you big, ugly motherfucker! Look over here!"

The bear was torn between the screaming man who was approaching and the smaller, closer prey crawling away. His first quarry was definitely easier, but it must have become quickly apparent that the attacking animal could be dangerous. The decision made, he dropped to all four legs, giving Remi his full attention.

Seeing Deidre nearly under the van, he looked for a way to save himself. He turned to the right, sprinting the ten yards to the bumper of the second van. He dropped his knife as he lunged forward and grabbed for the wiper blades. He needed to hoist himself up as his boots fought for purchase on the icy bumper and hood. His mind shot ahead to the next step. Once that high, he could try for the roof. His boots desperately pumped for any kind of grip, but couldn't grab hold. He had to muscle himself up onto the hood.

The polar bear, seeing his chance, swiped at Remi's leg and caught his right thigh with his powerful claws. Remi heard the denim rip and felt the incredible power behind the attack, as it shoved him sideways across the slippery hood. Five rods of white heat burned deep into his flesh. He cried out both in alarm and pain, but the angry roar of the bear drowned out his voice. One of the wiper blades broke in his hand as Remi started sliding downward. He grabbed for the hinged edge of the hood and found it. With adrenaline surging through his veins, he pulled himself up two more feet. The bear was standing now, his mouth open, salivating. Hoping to buy time, Remi rolled on his back to kick the bear with his good leg. Too late, he realized his mistake. His vital organs were now exposed to the menacing jaws and massive claws. There was no time to roll back, no time to pull himself out of reach of a certain death, no time to prepare. But he had been preparing for this moment all of his adult life. A single thought went through his mind, calming him.

It must be a good death.

He felt the earthquake hit with a sudden, single jolt, causing the van to shudder. The bear, stunned, was thrown forward, inches from his face.

Things went into slow motion; details became absurdly vivid. He saw the animal's teeth: white, wet, each wedge of dirty enamel catching a sparkle of light from the inn, the longer canines sharpening to powerful points; the warm, slimy drool dripping from the mouth, falling onto his neck, and running into the well of his shoulder blade; the eyelashes, long, thick, almost pretty, blinking above small black eyes too closely set; the long white length of muzzle ending in a nose that might have belonged to his dog, with black nostrils glistening, twitching; the breath moist, warm, and foul.

The surreal image baffled him. Remi wondered why the bear didn't rip his face off with those gruesome teeth. A loud, shrill horn screamed in his ears. He couldn't have lost that much blood. He couldn't be hallucinating, but neither could he make out what was happening.

A shot rang out just as a bullet whizzed in front of his face. Jesus! Why were they shooting at him? His muscle memory tried to duck for cover, but the weight of the beast above him pinned him down. The shot seemed to energize the bear, too, because he turned his head toward the sound.

Another shot, and Remi felt the bear collapse on him. He found himself crushed under the half-ton animal. A tooth grazed his cheek as the bear's heavy head fell forward, now quiet and still. The added weight forced him to release his hold on the hood, and he expected that both he and the bear would slide down the slippery surface. But neither moved.

In the distance, he heard men shouting, "Back up! Back up!"

Deidre's voice, panicked, cried, "I can't? How?"

More voices shouted. Something shifted again.

Remi wanted desperately to get away from those gleaming teeth and retched smell, but couldn't move. What if the bear woke up? He looked into the glassy eyes. Was the animal dead? Stunned? Pretending to be dead? Nothing about the last few minutes made sense. He had been ready to die the good death, but instead he was trapped in a living nightmare.

Deidre was at his side now. She was saying something, but it sounded like she was in an echo chamber far away.

"He's in shock," someone said.

That was the first thing that made sense to him.

He felt the bear being dragged off of him. He heard the weight thump heavily onto the frozen ground. Deidre was holding his hand. Others kept him from falling on top of the bear.

"Can you walk?"

He thought he could, but his injured leg crumpled beneath him. Two men supported him as Deidre ran ahead to hold the door. The others attended to the dead polar bear.

"What happened?" he asked Marvin.

"She smashed into him with the van."

"She? Deidre? She drove the van into the bear?"

"Probably killed both cars, but saved you."

"I don't understand. She was under the van—"

221

"Looks like she decided to get in the cab instead," said the other man.

"By the time I got out with my gun, she had it in first gear and just plowed into that white demon," said Marvin.

"Gutsy gal. Not sure I'd think that quick," another said.

"She could have smashed his legs, though."

"Better that than let the bear have a go at him," the other argued.

"Do you think it was one of those hybrids?"

"Don't know. The DNR can do the DNA," the other man said, then laughed. "That's funny, DNR, DNA…"

His leg was killing him now. His sweat was turning icy and he started to tremble.

Inside the inn, no one cared that boots dripped wet snow on the floor and rugs.

"Put him here," Deidre instructed, pointing to the couch in the lounge. "Has someone gone for a doctor?"

"Doctor don't come 'til spring, but we got a medicine woman. She'll come. Josey, go fetch Sarah's grandma. Tell her to bring her bag."

"Oh, no," he heard her mutter under her breath.

He knew she was worried, but he'd seen enough combat field medicine to withhold judgment. It could be all right.

Deidre started to tear his pants at the injury sight.

"Hey, don't do that. These are all I've got. Help me pull them down."

"All you've got?"

"I pack light." He tried to smile.

His attempt at humor worked. A smile threatened to ease her frown.

"Can someone get him some hot coffee or, no, tea?" she directed.

Someone brought a blanket, but he still shivered.

The tea came. He drank the hot liquid, but immediately retched it up. It embarrassed him. He hadn't vomited in public since grade school. Wiping his mouth on his sleeve, he apologized.

"Shock," someone repeated, and others nodded in agreement.

Clean towels were brought to stem the flow of blood.

Pushing the towels aside, he looked at his leg, then laid back.

"It won't need a tourniquet," someone said.

The claws had gone in at an angle. He didn't think his muscles were torn. He thought it looked worse than it was. Infection would be the danger. He felt better once he had made the mental diagnosis.

He saw Deidre's face when she looked at the wound. It was ashen, but she didn't look away. She just pressed the towel over it and held it in place to slow the bleeding.

Sarah's grandmother arrived. She had been the village "doctor" long enough to know how to disinfect the wound.

"Now you lay back there, young man, so I can fix you up."

"Had any experience with bear attacks?" he asked, hoping she knew what she was doing.

Those in the room hooted and laughed.

"Seen my share," she said, pulling things out of her bag. "Get more towels," she ordered as she opened a bottle.

"WHAA!" Remi exhaled loudly as she poured the alcohol over the wound. "What the hell!"

"Got to clean it."

"Good God, woman, what the *hell* is it?"

"Vodka."

"Goddamn!" he swore. "Give me that." He grabbed the bottle, took a long swallow, and coughed.

"They told me you were a Marine, that you attack polar bear. I didn't think I needed to get you drunk first," the grandmother said with a twinkle in her eyes. "Well now I know different. Better drink some more before I start stitching."

"Oh, God," he said, then took another gulp.

The mood in the room brightened.

Someone murmured, "He can't keep tea down, but the vodka, no problem."

The chuckles that followed signaled the end of the crisis. The villagers and others began filing out to help or watch those working on the dead beast outside. Two men stayed to help get Remi to his room.

Once in bed, Deidre tucked the blanket loosely around him.

"I guess cribbage is out for tonight," she said, lightening the mood.

"What makes you say that? Injured, in shock, exhausted, and drunk—hell, I can still beat you. Set it up." He grinned at her.

"I don't want to take advantage," she said closing the window.

"Leave it open."

"But it's cold and you're shivering," she said firmly.

He looked at her and relented. "Okay, just for tonight."

As she busied herself around the room, he asked, "Why did you keep walking toward the bear?"

"What?" She turned toward him.

"The bear—he was right in front of you, but you kept walking right up to him."

Deidre turned away again. "I didn't see him."

Confused, he repeated, "Didn't see him? He was right in front of you. I could see him."

"Well, I didn't."

"My God, Deidre, what was so important that you didn't notice a polar bear in your path? What were you thinking?"

"I—I was distracted."

"Over a polarizer?" he challenged.

"I didn't see him, that's all. Now can I get you anything before I go? You need to sleep, and I have to clean up the lobby, and then myself."

He wouldn't get any more out of her tonight, he realized, and he was suddenly too exhausted to try. He closed his eyes.

"See if you can get one of the claws before the villagers claim them." Quietly, he added, "And thanks for, you know, stopping the bear."

"—that would have eaten me if you hadn't put yourself in danger."

"So we saved each other, did we?" He smiled with his eyes still closed.

"We did. We saved each other."

WHEN DEIDRE looked into the lounge it was empty, most traces of the evening's excitement already wiped clean. She turned to go back to wash herself, but changed direction when she heard voices coming from the restaurant. Marvin and a few other men were talking, animating their conversation with small hand gestures in the way of nomad storytellers. They beckoned her to join them when they saw her standing in the doorway.

"I don't mean to interrupt," she said.

"Come on in. We were just talking about the excitement tonight."

"The whole village is talking about the white woman and the polar bear."

"What will happen to the bear now?" she asked.

"We'll call the DNR in the morning. They'll fly someone out to check the shooting."

"Check it?"

"When a polar bear is shot, the Department of Natural Resources has to make sure it wasn't a white hunter."

"Shootings almost never happen, not with live ammunition."

"Native people have no laws against shooting polar bear, but we prefer to live in harmony with our animal brothers. So when one dies, the government just likes to check."

"And it was too aggressive and too big. We think it was one of the mutant bears. DNA will tell."

"Mutant bears?"

"Hybrids," Harold volunteered. "The grizzlies are moving north now because of the warmer weather—you know, climate change."

"I've heard of it," she said politely.

"They're mating with the polar bear," a weathered Inupiat finished.

"This new bear is far more aggressive," a younger man with a scar down his cheek added.

"Bigger—"

"And stronger—"

"Not afraid to come into the village, even with the rubber bullets."

"They're ripping open the storage bins where we keep our winter meat."

"Smart and strong."

Every man was contributing to the story.

"These super bears are becoming a major problem."

"But I don't think hybrids can breed, can they?" She thought back to a biology class. With other crossbreeding—horses with mules, or horses with zebras—no offspring was possible.

"We don't know. We think they can."

"It's too soon. But DNR will want to study this bear."

The discussion fascinated her. "What will happen to the bear, the meat—can you eat polar bear? And the fur, the hide? I would really like two of the claws."

The men were silent, thinking. Then one explained, "The claws cannot go to you. No white man can own the claws of a polar bear now."

"The law forbids it."

"Why?"

"Their claws are like walrus tusks. White trophy hunters killed the animal, not for meat, not to defend, but for the claws and hide. The slaughter of the polar bear needed to be stopped," a gray-haired man explained. "That's why, for forty years now, it is illegal for the white man to shoot a polar bear for sport."

In one of the Fairbanks fur shops, she had seen a grizzly bear hide, complete with claws, on sale for two grand. In the lower forty-eight, she had seen claws selling for a hundred dollars each. Twenty claws could pay for the whole bear hide. At the time she had wondered if anyone had ever calculated the value of the claws into the sale price.

"How much for the whole bear skin, tanned?"

"Who would sell it? It belongs to the village."

"What will the village do with it?"

"Hang it in a public place, like the community center."

"Or maybe the library."

Deidre thought about the local library—it was a small trailer lined with books and certainly had no wall space.

"Or the clinic."

"Who decides?" she asked.

"The tribal council."

She gave the men a tired smile and thanked them for their help, and for saving Remi. The council would meet and decide. And they would have two more days in the village.

Remi spent a restless night. The pain was always just below the surface, waking him each time he moved. The nightmares, too, were fully energized by the harrowing memory of the beast's fangs in his face. Some were chase dreams, but some were old, familiar ones.

He woke up suddenly. His throat was scratchy from the shouting during the nightmare. Deidre was three feet away. He knew she was lying there awake, not moving. He was dripping with sweat and shivering. He had thrown off the blanket at some point, and as he rolled to pick it up, he cried out from the surprising pain shooting through his leg.

She was up and next to him in an instant.

"Blanket," he breathed, waiting for the pain to subside and wishing someone had left the bottle of vodka for him.

She shook the blanket over him.

"Damn, that caught me by surprise."

"Does it hurt badly?"

"Only because I rolled on it. Damn."

"You were dreaming."

"Nightmare."

"You had a few of them."

He was quiet for a moment. "Not sure what the options are. There are no extra rooms at the inn—"

"No, I didn't mean that. I don't care for myself. I just don't know what to do for you."

"That's easy, there's nothing to be done about it. I just don't know what to do about *your* sleep."

She wanted to sit on the bed, but that meant he would have to move over. Instead, she squatted next to him.

"What are they about, the nightmares?"

He didn't answer immediately. The one he just had was familiar and very fresh. It still hovered on the ceiling, waiting until he fell asleep again.

"You don't want to know," he said quietly.

She reached for his hand. "When someone has a nightmare, they experience it with all their senses like it's real. When a person hears about a nightmare, it's different. I only hear a story that only makes partial sense. I won't feel it like you do. But it would help me to understand. And," she added, "it might help you."

"It wouldn't—"

"It might."

He thought about that. A dim light from outside filtered through the curtains. He looked over at her face, so near to his. He could make out the lighted half; the rest was bathed in shadow like the chiaroscuro of a Renaissance painting. The smell of citrus and vanilla lingered in the air. Maybe it wouldn't hurt to tell someone, like she said. She wouldn't break out in a sweat, her heart wouldn't pound out of her chest, fear wouldn't charge through her veins. It would just be a silly story that hardly made any sense.

"Okay" he began slowly. "I've had this one before. It's crazier than most of them. There is a lot of commotion going on around me, and I know I should stay, but I turn to leave. I have to find something, and I see it. It's a foot, a white foot, you know, like on a store mannequin. I lunge at it, but it turns into a leg that starts kicking at me."

"What do you have on?"

"MCCUU's. Cammies. Desert uniform."

"Is it Iraq?"

"Yeah." He took a deep breath. "Like I said, a dumb dream."

"There's more. Tell me." She realized too late that she shouldn't have interrupted him. She should have let him tell his story.

"Why? It's only a dream. It's not real."

"Have you ever told anyone your dreams? Your nightmares?"

"No. Who would I tell?" He snorted.

"They aren't going away. Maybe you should try something different, like telling someone. Like me," she said.

He considered it for a minute. The definition of insanity, he knew, was doing the same thing over and over and expecting a different result. Maybe she had a point.

"It's ugly."

"That's okay." She squeezed his arm since his hand was buried under the blanket.

One, then two minutes passed before he began talking.

"I have to get the leg, that's all I know. I have to bring it back, but it begins walking away. I chase it and grab it but it keeps fighting me. Kicking me. The leg is incredibly strong. And slippery. It's not attached to anything. It's just this white leg that turns green and brown. So now I'm getting desperate, so I make a huge lunge and land hard on it, but it's like a jellyfish and just flattens out under me. I sit back and it reforms into a leg, and now I'm really mad, really desperate, and I grab it with all my might. I squeeze it as hard as I can so it won't get away, and suddenly it's like I've grabbed a fragile egg too hard and it crumbles in my hands, just turns to powder. I try to scrape the dust together, but someone comes into the space and the wind blows all of the powder away. And it's gone. The leg is totally gone. And I can't stop screaming. It's like I'll never stop screaming. And then I wake up."

They both remained quiet for several minutes. Finally, Remi asked, "So are you totally grossed out?"

"No. Just thinking. Is it always the same, this nightmare?"

"No, there are variations. Sometimes the fight with the leg goes on all night. Sometimes the leg turns white again and crushes like a porcelain vase when I grab it. But I can't glue it together because pieces just keep disappearing. Sometimes I have to chase it for hours. But the feelings are always the same."

"What do you think it's about?"

Now he felt uneasy. "I know what it's about."

"What?"

"It's a jacked up story."

"I don't know what that means."

"It means that something happened over there that I never talk about."

"Until tonight."

"I never talk about it."

She sat quietly, considering his words. Suddenly she looked very tired. "All right."

Good. He was off the hook.

But she continued, "I'll make a deal with you. If you can get through the night without any more nightmares, I won't ask again—tonight. But if you have even one more, you tell me what happened."

He calculated the odds. He didn't see how he was going to get any more sleep tonight. No more sleep, no more nightmares. "Okay, it's a deal."

Deidre, cold and tired, climbed into her bed. "If you need anything, anything at all, I'm right here."

"Thanks, honey," he said out of some long ago habit.

Honey. She turned the endearment over in her mind. Peace encompassed her as she quickly fell asleep.

Less than an hour had passed before another of nightmare struck him and woke her. This time, she shook him awake.

"Remi, Remi." She rubbed her hand across his brow, startled by how much sweat had gathered there. She wiped her hand on the bed sheet.

He struggled to free his arm out from the tangle of blankets intending to take a swing at her, but from the depth of his dream, he woke before he succeeded.

"God, Dee," he swore as he started to sit up. Then, realizing they were both safe, he fell back onto the pillow.

"It's okay," she said. "It's okay."

He raised his hands to rub his face. "I am one fucked up Marine, Dee. I'm sorry."

"Probably," she said with a smile, though in the dim light he only heard it.

"So I guess that means you want to hear the rest of the story, as Paul Harvey used to say?"

"Who?"

He waved her off. "Wrong generation."

How was he going to get out of this?

Last night, she had taken on a polar bear. In Italy, she had hauled a fifty-pound suitcase up ninety-seven stairs. She had charmed a would-be terrorist on an Egyptian bus. Okay, a bit of an exaggeration there, but she could have. Maybe she didn't like getting her socks wet, or using communal showers, or pissing in floor holes, but despite appearances, she seemed pretty tough to him. Maybe she could handle it—the sanitized version.

Decision made, he sighed, resigned.

"Back in 2004, when you were what? Fourteen? There was a battle in an Iraqi town called Fallujah."

"Believe it or not, Gunny Lamont, I *have* heard of Fallujah."

"Really? Well, that's something, anyway." He really didn't want to do this. "I was the Platoon Sergeant. Do you know what that is?"

"The boss?"

"Yeah, okay, I was the boss. There was an officer, the Platoon Leader, but I—well, anyway, I was responsible for seventy men in my platoon. I won't go into how tough that battle was, but in a word, it was hell.

"One day we were clearing buildings—kicking in doors. I didn't go out with the men every time, but I was out with them that day. I took point—do you know what that is?"

"You were in the lead?"

"Yeah. Kiss was stacked behind me: five other Marines were stacked behind him. Normally when we blow a door and go in there's a courtyard, but not this time. It was a hall with rooms on either side. There's a way we clear a building. The point man buttonhooks to the left, the next guy peels off to the right, the third goes straight, the next to the left, like that. Do you understand?"

She nodded.

"You can make exceptions. It's the call of the first guy in, the point man. If he sees some reason to change things, he does." Remi stopped here. Had he seen something? Was there a flash that had caught his eye? Why couldn't he remember it?

"There was a lot going on. I left half my squad to cover us and took the others to clear the building. I had six guys behind me, and we were out in the open, taking fire. We had to get off the street, but had to secure the building first. I should have buttonhooked to the left, but I didn't. I went straight and took the first door farther up on the right. I think something flashed there, but there was nothing when I got there. Kiss took my place and buttonhooked to the left, Barnes was behind him, Ranger behind him, moving across and down the hall. I got to my room, but the only thing there was a ratty dog in the corner. Then I heard an explosion behind me, to the left. Kiss had triggered a booby trap." He pushed on. "Sweeney was the first to reach him, then Barnes and Polansky. By the time I got there, they were pulling off his pack, going for the tourniquets."

"What happened to him?"

"Both legs were gone. Hence, the escaping leg dream. Help me sit up."

She pulled out his pillow and propped it against the wall as he pushed up with his arms.

"Better?"

"Yeah."

"So go on."

"That's it, that's the reason I feel so helpless about not being able to get Kiss his legs back."

"Because you felt you should have been the one?"

"I *know* I should have been the one."

She let that sink in for a moment.

"But tell me what happened then, after you got into the room."

Christ. This isn't going well. Just push through it this one time, Lamont.

"Sweeney was working on the right leg. He pulled the tourniquet too tight and it snapped."

"It snapped?"

"Yeah, it happens sometimes when your adrenaline is surging and you're super strong. You just jerk it too tight and the plastic breaks. Every Marine carries three, so while he was pulling out another one Polansky started on the left leg and I tried to hold his guts, tried to push everything back into his body."

"His stomach, too?"

"Yeah. It was real bad. Barnes, Ranger, and Demarti set up a perimeter so we could work. We stopped the hemorrhaging. It took a while before the corpsman could get to us. Then we were pinned down for another hour. Eventually they brought an armored vehicle and we got him first to the aid station they set up in town, then out of the country. I thought the stomach was going to kill him, but it turned out that wasn't the bad injury. It was losing the blood from the legs. And infection."

"Where were the legs? Could they be reattached?"

"They were in bloody pieces dripping down the walls." The words just floated out like dry, gray dandelion puffs in the wind, effortlessly, softly.

Why in the hell did he say that? He ran his hand through his hair. That was not the image he wanted her to have. What happened to the sanitized version? *Goddamn you, Lamont, God fucking damn you!*

"You must have felt awful. No wonder you have nightmares."

"I did something else." He really hated this part; it shamed him.

"What?"

He would say it one time, admit to it only this once. And then it would be over.

"After they took him away, we had to stay and finish the job, but I was crazy with anger. I just wanted to kill something, anything." He lost himself in the memory. "There's no excuse," he said softly. As he spoke, he once again felt the rage flow down his arm and through his finger and pour out from the barrel of his weapon.

Deidre waited without saying a word.

He looked up at her, his eyes threatening to betray him. "You have to understand, I was pumped full of guilt and rage and adrenaline."

She nodded.

"It was so stupid," he said quietly. "It wasn't enough, but it was something." He ran his hand through his hair again.

"What did you do?" Her voice was soft.

He inhaled deeply.

"I went back to that first room and opened fire on that miserable dog, blew him to smithereens."

She seemed unfazed. How the hell could she hear what he'd just said and push past it?

"Remi." She held his other hand. "I wasn't there."

He was in the habit of reading her thoughts. Now she was reading his.

"It's not the same for me. I don't have the smells or the adrenaline or the bonds with these men. Your story can't hurt me the same way it hurts you."

He thought about that for a long time. He thought about it after she had let go of his hand and gone back to her own bed. He thought about it as he heard her breathing become shallow and regular in sleep. He thought about it as the sun promised to end the long night. He thought about it until, at last, he fell into his own restless sleep.

THE SUN ROSE slowly in the autumn of this far northern land. The days were short, so they must be shared with the night. The villagers awoke in the pre-dawn hours, long before the gentle pink and baby blue streaks of light brushed the sky.

The hunters were readying for the hunt. They sharpened their already sharp harpoons, carefully coiled lines to rest in the floor of the angyapiks, measured the wind, and waved farewell to wives and mothers watching from the beach.

The restaurant was filled with both excitement and anxiety as Deidre lined up to get breakfast for Remi and herself. Remi had hobbled to a table, but heeding Sarah's grandmother's advice, kept his leg elevated while Deidre brought back the food.

"It sounds like today might be a good one for the hunters. Wind is down," she said relaying the words of the serving staff.

"Sounds like it," Remi said, trying to find a better position for his injured leg.

"What can I do?"

"Can you move that chair in? Yeah, that's better. Thanks."

He knew it pleased her to help him. It started to balance a vastly unbalanced relationship, she had said last night.

A draft blew in with the opening and closing of the main door.

"Are you warm enough?" she asked.

"I'm always warm enough."

"I've noticed."

Unlike Deidre and the other travelers, Remi was more like the Inupiat of the village, hatless, mostly gloveless, and wearing a coat he seldom zipped.

"What are you going to do today?" he asked.

"I thought I'd stay here with you."

"That seems a waste. Isn't there a tour of the village happening this morning?"

"Yes," she said hesitantly, "but that doesn't seem fair."

"What's not fair? I can't go, so you'll have to do it without me."

Deidre frowned. "When Cassie or I can't do something, the other stays behind, too."

"That's what I call a lose-lose way to live. That's like Jerry losing his legs, so I go sit in a wheelchair."

"Oh." She squinted her eyes, thinking. "Do you go see the world so Jerry can see the world?"

"Something like that. I hadn't thought of it in those terms, but yeah, probably."

He took a bite of sausage.

"It also satisfies my need for an adrenaline rush. You do know I'm an adrenaline junkie, right?" he said with a grin.

"Did you get your fix last night in the parking lot?" She returned the smile.

"Ah, last night. At least a week's worth."

They ate in silence.

Finally, Remi said, "I'm serious about the adrenaline. A lot of us who saw some serious action kinda like it. The rush, not necessarily the killing. Well, some of the men …" He paused taking a different direction. "What happens when we're in a long battle like Fallujah—I think we were engaged in active combat for something like six weeks—or we go on back-to-back deployments in a combat zone, we stay high on adrenaline. We're high for so long it becomes, I don't know, maybe a new baseline, a new normal. So when we get back, back home, I mean, life looks incredibly empty and boring."

Her eyes were focused on him. He wanted her to understand at least some small part of what made him tick.

"We all tried to go back home. A few didn't, couldn't make the adjustment."

A quizzical look on Deidre's face made him clarify bluntly.

"They killed themselves."

"Oh, no." A look of concern crossed her face. "Did anyone in your platoon?"

"Yeah, one. Kirby cracked."

"What happened?"

"They say he was being stupid and walked along the railing of a bridge on a dare. They say he slipped, but he didn't. The guy had balance like a cat. He let it happen."

"Are you sure?"

"I'm sure." He took a swallow of coffee. "His widow found his uniform all laid out, medals buffed, shoes polished, pants pressed. He was preparing for his own funeral. They didn't call it a suicide, but Laura and I know what it was."

"Do you still talk to her? Laura?"

"Not much. I did at first, but once she got remarried I figured she'd be okay." He looked at her. "They do that, you know: underreport the suicides."

"But why?"

"Public image. And the truth won't change things. We still have wars. We still need Marines. And Marines will still do their duty."

They sat quietly together, finishing their breakfast.

"Why is it hard to come home? I don't understand."

He thought for a moment. "It's tough to explain, but let me try. When you're here, when you're safe, even when you're training and getting ready to deploy for the first time, there is this romantic notion of war and battle and heroism that sort of surrounds you, you and everyone else who's never seen battle. And then you go." He struggled to find a way to communicate it. "It's like water. You expect the only thing you've ever known, let's say bath water, but instead it's frigid, buoyant seawater. It's all water, but really different. When you're training, you don't have the smells, for instance. You might be working hard and sweating like a pig, but fear sweat smells different, feels different, than work sweat. When you're running through a shower of bullets you're scared, but you still feel invincible until the guy in front of you goes down, and all of sudden it's real.

"When you're in the thick of it, you're not fighting for yourself, but for the Marines to the left and right of you. Everything you do is for them. And you trust they are doing their part for you. There are bonds that are forged in war that just don't compare to anything else you've ever known. It's like every other relationship is connected with rubber bands, but the Marines you've fought with, those relationships are metal links. Maybe that's not exactly right. It's hard to explain."

Deidre was paying close attention.

"When you get back, back to the fleet, you're surrounded by Marines who know the same things you know, so the world makes sense. But outside of the fleet—." He saw the question on her face, "—off the base, I mean, it's like going into an alien world where everyone speaks a foreign language you used to know but can't understand anymore. No one except warriors look up at roofs to pick out the sniper waiting to kill you. No one else notices the half-crumpled lunch bag next to the trash bin and wonders if it might explode. No civilian looks under the car to see if the brake line's been cut. We sit with our backs against the wall, with a view of the door. We avoid sitting near windows to avoid exploding glass. We like to have a weapon close at hand. Bridges make some of us nervous, the ones overhead and ones we cross. To stay alive, you have to grow extra-long and ultra-sensitive antennae that twitch all the time. You have to keep looking, always aware, always vigilant. Then, suddenly, you find yourself in America among a society of Disney cartoon characters dancing to 'It's a Small World After All.' How the fuck do you relate to that?"

Deidre looked at him, wordless.

"While we're at war, America is at the shopping mall. They have no clue. So we try to get back there, back to Disneyland, but how do you un-know what you know? You can't. You pretend for a while, but that will wear you out. You start to avoid people. You don't want them to know how different you are. You talk about inane things just to be part of it, but you're not really part of anything. If you can stay in the Corps, you have a better chance. But some couldn't take any more deployments. Some just went crazy or were forced out. Families made others quit. But for some of us, we left because we couldn't take any more bullshit."

"How long were you in the Marine Corps?"

"Eleven years."

"And you miss it?"

"Yeah, I miss it. I told you, I'm an adrenaline junkie. But more than that, I miss the men, my brothers. I left the Corps and went straight to work for Blackwater."

"The contract company in Baghdad?"

Remi nodded. He took a swallow of coffee, remembering. Some bad shit went down. He was finished. "Dee, let's talk about something else, would you mind?" He suddenly felt very weary. He could only deal with the memories for so long before they overwhelmed him.

"No, of course not. I am sorry—"

"Don't be sorry. At least you didn't ask if I killed anyone," he said. "How about a game of cribbage?"

Deidre got up and put her arms around him, silently holding him for a full minute until the tension left his shoulders. "I'll get the board."

They played through the morning, listening for any news of the whaling party. Nine boats had gone out at dawn. Just as the locals were filing in for lunch, word came that the boats had been sighted. Grabbing whatever they could eat on the run, the restaurant quickly emptied, except for Remi and Deidre.

"Go on," he urged. "I'll catch up when I can. And take your camera. Take mine, too."

By the time he got to the shore, the whalers, along with the rest of the community, had hauled the great leviathan onto the shore and begun butchering it. He hoped she had gotten some good pictures.

She waved when she saw him and hurried over. "I used yours. Look," she said, handing him his camera.

Remi took the camera and started to scroll through the pictures. He smiled and nodded approvingly. "Good. Good. This one is great."

Deidre leaned over to see the source of the compliment. The village children were standing or sitting on the whale's great black back. "I'm glad you like it. I know it's staged, but—"

"But it reflects the way they do things in the village. It's real. It tells a story. Good girl."

They watched the villagers butcher and divide up the whale. This bowhead measured forty feet long, about average. The harpooners found him far out at sea and had to tow him over eight miles back to shore.

"How much does he weigh?" Deidre asked one of the women.

"After we cut it up, we will weigh it. You come for the dinner tomorrow?"

"Where? I don't know—" She looked at Remi.

"Yes, you come. You white hunter. He white hunter. Both come and celebrate with the village."

Remi nodded. "Yes, thank you, thank you very much."

"You eat whale blubber. Very good for healing." She looked at Remi. Whale blubber, apparently, was very good for many things. She cut off a bite and put it in his mouth. "Good?"

"Sushi," he said to Deidre's raised brows. "Good."

"Very, very good," the woman said, turning back to her work.

They moved out of the way and found a soft place to sit a few yards away from the main activity. It was cold, and soon their pants began absorbing the melting permafrost. They hardly noticed the discomfort, though. Watching an entire village cooperating, each member having a task to do, and happy to do it, gave the day a festive feel.

"I'd like to be on a whaling boat," Remi said at last. "As a teenager, I liked hunting, but not anymore. But whaling, now that appeals to me."

"You don't hunt? That surprises me," she said.

He mulled it over a minute. How to explain it? "I told you I like my adrenaline rush, so I can see the fun, the danger, in harpooning something this massive and bringing it down. There is also a really good chance it's going to get away, or double back and capsize the boat, or pull the harpooner out if he doesn't let go at the right time. It seems fair. Now compare that to deer hunting. See, once you've hunted a two-legged animal, one that can shoot back, where's the sport in shooting a four-legged animals just grazing in a meadow? Something gets lost."

AS IT TURNED OUT, Remi's injury made him useless as a butcher and Deidre declined to leave his side. But they both recorded the event with their cameras.

The villagers all knew about the previous night's drama and were very willing to answer their questions.

"How do you keep the polar bear away when you are carving up the whale?"

They had seen a mother with a pair of chubby cubs heading down the shore toward the workers, but the trio was quickly discouraged when shots rang out. Where were the others, they wondered? Polar bear could smell fresh meat miles away. But only these had ventured close.

"We first cut much of the blubber off and put it on the front end loader. It gets dumped at the boneyard. That keeps everyone happy."

"And segregated," one of the men added.

"When we are finished, we will drag the carcass to the boneyard, too. That will give the bears fresh meat to chew on to help them through the winter."

They watched the careful carving.

"How is it divided up?"

Deidre knew that huge chunks of whale were hauled to some processing center, but the only place large enough to do the work must be the community center.

"The captain of the boat that held the harpooner who made the kill gets all the meat from the navel to the tail."

They looked at the disproportionate quantity of meat.

"Yes, it is a lot of meat," the villager said, "but it is this captain's responsibility to provide all the meat for the village for Thanksgiving and Christmas. There are nearly 250 people in our village, so you see why he gets so much."

It made sense to her.

"The men in the boats, the harpooners, get equal shares, but they must give food to all their family members from their share."

"What about widows who have no sons?"

"They are provided for by a nephew or a cousin or a brother-in-law. Everyone is fed."

They walked over to the large head. It was the last to be carved. The baleen was being carefully removed.

"How do you keep so much meat cold?"

"Once we dug deep holes in the permafrost. The meat stayed frozen and moist. In recent years, some of the people bought freezers and had them shipped here on the summer barges. Others liked the idea and began abandoning the old traditions. But the freezers produced dried out meat. By the end of the season, the food was not as good. So many of us are once again going back to the ways we were taught, in the ground, letting nature provide for us."

The sun was setting, but there was still much work to be done.

"We will work through the night. Otherwise, the bears will take what we leave. This is not a big whale, so maybe we will find another this season. Two in the fall, one in the spring. Or maybe the reverse. It depends on the caribou herd. We only take what we need."

Although they were thoroughly fascinated by what they were learning, Deidre only had to take one look at Remi's face to know he had overextended himself. Normally glowing with vitality, his skin now appeared pale and strained. He had zipped up his coat, and when she pulled her wool hat off her head and put it on his, he didn't object.

"You look exhausted," she said.

Time to get back to a hot dinner and warm bed. Tomorrow, they would enjoy their last meal with the villagers. Then the plane would come, taking them back to Fairbanks, and better medical care.

* * * * *

THE FAIRBANKS CLINIC walk-in clinic was busy. As they sat in the waiting room, they noticed an array of disheveled locals, parents with children, pregnant women, and people coughing, sneezing, and generally spreading germs. There were no broken bones, no lacerations. Those injuries were being cared for at the Urgent Care Clinic. She wondered if that hadn't been the better facility.

The wait was long. They read all of the available magazines, tried to amuse each other with small talk, but, in the end, it was simply a miserable wait. Finally, Remi heard his name and hobbled toward the nurse. Deidre watched as he disappeared through the doors. She had been examining his wounds carefully for infection, but so far there was no evidence of it, at least to her untrained eyes. She could see him improving daily, but until she heard a doctor's opinion, she couldn't be sure.

When he came out, Remi looked quite satisfied with himself.

"I was afraid he was going to have to restitch it, but the doc says Sarah's grandmother did a professional job."

"Give credit to the polar bear, too. He ripped you in nice, straight parallel lines."

"And no infection, though he gave me a prescription for antibiotics just to be sure. He said something about the frozen north killing off most of the germs, but a bite would have been a whole different ballgame."

"And activity?"

"Anything I want until it hurts. He says it's going better than he'd expect. It's healing fast. I'm pretty lucky."

"Yes, you are."

They headed for the car. Deidre cranked the engine, but before she could put the car in gear Remi put his hand on her arm.

"Deidre, it's time you tell me what happened that night."

She was prepared, and feigned ignorance.

"A polar bear attacked you."

"Don't play dumb with me. You know what I'm asking."

She looked at him with innocent eyes.

"And don't give me that look, either. I'm not your father." His hand tightened on her arm. "Something happened. You were walking straight toward that devil beast and you didn't even see him."

"Exactly. I didn't see him."

"How is that possible?"

It was early September. She had, what, seven, eight more weeks of sight? Could she tell him? Should she?

"Yes, you can tell me," he answered her unspoken thoughts.

She twisted in the seat to face him. "I have Retinitis Pigmentosa. Is that an ugly name or what? It's a degeneration of the retina."

There, she'd said it.

"And what does that mean?" he asked slowly, cautiously.

"It means I'm going blind."

He slowed the questions that were colliding in his head and grabbed one as it skidded by. He formed his next words carefully. "How does it happen? *When* will it happen?"

"You sound like my mother."

Remi blanched at the comparison.

"That's what she asked when we got the diagnosis, how much time."

He took a different tactic. "How does the retina degenerate?"

"There are different forms. I'm lucky. Mine is going from the outside in. Some people lose their center vision first. And what I can see is pretty clear. It hasn't gone blurry yet. Maybe it won't."

"I see."

"Yes, I'm sure you do, but I can't." The bitterness in her tone surprised them both.

"What can't you see?"

"The edges. My peripheral vision is gone. Night vision, as you noticed, is gone. When I walk from darkness into bright light, it takes longer and longer for my eyes to adjust. The reverse, light to dark, is even worse."

She was getting more and more agitated.

"I'm losing color differentiation. I'm, I'm—" She started to cry.

He shoved the console between them up out of the way and, despite the pain, scooted across the seat. He put his arms around her and held her as best as he could. He didn't say anything. He just let her cry.

"I didn't see him. I just didn't see him. Maybe if I had looked up and expected a polar bear to be there I would have, but what I saw wasn't… wasn't anything."

A life-altering decision based on something you saw or didn't see… If anyone understood that, it was Remi. She continued to cry in his arms.

"So will you be able to finish the Grand Tour?"

"Yes. Just. That was the plan, to see as much as I could, and once the vision is gone to go home."

"So November, then…"

"Or October, maybe."

He sat quietly, holding her. Then he felt a shudder pass through her body.

"It is so unfair. Sometimes I just want to scream. I did everything right. Why did this happen to me?"

He had asked himself that same question too many times. "We want to think the world is fair, is safe, that we're in control. But we're not," he said softly.

"I had goals, plans, my whole future!" Her voice was choked.

"Maybe only luck, or lack of it, determines our fate. I only know that sometimes bad things happen to good people."

They sat quietly as she cried in his arms. Then, he asked, "What can I give you in the next few weeks? What do you really want to see? What would help?"

He felt her begin to sob harder. "You're asking for my bucket list of lost opportunities? There's nothing there that you can give me."

"Try me. I'm pretty resourceful."

In an effort to soothe her, he only seemed to upset her further, if the intensity of her shuddered sobs were an indicator.

She was barely audible as she said, "I want to see my baby's face."

He felt his heart sink.

"I want to see my husband smile as I walk down the aisle on our wedding day. And my wedding gown, I want to see my wedding gown."

He swallowed. No, he couldn't help her.

"I want to drive a Ferrari on the *autostrata* for my fortieth birthday. And see a solar eclipse, a full one."

He stroked her hair.

"I want to know what it feels like to make wild, passionate love while I can see so I can have something to remember when I can't."

That made him smile sadly.

"I want to see the northern lights, and see the Tigers win the World Series, and watch the Russian Ballet perform *Swan Lake*."

It came out in a rush.

She started crying again. "I want to see us—my husband and me—grow old and gray and wrinkled and fat together. I want to pick out my china pattern and wall color and choose clothes that I like. I want to put on my own makeup and paint my own nails." She was crying harder now. "I want to be independent. But I can't be. I won't be. I'll be blind!"

He continued stroking her head, so perfectly round and small beneath his large hand. There was always an answer, but he just couldn't find it at the moment.

"My dear, sweet girl. My sweet, sweet girl."

He comforted her the only way he knew how, but he knew it wasn't enough.

CHAPTER 18

GARMISCH-PARTENKIRCHEN

THE INJURED LEG negated their planned hike of the Alps above Garmisch-Partenkirchen. Instead, they filled the time in a small *zimmer frei* once owned by a lovely German couple, Adolph and Doris, but now operated by their daughter. Remi had discovered this little gem on his first visit to Garmisch and had managed to find his way back on two other occasions.

The towns of Garmisch-Partenkirchen—two inseparable towns merging in the middle—were famous for three things: the Zugspitze, wood carvings, and quaintness.

Deidre had dug out her guidebooks the previous day, as they flew over the North Pole to Europe.

"We can take a cable car to the top of the Zugspitze and back. I think your leg can handle that."

In reality, Remi thought he could actually hike some of the trails, but if Deidre needed help he'd have no reserve strength. So rather than risk it, he let her plan their activities, knowing she would overestimate his injury. She seemed to blossom in her role as nurse, and he was content to let her play the part for a while longer.

The Zugspitze, the tallest mountain in Germany, attracted skiers from throughout Europe in the winter, and hikers in the summer. It had two glaciers, but in early September last winter's snow had melted, leaving behind an Alpine autumn.

They rode the cable car to the summit. The day had started out overcast, but during the ascent they broke through the lower layer of clouds to discovered sunrays bouncing off the pristine whiteness of puffy clouds floating under blue skies.

"There's a cross up there that's rather famous. But it might be too hard for you."

Remi wished she'd choose her words a bit more judiciously. Telling him something was too hard was like waving the proverbial red cape.

"We'll see," he said. "I've already been there, but there's no reason you can't hike it. The trail's not much of a challenge. Families make an outing of it."

Deidre had a habit of squinting her eyes ever so slightly when she was deep in thought. Remi had learned that look meant she was reasoning out a problem or reconciling a new thought with old ones already rooted.

"I'm thinking about what you said about lose-lose behavior, how Cassie and I never leave one another behind."

"Like when you go to the bathroom together?" he teased.

"No, I'm serious," she said, punching him playfully on the arm. He leaned away, feigning injury. "It seemed like the right thing to do, but not necessarily what I always wanted to do. Sometimes I'd imagine going ahead and doing it without her, but then I'd be ashamed of myself for being selfish."

"Why?"

"Well, she couldn't do it, so why should I? That wasn't fair."

"What's not fair about it? There will always be things that one person can't do and another can. There were times when Cassandra could do something and you couldn't, right?" She nodded. "So if she went ahead without you, would you feel bad?"

"Not bad. Maybe a little envious. Well," she said, thinking further, "not so much lately. Maybe it's just the way we've always done it, a habit."

"I'd break that one. If you handicap yourself by the abilities or fears or circumstances of someone else, you're going to miss out on a whole lot of living." He watched her considering the concept. "Everyone has different talents or interests, and I think it's the individual's responsibility to maximize those talents, not reduce himself or herself to the lowest common denominator."

"Something to think about, for sure," she said. "I'd like you to come, though. I like sharing, so later in life we can say, 'Remember when—'"

"—'you were attacked by the polar bear and I saved you?' Yeah, yeah, yeah. I can just hear it now, me sitting in my rocking chair—ow," he said as she slugged his arm in earnest, though the exclamation was solely for her sake.

That night as he walked from the bathroom to his own room, he saw her writing at the table.

"Another article? By the way, where's my copy of 'Egypt?'"

"Back home. I'll get it to you. No," she said, answering his first question. "I was just thinking about doing things alone versus doing them with someone else. You like to be by yourself, don't you?"

"Mostly." But lately, he realized, that had been changing.

"I don't. I like to be with friends. But I can see what you mean about doing things alone. When I'm blind, I can't expect Cassie to stop seeing."

"Maybe it will be just the opposite. Maybe she could start seeing for you."

"That's what I was thinking, too, though that wouldn't be fair either. To her I mean."

Now he had something to think about: the responsibility for living for someone else. Unconsciously he touched the cell phone in his pocket.

He turned the page toward him and looked up at her, inquiring, waiting for permission. She nodded, and he began to read.

Life is not a question with multiple-choice answers. At least, if that were the case, one might expect to get a percentage right just by marking the same letter. No, life requires thoughtful paragraphs, but, of course, you don't know that until you are deep into the thick of it with neither pen nor paper.

"So you think at twenty-one you're 'in the thick of it?'" he asked with a smile.

"Are you mocking me?" She smiled back at him.

"Gently," he admitted, his smile deepening.

"Well, it's the oldest I've ever been, so, from my perspective, yes, I'm fairly submerged in life. But not so old as to think I know much yet."

"So the lesson is to keep pen and paper handy."

BEING SMALLER, the neighboring town of Oberammergau, condensed "quaintness" to an art form with picturesque chalets, sparkling clean cobblestones, and charming shops. Among the delights of Oberammergau were the colorful frescos carefully painted on the whitewashed buildings, a perfect canvas for fairy tales and depictions of rural life.

"Enchanting," was the only word Deidre could find to describe that perfect little Germanic town.

It was September, the in-between season, too late for summer tourists, too early for Christmas markets and skiers. Whether in Garmisch or Oberammergau, mornings felt like theirs alone, a time to wander through the curvy cobblestone streets of Old Town, or stop in the church to hear an orchestra rehearse, or watch the shopkeepers change the window displays. They held hands as they walked. It helped to balance her when the stones were uneven, or that's what Remi told himself. It helped his leg, was Deidre's explanation.

The best way to reach Fussen was north past Oberammergau,

then south again to the Bavarian town.

"Or we can go south into Austria and north up to Fussen," Deidre said looking up from the map. "It looks awfully small. Why are we going to Fussen? I can't remember."

They sat at the breakfast table planning the day.

"Weiskirche," Remi said.

"White church," she translated.

"Neuschwanstein."

"Mad King Ludwig's castle."

Remi nodded. "Hohenschwangau."

"Castle of King Max."

"The end of the Romantic Road, and violin-making."

"Got it. Well, that should fill our time."

"I've got something for you," he said as he handed her a newly formed eye patch. "Here, put this on. Cover one eye for me."

"Why?"

"It may help when you go into places."

"What?"

"Just try it. I don't know if it will work, but—"

"I can't go out in public in this. I'll look stupid," she said, but put the patch on anyway.

"And you care what other people, what strangers who you will never see again, think, because?"

She smiled. "Because I'm vain."

"Yes, you are, but you are also curious and smart and love to learn, so do as I say."

"Yes, Gunny."

"And salute when you say that, Private."

She rolled her eyes, or at least the one he could see, and waved her hand somewhere in the vicinity of her forehead.

"I still don't know why I'm wearing this thing," she grumbled.

"Because I said so," was his simple answer.

The white church stood at the beginning of the road to Neuschwanstein and Hohenschwangau castles. After this short stop, they would continue their drive up the mountain.

It stood alone, a picturesque country church, small and unassuming, in the middle of nowhere. They parked in the small lot with mostly handicapped spaces. Deidre couldn't imagine what attracted so many visitors.

"The statue of Jesus was said to cry. That brought the pilgrims, some of whom claimed to be cured of diseases. But for me, the real treat is this interior design."

He opened the heavy door for her and they walked in from the back.

"Take off the patch," he said in a low, respectful voice. Deidre reached up and removed it, and something miraculous happened. She could see with that eye! She could see him clearly, in full detail. The interior was bright, but still far dimmer than the sunlight. And she could see.

"How did you know?" she asked in awe. "It's not possible."

He smiled. "I hoped it would work."

"But why? How?"

"It was part of our training. When we went out on night missions we were taught to keep one eye closed, in case of a flare. A flare in the dark will temporarily blind you in the eye that sees it, so you switch to the other eye that's been kept closed and protected. It's called dark adaptation. So I got to thinking the other night that if we kept the one eye covered, it would remain adjusted to dim light all the time. Then, when we go into dark places, you'll just move the patch and use that eye. The important thing is to protect one eye from sunlight, so a patch is perfect."

She reached up and drew his head down to kiss his cheek.

"Whether this is a miracle or you are a genius, you are once again my hero."

He hugged her. "My pleasure. Now turn around and look."

The first thing visitors saw upon entering the church was the altar at the front: the white and gold and soaring columns framing bright paintings. From this introduction, their heads began to pivot to all the artistic delicacies in the space.

"Yes," Deidre whispered, craning her neck to see the painted ceiling, frescos, and statues in the white interior. "A little gem."

"Baroque."

They sat in a back pew to absorb the awe of the space. No one else had yet arrived, though the church was a destination for many tourists.

"I've never even heard of this place," she said.

"A small thing."

"Are you religious?" she asked quietly. "Now, I mean?"

He didn't know how to answer her. Too terse, and it sounded harsh. Too much explanation, and it could overwhelm her. She had handled his nightmares, so perhaps…

"I find it hard to believe there is a God," he said simply.

She nodded solemnly.

Well, he thought, she took that well.

"Why?"

Ugh, more? "Abbreviated version." He took her hand. "When you're in the middle of a life and death battle, five battles, ten, whatever, and even if it's silently to yourself, you pray: you pray for help, you pray for safety, you pray to win. Everyone around you is praying, too. The funny thing is, you know the other side is praying, too. But you believe your god is stronger. Of course, so they do. Then someone wins and someone loses, so does that show whose god is better?"

"No, not necessarily," she said. "Maybe it's just whose god showed up."

He was stunned. How could she have known that? "Yeah, somebody's god didn't show up. And if there is one place in the whole cosmos where God needs to be, it's on the battlefield. Of course, He'd show up—if He existed at all."

"So he failed you," she said, looking at him.

"He didn't show up, that's all I know."

"But I feel Him here," she said thoughtfully. "Don't you?"

He tried to think if anything felt differently. Yes, it was peaceful, even safe. Yes, it was pretty, actually stunningly beautiful, but that was man's work, not God's. Did he feel the presence of God? If he did, then God would have to exist, and he knew that He didn't.

"No," he answered truthfully. "I don't."

They left the little church in silence, each absorbed in his or her own thoughts.

They drove up the road toward the castle high above them. They could see Neuschwanstein from the lower road, but it peeked in and out of view as they progressed up the mountain. At the point where car traffic ended, they parked and took a horse-drawn carriage to the castle.

"I know you think you can walk up, but let's not risk it," she decided for them. He smiled patiently, but silently thought that he would soon be putting an end to this "mothering."

They still had more hill to climb after the wagon dropped them off. At the final stretch, they heard music, and rounded the curve to see a harpist in a flowing dress, a lute player in costume, and a young troubadour singing centuries-old ballads. They stopped to listen and dropped a few bills into the trio's hat before continuing into the courtyard.

When they came back out a little while later, the troupe was gone, harp and all.

"What a fairyland," Deidre exclaimed. "It's incredible to think how this mad king came up with such a beautiful home."

"How many castles did he build, three?"

"I think it was four, if you count the apartment in Munich," she answered.

"And that concert hall built just for Wagner."

"My favorite was the river flowing through the kitchen for the swans—wasn't that just over the top? I can see why Neuschwanstein inspired Disney. It is truly a fantasy home for a princess."

"They think he was gay, by the way."

"Hence the fantasia and grace and charm of the castle."

They chatted the whole way down to the restaurant.

"Lunch here?" Remi suggested, nodding toward a Bavarian restaurant near the parking lot.

"Perfect."

They found a table and ordered a very German meal of *wiener schnitzel, spaetzle* and Black Forest cake.

"I'm not a virgin."

Recently, she had developed the oddest way of reading his mind. That very question had just been fumbling around in the recesses of his head.

"I didn't think you were."

Annoyed, she asked, "Do you think I sleep around?"

"Actually, I didn't think much about it at all," he said, grabbing another roll.

"Oh." She wanted to explain. "It was one time, when I was fourteen."

He put down the butter knife and looked at her.

"I was somewhere that I shouldn't have been. He pushed me down and did it."

"Rape?" he asked quietly, waiting for confirmation.

"Officially, probably, because I was a minor, but he was, too. Sixteen. But I don't really call it that. I didn't want it, but I was kind of curious, too, so maybe I didn't make it clear to him."

"Arrest?"

She shook her head. "I didn't tell anyone."

He thought for a minute. "That's your only experience?"

Deidre nodded.

Over dessert and cappuccino, she asked, "Are you an only child?"

He wondered how she did that, too, catching him off guard and asking about things he never talk about.

"I have a sister."

"You hesitated," she observed, sipping her coffee.

He shrugged. "I had a brother, too."

"Had?"

"My brother died when he was eleven. I was twelve."

She put down the cup and gave him her full attention. "What was his name?"

"Ronnie, but we called him Talon."

"How did he get that name?"

The question took him back home in the snap of a finger. "He liked birds, hawks and eagles, and said he wanted to fly, and sometimes just before falling asleep he said he thought he could. I used to tease him at night in bed. I'd get a feather and tickle his nose whispering that he was a bird and flying."

"You were a rotten kid."

Remi laughed. "You don't even want to know. One night he was waiting for me, and when I started the prank he sat up and scratched the heck out of my neck and shoulder. He'd filed his nails into points and, man, they got me good. After that he was Talon."

"Serves you right."

"Yeah, it did. We were twelve months apart so raised like twins, though I was bigger and stronger, but not by much. We lived on a ranch in Montana, a cattle ranch. We were old enough to help Dad work the place, and loved it."

"Did you have much property?"

"Fifteen hundred acres, and lots of cattle. We raised hay for the herd in case we had a bad winter. And across the east end of the ranch were thick woods for hunting."

"So how did he die?"

Remi regretted the conversation. It would dampen the whole fine day, and he had so few of those. Still, she knew sorrow, too.

"Our younger sister, Carole, raised an abandoned fawn. She named her Fawntine. The doe had free range of the ranch, and as she grew would be gone days at a time. She often headed up toward the east slope and the woods there. But after a while she'd come back, and we'd love on her and feed her corn and carrots. In the spring we planted clover behind the house, and that kept her close.

"Carole tied a red bandana around Fawntine's neck so people would know she was tame. She wasn't afraid of humans. That dumb deer would walk right up to a hunter pointing a gun. But the neckerchief saved her more times than I can count, I imagine. Dad said that come hunting season we should spray paint a big red X on each side in case a hunter only saw her body.

"The first day of hunting season in 1987, I'd just turned twelve, Carole came running to the barn in a panic holding Fawntine's bandana. She had lost it somehow, and that's when we remembered we'd been so busy bringing in the hay we all forgot to paint her sides. So Talon grabbed the spray paint, and I took the neckerchief, and we raced off to the woods to find her.

"Finding any deer is a challenge. You hunt? No, of course you don't hunt. That was dumb," he muttered. "Well, seeing a deer is a challenge, but finding a particular deer, even a tame one, is close to impossible. But we were kids, and were positive we could do anything.

"We'd been out for about three hours. The sun was at the crest of the west mountain, thinking about going down. And we were getting hungry. Still no Fawntine. I was getting ready to call it a day and head back home. It was maybe an hour back to the house at a slow trot. I think Talon was thinking the same thing. I saw him running down a slope toward me when I heard a *pop*. Just like that, a *pop*, like a toy gun. At first I thought he had tripped and rolled, but he didn't get up, so I ran to help him. First thing I saw was blood. He was shot through the stomach and bleeding bad.

"I started shouting for help. The hunter had to be close enough to hear me. I saw him down in a small swale. At first, he started to run up the hill toward us. Then he stopped, stood still for a minute, then turned around and ran. I thought he was going for help, but no one ever came. He just left.

"I went back to Talon, thinking help was coming. He cried, saying it hurt bad and he was going to die. I was so freaking scared. I didn't know how to stop the bleeding. He was too big to drag out of the woods. I couldn't leave him because wolves were beginning to come back to the backcountry, and coyotes. He kept crying, and I felt so helpless. I was crying, too. I don't remember what I did to stop the bleeding. I know I tried things, but I don't remember what. Only nothing was working. Finally, I just sat down with his head in my lap, trying to comfort him, waiting. It was like being in a slow motion nightmare that went on and on. I remember my hands were covered with blood, and that bothered me. They were wet and sticky.

I had new jeans on. It's funny that I remember that. I tried wiping the blood off on the ground, but the leaves and dirt got stuck in the blood, so I wiped them on my jeans. I was worried that I ruined them.

"It was too dark to see, but I could feel Talon shivering. I was shivering, too. I held him until he stopped crying. Then he stopped moving. I held him until he felt cold on my lap, colder than the night air. It was the most alone I've ever felt in my life.

"It was just before dawn when they found us. My brother was dead. My jacket was wrapped around his middle, and I was nearly frozen. They came, my dad and the neighbors, and carried us down the hill. They never found the hunter.

"I lost my innocence that night. It was like the cold fingers of death had wrapped themselves around my soul with a promise to come back for me someday. I had been spared this time for reasons I didn't understand, but I knew death was always watching. It was just a *pop* away.

"The ranch never felt the same for me after that. I went to college in Bozeman for a couple of years, but that didn't feel right either. So I joined the Marine Corps after my sophomore year. I just needed to get away from the ranch, from the memories."

They sat quietly, each in thought.

"Was that the first time God abandoned you?" she asked.

He looked up at her, startled, and nodded.

AS TRAGIC AS the story was to tell and to hear, what disturbed Deidre most was the way he told it, detached, like an observer. He wasn't there. He wasn't here. He was lost somewhere in between. And what frightened her most was that she didn't know how to reach him.

CHAPTER 19

VENICE

"MAYBE GOD DOESN'T approve of war, so he never shows up."

The platform at Santa Lucia was crowded. Deidre reached up for the suitcase Remi was dropping down to her. He grabbed the last bag and climbed down the two steps from the train.

"Where did that come from?" he asked, looking at her as they muscled their way through the crowd.

"Well, the capricious outcomes. It doesn't seem like there's any direct hand orchestrating things."

"The military generals would disagree."

"You know what I mean."

"You sound like an existentialist discussing the notion of the Absurd."

"Since my diagnosis, I find it plausible. Bad things do happen to good people sometimes."

"Lighten up, Sinclair. We're in Venice, the Serenissima, the Queen of the Adriatic, the bestower of birthday wishes and fulfiller of dreams. Let's go play. We've earned it," he said as they pushed their way out of the train station.

From their vantage point at the top of the train station stairs, she got her first view of this lovely lady, this Queen of the Adriatic. As they looked out at the Grand Canal with all its bustling boat traffic, they saw *vaporetti* to the left and to the right, commercial boats making deliveries, water taxis, a *polizia* cruiser, and private boats motoring like cars, all churning through the main watery thoroughfare.

Across the canal from the station stairs was a grand church with a green tiled dome and cupola. The ancient buildings stood strong, and proudly looked back at the tourists who looked at them. Pedestrians walked between the buildings and the stone edge of the canal, mainly tourists, but many Venetians, too. Though a tourist town, Venice was very much owned by its residents.

"I never tire of her," Remi said with a sigh. "I never, *never* tire of her."

This was his city, the only place he truly gave his heart to.

He looked over at Deidre. For once, she had nothing to say.

"What are you thinking?" he asked.

"The energy. The—I can't describe it—the happiness, or maybe it's my own happiness. It's all confused. But it is magnificent."

He smiled as they started down the stairs to the *vaporetto*. "Just wait until I show you San Marco." His voice was filled with boyish anticipation.

They stood at the rail of the waterbus, looking out at the shore hemmed with historic buildings and crowded with tourists. This was the one place where crowds felt tolerable, except at the train station, and in San Marco at Carnevale. Otherwise, he felt safe.

"There's the Ruskin House," he said, pointing to a red building. "And back there, that's the Redentore."

"The what?"

"A plague church."

"What is a plague church?"

"You've heard of the different plagues that swept through Europe, right?"

Deidre gave him a look that telegraphed, *You're really asking me that?*

"Well I don't know what they teach in schools these days," he said with a shrug. "People back then believed the plagues were punishment for their sins."

"Like when AIDS hit the gay community," she said.

"Exactly. They vowed to reform and build God a magnificent church if He spared them. So they did, and apparently, He kept his end of the deal, too, because Venice still stands."

"And everyone lived happily ever after."

He smiled. "Later, we'll go down the Grand Canale—"

"Isn't this the Grand Canal?"

"Actually," he explained, "it's the back side, a shortcut to our *pensione*."

Without realizing it, Remi had fallen back into using the Italian pronunciation, adding the vowel to lift the tail of a word, making it light and lyrical.

"Oh, that is a pretty church," Deidre said. "My favorite so far."

"San Giorgio," he said as the *vaporetto* turned east around the point of the church.

"Now look behind you."

"Ohhh," she breathed. "It's wonderful."

"The Santa Maria della Salute, 'Salute' by the locals."

The stairs leading up to the doors were perfectly proportionate to its magnificent façade. The combination of dome, cupola, and morning sunlight created an illusion of perfect harmony and peace.

"If this is a plague church, I don't want to know. Don't tell me."

"It is, but I won't say anything—Ow." He pretended to feel pain from her wimpy punch.

"I want it to be a celebration, not a bribe."

"Okay, pretend I didn't say anything," he said with a grin. "It's really easier to not believe in God. Then you can simply revel in the architecture and aesthetics of the thing and not get tangled up in the meaning and politics and all the other trappings."

"Or you can just believe that God is out there waiting, but staying out of the mess for a while. At some point, He'll re-engage and straighten us all out." She paused, then added, "Or not."

"Good point. But why pray if He isn't going to sully his hands with us?"

"Let me think on that."

"Do that later, because we're getting off at Arsenale, the next stop."

They hopped off the *vaporetto* with their luggage and started walking along the Grand Canal.

A wide staircase over a wide canal rose in front of them. The arch of the bridge was particularly high to accommodate the large boats docked at the Arsenal located at the end of the canal.

"All these stairs," she observed.

"Never ending in Venice."

"I'm glad I packed light."

"Me, too," he said. "And remember what I told you, no jeans and no tennis shoes."

"They don't wear tennis shoes?"

"Only on the tennis court. Otherwise, it's considered disrespectful. Except for the kids. It's assumed they will be disrespectful, so they can get away with it. The thing is, we don't want to dress like tourists or act like the ugly American."

In the days that followed, Deidre identified the North American tourists easily, by just those things: tennis shoes, blue jeans, cameras, and maps.

At the base of the broad bridge, Remi grabbed the two larger suitcases while Deidre picked up their carry-ons. His camera bag was slung over his shoulder. Hers was in a backpack.

She followed him past the Naval Museum to a shop on the corner with a large window across the front and a smaller one looking out toward the bridge. Inside the shop, the air was soft with the smell of leather. *Il Mercante di Venezia*, the Merchant of Venice, was a book-making shop.

"Roberto!"

The man looked up.

"Remi. My friend." He rose for an embrace. "How are you?"

The men kissed each other on both cheeks.

"*Bene, bene, et tu? La familia?*"

"You remember a little Italian? It is good. I am good, we are all good."

Roberto, a man nearly as tall as Remi, looked over his shoulder at Deidre, who stood waiting at the door.

"*E l' amica?*"

"*Si*. This is Deidre. Deidre, meet Roberto, our landlord."

"*Piacere*, Deidre. Welcome to Italy. Welcome to my shop," he said with a flourish. "But Remi, your leg. Why do you favor it?"

"Oh, a little accident in Alaska."

"He attacked a polar bear that was attacking me," Deidre summarized.

"You are joking," Roberto said with a smile, sincerely believing they were.

"Well, there were a few more parts to the story, but that's about right," Remi said.

"A polar bear? Really? Where?"

"Alaska."

"Remi, Remi. You travel all over. But more later. Let me call Vittoria to see if the apartment is ready. One moment, please."

As Roberto went into the back to place the call, Deidre whispered, "I am overcome with the warmth of your friend. And this shop! It's wonderful."

Remi beamed with happiness.

"It feels like home."

Remi had been to Venice many times in the nineties, and twice since his discharge. He didn't know it then, but he had left a part of himself in the city, to be preserved. And the city had kept it safe until he returned. Only in Venice could he become the man he had been before Operation Iraqi Freedom, before Enduring Freedom, before the ravishes of war had poisoned his soul.

"Look around," he said. "They're all crafted by Roberto."

Deidre began looking through the shelves of neatly arranged books. Some were lined. Some were not. Some had handmade paper embedded with small flowers or leaves in their creamy pages. There were telephone books and diaries and photo albums with onionskin pages to protect the pictures. Some covers were pliable, while others were stretched over cardboard. There were leather cases to carry CDs and pouches for travel documents. In the window, Roberto had kaleidoscopes and hourglasses, glass pens and bottles of ink, compasses and old maps. It was a visual banquet.

"The house is ready," Roberto said when he returned. "Here is the key, but Vittoria is waiting at her mother's. I will see you later, Remi. *Ciao,* my friend." He gave a quick kiss on each cheek. "*Ciao, signorina,*" he said with more kisses.

"*Ciao, Roberto. A piu tardi.*" And they left.

"What was that at the end?" she asked as they made their way over another bridge before turning down Via Garibaldi.

"*A piu tardi*? See you later. My Italian is terrible. They tease me all the time."

"So you've stayed here often?"

"As often as I can. Maybe I'll move to Venice someday. This feels more like home than any other place."

Rolling their suitcases behind them, they made their way through the residential heart of Venice. Remi nodded as they passed a tall black gate propped open. "This is the Garden District, and this is the garden. Way back in there are pavilions for the Biennale, an international art display held in odd years. Each country has its own building."

"Is it good?"

"It can be. Reviews are mixed. Some countries are better than others. It's on this year if you want to see it."

"Since we're here, yes."

"And the Venice Film Festival. We can check that out, too. I think we're too late for the Marathon. That was last week."

"Do they have something going on every week?" It seemed incredible.

"Not every week, but there's a major festival at least every month."

Along the wide street they saw restaurateurs pulling out tables, people stopping to choose their dinner or chat with the fish vendor, and two men with a cart of sloshing wine in demijohns struggling to get over a canal. Overhead they heard the screech of resistant pulleys as clothes were strung up to dry, the lines joining one side of the broad street to the other.

"It started out for real, but now it's mainly a joke for the tourists. They come to see the clothes hanging out."

Red long johns, brassieres, tennis shoelaces tied together, fluttering slips, bloomers, and other intimate apparel items dangled high above them adding to the merriment and tongue-in-cheek feel of a city that knew how to laugh.

The wide street was met by a small canal. Now only a narrow strip of sidewalk edged each side of the water. An open flat bottom boat converted into a fruit and vegetable market was docked at the end. The crew, also acting as merchants, were taking orders and handing up the food to waiting hands. The Venetians lining the canal to shop pushed to get in, called out orders, and negotiated prices.

"I don't know if you remember Rome," Remi said, "but Italy

has perfected the term 'survival of the fittest.' We'll dump our bags and come back to shop. By the way, do you cook?"

"No."

"Me neither. Maybe we can get a cooking lesson or two. I love everything about Venice, including the freshness of the food, but the restaurants here don't impress me. I've got a few favorites, but mostly the food caters to the tourists and is either mediocre or ridiculously overpriced."

"Maybe we can find some local places to add to your list."

He smiled down at her. "Like in Nice."

At the beginning of the Grand Tour she might have assumed they would eat at places like the Gritti Palace or Cipriani, but now he saw that spirit of adventure blossoming, along with her appreciation for the small things, the things you had to dig for, seek out. She was the same girl, but definitely more grown up.

I like her. And I don't tell her that often enough.

He would miss her when this was over. He'd been on his own for so long it took a major adjustment to let the girls into his life, but now, he thought, there would be another transition getting back on his own again. The summer trips, Europe and Alaska, had been revisits. He wondered what it would be like to take her some place that neither had been before, a place to be discovered together.

"What are you smiling at?" Deidre asked.

"Am I smiling?"

"The mouth definitely curled in the corners."

"I guess I was thinking that I like you a lot."

Her face lit up. "Really?"

"When you're not being a pain in the ass," he teased. "Come. We're almost there. Just at the end of this *calle*."

As he turned the key in the courtyard door, Remi felt like he was coming home after a long time away. They walked into the intimate courtyard. Yellow finches in hanging cages greeted them with a merry song. A round picnic table with chairs and an open umbrella sat in the middle. At the far side of the courtyard, two sets of French doors were open to welcome them into their apartment. Along the right wall of the courtyard was another door, and above were three Ottoman windows, also open.

"Down here is Roberto's apartment, Roberto, Vittoria's brother, not her husband who owns the shop. And above his apartment, there," he said pointing to the decorative windows, "is the home of their parents, Giulia and Franco. We've got top and bottom of—"

"Remi! *Ciao! Ciao!*" Giulia called down from one of the windows.

Vittoria hung out another. "*Ciao, raggazzi.* I am coming down." She disappeared.

"*Come` va?* How have you been?" Giulia asked.

"Good, Giulia. Good. This is Deidre, my friend."

"*Ciao*, Deidre. Tonight you will come for dinner."

Vittoria came into the courtyard and hugged Remi with a kiss on each cheek.

"Deidre, I am Vittoria. Welcome to my home."

Upon hearing the commotion, Roberto, the brother, came out, and the sequence was repeated. Soon, Giulia joined them.

Suitcases forgotten, they hugged and kissed and chatted and complimented, and Deidre thought she had never met such warm and genuine people in her life. There was no awkwardness, no stumbling to find something to say. Their English was excellent. Roberto's fluency was easily explained. He had lived in New York City for years. Giulia's humble apologies that hers was not well practiced went unnoticed since she kept up with her children and guests just fine.

"If you need anything, I am just up here." She pointed to her apartment. "Now I must start to work."

"And I am off to Milano tomorrow," Roberto said. "I should be back in two weeks. Vitti said you will be here for three, so we will have time when I get back."

Deidre would be sorry to see him go. The mischief in his eyes was absolutely endearing.

"Such a pleasure to meet you, Roberto," she said, extending her hand.

He took it, but bent in to kiss each cheek instead. He smiled warmly at her.

"But I will see you tonight at my mother's for dinner, yes?" He turned to Remi. "How did you find such a beauty? You make it hard to leave," he said to her.

Vittoria slapped at her brother. "Now go on. They haven't even seen the apartment yet. Come on, *raggazzi,*" she said, lifting one of the carry-ons and leading the way. "It is all ready for you."

The apartment was exquisite. From the courtyard, they walked into the dining room with a table and four chairs. A corner nook held plates and bowls. Behind that, a white kitchen with a window looked out onto a small canal. With pullout drawers full of pots and pans, silverware and utensils, mixing bowls and serving platters, dishtowels and pot holders, it was complete. An open, polished wood staircase sat to the left of the dining room between the two sets of French doors. The rest of the lower floor was the living room, comfortably furnished with a couch and chairs, fireplace and a television. The white marble of the floor glistened. Upstairs held an elegant bathroom as large as a bedroom with a shower and separate tub, toilet, and bidet. The two bedrooms, a queen with a floor-to-ceiling closet along one wall, and a second with twin beds and a place for the suitcases, completed the top floor.

"What a special place," Deidre said as she peered into each

room.

"They renovated it fifteen years ago, but it could have been done yesterday."

"I love it. And the family… there is something very wonderful here. It surrounds me."

"Ah, you're seeing with your heart now." Remi smiled.

The feeling continued at dinner. The guests and family gathered around the big table in Giulia's home enjoyed a lively evening of eating, laughing, talking, and relaxing. Vittoria's two sons, her brother, husband, parents, and grandmother, ten in all, enjoyed hearing the stories of their American friends. They were especially thrilled by the story of the polar bear. And the Americans enjoyed listening to stories about former guests, the trials of Carnevale, and the corruption of Venetian politicians.

By evening's end, drowsy from the wine and food, Deidre and Remi made their way down the stairs to their own apartment. Roberto, the brother, said his final farewell before leaving for Milano. Roberto, the husband, said he would see them at the shop in the morning. Giulia asked if Deidre would like a cooking lesson during her stay. Vittoria gathered her chicks like a mother hen while calling out a good night as they left, promising to visit on the morrow.

Arm in arm, they walked the short distance across the courtyard and into the unlocked house.

"I love this family! I wonder if I have ever had such a wonderful evening in my life," she said.

Remi smiled contentedly. "They are really great, aren't they? They're like family to me."

"I've only known them a day, and it feels that way to me, too."

"You look like you're going to pass out."

"Long day. Happy day, but long."

As they headed up the stairs, Remi felt a powerful urge to kiss her, to make love to her. He restrained himself, but barely. Deidre took the first room with the queen size bed. Remi fell into the twin bed that would just about hold him, if he slept diagonally. He thought he would fall asleep immediately, but found that the sexual stirrings she had ignited required attending to. Finally, he drifted into a peaceful slumber, not even pausing to reflect on how the day had been. Instead, a germ was taking root in his mind, a way for him to give her something. Maybe he could… and then sleep.

CHAPTER 20

AFTER THE CONCERT

SHE CAME DOWN the stairs wearing that damn silk dress. The moment he saw it, he thought it could be trouble. As she moved, it flowed over her like an oil slick on water, a film of color in motion. It was a deep, rich aqua blue, free of adornment, so the eye focused just on the garment and the woman who wore it. It was high in front, too high for his taste, but when she turned he could see the deep scoop down to the small of her back and a short zipper that pulled the fabric tight across her hips. The dress was short with a slight pleat up the left leg, and as it caressed her body, it embraced every curve and accentuated all her willowy assets. When she moved, he could see the silk's feathery touch brushing against the skin beneath. Perhaps modest by Italian standards, the dress covered her while still giving the illusion of transparency through which he could see her fine collarbone, the delicate ribs, and the small, soft puffs of her nipples. No bra, then. Nice. He hadn't intended to stare, but there it was, an adolescent response, and her eyes saw it. He could feel the old ache in his loins.

They had been in Venice a week, but it felt like all his life.

He looked down at the drink he was mixing, cleared his throat just in case.

"Here," he said, and handed her a glass, risking another glance. Then he poured a double shot of Campari into his own. Still looking down, he said, "You look lovely, by the way," and glanced up in time to catch her small smile as she turned away.

The sun was setting. She walked through the French doors to their courtyard. The dress hugged her heart-shaped posterior, accentuating its perfect roundness. No panty lines, either.

Deidre sat at the table, legs crossed, sipping the red liquid that got lost in the color of her lips. He couldn't help but watch the way the dress slid up her thigh when she sat, his imagination taking it up the next few inches. He went from perfectly normal to holy shit in the time it took the fabric to expose more leg. And now his pants felt too tight.

They finished their drinks.

"Shall we go?"

Out on the quiet street, Deidre slipped her hand into his. There were no cobblestones. His leg was good. He had to suppress the smile that threatened to reveal him. As he followed her up the steps over the small canal, he could smell her hair. Along the way, he allowed himself the indulgence of guiding her on the small of her back, or taking her arm to maneuver her away from an oncoming soccer ball as they skirted a small game in the middle of Via Garibaldi. People were looking at them, and he wasn't sure how he felt about it. Proud? Protective? The men, especially, made no pretense about what they were thinking. Instinctively, he put his arm around her waist and drew her to him, making a statement, marking his territory. The warmth of her under his hand spread up his arm and through his body.

Remi was glad to board the *vaporetto*. Gliding on the water provided enough distraction for him to keep his desire in check. His plan had been to slowly seduce her tonight, the operative word being 'slowly,' but damn if that wasn't going out the window fast. Did she know what that dress did to him?

They made their way through the crowded Piazza San Marco and past the Basilica to the concert hall. More looks. She attracted a lot of attention. He liked the shadows; she caught the spotlight, and was basking in it. He felt that spotlight encompass him, too—they looked good together—but center of attention wasn't his thing anymore.

As the orchestra was tuning up, the strings of the violins pulled them into the elegant but relatively small concert hall. He found their seats. Somehow he would make it through Vivaldi. What was it Deidre had said? "The Four Seasons?" Maybe they would just play "Spring." That always seemed like the shortest season. As the musicians tuned their instruments, he looked at his watch. How long until he could get her back to the apartment?

"It's chilly in here, isn't it," she said, pulling her wool shawl across her bare back.

"Do you want my jacket?" He had forgotten there was no heat until mid-October, and little heat, if any, in public places like this.

"Hmm, no." She adjusted the shawl.

As she did so, the program slid off her lap. They both bent to retrieve it, and his hand grazed the firm curve and tip of her breast. His brain translated the touch as fast as the current surged from fingertips to loins. *That was very nice.* He smiled to himself. She pretended not to notice, but how could she not?

The music began. Somewhere, near the opening notes, as best as he could remember, it seemed to seep into him, the rise and fall of it matching his own sexual rhythm. He thought about the accidental touch and the heat it radiated. The memory of that touch came back again, warming him between movements, during a particular crescendo, and for no reason at all. The Campari must have compromised him. He would have to clear his head if he was going to maintain the control he needed. Then she reached over and entwined her fingers in his, her fingertips resting on his inner thigh.

Oh, hell.

Finally came the applause, the scratching of chairs as the audience rose to leave, then the chill of the evening as they stepped outside.

They walked back to the apartment in the cool darkness, her hand linked through his arm. Seven or eight bridges down the Riva. But he didn't need to count. He could find Garibaldi; it was not a street you could miss, one of the actual avenues of Venice.

The shops were still lit along the Grand Canal, but the artists had packed up and the vendor carts put away. The tourist lines for the gondolas were gone, too, though the *gondolieri* stood near their station, the orange glow of their cigarettes waving as they spoke with their hands. He recalled an old joke he had once heard. If you want to stop an Italian from talking, make him sit on his hands. He smiled at the truth of it.

"Look how the water captures the light," she said, her voice low and wistful.

"Can you see it?" He was pleasantly surprised. How much time, he wondered, did she have left?

"I can remember it."

Shit. She was right, then; her night vision *was* gone, or nearly so. She hadn't worn her patch tonight. Maybe that would have made a difference. He wasn't ready to give up, not yet.

He held her more securely, her arm under his, their hands clasped. They were in no particular hurry, or so he tried to tell himself.

"Promenading, isn't that what the Italians call this?" he asked.

"Hmm, it could be. Such an old fashioned word. It reminds me of the Promenade des Anglais in Nice."

"The Avenue of the English," he translated loosely.

They passed the Hotel Danieli. Thank God, he had cancelled that reservation. Another of her father's brilliant ideas.

"I should have brought my camera," he lied.

He could see the gondolas on the Canal, prow and stern aglow with lantern light. They crossed a bridge over a small canal. From the interior of Venice, they heard a gondolier's "Ahoy." The sound was distant, but distinct.

"The fog's coming in," Remi observed. The pink streetlights were beginning to halo, and the damp seeped through the neck of his jacket.

"San Giorgio looks so soft and solid at night." She shivered.

Remi put his arm across her shoulder and she leaned into him. Since her revelation about the eye disease, and the physical comfort she apparently drew from his embrace, he noticed a shift in their touch. It was both frequent and natural, intimate but not sexual, somewhere between old friends and not-quite-lovers.

He looked across the canal to the church. It did look soft with its rounded dome, and stocky when compared to its length. The proportions gave it a homey solidity. She was right.

"You remember it," he said.

"Yes. I remember everything." She tried to smile.

It was over two miles to their apartment, and by the time they arrived the plan was clearly formulated in his mind. The question, he knew, was whether he could contain his desire for her.

"I love the walk, but I should never have tried it in heels," she said, bending over to slip them off, rubbing first one foot, then the other. Her rounded derriere seemed to call out an invitation to him. To keep his hands from caressing it, he took off his shoes, too.

He had meant to make another drink, but instead followed her upstairs, then into her room. As she turned, a question on her lips, he turned her back away from him and stood behind her, his left hand holding hers, his right hand circling around her waist, pulling her to him, swaying to silent music. She followed his movement and started to say something.

"Shhh. Don't speak," he whispered. "This is for you."

He felt the shudder go through her, and a hint of a smile curved his lips.

They had walked in the darkness for an hour. Her eyes could probably see now. He had deliberately left the apartment dark. He wanted her to see him.

He lifted his hand up to her breast, cupping it, feeling her through the silkiness, his fingers gliding smoothly. Her hand lightly on top of his, following as he moved from one breast to the other, her nipples alert under his touch. He felt her tense, not in resistance, but in excitement. He pulled her dress off one shoulder and slid the fabric down her arm. She lifted her chin, letting her head fall back against him. His fingertips lightly felt the curve of her jaw and stroked her neck from her chin to the top of her breast, his mouth warm in her ear. Slowly he traced the upper contour, feeling the fullness, small but firm, and let his fingers wander down between the mounds while his mouth caressed her neck and shoulder. Then gently sliding his hand under the dress, he cupped her breast. He felt the velvet of her skin. He slowly moved his hand upward, feeling the nipple grow firm under the ripple of his ascending fingers.

"This is for you," he whispered. "Just go with it, feel it."

"Remi—"

"Unless you want me to stop, no words."

He reached down with his other hand and ran his fingers up the slit in her dress, stroking her thigh, lifting the hem, inching higher, stroking higher. He could feel her heart keeping pace with his own. Her breathing was shallow, as if she had stopped breathing altogether, as though breathing might somehow distract him from his exploration. Her response was intoxicating.

He was slow, deliberate, in control. He hoped he could stay that way. If he could stay detached and not get caught up in her maybe he'd have a chance.

"You're too beautiful," he breathed. Her head was back. He ran his fingers over her face, her opened lips, down her neck again, and over her breasts.

They continued swaying, her back and bottom pulled against him, the hard pulse of his erection pressing into her soft flesh. He knew she could feel him. His hands explored her, his questing fingers sliding over the shimmering silk. She didn't resist, allowing him to experience the emotions with her.

Effortlessly, he lifted her onto the bed. She was light, and his strength seemed to arouse them both. He could take her at any time. She was his. She couldn't resist, and that, too, intensified the tidal surge of tension.

One leg between her thighs, he saw her face now, kissed her neck and ear. She tried to turn and kiss his lips, but he forced her chin upward, vulnerable, to kiss her throat. He moved his hands down her hips and under her dress to her thighs, pushing them farther apart. Slowly but purposefully, he slid his hands up, his thumbs leading on the sensitive inner leg until she arched her back and softly moaned in acute anticipation.

He kissed her then. Moving up, he held her head with both hands, stroking her cheek, brushing her hair from her damp brow, his kisses soft at first but then harder, his tongue penetrating her, tasting her. Still kissing her, he rolled to one side as his hand reached between her legs.

His fingers slipped between the soft folds of flesh to find their mark. Wet. God, she was so wet. She gasped and moaned louder, and then seemed not to breathe at all, waiting. He held her perfectly suspended there, in that place of ultimate longing. He would make her linger; he wouldn't satisfy her, not yet. The power of it consumed him.

She was arching toward him, pulling his head to hers. The room was suddenly stifling. He pulled off his shirt in one graceful motion, his muscles glistening with sweat. He pulled her dress down over her shoulders, exposing her breasts. The nipples were hard, standing erect, puckering at the base, darkening. He moved the flat of his palms in circles over each nipple, feeling them grow even harder.

He lifted her hips with one hand, unzipped the dress, pulled it off, and tossed it aside.

The light of the lamppost across the canal filtered through the thin curtain, illuminating the room. She was beautiful: chestnut hair falling around the pillow, skin white against his dark silhouette, breasts like small mounds, each tipped with a beckoning bud of promise. He kissed one while his hand stimulated the other, his lips now avoiding the sensitive nipple. She wanted him to kiss them, to stroke them, to suckle them, so he refused, teasing her. Later, when she could no longer stand it, he would satisfy her. A groan escaped her lips. Her eyes were closed, her back arched again. He could see she wanted him, needed him inside her. How in God's name could he maintain his resolve?

He heard her, an urgent whispered prayer, "Please. Please."

He sat up, straddling her, pulled off his belt, and opened his pants, releasing some of the pressure.

What am I doing? I shouldn't be getting this close, his reason shouted, but his heart whispered, *No further. Just this.*

He moved down her body again, spreading her legs, his tongue tasting the sweet wetness of her. She gasped again and moaned softly, "Oh, God. Please, oh, God."

He was as excited as she, but this was her climax. One hand reached up and rolled a nipple between thumb and finger, his other hand found her clitoris and began stroking the length of it first with his fingers then with his tongue. She gave a small cry. She was so close, right at the edge. He had intended to tease her some more, but he was too aroused himself. He inserted his fingers, one, then two, and felt her rocking against him as he stroked inside her. Deeper, he probed. Faster. Slower. He controlled her moment of release.

"I own you," he said, believing it at that moment. Whether it was his own words or her response to them, he couldn't tell, but he thought he would explode from wanting her.

He left off everything except the stroking, in and out, to the rhythm of her, finally hearing her cry, "Oh God! Oh God! Oh God!" He felt the contractions on his fingers. He continued to stroke, pushing deeper still. It was a strong orgasm, and lasting longer than he thought possible. His heart pounded at a pace that matched hers, thundering in his ears. He was both spectator and participant.

He stared down at her face, glowing in the lamplight, and felt his heart squeeze. How long had it been since he'd made love to a woman? Years ago, a lifetime ago, before the war. Sex, yes, but not lovemaking. This felt good. It felt right and normal and he wanted to thank her for it.

He felt her coming down and he eased up next to her, his fingers still inside of her. Her breathing was slower now, but her heart still pumped hard. She reached for him. She didn't say anything at first, just lay limp beside him. He withdrew his fingers from her, and her hips moved in protest. He brought his fingers to his nose and inhaled deeply. He wanted to be drunk with the smell of her and the taste of her.

"Come hold me," she whispered.

He moved up alongside her, spooning hard against her body as though he had to contain her and gather the pieces before they floated away. He was still aroused, but the urgency had lessened. Still, it could be reignited with a touch.

He knew the holding was a big part of it. She would want that containment, that reassurance. He brushed the hair off her cheek, stroking it back, touching her lightly on the arm, embracing her. Both of them drifted softly into peace, hers more peaceful than his.

Deidre stirred, turned, traced the lines of his face.

He knew it was coming.

"I love you," she said.

God, why do women always do that, say they love you after sex? Well, after good sex anyway. So it was good for her.

He smiled inwardly. He didn't need to ask. Her body had told him it was good, and that was enough. He smiled a slow, drowsy smile at the memory of it and linked a strand of hair behind her ear.

"You are beautiful."

She kissed him, first softly, then slowly, then more eagerly. It didn't take more than that, and he was ready.

"You didn't finish," she whispered.

"No." His voice was hoarse, even to his own ears.

She moved down and tried to remove his pants. He resisted.

"That wouldn't be a good idea."

"Are you a virgin, then?" she taunted.

"Hell, no! Do I make love like a virgin?"

She laughed at the trace of fake indignation in his voice. "Hardly." Then seriously, just shy of demanding, she said, "Take them off."

He felt his heart skip a beat, then another, as he lifted his hips so she could pull them off.

Just this far. I can control it.

This is bad, this is really bad. His rational voice tried to reason with him, but it was drowned out by his desire.

She straddled him and kissed him tentatively, then bolder. He had invaded her mouth with his tongue, now she probed his. Her hands searched for his nipples and found them. They were hard, like pink pearls, under her touch. She slid down and gave him what he had denied her, sucking gently at first, then with more insistence. He couldn't stand it and pulled her up to kiss her again. He rolled on top, kissing her hard, but she pulled away and turned him on his back. He couldn't refuse her anything. She slid down and sat on his thighs as if looking him over, wondering what to touch next. His cock quivered slightly, and she took it first with her hands, then with her mouth. Warm and wet. But she didn't slide down deep enough, and he was too sensitive for her tongue's naïve exploration. He pulled her up, flipped her over, and was on top again. With one hand he held both of her wrists over her head, pinning her thighs under him.

"Close your eyes." She complied. "Do you trust me?"

"Yes." Her voice quivered.

Good. His heart was slowing again. He was regaining his control. "Don't open them until I tell you."

She nodded. The breathless anticipation was increasing. He gave her arms a small jerk to remind her she was completely powerless, and saw the vein at her temple throb faster.

"And don't speak."

He looked around the room. She always took a glass of water to bed, left it on the nightstand. Still holding her wrists with one hand, he put his long fingers in the glass and let a single drop fall on her breast. It startled her. Then he took his wet fingers and touched her lips, running his forefinger over the lower lip, then pushing between the lips until she opened her mouth and sucked it. He moved lower on her hips and dipped again, letting the cold droplets fall in a circle on the smooth softness of her belly and roll into her navel. Another small gasp. He waited. Time stopped. He could feel the tension as she waited in suspense. He flicked a nail over her nipple, and she turned her head as if in pain. Like when her mouth drew him into her, it felt so good it hurt. The tease continued as he touched her unexpectedly, softly, urgently, taking her up, letting her relax, flicking a tongue over a nipple, stroking an inner arm, running his fingers down her side just at the curve of her breast, drawing a hand up her inner thigh and stopping just short, sucking her breasts, fulfilling her need with his lips while exciting her with fingers between her legs. To the edge, but not over it, allowing her to come down, then quickly propelling her almost over the top. But not quite. She struggled to be released, she opened her eyes, she pleaded with him to take her, she broke all the rules, but he wouldn't, couldn't, make this easy for her.

He kissed her hard, forcing his tongue into her mouth, and she sucked it. He released her and ran his hands down her breasts and hips and legs and into the wet center of her desire that only wanted to be filled with him.

Tiny stabs of fingernails pressed hard into his back, the pain mild but unexpected. Every cell of his body ached for her. If he possessed her, she possessed him. His plan dissolved, his will evaporated.

She was totally ready for him, totally his. What was he waiting for? He couldn't make it any better for her than this.

Then his brain turned off and nothing else mattered. The sheer explosion of desire, the heat racing through him, propelled him to enter her. His need was greater than even her need for him. He didn't mean to be rough but he was, sliding his hand under her, lifting her to meet his erection. The adrenaline was surging; she weighed nothing to him. And then he thrust in, feeling the soft, slippery heat of her flesh open to him. He pounded against her, deeper, and deeper still. Sliding out, thrusting deep, again, again, the rhythm of it shuddering through his core. He could go on inside her forever.

Then time stopped. His world was suspended with sweet release. He heard a sound. His? Hers?

Nothing at all existed but this exquisite moment of omnipotence, release, possession, and possessed, all flowing together.

His muscles weakened in euphoric relief, and he half collapsed on her.

He knew she had come, too, but when he stopped thinking he lost awareness of two separate beings. What was him, was her, Her body his, His body hers.

His heart was still pounding in his ears. He was coming down now, but still breathing heavily. His mind reengaged. He tried to shut it out, to stay in this state of ultimate bliss where everything was good. But reality insisted on seeping in.

God, he'd fucked up. He hugged her tight, until she gasped for breath. He released her a little, stroked her hair.

She was crying small, gentle sobs.

He was sure he hadn't hurt her.

"Are you okay, sweetheart?" he asked anxiously, smoothing her hair.

"It was just so good." Her voice trembled.

I love you, she had said. He wanted to say it back, but didn't trust himself. Did he love her, or was it just the afterglow of spent lust? It didn't matter. He was tired of thinking. What did he always say to her? Turn off your brain. See with your heart. What did he see with his heart? Yes, he loved her, loved her with every ounce of his being. But he would tell her later, on his own, so she wouldn't think he was just saying it because she had said it. Oh God, he couldn't love her. It wasn't in the plan. But he did.

"I'm lost," he whispered softly in her hair, smelling the citrus and the vanilla; but she didn't hear.

SOMETIME DURING through the night he had gone to his own

bed. While he thought his conscience would keep him awake, he had, in fact, slept with such contentment that no nightmare could invade. He woke up wrapped in a strange kind of peaceful happiness. The morning light was just edging through the curtains. As he passed her room, he wanted to look in, to make sure she was all right.

Who was he kidding? He wanted to look in to see her fucking gorgeous naked body, and maybe just ravage it again.

Instead, he walked on to the bathroom to shave and shower off the lusty smells still lingering from her bed.

By the time she woke up, he had brought back two apricot-filled brioche from their favorite bar-café. *"Due brioche con marmellate, per te, signorina."* He had learned that one quickly. "Two croissants with marmalade for you, miss."

Her hair was wrapped in a towel and an ivory silk robe clung suggestively to her curves. It was all he could do to keep from going to her. Where was the thick white terrycloth robe she always wore? He took a step toward her, then stopped.

What the hell was he doing? How had he let it get so far out of hand? Christ! He could have gotten her pregnant! He felt the sweat sliding down his back. And Sinclair—If Deidre told her father—God, Sinclair would hire the Mafia and arrange a hit on him.

He took a step back, frowning as he dropped the sack onto the table. "You'd better get dressed. We've got a lot to do today." And, with that he walked out of the apartment.

CHAPTER 21

MORE VENICE

DEIDRE WAS BAFFLED. No, hurt. Last night… it had been so surreal. She hadn't imagined it. The subtle throbbing between her legs was evidence enough. Last night was everything. And today, it was gone. More than gone. Remi was gone, emotionally unavailable. What had she done wrong?

They spent the morning in awkward silence as they explored the small canals of Venice. When he did speak, Remi kept the wall of professionalism firmly between them. He pointed out interesting Byzantine windows with Ottoman peaks; a crazed wall with cheerful flowers on the sill; the contrast between the fresh flowers and peeling paint; the distorted reflections of the buildings in the canal and how the water's currents moved the color in undulating patterns. And then there was the lacy workmanship of the wrought iron of a tiny bridge in a remote canal—

"I thought we were past this, this silent, brooding man saddled with a load he doesn't want to lug."

"We are past it," he said ostensibly looking at some far more interesting object through his camera.

"But last night—"

"Last night was a mistake, I mean, the second time was."

"It didn't feel like a mistake."

"Well, it was. I take responsibility. I'm the adult here and—"

"And I'm not an adult?" she demanded as she grabbed his arm.

He looked at her then. He softened as he gazed down into her face. What was he supposed to say?

"Look, all I wanted to do was to give you some memories to

hold onto when you're, when you're—"

"Blind."

"Yeah. Blind—God, I hate that word." He turned aside and ran his fingers through his hair. "That day, when you cried in Fairbanks—"

"I remember."

"You talked about all these things you felt you'd never see, never know, never experience."

"My bucket list of lost opportunities."

"I wanted to give some of them to you, that's all."

"You made love to me because of my bucket list?"

"And some other things, too. Not all of them, of course—"

"Wait a minute. Last night was just a mercy fuck?"

The word froze him, as fury surged through his body, returning her anger twofold.

"That language doesn't become you." His voice started low, threatening, but quickly amplified. "And no, goddamn it, it was not a mercy fuck!"

"Then you wanted to make love to me, except, what did you call it? 'A mistake!'"

"How do women do that? They can take anything a man says and twist it into the opposite of what he means. Do you all get lessons in this shit? Or do you do it just for sport?" He was mad, really mad.

They stared at each other, smoldering, glaring.

He tried to get a hold of his anger, but it wasn't working. Remi had to step away, but was careful to stay in sight. Slowly, he gained some control of himself.

By the time he came back to the bridge where he had left her, he was wondering how to repair this. He ventured a quick look at Deidre. Her anger was dissipating, too.

Looking off into the canal's murky water, he said, "I can't give you your baby to see." He took a deep breath. "And there isn't a solar eclipse in the near future. I checked."

"You did?" she murmured.

He still couldn't look at her. "Yeah, I did."

He walked over to the end of the bridge, and knelt with his camera to his face. "And we can't go back to Fairbanks hoping to catch the Northern Lights. That isn't a good use of time. And you can't see them anyway. And," he hesitated, changing the focus on the camera, "And—"

"Would you just stop! Just stop using that damn machine like some kind of shield. You tell me to see what's going on around me, but what do you see? You see a frame, a camera that you hide behind, a lens, glass, a barrier between you and the world! Just put it down for once and look at me!"

The truth of it struck him like a slap in the face. He stood up slowly, letting his camera dangle from his hand. Was it true? Photography was his salvation. But was it also his excuse?

He looked at her, saw the tears balancing on her lower lids, and in two strides stood before her, set the camera down, and took her hands. As he looked into her eyes, she seemed somewhere between the teenager of last summer and the woman of last night. Someone he wanted to protect. What could he say to her? That she was right?

He couldn't look at the truth of her anymore so he clutched her tight to his chest, though she hung limply in his arms. He felt her tension ease, and his own defenses dissolve. What could he say? What was inside of him? What was true?

"I've been thinking."

"That you're a jackass?"

"Yes, that, too." He stroked her hair. "I was thinking, I want you to pick out your wedding gown when we get to Paris," he said.

"We'll find a shop where we will spend all day looking at dresses, all week if that's what it takes. You're going to make a beautiful bride, and we're both going to see it while we can. I'll photograph you." He hesitated. "If you're willing, if you'll let me."

She hugged him fiercely.

He wanted to see her face, so he pulled her away from him. The transformation was startling. She simply glowed, despite the glistening tears in her eyes. He wiped a seeping drop from her cheek and felt warmth flow through him. If he could bring her this much happiness, maybe there was something still salvageable.

"Yes! Yes! I will!"

"So you like the idea."

"Oh, you crazy man, you are the most wonderful, the most sensitive, the most—"

He kissed her then to stop the gush of words. He wasn't wonderful, wasn't sensitive, but, damn, he wanted her to be happy. The passion of her kiss told him he could do it. He could reach her. He could touch her core and keep her safe. And in her arms, he was safe, too.

DEIDRE COULDN'T believe how fast it had happened. Last spring she was sitting in a classroom listening to this fascinating speaker, and now, five months later, they were engaged. She was about to marry the most wonderful man.

Not only that, he had awakened her body.

Her dating history was incomplete, sporadic. Too beautiful, too rich, too smart, too protected—in high school, she had intimidated her peers. And though she attracted a lot of attention, nothing about college boys interested her. She had begun to question if her standards were too high. Would she ever find someone to love and be loved by, in the same package? The question had been superseded by the diagnosis last spring, but was always there, peeking out of the blanket that had been casually tossed over it.

Now, here in Venice, she had stepped out from the shadows of childhood and was loved by a real man. By a perfect man. An experienced man. A knock-your-socks-off gorgeous man.

You were so worth the wait, she thought, looking at him now.

They sat on the short wall across the small canal from the restaurant, and watched the gondolas float by, as they waited for it to open. Trattoria Sempione was his favorite haunt in Venice. It was the perfect place to celebrate.

Remi was skipping pennies across the water when Deidre turned to him.

"Why didn't you stay the night?" she asked, looking at the sparkling water.

"The nightmares."

"I haven't heard them since we got here. In fact, not many in Garmisch either."

"No. It's been good here."

It was a warm evening for late September. The gondoliers wore no jacket over their red and white striped T-shirts. The air smelled slightly of salty fish, algae, and traces of mold in the close interior of Venice. The ivy leaves were turning red, a few dropping into the canal, as they hugged the brick wall of the restaurant. Reluctantly, the lush greens of summer were surrendering to the coming fall.

"I did dream last night, though," Remi said.

"I never remember my dreams."

"Not a problem for me. I never forget mine. But this one was different. A new one. I was looking for sapphires on a table. The sun was bright and the gravel was wet, so everything sparkled." He paused for a moment, thinking. "Have you ever looked for raw sapphires?"

"No. Have you?"

"Yeah, when I was a kid, in Philipsburg, near my home in Anaconda."

"You were a cowboy," she said.

"Yeah, I told you, cattle, Black Angus."

She smiled. "That suits you. But tell me about the dream."

"Well, outside this small town called Philipsburg, population, oh, maybe six, seven hundred, they used to mine for silver. Dad and his partner had a claim, but they closed it down when the silver got harder to mine and the prices dropped. It was about then that the town discovered that many of those silver mines also had sapphires, so they switched to gemstones. Lots of shops in town made it a commercial enterprise, having tourists mine for sapphires."

"Like real sapphires? The real thing?"

"Yeah, they're real, but they're usually little bitty things. So the shops contract with the mining companies to sell them raw gravel. They bag up the gravel and sell the bags to tourists."

"Like you," she jabbed.

"We weren't tourists. We were neighbors, just forty miles up the road." He grinned, fending off the subtle dig. "Sometimes Dad would take me, Talon, and Carole to buy a bag of gravel. We'd each get our own bag. We'd try to guess which bag had the best sapphires before choosing one. Not that we had any way of knowing." He laughed. "They would wash the gravel in the rain barrel using a sieved box, and then they'd flip it over on a white tabletop. Sapphires are heavier than the stones, so when you invert the pile they land on top. For some reason I'll never understand, they also tend to be in the middle of the pile, not the edges." He shrugged. "We'd get tweezers and empty pill bottles and pick through the gravel."

"Shiny blue stones must have been pretty easy to spot."

"Sapphires in the raw aren't blue. Mostly they're clear, like quartz, or sometimes have a tinge of color, but never that deep blue you're used to."

"Really?"

"You have to heat treat them to bring out the color, and they come in all kinds of colors. Did you know rubies are just red sapphires?"

"No way. You're making that up."

"Blue is the most common color, but I've found yellow, green, and orange and once even a pink one."

"Any with a star on it?"

"Naw. These are Montana sapphires. We don't have any star sapphires that I know of. But let me finish the dream. Not that it's all that important…"

"No, finish it. Sorry. I get sidetracked."

"So I'm standing at the table looking at thousands of tiny stones all wet and sparkling in the sun. I'm young, just a little kid, but somehow as big as my father. He comes up and looks down at the stones that I've been staring at for five minutes and says, 'Wow, now there's a beauty. Bet it's a carat.' But I can't see it. 'Where?' I ask. 'In the center. You lucked out with that bag.' Then he walks away.

"So I'm looking at this square of wet stones, staring right at the center, but I can't see any sapphires at all. Then, all of a sudden, I see one, a little one in the center of the pile, lying right on top. And then another next to it, and another. Four altogether, just sitting there right next to one another, pretty as can be. Now how could I have been looking at that silly pile of washed stones and not seen the sapphires? I called out to Dad. Then—you know how dreams are." Deidre nodded as he continued, "I looked back and one of them had grown to this huge stone, like Dad said, a carat, probably a carat and a half. God, I was so excited. I mean, a point three is pretty exciting, but no one finds a one point five carat sapphire in Montana."

She smiled back at his beaming face. "So what does it mean?"

"I have absolutely no idea," Remi said, "but it was the best dream I've had in years."

He looked at his watch, then pulled her down from the wall. "Come on, they're opening now."

THE NEXT MORNING, she found Vittoria.

"How do women get birth control in Italy?"

Never one to mask what she was thinking, Vittoria grinned knowingly.

"What do you want, the pill? Or a diaphragm? Or, I don't how you say it in English—that thing the doctor puts in the womb—"

"IUD? Yes, that's what I want."

"Let me call a clinic. This is a Catholic country, but the women know how to keep from having babies. Come with me. Maybe we can go today."

She was relieved. She hoped it would be today, because, if she was very lucky, tonight might be a repeat of the last two nights. But she needed protection.

MORNINGS CONTINUED to be their favorite part of their day. Even after a long night of lovemaking, they found themselves awake, showered, and dressed before seven. The destination was the bar-café down from Roberto's shop.

The days were growing shorter and the mornings much cooler, but day after day the sun smiled down from a cloudless sky.

They sat at a table on the Riva looking at the *vaporetti* churning along carrying early morning passengers heading for work. The Grand Canal had no chance to grow calm with the many boats. One morning a large cruise ship had been tied to mammoth moorings, blocking the view for everyone. The locals celebrated the stop since it was well-known that tourists shop at the first stores they step into. And indeed, they had poured out of the giant ship by the hundreds, and Roberto had sold a month's worth of books in a day.

This morning, though, the ship had gone to another destination, and their view had returned.

"I have a confession," Remi said. "Operas and concerts are not my thing. I know I've been told they grow on you, but on me they grow like mold."

Deidre seemed unfazed. "Can you stomach it once a year?"

"I don't think so. And add the ballet to my list, while you're at it."

"Oh, now you're hitting where it hurts."

"I'll make a deal with you. If the Russian Ballet is in Venice or Paris and performing *Swan Lake*, I'll take you."

"And the chances of that are?"

"Nil. I looked."

She kicked at him under the table, but his reflexes were ready for her.

She sat back, a look of total contentment on her face. "I don't like American coffee, but cappuccino here in Italy is totally different. And this place has the best."

"I'll take your word for it." Remi continued to order *espresso corretto*. He'd take his coffee, though, any way he could get it. "The brioche are good here. I've had them all over Venice, but nothing compares to this café."

When they arrived at seven, every morning except Sunday, the brioche were just coming out of the oven. And everyday the same young woman cautioned them to watch their tongues. "Hot *marmellata*," she warned.

Deidre tried the chocolate croissants and the plain, but the apricot-filled were far and away her favorite. She always regretted the last bite, because it *was* the last bite.

"There's a shop near San Stefano I want to find today," Remi said as he finished his, too.

"What is it?"

"An artist who works with wood."

"Something special?" she asked, stretching her lovely arms over her head.

"Very." Remi resisted the urge to reach under her jacket and stroke her exposed stomach. "Let's go to the Rialto first for a picture I want to get. Then we'll head over to San Stefano."

They paid the bill and crossed the Arsenale bridge. She liked the way he had a map of Venice in his head. In the first days, she confessed, she could make neither heads nor tails of the city.

"That's all you need. Just learn the head and the tail," he said.

To help her, Remi had taken a map and pointed out the three bridges that crossed the Canal, as well as the train station and the bus depot at Piazza Roma. He showed her, too, the cluster of the three great churches, San Marco, San Giorgio, and the Salute.

"Venice is a big fish. See the head and tail. See the fin down here? This is the shortcut we took from the train station near the Ruskin House."

Now that she understood the basic structure of Venice he took her into the heart of the city to where the yellow signs with red arrows were painted high up on corners of buildings. They read "Rialto," "San Marco," "Statione," "Accademia," "Roma."

He pulled out the map again and showed her how the pieces fit together.

"So that's the trick," she said. "I was convinced you were a genius."

"No such luck. Mere mortal," he said with a grin.

Soon she was navigating like a local.

"Venice will be hard when I'm blind," she said one day. There was no bitterness, not even wistfulness in her voice. Just a statement of fact.

Remi didn't know what to say. She was right. No, she had understated it. Venice would be impossible.

They hopped onto the number one vaporetto. "You haven't had a nightmare for a long time," Deidre said.

"I don't get much opportunity. I have to sleep to have nightmares."

"Are you complaining?" She grinned.

"Do you hear me complaining?" Then he added, "Bear in mind I'm an old man, though, and could have a heart attack at any moment."

"Sounds like complaining to me."

He turned her head to face him and kissed her. "Not complaining."

The number one was a local and took on and dropped off passengers at every stop along the Grand Canal. They weren't in a hurry. They had found seats at the front outside deck, but the chill in the October morning prompted them to move to the back deck, also outside, where the sun reached them and the boat blocked the wind.

They got off at the Rialto and made their way to the top of the bridge. They hung over the wide stone edge and snapped pictures of the lazy morning traffic. They climbed down the far side of the bridge and headed up the Fondementa Del Vin to a narrow wooden pier lined with gondolas. The tourists were asleep and the *gondolieri* were having breakfast, leaving the gondolas bobbing at the pier, peaceful and empty.

Remi found what he was looking for. Some of the gondolas were worn, their seats frayed or even torn from use. Sometimes the paint was dull, or the bottoms needed cleaning. Others were pristine, like the one he spotted now. He leaned over and moved a gondolier's straw hat from one seat to another.

"What are you doing?" Deidre whispered looking around nervously.

"Arranging the picture."

"You'll get caught."

"I'll move it back when I'm done if that will make you happy. But really, he won't notice which chair the hat was tossed on."

The sun caught the blue brocade of the chair and hat perfectly. The gondola's black, gleaming side and gold ornamental angel sealed the setting. He took the close-up then changed the lens for a long shot to include the water and bridge. Deidre slipped under his arm to take the same picture. When they compared their pictures, they were interested to discover the slight variance in the way they saw the scene, each a little differently. Remi's pictures were always technically superior, but sometimes—not often, but sometimes—she liked hers better.

They replaced the hat, then headed toward San Stefano.

Remi hoped he could find the artist's shop again and that it was still in business.

They walked through the fish market that, thanks to Ernest Hemingway, was now a tourist destination. Not much had changed. The covered stalls with their fascinating array of fish, the stone floor slippery with water and fish parts, the strong smell brought from watery depths, the customers, the merchants, the homeless man capable of sleeping in the corner amid the activity—this was the famous Venice Fish Market.

They walked to the other market near the clock that turned counterclockwise, the one that sold fruit, vegetables, and sweets. In the small *campo,* they found the statue of the hunched gnome.

Deidre insisted on looking for it early on.

"According to the story, if a man was accused of a crime and was brought to trial by the court in San Marco, but, if there wasn't enough evidence to find him either guilty or innocent, he was given a chance. With a head start, he would race toward the statue. If he could reach it before his accusers overtook him, he would be safe, free, declared innocent. Otherwise, his fate was left in the hands of his accusers. It's like tag," she said in conclusion.

"The Medieval version of fun." Remi shuddered.

They stopped for a bag of late season raspberries and a wedge of coconut to chew as they meandered through the city.

"I think we pray to help ourselves, not to change God's mind," she said.

He was getting used to the way she would pick up an old conversation as if it hadn't been interrupted.

"What do you mean?"

"Do you really believe that if I ask God for something, I should be able to change His mind?"

"I don't believe in God, remember."

"Well, hypothetically, then. It doesn't make sense. God knows what He wants. He isn't fickle. I mean, we may not understand it, but I certainly hope God understands why things happen."

"You're assuming there is a purpose. I thought we'd agreed that God is staying out of things."

"Well, if He isn't. If things are predestined…"

"So much for the notion of the Absurd."

"No, I still believe that bad things happen to good people, but maybe there's an unknown purpose. But back to prayer. When we pray, a change can take place within ourselves."

"Such as?"

"I was thinking about the Lord's Prayer and the phrase, 'Thy will be done.' That's what we're supposed to pray for, the ability to accept the inevitable."

He thought about what she had said. Was that it? Was he unwilling to accept God's plan? But he didn't believe in predestination. He believed in free will. And life had taught him that, regardless of his best intentions, nothing was free about it, nothing was within his control. He was no more potent than a chunk of driftwood floating down a fast-moving river, getting knocked around on every rock and root in the water. He was racing to the end, to death, and how in the world did any of that make sense? Accept it? Hell, no? He'd fight with everything he had in him. Otherwise, what was the point of going on?

"Let me take your point to the extreme," Remi said. "If a guy is holding a knife to your throat, I should just let him because you're going to die anyway, someday, and it might be God's will that today is that day. So I should just accept it?"

"That doesn't particularly appeal to me. No, be a hero. So maybe we need to think about predestination versus free will, whether God is involved or else waiting it out on the sidelines."

"Or if He exists at all. To be continued," he said, turning a corner. "I think we're close. Yep, there it is."

He enjoyed talking with her. She made him dig a little deeper than he would have on his own. And he also loved the look on her face when she was amazed, like now.

Deidre looked at the store window. A cowboy's overcoat hung from a peg. A pair of boots, one leaning on the other, stood nearby. Both were pale brown bordering on yellow, like camel fur. Beyond the clothes, they could see household objects: a telephone, a pillow on a couch, a lamp, and a rug with fringed edges draped across a clothesline.

But it was the material that made the objects astonishing. They all were made from wood.

Deidre was thrilled. "Look at that hat. But it looks like felt. And the coat. It looks like soft pliable fabric that would be pliable in my hands. I *have* to touch it."

"Come inside. He's already open. You won't believe what he has."

They spent the next hour admiring the art pieces.

"What an incredible talent."

She could tell the cowboy hat was Remi's favorite, and one of hers, too. She planned to come back and buy it for him later, when he was off exploring somewhere. Perhaps she would save it for a wedding gift. She wanted to hug herself, or him. She was so happy.

ONE NIGHT, THEY persuaded Vittoria and Roberto to come to Sempione with them. Their friends resisted at first. Apparently, every Venetian knew something about every other Venetian.

"How many people live in Venice?"

"About fifty thousand."

There was some history generations ago—no one could remember what—that left a bad taste in the mouths of Vittoria and the family regarding the family who now, or once owned Trattoria Sempioni. Still, who could resist the joint forces of Deidre and Remi for two weeks?

They reserved the window seats overlooking the canal.

It was a wonderfully warm October night that felt more like early September. The long days of September, however, had surrendered to the long nights of fall. The last rays of the day caught the golden peaks across the top of the basilica as they walked through the Piazza of San Marco.

"How is it in Italian? Does night fall, or does darkness fall?" Deidre asked.

303

"*Si,* it is the same," Roberto answered.

"Because it really doesn't," Deidre continued.

Vittoria laughed. "So what does it do, go up?"

"Exactly," Deidre said. "Night rises. Look." She stopped in front of the great church. "Watch the sun. No, watch the shadows, the darkness. It climbs up the basilica. The darkness rises up; it doesn't fall down. Night doesn't fall; it climbs up."

They stood for a moment watching as the basilica proved her point.

"And in the morning, you're saying," concluded Remi thoughtfully, "that as the sun rises, the light actually falls."

"Well, doesn't it? Think about the bell tower. The angel on the steeple gets lit first, then the sun works its way down to the roof, then down the walls to the ground. The morning light falls."

"You are one screwy girl." Remi grinned.

"Who thinks of things like that?" Vittoria asked.

"Americans. They have no respect for tradition," Roberto said. "Even if you are right, for myself, I like my mornings to rise and my darkness to fall."

The talk was lighthearted and fun. She certainly kept them on their toes.

Most evenings Deidre wore her patch for an hour before sundown, so in the darkness of evening she retained some vision with that eye, at least straight on. She couldn't be happier with the invention.

They walked under the clock tower to the end of the street past Cartier, and turned with the crowd. Remi led the way. Instead of making the second left, to the *calle* lined with bright shop windows and meandering tourists, he took the first. Here, behind the Hotel Splendid Suisse the alley was narrow and vaguely smelled of urine. It was well lit, however, and swept clean. "But mostly it's free of tourists," he explained.

"*Complimenti,* Remi," Vittoria said. "You know the back ways of Venezia now."

The alley came out at the little canal, and following it they crossed in front of the Hotel Splendid Suisse. In front of them, leaning on the wrought iron railing over the small canal, the proprietor of Sempioni enjoyed the last remnants of summer. Luigi recognized Remi and Deidre at once and greeted them with kisses, followed by handshakes for the newcomers. Apparently restaurateurs couldn't afford to remember the history of past generations, Deidre thought, or else he hadn't heard about the feud.

Luigi ushered them into his restaurant. As he led them to their table, he called out to no one in particular, "*Prosecci,*" as he snapped his fingers over his head, calling for the glasses of wine.

I love the drama of the Italians. Deidre smiled openly.

It was early in the evening. Just one other table was occupied.

Still warm enough to keep the windows open, each table was pushed out a few feet onto a private balcony. The gentlemen seated the ladies so they would have the best view of the canal. The Italian champagne arrived as the last seat was tucked in, and everyone toasted "*Salute!*" to one another.

Deidre gazed out across the water to the wall where they had sat on the evening of the day he had proposed. She sighed contentedly. Since childhood, she had imagined honeymooning in Paris, probably thanks to her grandmother's influence. But now, Venice seemed like the better place. It wouldn't, couldn't, be as good once her sight was lost, but…

Suddenly, it occurred to her that she was having her honeymoon before the wedding. Right now, while she could see. Remi was providing her with another extraordinary gift. And next week there would be Paris, too. He was making it all happen before her eyes, before her seeing eyes!

It seemed his love and consideration for her just kept growing. How could she bear so much happiness? Looking over at him tonight, laughing with Roberto and Vittoria, relaxed, happy, hers—her heart just ached with love.

They ordered everything: an *antipasto* (appetizer), a *primo* (pasta), a *secundo* (meat), a *contorne* (side dish of vegetables and salad), and, of course, a *dolce* (dessert). And finally, a *digestivo*, a digestive, to help all that food work its way through the body. As promised, Remi had introduced her to a non-bitter *digestivo* their first day in Venice, the incredible *scropino*. At the table, their waiter, Rinardo, whipped the lemon ice in a bowl with the Prosecco and vodka to the perfect consistency, then poured the drink into narrow flutes. Like everything else this evening, the service was impeccable.

The group was merry. Remi was the epitome of charm. Deidre could see even sensible Vittoria being drawn into his web. She liked seeing him so at ease and sociable. This was a new and surprising side of him, and she was eager to learn all the sides. He wasn't a cube, like the men she had dated in the past. He was a disco ball, a complex multi-sided, three-dimensional sphere. Every day would be a new adventure on her way to knowing him.

The gondolas had been floating by all evening. Often the gondolier, at eye level with the diners, would call out a greeting, particularly to the lovely ladies, and they, of course, would reply. Toward the end of the meal, one man stopped his gondola to flirt with the women. It didn't matter that their men were seated next to them. The women were at the window, and so was he. In Italy, flirting was a sport that needed to be perfected at every opportunity.

Soon, the gondolier caught the eye of Luigi and a moment later the proprietor handed him a glass of wine. The gondolier accepted with a flourish and continued talking to the happy group. After a while, Deidre stood up and looked over the ledge. There, below them, sat a boat full of passengers.

"Aren't they paying you?" she asked, sitting back down.

"They are," he said with a smile. Then dropping to a loud whisper, he continued, "but they are Spaniards, and rude, and they don't speak English. They can wait while I drink my wine."

Finally, he placed the empty wine glass on the wide sill and said, "I regret I must go."

They called a farewell as the gondolier and the stranded Spaniards headed for San Marco.

Vittoria was more reserved than the Americans. *Gondolieri* had reputations for being, "How do I say it? Loose in the pants?" she reported.

Remi challenged her. "So how many times have you been accosted in a gondola, Vitti?"

It was then that she admitted that though she was a lifetime Venetian, she had never actually been in a gondola, except on her wedding day.

"It is mostly for tourists," she said.

"You sound just like Remi when you say that word." Deidre laughed.

"The tourists keep us alive. But it is the end of the season now, and all of us in Venice are tired and wish they would just go away."

"Us, too?" Deidre asked, pretending to be dismayed.

"You are friends, family. You are not tourists." She waved away the silliness of the notion.

As if on cue, Roberto's cell phone rang. He answered and spoke in Italian while Vittoria listened and translated.

"My brother. He is back from Milano. He is unpacking the car at Tronchetto and his friends aren't coming." She listened some more. "He wants Roberto to come help."

"I'll go, too," Remi said.

"We can all go," Deidre added.

Remi looked at Roberto as he put the phone away. "Can you and I manage it, do you think?"

"*Si, si*. He only had two friends to help before. With you and me, that is all he needs."

Turning to Deidre, Remi said, "Stay and talk with Vittoria. Or go promenading." He smiled. "We'll meet you back at the apartment. You'll probably get there before we do."

"Don't expect them before midnight," Vittoria said.

"Midnight?" How long could this take? Deidre wondered.

"We have to go back to the apartment to get Roberto's boat, then go to Tronchetto. We won't get there for an hour, then another to load it, and half an hour back," Roberto explained.

"Or more," Remi's practical side added.

"It's how we do things in Venezia. Even when we work fast, nothing is fast." Roberto pushed his chair to leave.

"But for you two ladies," Remi said, handing his credit card to the waiter without looking at the bill, "you will enjoy the rest of the evening for us." He kissed Deidre, and said, "I'll see you at home, honey." And they were gone.

Once the men had left, Vittoria suggested they walk through the city. The crowds were thinning, with most tourists either in restaurants or hotels. Arms linked, they strolled to the far end of San Marco's *piazza*. Deidre had put on her patch during dinner, so she had some night vision.

"There used to be a canal here," Vittoria explained.

"Under the pavement?"

"Yes. There are paintings. There was an orchard, here, too, owned by the nuns."

Deidre wondered what it must be like to live in a city so old its history was known from paintings.

They continued past the Moise church and turned down a small *calle*. In front of them, a large sign read, "Hemmingway's Bar."

"Would you like a Bellini?" Vittoria invited.

As they entered the crowded room, a young man greeted them and found them seats in the next room. He made no mention of the patched eye. Deidre looked around and wondered if this was the real thing, or just another tourist trap. When the waiter brought their drinks, she asked.

"Oh, yes, Hemmingway was a regular here, and since he was famous and brought us much business, the name was changed in his honor."

"It continues to bring in business," Vittoria muttered.

"Were there many Americans who spent time in Venice?" Deidre asked her friend. It occurred to her that she knew little about ex-patriots who had lived in the city.

"Ezra Pound is buried in the cemetery at St. Michaels. George Eliot spent her honeymoon in Venice, and Hemingway wrote a book while here. The Brownings, Elizabeth and Robert, spent many years here, but, of course, they were British."

"I saw the Ruskin House."

"Yes, there is that." Vittoria thought for a moment. "Cole Porter lived nearby for a while. And Woody Allen almost bought a haunted *palazzo* on the *Grand Canale*."

"He did? Oh, I'd like to see it!" Deidre said.

"Finish your drink and we'll go."

Soon they were on a *vaporetto* gliding up the canal, the wind picking up the cool water and dampening their faces as they huddled at the rail.

"There," Vittoria said, pointing. "The pink one with the circles. It is called the *Palazzo Dario*."

It was a small, pale pink, four-story structure with decorative marble circles.

"They say that everyone who has ever owned it has experienced a tragedy of some kind."

"Fact or fiction?" Deidre asked.

"Who gets through life without a tragedy?" Vittoria asked philosophically.

A small shudder passed through Deidre. *Who indeed?*

"The first suicide was the daughter of the Venetian Senator who had the *palazzo* built. Since then, there have been suicides or murders or bankruptcies of every owner in the past five hundred years. Venetians won't buy it. Even the Guggenheim refused to take it."

"Amazing," was all Deidre could think to say as the palace disappeared behind them.

The women caught a *vaporetto* heading in the opposite direction toward home. Soon, they were linking arms and strolling back in a euphoric fog of too much wine. Their conversation was light and laced with laughter.

At the door to the courtyard, they hugged their goodnights and made plans for the morrow.

In happiness, Deidre twirled around in the courtyard and hugged herself. *I could live here. Yes, Venice could be home. I just have to keep my sight.*

CASSIE HAD BEEN Deidre's best friend for so long she had forgotten what friendships with other women felt like. But Vittoria was easy to be with, easy to talk to. They were different in background, family dynamics, country, and culture, yet they shared the same values and outlook on life. Vittoria was older and her life experience helped with wise decisions. Deidre looked up to her and soon thought of her as the older sister or the younger aunt she never had.

"I love Remi," she confided one day. "I know we will be happy. But sometimes I wonder about his need to be alone so much."

Vittoria was surprised by all parts of that statement. "So it is serious with the two of you?"

A strange feeling came over Deidre, a warning. Vittoria knew a different side of Remi, more about his past. Cautiously, she asked, "Has he come here with other women?"

As soon as she'd asked, she wished she hadn't. She didn't want to look behind the curtain, didn't want to look at his call list. But here she was, at it again.

Vittoria hesitated. "There are two Remis that I know: the one before the war and the one now. The one before, that Remi liked women. He didn't travel with them like he is doing with you, but they sometimes spent a week or more with him. After the war, he has been always alone. You are the first one he has brought to meet us. So I don't know why I am surprised that he is serious about you. He just didn't say so with words, I guess."

"We're getting married, actually."

Vittoria grabbed her hand, looking for the missing ring.

Deidre laughed a little nervously. "I imagine we'll buy it together. Probably in Paris."

"Is that where you will go next?" she asked.

"Yes. Tomorrow. He said he wants me to buy my wedding gown there."

Vittoria stepped back and held her at a distance, digesting the announcement. "I did not expect to hear that. But I am very happy for you both." She hugged her with sincerity.

"That is why I worry about how solitary he has been, and if he will need more space than I want to give him. You have known him

311

for a long time. What do you think, Vittoria? Will I be too needy for him?" She didn't add anything about the sightless future that would add a significant dimension to her need.

The Italian woman thought carefully before answering. "You do not seem needy to me. You are independent enough, I think. Remi knows you. We have just met. If he tells you he wants to spend the rest of his life with you, he must know himself, and know you well enough that it will be all right. And if not, both of you can change a little for the other."

The answer made Deidre uneasy, since her biggest fear—after having to learn to live a different life—was losing her independence and having to rely on a man who himself was so very independent. But Vittoria was right. He knew the honest situation, and was going in unafraid. That would be enough. She believed in him. He had told her not to overthink things, and to see with her heart. Why would she want to spoil this happy time with needless doubts?

CHAPTER 22

PARIS

THE NEXT MORNING, a water taxi waited in a back canal near San Pietro to take them directly to the Venice airport. From there, they boarded an Air France flight to De Gaulle Airport. Remi hailed a cab, and by evening they were enjoying champagne at the Ritz in the heart of Paris.

Deidre had half decided not to go through with it. "I need my mother, my bridesmaids. There's a whole tradition that comes with picking a bridal gown."

Remi just listened. If nothing else, he had learned patience in the past few months. He waited for her to argue it front to back and back to front with a sideways argument in between. Eventually she talked herself out of, then back into, the idea.

"It's all about time, isn't it? I don't have any," she concluded.

And we're running out of it, Remi thought to himself.

"If you decide you don't like it, or your mother or bridesmaids don't like it, go buy another one. You don't have to get married in it." He had come to appreciate the excesses enjoyed by the Sinclair family. Not his values, but he recognized theirs.

"But wouldn't that be wasteful?"

He smiled gently. "Yes, but if it makes you happy… You're only getting married once."

Surprised, he caught her as she threw herself into his arms.

"Yes, I am," she said, kissing him fiercely.

THEY ACTUALLY WENT to two bridal salons. The first was too haute couture.

"Let's go somewhere else. I feel like Vivian shopping on Rodeo Drive," she whispered, *Pretty Woman* fresh in her mind. She had popped in the movie when she was home in August. Since the driving lesson in the desert, she had wondered, what in the world was a Lotus Esprit?

They left without waiting for the designer to return with the dresses.

"Thank you," Remi said as they stepped outside, his relief almost palpable. "I felt completely like a fish out of water."

The second salon was better, much better. The staff was down to earth, excited for her, helpful, and made the day fun. Three of them ran in and out with dresses at Jeanne's command.

"When is the wedding?" she asked in perfect English.

"We haven't even started planning it. I just got engaged in Venice a couple of weeks ago."

"Venice. Ooh la la, the honeymoon first. Very modern." She smiled. "You look like a modern girl." She studied the mermaid-style dress Deidre was wearing. "But this one is not for you. Do you agree?"

Deidre looked at herself in the mirror. "No, not this one. You're right."

Jeanne said something in French to the waiting attendant as another entered with a lovely armful of chiffon. Jeanne helped her out of the serpentine dress and into the princess gown. "He is very handsome, your fiancé," she said, nodding approvingly.

"I think so," Deidre said gaily.

The princess style was too young-looking. Yes, she was young, but she needed to appear older to match Remi.

"Let me show him this one, to see what he thinks," she said. He had told her not to leave him waiting in the salon too long. He wanted to see the various dresses, too, she thought. He was a part of it, after all.

"You are not afraid of that old custom of keeping the dress from the groom until the wedding, then," Jeanne said with approval. "Yes, very modern." She helped Deidre step down from the low pedestal in the dressing room.

Remi amended his original intent and began shooting her as she modeled various dresses. He caught her making faces, lifting a hem to look at a shoe, swirling around to see how the skirt flowed, shaking her head, grinning, frowning.

It was all there, documented for her, even if this was the only memory she would have of choosing her bridal gown.

He wondered if she would show—

He felt a turning in his stomach, a twinge of jealousy he had no right to feel. He wasn't going to let his mind go there.

He'd been looking at her through the lens, but he lowered the camera and saw her as the woman he had made love to just last night. She would make a lovely bride, a spectacular bride.

Without any warning, the words just came out. "That one."

Deidre looked up. "This one? You like it?"

"Yeah, I do."

She looked in the mirror again. It was simple, but elegant. It had a sleeveless bodice that swirled with seed pearls and crystal lace. The silk and satin skirt was layered and gently overlapped at irregular lengths, like the delicate petals of an inverted rosebud just opening to catch the morning sun. She straightened her bodice and smoothed the skirt. Then she turned to catch his eye in the mirror.

He should have been taking pictures, but he couldn't take his eyes off her.

"I like it, too. Do you think this is the one?"

"I can't imagine anything more beautiful."

The smile glowed through her skin.

"Are you talking about the dress?" she asked coquettishly.

"The whole package," he said with a strange intensity.

"Then this is the one. It doesn't even need any altering."

"Then let's take it with us and find wonderful places in Paris to wear it."

She wanted to be practical. It might get dirty, but the thought of dancing through Paris in her wedding gown—why it was almost like seeing herself on her honeymoon. Paris. They would continue their honeymoon here, as she had always dreamed.

Remi produced her father's credit card. "I don't even want to know the price."

He didn't, she thought. Five figures. He would simply blow a gasket if he knew.

To the shock of the staff, she didn't take the gown off. They just left the salon with her clothes stuffed in his backpack and headed straight for the Louvre.

That night, they poured over the photos he had taken. Deidre wanted them all. Remi's professional eye deleted a few obvious misses. He sorted the rest into A and B categories, the A file being substantially smaller. He then sent all the pictures to Deidre's laptop, but according to category. As she looked through them, she agreed with most of his assessment. The A folder was much better.

Deidre dreaded telling her mother anything about the engagement, the honeymoon, the wedding gown, and certainly not Remi's skill as a lover! But she shared all these things with Cassie on the phone, in pictures, and through Skype. Cassie was the only one who knew everything, and was an excited echo to Deidre's euphoria.

The last two weeks in Paris were the happiest of her life. Not even the daily rain could dampen her joy. They explored the Louvre and climbed the Eiffel Tower. They walked through Rodin's studio and garden and left flowers at the memorial for Princess Diana. They feasted and frolicked and laughed their way through a dozen restaurants, bistros, and cafés reserving just enough energy to fill their nights with passionate love. He left her breathless.

She was writing at her desk when Remi knocked. Although he had a key, he insisted on knocking. He hadn't had a nightmare in weeks, but he wanted his own room across the hall to spend the quiet time he still felt he needed. The nights, he spent with her.

He had showered and shaved and was wearing a fresh shirt. His blazer hung over his arm. He looked fabulous, she thought.

"Going somewhere?"

"Well, I thought if there was a lovely lady around I might invite her for a stroll along the Champs-Elysees. Or a ride down the Seine? They light up the Eiffel Tower at night. Or we could find a restaurant in the Latin Quarter with decadent desserts? Anything sound tempting?"

"All of the above?"

Remi laughed. "We have a week left in Paris. Shouldn't we spread it out a bit?"

"Well, it has mostly rained since we've been here. But it stopped tonight. Shouldn't we live in the moment while we can?" she said with just a trace of wickedness.

"Throwing it back at me, are you?"

Deidre nodded with a smile. "I've been a very good student."

"Yes, you have," he said, bending down to kiss her. "And as a reward, you get me in your bed tonight."

"Accepted. But, the choices? I only get one?"

"You only get one."

"The Seine, then."

"The river?" he asked, patting his stomach. "I thought you'd go for the dessert. Okay, but I recant. We'll eat, too. Wear something warm. I'll meet you downstairs by the concierge." And he left.

Deidre wondered when this incredible happiness would end. How had she managed it, to make this larger than life man fall in love with her? It would end someday, of course, or diminish. Epic love and happiness couldn't go on forever. But maybe it could. It felt like a fairy tale, and though they all ended with "happily ever after," evil witches and poisoned apples sometimes got in the mix. Maybe things would change once she lost her sight. She was so glad Remi knew about that and loved her anyway. Or maybe, by some miracle she wouldn't lose any more. The progression had seemed to stall. How long had it been? Since the white church, when she had sent up a silent prayer. Could a miracle really be hers? For over five weeks, her vision had changed hardly at all. For four glorious weeks, she had floated in perfect bliss. If only there was some way to keep time from moving forward. If only it could stay this way forever.

Maybe a Christmas wedding at home. Could she hold on to her sight for just two more months?

DEIDRE DIDN'T HAVE her patch. She needed a couple of hours with it on before it served its purpose, and Remi's sweet surprise had left no time for it.

He had his arm around her as they sat in the boat. The Seine was ablaze with the lights from the city. The ancient river seemed full of dark secrets, secrets so deep that even the river itself had forgotten them. Yet floating on the surface were shards of broken color, each sparkling, dancing, whirling with hope and promise. If only she could scoop out a handful of color and press it to her heart, she thought dreamily. Then nothing bad could ever happen to her.

"Hmm," breathed Deidre.

"You're purring," he said.

"I'm a cat," she said. "Didn't you know?"

"A cat. Independent. Hmm, no, you like being held too much to be a cat."

"A ragdoll cat, then. They're extra cuddly."

"What am I?"

"A dog."

"A golden retriever?"

"No, they're too nice."

"Thanks."

"A German shepherd. No, border collie."

"Why a border collie. You like my long hair?"

"No, because they're smart, and they know what to do, and they have lots of energy. And I like your hair, too."

"Border collie. Okay. Not a bad choice."

They enjoyed the silence of the water. Tourist season was over, and the boat was mostly enjoyed by lovers with passion to warm them in the autumn air.

Deidre stroked his scarf.

"Cashmere," she said.

"Yes. I bought it in a shop yesterday. Do you like it?"

"My favorite. This one was expensive."

"Like everything in Paris."

"No. The quality of this one is especially fine."

"Isn't cashmere the definition of fine quality?" he teased, bending to kiss her.

"Not all. Imitators, you know. Do you know where it's from?"

"The shop? I could find it again."

"No, cashmere."

"The wool? A goat, I think."

"Yes, a goat from Kashmir. It's the fur under its chin."

He hugged her closer. "Goat chin fur, huh? 'Cashmere' is a better marketing term."

"Do you know what is warmer than cashmere, and softer?"

"Me," he said, hugging her closer.

"Besides you," she said, snuggling tight.

"Warmer than cashmere. You're going to tell me elephant ear hair."

She laughed. "No, silly. Qiviut."

"Qiviut, of course. How stupid of me to forget. And where, pray tell, does qiviut come from?"

"The muskox."

"Yes, the muskox. I remember seeing qiviut the last time I was grooming my muskox."

She tried to punch him, but he held her too close.

"You're always trying to bruise me," he complained with a grin.

Ignoring him, Deidre continued, "If you brush the under wool and gather it, you can spin it into qiviut yarn. And from that, you can knit it into a hat or scarf, or something."

"I knew that."

"I wonder if blind people can knit. Probably not."

He was silent for a moment, then quietly said, "Don't rule it out. I'll bet dollars to donuts you'll do anything you set your mind to."

She wished she hadn't brought up the blindness. It was such a downer.

"How much can you see?" Remi was in the habit of asking. It helped him gauge their activities.

"The same as Venice. Night vision isn't there if I forget the patch, but straight ahead daytime sight is good."

"So as we sit here in the dark looking out at the city—?"

"I can't see anything."

He paused. "Well, that was pretty thoughtless of me," he said quietly.

"Not at all, honey." She thought she'd risk the endearment. He seemed okay with it. "I think this is perfectly lovely. I can hear the boats, and feel the spray on my face, and feel the boat rock. I am in Paris sailing down the Seine! What is thoughtless about that?"

He squeezed her shoulder, and she sensed his contentment.

"When I'm totally blind, there will be lots of things I won't be able to do, but that doesn't mean the world stops for everyone else. We'll just figure out a way to include me when we can, that's all."

"I can see the Eiffel Tower. Can you see any of it?"

She squinted her eyes. "Not yet."

"Okay, we'll get closer. It will look like a narrow triangle of white lights."

She studied the direction where his arm was pointing. Still blackness.

Her mind saw it, though, strong and bold, all metal and modern. She was pleased how well the photos of their visit there had turned out. They were among her favorite. It had gotten foggy that day so the tower was blurred, but she was in the foreground spinning around, her hair flowing out from her head. So many of her favorite memories were in the fog. Was there something symbolic about that, she wondered?

"I see it! Right there. It's faint and blurry, but I see the triangle of light. I can see it!" She turned to hug him, his warm arm holding her against the heat of his chest. She turned quickly back. "Where is it?"

Putting her chin on his bicep, she looked down the length of his arm.

"Now I feel like a Labrador pointing out a pheasant." Remi chuckled, continuing to hold his arm out. "It's getting bigger, we're getting closer."

Yes, she saw it.

It grew until they passed it. They watched until it was too small for her to see anymore, and only then she settled back into the crook of his arm, feeling his body heat warm them both.

"So our Grand Tour ends in a week," she said. "Then what are we going to do?"

They had yet to make a single plan for the wedding. She wasn't in a hurry. She didn't want this happiness to pass too quickly. What had Remi said in Cinque Terre? Enjoy today because you don't know what tomorrow will bring. Enjoy the moment. A good lesson to learn, she thought.

"Are you going to go back to college?" he asked.

That surprised her, but of course he would want to know. How else could they plan where to live at first?

"What do you think?"

He considered the question. "Your major is fashion design. Still going to finish that?"

"No. That would be foolish. I thought I might try creative writing."

"That has some merit." He continued thinking. "Maybe attend some kind of school for—to see what your limitations might be. Talk to a counselor to find out if there is anything else that is practical for… you know."

She did know. For being blind. He could listen to her talk about it, but he had a hard time articulating that blindness was her fate. Maybe he believed, like she did, that by some miracle she wouldn't really be totally blind.

"We could do that," she agreed.

"I think I'm going home to Montana for a while," Remi continued.

Deidre sat very still.

"For very long?"

"I don't know. I have some things to settle with my sister."

Deidre relaxed. A short visit to get ready for their new life.

"Then I thought I'd head south somewhere. South America, Africa. The weather should be nice enough. I've noticed the cold isn't good for my leg."

"But—" She caught herself. "When will you be back?" Her heart swelled and pounded in an empty cavern as her stomach fell away. She felt a sudden flood of heat, and her head buzzed in dizziness.

"Don't know. I thought about Europe in the spring and summer again. Depends on the leg, I guess."

First person, singular. *He's leaving me! And so casually*!

The assault to her brain traveled down through her body at the speed of sound, the speed of his words. His cavalier tone struck her viscerally, each blow fiercer than the last. His voice was only slightly louder than the booming of the blood surging through her chest and head. She forced herself to keep breathing evenly. She stepped out of the pain, hovering above herself. Her former self, the woman she had been two minutes ago, sat curled in his arms.

He must have felt her muscles tensing because he readjusted his hold on her.

She had to pretend she expected it, his going on with his life without her. But that would require something superhuman.

Talk. Talk about something, anything!

"How *is* your leg? You don't seem to be limping much at all, and I looked at the scar last night. It's healing really nicely."

She felt caged, trapped on this boat, caught in his grasp. A fly in a web. How could she get away? How would she get through this?

I want to die. Right now, all I want is to die, to disappear, to not exist.

She couldn't live through this pain; it wasn't possible.

They had made love last night, and the night before that, and the night before that. In fact, every night since that first night, they had made tender or passionate love. Two, three, even four times a night—though sometimes it was in the day—they made love. Their bodies seemed insatiable. Remi stayed until dawn, and the nightmares stayed somewhere else. They were happy. They were going to get married; only now he was going away.

When had he decided to leave her? What was his plan? At the altar? Or had he never intended to make it to the altar at all? That's what it sounded like. He didn't—hadn't—made any plans to marry her. It sounded too casual, like it was all part of a different plan. Why would he do this to her, lead her on? For sport? It didn't make sense. Nothing was making sense!

"—you know I'm going to miss you," he was saying.

He continued talking softly, caressing her cheek and hair with his fingertips, her soul with his words, but she had transformed into a lovely statue, unreachable.

I'm not going to miss you. I'm going to curse your name every minute of every day for the rest of my life, you two-faced cad. I hate you. I hate you!

* * * * *

HER WORLD, AND everything she knew and believed and hoped for, lay shattered at her feet. Over and over in the background of her brain, the backdrop for all her other thoughts, she recited, "Humpty Dumpty sat on a wall. Humpty Dumpty had a great fall. All the King's horses and all the King's men, couldn't put Humpty together again."

The pain was too intense. The only thing that made sense was escape. Escape from the pain. Escape from Remi Lamont. Escape from Paris. She needed a plan. A plan was movement. A plan meant changing the scenario, changing the moment, changing the outcome, if one was lucky. She had learned that from her father. This outcome wouldn't change, but the moment, the pain—that might change.

She pulled the covers up tighter to her chin. Hours had passed and still she couldn't sleep. It must still be night. Did Remi close the drapes when he was here last? No, she remembered the morning sun hitting her mirror yesterday and bouncing back to wake her. And she had turned him away last night, so he hadn't touched the drapes since then. She never pulled them. What was the point of requesting an east-facing room if you didn't let the sun wake you? The maid, then. But why would the maid pull the drapes in the middle of the day? What time was it, anyway? She rolled over to look at the clock. Where was it? Who had moved the clock? Perhaps the face was turned away. She began feeling the nightstand, knocking over the clock and discovering the lamp in the same motion. Irritated, she snapped on the lamp. What the heck! The bulb was burned out. She threw off the covers, her irritation cutting through the pain in her heart. She'd open the drapes, but what an inconvenience. The Ritz, of all places, ought to know better.

As she sat up and swung her legs out of bed, a pinprick of light from the direction of the window cut across her field of vision. She didn't move. The shiver that traveled down her spine wasn't just from the cold. She felt her way to the window and pulled apart the flimsy sheers. The heavier ones were where she had left them. She peered out, looking for the city lights, but again, all she saw was a useless point of light in front of her, like she was looking at a tiny penlight in a dark room.

"Oh, my God," she breathed. "It is really happening."

Maybe it was only night and she couldn't see the city lights. She felt her way around the bed and turned on the lamp on the other nightstand. It, too, was dark, but this time she put her hand on the bulb and felt it grow warm, then hot.

She stared at it. It was on, she knew, and the pinprick of light that she saw pierced her hope.

The cold fingers of reality strangled her. Her chest contracted, squeezing air out of her lungs. Chills covered her skin. Her heart raced in fear. She wrapped her arms around her body to hug her sides, but then put them out again to feel her way back to the bed. Pulling the covers around her was a small comfort, a cocoon of temporary safety where she might recover from the shock.

She knew it was coming, but she had never truly accepted it. She had been so victorious in keeping the disease from stealing all her vision. For weeks, her eyes had seemed to abort their steady campaign toward blindness. The advance had stalled. Nothing changed for a month. Through sheer willpower, she imagined, she had defeated this insidious enemy. But now, in just a blink, when her attention was diverted elsewhere, when her defenses had slackened, it ambushed her. And defeated her. The truth of it immobilized her. She would never emerge from this bed again. She would lie here until someone found her paralyzed body, rigid in the cold grip of death.

She didn't know how long she lay shaking in the bed. She didn't sleep. Her mind was too agitated for rest. She heard the maid tap on the door, but sent her away. She heard Remi's firmer knock, but remained silent. She felt relief when she heard him draw back, his keycard unused.

She had to leave. She could not face him. Not now, not ever. She had to reach her father. He would come and take her home. But Remi might come back. She needed another room, maybe another hotel? No, not another hotel. How would she find one? Just another floor then, a safe place to hide until her father came to get her.

Her father. She had to reach him. She felt her way to the desk where she had tossed her purse last night. She felt for the smartphone and pulled it out in relief. Her fingers swept across the smooth, unbroken screen.

Oh my God! How could she find the phone app? How would she dial? Oh my God! Oh my God! She screamed silently, her hand across her mouth to stifle the sound that was sure to burst out. She held the back of the chair for support.

"Calm down. You can do this. Find the hotel phone. It's here on the desk. Someplace. It has to be here. One step at a time. You can figure out the push buttons. Just start with getting an outside line," she rehearsed. "Okay, it's probably nine. If that doesn't work zero will get the front desk."

The phone was where it should have been. The keypad was raised but there were twelve pads to depress, and other buttons, too. She tried to visualize the formation. Top row: one-two-three. Second row: four-five-six. Third row: seven-eight-nine. Where was the zero in the fourth row? The center, yes, she was sure it was the center button, fourth row.

She took a deep breath. She felt as if she had just reached the top of a steep mountain. *Now make the call.* Outside line, international code, Dad's cell—

Another blanket of terror engulfed her. What was his phone number? She had never memorized it. Why bother, when all she had to do was touch his name on the phone?

She started to weep in utter defeat when the unused phone in her hand switched from a humming dial tone to an incessant beep. She hung it up quickly, missing the cradle on the first try. She wanted to scream. Yes, scream! But Remi might hear and come. No. NO! Never Remi. Never again would he rescue her. She'd find a way to get away from him.

Think. Think. Cassie. No, she didn't know Cassie's number

either. What did she know? Only her own numbers, both cell and home. Home! Yes, she knew her home number. Someone would find Daddy.

She slowly, painfully worked out the number. It took eight tries but she finally heard a series of clicks followed by her mother's voice. It had never sounded so sweet.

"Mother, I have to talk to Daddy. It's an emergency!"

REMI COULDN'T figure out where Deidre had gone. She always left word where she was going and when she'd be back. Perhaps she wasn't feeling well. Sometimes, he noticed, she had cramps and would beg off the day's outing. That would explain the disinterest in sex last night. She had grown quiet on the river ride and declined dinner, saying she was tired. It was the first night they hadn't slept together in a month, and he missed her. He didn't want to wake her, though, if she was sleeping. She had said sleep was the best cure for cramps. He left word at the desk, that he was out for the morning, taking pictures.

It was a glorious autumn day. As he walked the Paris streets, he felt weightless, like he could simply float. Last night after she had left, his arms felt empty. They were empty now without her. He realized that she was inside him, a part of him. She had been since that first night they made love, or was it the day she told him about her blindness and he'd comforted her as she cried? No, before that even, before the polar bear attack. He must have fallen in love with her when he saw the expression on her face the day she called Jerry. That look of relief and gratitude and something else. Something that looked like love. She had loved him. He had missed it then, but recognized it now. That look on her face after the call, that was when he started to let her in.

So what was he going to do about it?

It had taken most of the night, but he had made a decision. To hell with their age difference. To hell with his empty bank account. To hell with his nightmares. He'd faced worse odds before. He'd overcome tougher obstacles in his life, in his career. What happened to that Marine? When did he become such a wuss? No more. He'd show his hand, and if he lost, well, at least he wouldn't be "that cold and timid soul who never tried," or however the quote went.

For the past month and a half, two months, he'd been happy. God, he never thought it possible. He was actually happy. That blue sky he was always looking for—it was there day and night. He hadn't even noticed when it arrived. It was just there one day. He had finally come home from the war, home to her. The very thought of that, coming home to Deidre, filled him with so much joy he might have choked if he had to speak.

He wouldn't give up photography. No. He'd take her with him. Maybe she wouldn't be able to see, but he could describe the scenes to her, making them more real for him, too. She would be in on all of it. He would keep her safe. The thought of having her at his side for the next forty or fifty years was a drug as potent as a hit of cocaine. He'd never gotten hooked on that stuff, but he wanted very much to get hooked on her.

Everything about Paris looked incredible this morning. The early morning rain had cleaned the city of dust, and cleaned his mind of doubts.

Last night, when they had begun talking about what would happen after the Grand Tour and he considered South America, Africa, Europe—it just sounded so empty all of a sudden. Without her in his arms, pressed against him, he realized he'd missed her like he'd never missed anything in his life—not his parents when they died, not Talon after he died, not even his brothers in arms. He'd known Deidre five months, but already she was a necessary part of him.

Wasn't he good enough, after all, to make her happy? She seemed happy—no, she *was* happy. He was making her happy. And just as important, he knew her. He knew what made her tick. He knew how scared she was about the blindness. God, she had cried in his arms. What other man could ever share that moment with her? No one. Who took her on her Grand Tour? Who saved her from a polar bear attack? He did. Who helped her pick out her wedding gown? No one but him. If she argued with him, he'd help her remember all the reasons she should love him.

He smiled at that. "You can't argue a person into loving you, you dumb ass. Either she will or she won't," he said out loud. But watching her these last few weeks he thought the odds were pretty good in his favor.

Deidre Lamont. He liked it. Deidre Lamont. Just the sound of her name, combined with his, filled him with happiness. The scene of Gene Kelly swinging around a Parisian lamppost suddenly seemed very appropriate.

He thought for a second. Maybe he wasn't mixing his metaphors again but was he was mixing his movies?

An American in Paris.

Singing in the Rain.

Gene Kelly was in love.

And so was he.

Who cared which movie had the lamppost—other than Deidre. Well, he wouldn't tell her. Or maybe he would, and she would laugh.

He couldn't stop smiling. She was so beautiful, so smart. What did he love about her the most? There was nothing to consider here. It was her mind. Yes, she was sweet and thoughtful, and yes, oh so beautiful. She was sexy as hell. She would never embarrass him. She was always teaching him things. He taught her things, too. He realized on this trip how much pleasure that gave him. Someday he might run out of things to teach her, but for now he was glad that he could impress her.

But her mind: he liked how it worked, how she reasoned out things, arguing with herself until she got it just right. And she remembered everything. If only he had a mind like that.

And then there was the whole issue about her sight. What would it be like to be married to—to be *with*, he corrected; no, *married to*, damn it. What would it be like to be married to her when she became totally blind? He gave a mental shrug. So what? They'd figure it out. People married people who were blind. People who were blind lived life just like anyone else. Well, maybe not just like them, but they could work it out. He was up for it, without a doubt. They were both resourceful.

Where would they live? Detroit? Near her parents? No. That was non-negotiable. The Sinclairs were too domineering. He'd try his best to get her out to Montana. He wished that had been on their travel list when she could see. He should have thought about that earlier. She probably could visualize it, though, through movies or TV. Big country, big sky, mountains, lakes, lots of cattle. He suddenly felt homesick. Yes, he'd have to take her to Montana to visit, at least. Maybe he could take her next week, after Paris, while she could still see. What would Carole think? He chuckled to himself. They were as different as night and day. Deidre, sophisticated, worldly, educated, and his sister, well, in a word, a mom. But they would like each other. She had hated Sadie, but she'd love Deidre, he was sure.

He wished his parents were alive to meet her. How they would dote on more grandkids.

He surprised himself. Grandkids? He had never thought of himself as a father before. And Deidre, a mother? Sure, why not. But not for a while, not until they had time to just be together, to learn everything there was about each other, to figure out this whole blindness thing.

But a kid. He was surprised how great that suddenly seemed. How had he never thought about that before? A son, or even a daughter, someone to teach about ranching, maybe. He'd have someone to ice fish with on Lake Georgetown. Maybe Deidre would like that, too. He thought for a moment. Yes, she could go ice fishing even when she was blind. Fishing's mostly about touch.

And to teach him how to drive, and how to shave—poor kid. He hoped his son wouldn't be cursed with his dad's heavy beard.

What a glorious day!

Before he knew it, his stomach was telling him it was lunchtime. He didn't know where he was at all. He and his thoughts had merely drifted through Paris. Across the Seine, he saw the Tuileries Gardens. How the heck had he gotten there? And he hadn't taken one shot, either. He looked up and down the river for the nearest bridge that would take him to the other side. He'd better head back or she'd be worried. And, besides, he had something very important to tell her.

THE RITZ PROVIDED wonderful service. Somehow the staff knew each guest on sight. As he passed the reception desk en route to the elevators a handsome Frenchman called him over. There was a note waiting. Deidre was under the weather and needed to sleep. She'd call him in the morning.

He thanked the clerk and dropped the note in the trash. He'd let her sleep and check in on her in a few hours. Right now he was famished. He walked by the Bar Hemingway, but it held no interest. A beer with lunch, good wine for dinner—that was it. The need for anything more was a distant memory.

He stepped into the L'Espadon. Far too elegant for lunch, but perfect for the little talk he planned to have with Deidre tomorrow night. "Proposal" seemed too strong a word. He wouldn't have a ring for her. But later, when Sinclair paid him, they would go pick it out together, so she would have the perfect ring, one she'd never take off.

"I'd like to make a reservation for two for tomorrow evening, 7:30. Name's Lamont."

Good, that was done.

He headed out the door to find a cheaper venue for lunch. He still couldn't waste Sinclair's money without feeling some guilt.

But it *should* be a proposal, his thoughts continued.

And love. He'd never told her he loved her. He could kick himself for all the missed opportunities. Well, he'd fix that, too.

THE NEXT MORNING Remi was again eager to see Deidre. They hadn't been apart for this long since that cell phone incident in Turkey. She hadn't answered her door last night and he had been reluctant to use his key. She'd call if she wanted him. He should just let her sleep. Still, he thought, she might have called him.

He dialed her room. No answer, so he tried her cell phone. It clicked to voice mail. Maybe she was in the shower. He went down to the lobby to talk with the concierge. He wanted to see what Paris had in the way of carriage rides. As he made his way back to the bank of elevators, he saw the doors closing on an attractive woman. For a moment, he thought it was Deidre. No, much too old. Though her hair was falling in her face as she looked down at her shoes, she had the look of Janet Sinclair. He had really only seen Deidre's mother a couple of times back in May, though, and there was no way it could be her. But this woman was a stunner.

On his way up to the room, Remi called Deidre's cell phone

again. And again, there was no answer. He dug in his pocket for her keycard as he got out of the elevator. When he approached her room, he saw a "Do Not Disturb" sign hanging from the handle. He hesitated. Should he? What if she was in trouble? It had been too long since he had heard from her. But when did the sign get put on the door? Was it there when he passed by her room that morning? He couldn't remember. Well, he'd give her until lunchtime. If he didn't hear from her by then, he was going in. In the meantime, maybe he shouldn't let the day go to waste. The light was perfect this morning. Grabbing his camera, he left the hotel. Maybe he'd look through the windows of a jewelry store or two.

SAFELY ENSCONCED in her new room on the second floor, Deidre waited. What else could she do? She could walk around the room and try to envision where her things were; she had spent last night—or was it the day?—packing. Or she could sit. The black world immobilized her.

Her mother had said her father would be there in the morning. While they were talking, Janet had pulled up various airline schedules. Several flight possibilities would work, and it looked like there were Business Class seats in nearly all of them.

Deidre pleaded for the earliest flight possible.

There was a flight landing in Paris at 8:05 a.m. and Deidre and her father could be on the 2:00 p.m. flight back to the States.

"Yes, Mother, reserve that one. Please. Please. Tell him to hurry."

The problem was, she had no idea of the current time or how long it would take her father to get through customs.

Sometimes she heard the church bells, but she'd lose track when the quarter, half, and three-quarter chimes left her wondering about the hour.

At first she was afraid to call room service, not knowing if it was breakfast or lunch or dinnertime. Then she shook that off, realizing a place like the Ritz served their cliental twenty-four hours a day. She had finally called in desperation and discovered she was between lunch and dinner, but, of course, she could order anything she wanted. Unfortunately, the menu was useless.

What should she do about breakfast now? In truth, she had no appetite. Even yesterday, the room service was as much about finding out the time as it was about food. Her stomach was in knots, and after a few bites she felt the need to throw up.

She wasn't sure if she had left anything in the other room, either. Her father could look when he arrived. Her keycards had gotten mixed up, but he could try both. He'd know what to do. The bellboy had put the do not disturb sign on the door. That was smart. Now she had done as much as she could.

So she sat, until finally, after what seemed like hours, there was a rap on the door.

Daddy! At last.

Or could it be Remi? Could he have found her?

She wanted to peer through the peephole, but, of course, that option was gone. She pressed her ear to the door, hoping for a clue.

"Deidre? It's Mother."

Mother!

She swung the door open. "Mother!"

Suddenly she felt warm arms surrounding her, comforting her, protecting her. Now, finally, she felt safe enough to cry.

Her mother's voice was soothing, soft, and familiar. It was her own response that was strange. She had no more defenses. She surrendered totally to the need for comfort.

"He left me, Mother. He left me," she sobbed.

"Remi? He's gone?"

How could she explain it?

"We were engaged. We were going to get married," she stuttered.

"You were going to elope?"

"No. No! Not like that. We were going to get married at home at Christmas."

Her mother must be very confused. But it was so hard to explain.

"We bought my wedding gown," she sobbed.

"Oh, Deidre. What were you thinking?"

"I don't know. He told me to see with my heart, to learn to trust him. And then…and then he said he was—he wanted to leave, to be alone."

"Because you can't see?"

"No, no, he doesn't even know about that. I mean he knows it will happen, but then it *did* happen after he talked about going away, and I just want to die. I just want to die."

They sat together on the bed for a long time until the tears and the story were spent.

Finally, Deidre asked, "Mother, why are you here? Where is Daddy?"

"I am so sorry," she said, brushing the tear-dampened locks from her daughter's face. "He's in Cambodia, for business. He couldn't get here until tomorrow. I didn't tell you because I was afraid that would be one more worry on your shoulders." She picked her words slowly, but the meaning was clear.

"But Mother, how did you get here? Did you fly? You must have flown! Mother, did you fly?"

Deidre could hear the smile in Janet's voice. "White-knuckled it all the way, but made it. When I entered the plane, the pilot was standing there—at least, I think it was the pilot. I told him to remember the first rule of flying."

"I don't know that. What is it?"

"Landings equal takeoffs."

Deidre laughed. She was surprised that she still could.

"He laughed, too, and told me he promised to land." She hugged her daughter. "Now, let's make sure everything is ready to go. I have a cab coming at 11:00."

"What time is it now?"

Janet looked at her watch. "10:15."

"I'm packed, I think."

"You think?" She heard her mother slowly form the words. "How much sight do you have left, Deidre?"

"It's gone. It's all gone."

NOW REMI WAS getting worried. It was noon and still no word from Deidre. Grabbing the keycard, he went to her room. He tried swiping it several times but the door wouldn't open. He tried his own key. Maybe he had switched them. No, it didn't work. He went back to his room. His keycard was fine. Frustration welled up as he stomped toward the elevators.

At the desk, he said, "My key for room 318 won't work. Can you recharge it, please?"

"Of course, Monseigneur," the young woman at reception said, smiling warmly. Even with a staff this professional, he couldn't miss the subtle but seductive invitation in her voice or the look in her eyes. "And the name, please."

"Remi Lamont. Oh, you mean the name on the room. Deidre Sinclair."

The smile didn't waiver, but he felt something shift. A chill drifted between them.

Immediately, he saw the problem.

"I am sorry, Monseigneur. I can only activate it for Mademoiselle Sinclair." She continued to smile, though the look seemed to accuse him of something nefarious.

Remi ran his hand through his hair.

"Look, we're traveling together."

"I am sure," she said.

"No, you don't understand. I haven't heard from her for two days."

"Perhaps she has checked out."

"No, we're traveling together! I told you. We are here for five more days."

"Let me look. One moment, please." The clerk clicked the computer keys.

This was a waste of time. He needed to get to her. Something had happened, he was sure of it now. Why had he waited so long? He could kick himself. He had to find a way to get to her. Suddenly, every minute seemed precious. The clicking stopped and he looked at the pretty woman expectantly.

She smiled, but there was no warmth in it. "Yes, it is here. Mademoiselle Sinclair checked out today. I am sorry, Monseigneur."

CHAPTER 23

BACK IN NEWARK
December 2014

"YOU DIDN'T CALL," Jerry said casually as he brought the beer to his mouth.

"I knew you were good." Remi avoided looking at him.

"Yeah, we both know I'm good. But what about you?"

"Good, real good," he said enthusiastically, too enthusiastically.

The room went quiet except for the hum of the refrigerator.

"Heard from what's-her-name?"

"Who?"

"That Deidre chick."

"Oh, *that* 'what's-her-name'."

Jerry grinned. "Yeah, that one." He reached over, grabbed a sealed envelope, and pitched it to Remi.

"What's this?" He looked at the envelope. It was from Deidre, addressed c/o Jerry Kiss. He had only seen her handwriting once, that note in Rome: the Demilitarized Zone, the DMZ one. Someone else, the front desk had probably written the I'm-too-sick-to-see-you note in Paris. But this time it was typed. He opened it casually.

"Nah. I expect that chapter's closed."

"Thinkin' about starting the next chapter?"

He pulled out the two sheets. It was her article on Egypt. He carefully folded it and put it back in the envelope, then leaned over to drop it in his bag.

"I got married."

Jerry sat forward, eyeing him like a hawk on a mouse. "You're shitting me."

339

"No, for real, in Vegas, last month."

"Holy shit," his friend said quietly. "Known her long? I mean, you just got back in country, what, a couple of months ago?"

"Yeah, I've known her long. I married Sadie."

"What! Again?" Jerry fell back in his chair.

Remi laughed ruefully.

"You married Sadie—*again*!" Jerry repeated.

"Yeah, again," he said, taking another swig of beer.

"What the *hell* were you thinking?"

Remi laughed again. "I was staying in town at my sister's place. We went out to eat and Sadie happened to wait on us. Next thing you know, we were in the alley making out."

"Goddamn it, Remi, you're smarter than that. I don't care how horny you were—fuck!"

Ignoring his friend, he continued, "So we thought we'd try again. A week later we were in Vegas."

"And how did that go?"

Remi finished his beer.

"We got married," he said with a lopsided smile. "It seemed like a good idea at the time."

He pushed his arms across the table in a stretch and yawned. "She bought a lot of crap. We gambled some. Mostly, we got drunk and fought."

"Remi, you know she's a train wreck. Goddamn, bro, how much deeper are you going to dig that hole?"

"I guess it took me coming to the pool to find her sucking face with some teenage waiter at the hotel to slap me out of my stupor. That was a week after the wedding."

"Tell me you got a quickie divorce."

"They're working on it."

"Go on."

"Well, things were going pretty good in front of the judge—"

"And then?"

"And then it came out that we were married before."

Jerry arched his eyebrow.

"And all of a sudden, the judge looked over at me and said in this fatherly this-is-going-to-hurt-me-more-than-it's-going-to-hurt–you voice, something about how I knew what I was getting into the second time, and maybe I needed some incentive to remember it for the next time—"

"So how much does she want?"

"Oh, God, Kiss, you know her so well. At first she wouldn't settle for anything less than the ranch."

"Your folks' ranch?"

"Yeah, and Carole's half, too."

"You're making me sick. Why don't you just off that fucking whore? Or let me get one of the guys to do it. You've got to stay clear of it, though. Jesus, there are half a dozen—"

"It's okay, Jer. We settled for my share of the silver mine."

"You got a silver mine?"

"Quarter share. Carole and Dad's partner have the rest. It's up in Philipsburg. Hasn't produced in decades. The partner is waiting for silver to go up before he opens it again."

"If he didn't open it three, four years ago when silver shot through the ceiling…"

"Exactly."

"So you bought Sadie off with a closed silver mine. Well, well, well," Jerry sighed with a smile. "Best news I've had all day. Unless it strikes, of course."

"The way my luck's been running these last few years, it probably will. But I'll take that gamble if it gets me out of this marriage." Remi went into the kitchen, calling back to his friend, "It should be finalized in a week." He returned with two more beers.

"So you want to tell me where you've been for the last three years?"

Remi sat with a satisfied smile. "Russia."

"No shit. How the hell did you pull that one off? Last call you made you were crying in your beer in the City of Lights."

Remi's face darkened as he recalled Paris.

"Left France. Went down to Kenya. Sinclair paid me, by the way."

"So the old man lived up to the agreement, eh? I wondered."

"Next thing I knew, I was on the Serengeti when my cell phone rang. It was the Foreign Service offering me a job."

"The who? Doing what?"

"This guy just called me up in Africa and asked if I'd like to be the Embassy photographer in Moscow."

"What the fuck," Jerry said.

"Yeah, apparently their guy took a powder and they needed someone quick. I still had my security clearance, and this MSG Marine I met in Istanbul—Did I tell you about that?" Jerry shook his head. "Well, anyway, my name came up, and two weeks later I was snapping pictures in the American Embassy in Moscow at some charity event."

"God, our tax dollars at work."

Remi nodded smugly. "And a pretty dollar you paid, too." He got up and rummaged through his bag, continuing to talk over his shoulder. "Mostly it was PR stuff, but I got to take pictures of the landscapes and people, just stuff to throw up on the walls." He found what he was looking for and sat down again with a book and a magazine. He pushed the book toward his friend.

It was a large coffee table book, the kind you set out for guests to thumb through, the kind with oversized glossy photos and color that jumped off the page. Jerry opened the book. It featured all walks of daily life in Russia. The first showed a grandmother making a pot of borscht. The steam coming off the red soup was almost aromatic. The next captured a group of men dancing, arms grasping shoulders, legs kicking out from a squat.

"That's tough," Jerry said. "I remember trying that at boot camp."

For once Remi didn't flinch.

The next picture was taken at a flea market. A woman tried on an Arctic fox hat while others stood by admiring it, the vendor most of all. There were several more from that market: musicians, a child singing, and a table of lacquer troika boxes.

He closed the book. "So for nearly three years you took pictures in Russia." His voice carried an accusatory tone Remi wanted to avoid.

He pushed the magazine toward Jerry. "Turn to the last page."

Jerry lifted the magazine. "The Delta In Flight Magazine." He flipped it over to the ad on the back cover.

"No, open it," Remi instructed eagerly.

He pulled back the cover to the last page to reveal a stunning photo of a lioness chasing a zebra. Both were in perfect focus, the movement derived from the slight blurring of the trees in the background. He looked down to the credits. *Photo taken by Remi Lamont.* Jerry looked up at the expectant face. "Nice, real nice."

Remi beamed. He reached for the magazine. "I've got contracts with Delta, Southwest, United, Lufthansa, practically the whole industry. All I have to do is send them monthly photos. I've got so many archived I don't have to work another day in my life if I don't want to. Finally, after all these years, I caught a break."

"I'm glad for you, buddy. Still pissed off, but glad."

"I know you are—glad and pissed off—but just be glad for me

right now, okay, at least through dinner. Then maybe I can get you drunk enough to forget about the pissed off part." He stood and punched him in the arm.

"Is that your way of inviting yourself for dinner?"

"Dinner and a bed."

"Shit. You don't want much, do you? You can have the couch. I sleep alone."

They left the apartment. The same group of hoodlums were throwing the same basketball that he remembered from three and a half years ago, only they were bigger now. Some were hurrying over to them.

"Hey, Raz," Jerry called out. The ball carrier finished his dribble and hooked it into the basket before jogging over to catch up with his friends. The hoop looked low, Remi thought.

"Hey, what's up, bro?" the Globe Trotter wannabe said, approaching Jerry with some secret handshake.

The four boys knocked fists with Jerry. Some saluted. He saluted back.

It irritated Remi, that sloppy salute and Jerry playing along. Was he still playing at being something neither one of them would ever be again? And what's with this "bro" shit, like they were brothers in arms? Like they'd gone through some shit together?

"I seen you before. You a Marine, too?" one of the kids asked him.

"Used to be."

"Jerry says, 'Once a Marine, always a Marine.'"

Then why don't you fucking try to be one?

"Does he? Well, that's what they told us." He felt his hands curl up into loose fists, just in case.

The group got Jerry to promise to shoot some hoops the next day and, finally, went back to their game.

"So you've got yourself a little gang of admirers, have you?"

Jerry looked at him quizzically and shrugged. They had reached the bar and grill. Time to eat.

Remi forgot the punks in the empty lot. He began painting verbal pictures of Russia for Jerry to see—the darkness in Siberia, the nightlife in Moscow, and the glamour of the castle despite the overcast dreariness in St. Petersburg.

"The sun only comes out twelve times a year there. Tried three times to get a picture of the Winter Palace. Couldn't get a good shot to save my life. No sun, ever."

They lingered over a pleasant meal, at first, neither in a rush to get back. But it was getting dark. Not the neighborhood to be in after dark, Remi knew. Maybe Jerry kept the punks around as a watch patrol or something. Though Jerry was relaxed, Remi was growing antsy, so they left.

The liquor store was just across the street.

"Quick detour. Going to grab some beer," he said, darting across the empty street.

He had started drinking more in Russia, and Sadie compounded the habit. He hadn't had anything to drink since moving out of the Vegas hotel until today, though, and today he'd already had too much. He'd clean up his act tomorrow.

Jerry was waiting at the kitchen table, a pile of newspaper clippings pushed to one side.

Remi put four beers in the refrigerator and opened two, setting them on the table as foam seeped over the tops. Jerry accepted the bottle and asked, "You going to look her up, you know, what's-her-name?"

Remi looked up in surprise then answered. "Hell, no, man. I told you: I'm too old, too broke, and too poor to start with her or anyone else. Sadie is proof in point." He was going to keep it light.

Jerry nodded. "But you're not that broke anymore from what you're telling me."

"Not that kind of broke, you knuckle-head."

"And the PTSD was getting better last time you called."

Quietly, he said, "Deidre and I have no future. We got over each other a long time ago."

They drank in silence for a minute.

"She's here, you know."

"Who's where?"

"She lives in the city," Jerry said.

"Who? Deidre? In New York?" He tried to act cool, mildly disinterested, despite the feeling in his gut. "What's she doing here?" Then he added with unrestrained interest, "And how do you know?"

"I've been keeping track of her," Jerry said just as coolly.

Remi turned that thought over in his mind, but asked the more pressing question. "So why is she here?"

"She works here."

That broke the fragile crust of his indifference. "But she's blind. Or is she? And, besides, her daddy's rich—"

"And her mama's good looking." Jerry crooned.

"Yeah, yeah, so what gives?"

Jerry wheeled his chair to the roll top desk, a new acquisition since Remi's last visit. He pulled out a *New York Times* page dated January 2013, and handed it to Remi.

"Read this."

Assuming it was the society page, Remi groaned. But, no, he saw, it was under the travel section.

"Read it out loud," Jerry urged.

"Hell, no," Remi said to the grinning face of his friend.

"Come in the kitchen and read while I do the dishes." He rolled into the kitchen.

Remi followed, carefully spreading the newspaper on the table. He sat with his back to Jerry and began reading.

A TINY SHOP IN VENICE
By Deidre Sinclair

Across from the island of St. Giorgio, where the Grand Canal of Venice empties into the San Marco Basin, there is an exquisite bookbinding shop called Il Mercante Veneziano. The shop is located at the end of a row of buildings, giving it the advantage of having windows across the front and side, windows that face the canal and look out to the Riva. It measures no more than fourteen feet by fourteen feet, and that may be an exaggeration. Within, Roberto Manera is turning the rich leather into the cover of a book. An animated boy of six or seven is chatting away beside him, the obvious owner of the bicycle parked in front.

I enter the tiny shop with its well-worn wood plank floor and heavy beamed ceiling. Modern halogen lights brighten the room. Lining the ancient walls are shelves displaying books of various sizes and colors of leather. I pick up a brown, thin, soft-sided volume. The leather bound book is called pala. It is like a diary filled with creamy blank leaves. The leather is supple within my hands and has the subtle smell one would expect of quality material. With an almost reverent respect for tradition, the bookbinder makes all books of this particular style brown. Next, I pick up a diary with a millefiori disk embedded within its hard leather cover. The famous medallions are a creation of Murano artisans who bundle and adhere colorful glass rods together, then slice the bundles into disks that form a petite flower design. At the moment, Roberto is placing a millefiori, translated, "a thousand flowers," onto the cover of another book, and works the leather around to secure it in place. It is a jewel. I pick up a burgundy-colored address book, then thumb through a forest green organizer. I carefully reach up to the top shelf and take down a heavy black photo album with thin white sheets between black pages. The white sheets protect the photos from sticking together in humid weather. I remember seeing this process in a wedding album from the first half of the last century. It is a rare find, but not yet what I am seeking. Finally, I find the perfect book. The pliable navy volume is tied shut by a long leather strap wrapped around it. The book measures a little larger than four by six inches. Between the covers is handmade cotton paper with soft, uneven edges. It will be my travel diary for those Hemingway Moments. I smile.

Roberto Manera, a tall, loquacious Italian, sends his son off to play. He is pleased that I so appreciate his wares and is quite willing to talk to me about his store, his profession, and his life.

Obviously, I am not the first to discover this wonderful little shop. Over the years, Roberto tells me, he has served many famous clients. In a matter-of-fact tone, he explains he produces the guest books for several major cruise lines, including the Grand Princess and Disney cruise ships. Recently, he has been commissioned to make books using three-ring bindings for a Hollywood screenwriter who wants his scripts organized yet beautifully displayed.

I asked him how he came upon his trade.

Roberto opened the shop in 1994. It was a risk. He had a well-paying, secure office job, not easy to find in Italy, and he was newly married. The building he wanted to renovate was not in the trendy San Marco area clogged with tourists. Instead, it was farther east on the Riva degli Schiavoni, down toward the Garden District, an area undiscovered by many tourists. Supported by his bride, whose family had always been merchants in Venice, he took a deep breath, quit his job, and began doing what he loved best: working with leather.

He had received his training at his first job, which entailed the restoration of antique books. Some of these documents were hundreds of years old. The fragile pages often required serious repair. But the bindings, stiff and threatening to fall apart in his hands, intrigued Roberto the most. He gently rubbed the old leather with vegetable and animal oils. Patiently, he massaged the covers and spines of manuscripts written as long ago as 800 AD. Gradually, he could see the ancient books coming back to life as the leather absorbed the oils.

"*I was amazed to see these books restored to their original color and pliability,*" *he said.* "*They became soft like a baby's cheek.*"

The secret lay in the original tanning of the leather.

"*To produce leather that will last generations, you have to process it in natural animal oils. It takes twenty-four hours or more to do it properly. Today, we have no time. Instead, we turn to chemical tanning using chromium, which reduces the process time to an hour or less. But there are problems with today's leather.*"

Roberto explained that chromium processing causes leather to eventually harden and flake. It does not tolerate heat well. The leather seats and console of cars are examples. Within a decade, the leather is cracked and peeling. Leather coats, too, start out supple but over time start to show craze lines that cannot be worked out even with the finest oils.

"*I looked for two years to find the right processor of leather. In Florence, I found two. But they are very expensive. And I cannot always get the colors I want. Sometimes I have to wait.*"

Throughout Venice, many shops sell leather books, but the owners use the chemical processing and sell them for much less. Roberto told me that only he and one other artisan work the materials in the old way.

"My books are not for everyone. My work attracts a special type of person, someone thoughtful who has an appreciation for the finest quality. My books will last hundreds of years."

I look down at the travel journey I have just purchased. Will my travel notes during my Hemingway Moments be worthy of a book that will last hundreds of years? It is a bit intimidating!

Of his life, Roberto says, "Every day I come to my shop and look out at the Grand Canale, and San Giorgio. All the sun is coming in. There is no better view in Venice than this. In the office where I used to work, there were no windows and I had no freedom. That is no way to live life. Here, the family is all around. My son rides his bicycle in front of the shop and we have much time to be together. I can walk home in five minutes for lunch. My work is wonderful. I have the best life. Is there anything more?"

I left the shop that day with more than a leather-bound book. I left with one man's answer to a universal question—the meaning of a good life.

Remi lowered the paper and looked over at Jerry. "God, she's good. She nailed it perfectly."

"She writes for the *Times*." Jerry rolled to the table across from him.

Remi didn't hear. "I mean, she got it exactly right. The shop, Roberto, the smell of the leather."

"She writes about those months she was with you."

"She writes professionally, then." That made him smile. "Well, she's damn good at it."

Jerry pointed to the pile of clippings. "These are all hers. And, yes, she is blind."

"How do you know?"

"We had coffee once."

"Where?"

"Here."

"I thought she was blind. How did she get here?"

He shrugged. "I don't know. She just called me up and asked if we could meet."

A collision of thoughts and emotions jolted through his head, each fighting to be recognized.

"How's she doing?"

Jerry rubbed his hand over his face. "You mean learning to be blind? Or living in New York? Or writing? Or missing you? What's the question here?"

"All of the above, but start with the last one."

Jerry mulled over his answer.

"She's as closed off as you are about what happened in Paris, so I've got no answers for you. But the girl absolutely lit up like the goddamn White House Christmas tree when I said your name."

He hadn't expected the skipped heartbeat. He was over her. No, he wasn't. He was fucking furious with her. He wanted to smash the table for all the pain she had caused him. But he also wanted to take her in his arms and kiss her until she fainted. He wanted to hope, and he wanted this conversation to never have taken place. As each new thought tumbled over the previous one, his face changed. But flooding over everything was pain.

"Talk to me, Remi."

He couldn't, not yet. The brain activity was still too volatile. He put up his hand and shook his head.

"Remi, she's going to run out of material, out of stories."

Remi shook his head again.

"She's going to need you."

He ran his hand through his hair. "I can't hear that."

"Well, so much for 'getting over each other.'"

Minutes ticked away as they sat in silence.

"I love you like a brother," his friend said, "so let me talk to you like one. When I met her, I wondered if this was the same woman you complained about so much." Remi continued to look down, but Jerry knew he was attentive. "She was as beautiful as you described, but, wow, what a sweetheart. I always pictured this, well, this debutante, some little rich bitch. But she's not like that."

"No, she's not like that," he softly echoed.

"I'll tell you honestly, if you weren't my best friend I would've made a play for her myself."

At first he thought that was a joke, but as he looked at the man across the table he wasn't totally sure.

"But I know how you feel about her."

"Really!" That did it. "*I* don't know how I feel about her! How can you?" he shouted.

"That's bull," Jerry shouted back. "For six months she was in every sentence of every conversation you had with anybody. And then it stopped, it ended, like a shot through the heart. And I saw you die again. It was Fallujah all over. Only this time, you ran."

"I didn't run! I got a job!"

"And you stopped calling. Why? They don't have cell phone service in Russia? No. You stopped calling because you knew that I knew she broke your heart. And the only way she could do that is if you let her in, if you loved her."

"Fuck you, Kiss!" Remi said, standing up and slamming the beer bottle on the table. "So you've got all the answers here. You've got it all figured out. Some broad gets under my skin for a while and suddenly I must be in love. And when she walks out, I must be heartbroken. Is that your professional diagnosis, doctor? Why don't you go and become a fucking shrink if you know so goddamn much! Why don't you do something instead of rolling around in that goddamn chair! You think saluting those damn punks out there makes you somebody? Well, buddy, you'd better think again.

"And one more thing." He was on a roll now. "Why did you make her come to you? She's blind, for cryin' out loud. Why didn't you get off your sorry ass and get on a train and go into the city? And for that matter—" He might regret this but he was going to say it anyway—"stop using that damn chair as an excuse for doing nothing. There are guys in worse shape than you out there in the Special Olympics, inspiring people, teaching, working for a living. But all you do is sit there and live your life through me and the other guys. You ask why I can't get over it? It's because you've saddled me with the chore of living a life for you, too!"

It was out. Let the cards fall where they may, he thought bitterly.

"Goddamn it! I need some air."

The door gave a satisfying slam behind him.

The next hour was a tough one, though. Once the adrenaline subsided, the pain seeped in. He paced up and down the block, hoping one of those kids would cross his path just once. But he was alone, alone with his thoughts, and right then, that was about as bad as it got.

When he walked back into the apartment, Jerry was deadly silent. He pushed a piece of paper toward Remi. "Don't call me until you've taken care of this. That's all I have to say."

"I'm sorry. I was way out of line."

Jerry nodded. "You were. I'll wait for your call. You can let yourself out."

He looked at the paper. It was a New York address. He jammed it into his pocket. Without another word, he grabbed his jacket, his bag, and left.

The challenge lay heavy in the pit of his stomach. Would they be all right? As long as he did the deed. And therein lies the rub, as Shakespeare cruelly pointed out.

Remi had planned to spend the night with Jerry. Now he had to find a place. Newark, the left armpit of the country was a hard place to navigate at night. Maybe he should go into the city and treat himself. A nice hotel, a good meal, a walk around Times Square, maybe a cheap ticket for some Off Broadway play. Better than Newark. He headed for the train station. He pulled out the paper in his jeans. Her address. He shoved it back in his pocket. Prioritize. First objective: get a room.

CHAPTER 24

HARLEM

IF REAL LAVENDER could be found any place in December, it would be New York City. He was on a quest for it now.

He had spent last evening and most of the night reminding himself that he was in the right, and the next move was hers. She had walked out on him with no explanation. Not even a Dear John letter. Yeah, the Grand Tour would have ended eventually, but somehow he never quite believed it. Throughout those months, there was this thing that was growing, like the twisted roots of a tree, or a fast growing cancer, this thing that was worming its way into his heart. He had played with the idea, rejected it, danced around it, yanked at it, and ignored it. But it wasn't until she had performed anesthesia-free surgery on his heart that it became crystal clear. She was the closest thing he had ever known to love. And if it was love, then somehow it would work out. He came to understand that in those last days in Paris. The tour would end, but they wouldn't. That belief must have been growing at the core, buried beneath the denial all along. Otherwise he would have had some defense, he would have stood a chance of survival when she left.

Sometime, just before dawn, he knew that was what it was. He had just reached the point where he let himself jump and was in a full-blown free fall when she had shredded his parachute. Her disappearance was so sudden, so painful, so damn unfair, that he stopped everything. He stopped caring, stopped feeling, stopped being human. The camera no longer became an extension of him. He became an extension of the machine, seeing the world, recording it, but not being part of it. He cut himself off from everyone. He almost signed up with Blackwater again, but at least something was working for him when the Embassy gig appeared. Otherwise, a nice suicide mission for the CIA seemed like a good option, and then all the pain would stop.

She had left. Just left. God, he hated her. For over three years, he'd been hating her. And then Jeremiah Fucking Kiss hands him her address and he's out looking for lavender.

"I am one fucked up son of a bitch."

He shook himself. He had been muttering out loud, he realized. No, louder than a mutter. He was walking down Fifth Avenue talking out loud, and the surprising thing was that not one person took notice. New York City never disappointed.

HE ASSUMED SHE would be in the heart of Manhattan, perhaps overlooking Times Square or the Hudson River or Central Park. Greenwich Village, at least. So when he found himself looking at a third floor walk-up in a gentrified section of Harlem, he double-checked the address. The lavender suddenly seemed frivolous. He was tempted to toss it, but after the trouble he had finding the real thing... Well, he'd decide when he saw her.

He barely knocked twice when the door opened. He expected a call-out, a peek through, a cracked door with the chain still on, the unlocking of four deadbolts, something, not an immediate opening of the door. The man blocking the entrance was even more startling. A boyfriend? Husband? A wrong address? Jerry didn't say how long ago he had met with her. The article was dated January 2013. A lot could happen in a couple of years. Was this a mistake?

"Can I help you?" the man asked.

Well, he was here now. May as well get it over with.

"I'm looking for Deidre Sinclair. Does she live here?"

"And you are?"

"Remi Lamont."

"*The* Remi Lamont? The larger than life, Remi Lamont?" The younger man was clearly impressed.

"Not a common name, so probably," he replied, his tone just a little pissy. Well, at least he knew he had the right place.

He heard female voices from inside the apartment. Someone else was here, too.

"Yeah, yeah, she's here. We were just talking about you!"

Fuck.

"Come on in. You are going to blow her mind. I'm Alan, by the way."

Remi missed the outstretched hand as he walked into the foyer, his eyes looking for her. He set the flowers on a side table and pushed by Alan.

"She's in the living room." Alan held out his arm to indicate the way, but Remi was already following the voices.

A step away from the room he heard a woman say, "You *always* think it's Remi." No, not a woman. It was Cassandra.

He saw them on the couch and his heart squeezed in hope and dread.

"Deidre?" His voice was soft.

"Oh, my God, it is Remi!" Cassandra squealed, but Deidre was already up and walking toward him.

How much vision did she have? She didn't seem blind. Then she reached for him and missed by a bit, but he rescued her by pulling her into his arms. To hell with the husband, or boyfriend, or whoever this Alan was to her. If this was the last hug they ever had, well, he got it. And if the guy wanted to punch him in the nose… Please don't be married. Just don't be married.

She certainly didn't hug him like she was married with her husband standing there watching. And when she whispered his name, he knew Alan was history.

Cassandra was there now, jumping and screaming and hugging both of them, and he reached around with one arm to include her.

"Can I get in on this?" asked a bewildered Alan.

"Of course you can, honey," Cassandra said pulling her husband into the circle.

In a matter of minutes, he met Alan—again—kissed Cassandra on the cheek, helped her tug on her coat to go, and heard Deidre instruct her to give the third ticket to, "someone on the street who's never heard an opera." Cassandra said she hoped to see him tomorrow, kissed him again, and with her husband in tow ran down the stairs calling farewells and throwing kisses as the door shut.

Alone.

"I can't believe you are really here." Deidre was breathless.

She was even more beautiful than when he last saw her.

"Come sit in here, so we can talk."

"Before we say anything—and we will talk, I'm warning you right now. I will get some answers…" Then his voice softened. "Before we say anything, I need to kiss you."

Without waiting for consent, he pulled her to him, praying to God she would have him. What had Cassandra said? "You always think it's Remi." Had she really been waiting? Could there really be an explanation for Paris?

The kiss was long and passionate, both given and received. Her heart was pounding as hard as his. He pulled her face away, brushed back her hair, and looked at her. She had cut and straightened it. She wore it smooth, shoulder length, curled under at the ends. She smelled faintly of Fath de Fath, but everything else about her was unchanged. Yet somehow better.

Finally, Remi said, "I have three things to say to you. I loved you. You broke my heart. And, why?"

She pulled him down on the couch to sit next to her. She took his hand in both of hers and turned toward him.

"I'll tell you whatever you want to know, but..." She needed a moment to compose herself, "But, Remi, the 'I loved you'—is it really past tense?"

He gazed at her. It was disconcerting to think she couldn't read his face. Though she was looking at him, it was through her sense of hearing and touch that she made sense of things.

"God, Dee, don't ask me to drop my defenses. They're all I've got, the only thing that's held me together for three years. Talk to me. Tell me. Make me understand."

She nodded. "So it isn't necessarily over for you? Because it isn't for me, not at all."

"Just..." He put his head down and his other hand up. "Just talk."

* * * * *

"YOU KNOW WHAT a perfect storm is, right?" she asked in a quiet voice.

Remi nodded.

She continued, haltingly, "I'll take that for a yes."

Oh, shit, he thought. "Sorry, yes."

"Okay. I found myself in the middle of a perfect—that's a horrible word; there was nothing perfect about it. No." She inhaled deeply. "I found myself in the middle of an inferno, or maybe a tornado."

"Go on," he said.

"Do you remember the first time we were together in Venice?"

"By 'together,' do you mean made love?"

"Yes. And we did make love, didn't we? It wasn't just sex for you, it—"

"We made love," he said quietly.

Deidre turned the idea over in her mind for a moment, savoring the truth of it.

"I don't want to talk about Venice, Deidre. I want to know what happened in Paris." He would be as patient as he could be, but he didn't want to recreate their whole relationship.

"I know, but trust me, this is directly related to Paris." She took another deep, quivering breath. "The day after the first time we made love, we had a fight. Do you remember?"

He nodded, then quickly said, "Yes, on the small canal."

"You said—" She stopped and inhaled deeply. "Remi, this is so hard." Her voice was just above a whisper.

He gave her time to gather her courage, but he couldn't imagine what in the world she was getting at.

"You said—you told me to go buy a wedding gown. You said you were going to take me to Paris to buy my wedding gown." Her voice was trembling.

"I know. Yeah. You wanted to see yourself in your wedding dress before you went blind."

"Remi, when a man makes love all night to a woman and the next day tells her he's taking her to Paris to buy her wedding gown, and when he sits there and after thirty dresses says, 'that's the one'—"

Slowly a light flickered in his brain. "Oh, my God. You thought—"

"I was trying to see with my heart."

"And that's why I was 'the most wonderful, most sensitive man,' or whatever. Oh, Dee. Oh, Dee." He shook his head sadly in terrible regret. "I just wanted you to have the pictures, the experience…" His voice trailed off, lost in the memory.

"I know that now. I figured it out eventually. But I was humiliated. Everyone else, and me especially, thought we were engaged. The girls at the bridal salon were all excited and talking to me about the wedding, and I was making a million plans. I even told Vittoria. I was so happy!"

He squeezed her hand. Then he reached out to pull her to him.

"I am so very, *very* sorry."

"Didn't you even think how it sounded, how I took it?"

"No," he answered honestly. "I was in a different place."

He put his arm around her, rocking her, understanding how his gesture of kindness had backfired. But her reaction had been so extreme. He still didn't understand that.

"Didn't it cross your mind, ever, that maybe we might—?"

"All the time," he admitted.

"All the time? Then how did this happen?"

"And I rejected it over and over again. You parents would never have approved."

"No, they wouldn't, but Remi, you should have told me. I wouldn't have cared what they said."

Each got lost in his or her thoughts. What if he had spoken up earlier? What if they had married? What if her parents forbade it? What if they had eloped? So many questions.

Finally, Deidre sat up again. "So there's still more."

"Lots of parts to a perfect storm."

"Yes." She reached out to find his hand again. "Remember when you asked me if I had protection?"

This was not a question any man wanted to hear, ever. "Yeah, just before we left Venice. I just wanted to make sure," he said hesitantly.

"I had an IUD put in while we were there."

"IUD? What happened to the pill?" Every woman he ever knew

was on the birth control pill.

"I've never been on the pill." She shot him a quizzical look. "Anyway, it takes a month before the pill starts working, so I needed something right away."

A blade of ice began chiseling its way through his internal organs. Where was this topic going? There seemed to be only one direction.

"It's not a hundred percent safe." Another deep breath. "I don't know if the doctor put it in wrong, or if it happened the first or second night, before I got it, but I was pretty sure…" Her voice trailed off.

Remi finished it. "You got pregnant."

She nodded.

He looked quickly around the room. There was no sign of a baby. Did she abort it? Put it up for adoption? Leave it with her mother? No, she wouldn't have done that. But what would she do? She might have gone for an abortion. Like a deep blow to his chest, it occurred to him that he didn't know her at all. Pregnant, and she never told him! Making all the decisions without him! He felt the anger rising, his patience thinning, the ice turning to acid in his gut.

"And then there was the third thing—"

"Whoa, whoa, whoa. Oh no you don't. Where's the baby? What happened to the baby?" He nearly went to shake her, but somehow her small hands holding his one large one kept him immobile.

"I'll get to that, but you have to hear it chronologically to understand why I left."

"Well it seems to me that was one big reason to stay!"

She dropped her head to her chest. "You're right."

He felt like jumping out of his skin. "Was it a boy or a girl?"

"Remi, don't—"

"Do you know? Did you kill it?" He could strangle her right

here, right now.

Deidre shook her head silently.

"A boy or a girl?" he asked again, his voice low and threatening.

A fine tremor enveloped her. "A boy."

She gave him away. She gave their son away.

He pulled back from her, stood, and thought about leaving. He couldn't stay in this vacuum where his every breath was being sucked out of him, where there was no air. Not one more minute! He took a step toward the door. But, no, he had come for answers and, by God, he was going to get them. All of the answers, including what had happened to his son.

"Remi, please come sit with me. I can't see you, so I have to touch you. I have to make sure you can hear me," she pleaded.

"No." He said moving across the room to an empty chair. "I can hear just fine from here."

"Please," she pleaded.

Let her touch him? She could go to hell first. "No!"

"How can you be so cruel?" she asked bitterly. "Don't you think I've suffered, too?"

"You've had about three years to adjust. This is all kind of new for me," he said, the sarcasm thick. He saw her lashes shining with fresh tears, but he didn't care. "Go on, Deidre, tell me the rest of it." His voice was as hard as jagged stone.

He knew she was trying to organize her thoughts. That's all right, sweetheart, he thought angrily, I've got all night. He stood up again, restless, and started walking around the room. He picked up a conch shell she had bought in Nice, a glass pen from Venice, and noted the rug from Turkey. He touched the much smaller marble reproduction of Rodin's *The Kiss*, the curves of the embracing couple sensuous even to his untrained fingers. His map with the gold circle was framed and hanging. There on the adjacent wall was a polar bear skin, head mounted, teeth glistening. He suppressed a small shudder. *So she had gotten it, after all. But she always got her way, didn't she.*

He sat down again.

Deidre pushed her hair back with both hands, squared her shoulders, and looked in his direction. "All right. I'll go on. But I want you to know you are probably lucky I'm blind."

"Oh?"

"If I could see you, I'd be glaring at you right about now. But with the blindness, I have to stop and think everything through. That's the only reason I'll go on, because I realize you have a right to know everything in whatever order you want, even if you are—well, you know what you are."

"An asshole."

"Yes. Good. Now that we've established that fact, I'll continue.

"I had reasonably good sight while we were in Venice and when we first got to Paris. I mean, I could get around during the day. It was like I willed my vision to stay put, at least that's what I told myself. I thought if I wanted it badly enough, I could keep the darkness out. I had a real reason to. I was going to get married, and there was a wedding to plan, and a man to love. But when that reason evaporated, it was like I gave up."

"You're not a quitter," he said flatly.

"No, you don't understand. It took so much energy to keep on seeing, but I was energized by you, so I had the strength. I just didn't understand the physics. But you don't have to understand physics, do you? The laws of nature will occur with or without an understanding.

"I had two fault lines within me, two straining tectonic plates: my will to see and the disease to blind me. It only took a single moment of distraction for the disease to get the upper hand. The earth shifted violently, a nine on my Richter scale, and overnight my sight was gone. The balloon burst; the air rushed out in a pop. It just took that one thing for all the darkness to fill the void. One night I went to bed seeing, and the next morning all I had left was a pinprick of light. I couldn't even see if I had started my period or not. I was totally helpless and, oh, Remi, so very scared." Her voice quivered, just above a whisper.

He sat silent, taking it in. He wasn't sure what he felt.

"I couldn't come to you."

"Why the hell not?"

"I thought we had plans to get married, but you had plans to go off with your camera. You had no interest in me! I was so humiliated, mortified! I swore I'd never turn to you again… I was alone in Paris, blind, and probably pregnant." She was sobbing now, allowing the pain to bubble up from some deep, dark well within her. "It was all because of you, all of it, and I felt you had left me to deal with it by myself!"

He sat forward in his chair. "But I didn't leave you. I wouldn't have left you. I was right there. How the hell did you get that so wrong?"

"I had everything else about you wrong. You didn't want to marry me. You didn't love me. How, how—" She gulped. "I couldn't risk any more mistakes. I had no more reserves."

He felt it, what she must have been going through. He got it, finally. His heart ached for her, imagining her panic, her despair. He was a twelve-year-old boy again, holding his brother, scared out of his wits, waiting, alone, helpless, overwhelmed.

He went to her then, bent and lifted her to his lap, where he could properly hold her, comfort her.

"Oh, Deidre. Oh, Deidre. Shh, shh, shh." He rocked her. Her arms were around him and her face was in his neck.

"Oh, God, sweet girl, I was just across the hall, ten steps away. I was right there. And I did love you. And I did want to marry you. It just took me longer to figure it out."

"You wanted to marry me?" her muffled voice asked, small and far away.

"I did. I had reservations downstairs for that night, to tell you, to ask you." He felt her hug tighten as she cried. "Your dad hadn't paid me yet, but I bought a cigar so I could propose with a cigar band. I thought you'd get a kick out of it.

"Deidre, Deidre. Shh. Shh. You've had a pretty rough time, haven't you." He continued rocking her.

He felt her nod, felt the sobs shudder through her, but less violently now.

"Okay, okay. You can cry now. Go ahead and cry. I'm here. I've got you."

She did. They sat that way until the light left the room. In the darkness, he felt her start to breath normally again. The tears, still wet on his shirt, seemed spent. He could wait to find out about his son. She wouldn't withhold it from him. He knew that now. She wasn't mean. She was a sweetheart, like Jerry had said. She just got dealt a lousy hand when all her life she'd held a royal flush. Even he remembered being young and fresh and naïve about life, thinking it was fair, and then discovering that was all just a bunch of crap. And he had been raised tough. She was raised soft. What in her first twenty-one years had prepared Deidre Sinclair for those days in Paris?

Remi felt her stir.

"Mom came to get me."

"Your mother?"

"I was shocked."

"You know, I thought I saw her enter the elevator in Paris, but knew it couldn't be her. She doesn't fly."

"She flew. She came. At first, I was afraid she would make everything even worse than it was. But it was all right. She helped. She knew right away I was pregnant. Morning sickness. We kept it from Daddy about a week. I don't know if he just guessed, or if Mom told him, or maybe he got a hold of a medical record. I don't know, but it was bad, real bad."

The memory was obviously painful. "The night he found out," she said, "I had gotten up for some water and walked past their bedroom. I—Remi, I'd never heard him cry before." Her voice broke. "I didn't think there was any more pain to feel, but, Remi, hearing him, it just broke my heart."

He hugged her tighter.

After a few minutes, she continued. "From Father's point of view, it was all your fault, of course. I couldn't possibly have been responsible in any way."

"No, of course not," he said, remembering their conversation at the Marriott.

"I didn't know at first, but I found out about a year later that he—God, this is so embarrassing—he sent you away."

"No, Deidre, he didn't send me anywhere. I never spoke to your father."

"He arranged for some Embassy job, so you wouldn't come back, so I could move on with my life without you complicating it."

The calculation took a fraction of a second before he said, "Oh shit. And the hits just keep on comin'."

"I know. I know. You see, I kept expecting you to show up. I told Cassie you'd find me, you'd come, but you didn't. Daddy was so kind and told me you obviously had just viewed our time together as a paycheck and a chance to get some clean pussy—"

"What!"

"His words, not mine. Sorry," she scrambled. "He said I needed to accept the fact that I had totally misread you."

"Obviously, I set the stage for that assessment…"

"It did seem that my judgment about you was somewhat flawed."

"And the baby?"

"The baby." She sighed as if preparing for another defeat. "A tiny baby boy. He came way too early, twenty-two weeks."

Remi did the math. "That's just five months."

She nodded. "I got to hold him. Remi, he was so, *so* small. There was no weight to him at all."

"He died," he whispered, the reality collapsing all emotion into a momentary void of grateful nothingness before the pain rushed in.

"He lived for about an hour," she said. "I named him David. It means 'beloved son.'"

He squeezed her. "I like David," he said softly, his eyes beginning to burn.

"I had a priest come and give him last rites."

"You aren't Catholic, why—"

"You are. Even if you don't believe in God. I remember you said you went to a Jesuit school."

"Oh, so you thought I was…"

"I thought you would want it. The priest baptized him, too. There was time."

Although he was no longer a believer, an inexplicable peacefulness settled on him knowing his only son had been baptized, and was given the last rites, and his soul, if man had a soul, would be saved.

"What is—when was he born?"

"March 15."

He nodded. "The Ides of March."

They sat quietly until finally he asked, "Where is he buried?"

Detroit. He'd have to go back to Detroit when he swore there was no power on earth that could ever make him return to the place that had brought him so much agony.

"I had him cremated."

He nodded, relieved. "And his ashes?"

"They're here." She touched her chest. That's when Remi saw the bear claw for the first time, hanging from a gold chain and attached by a gold cap. "I had the claw hollowed out and some of the ashes put in."

"Oh, God," he said, half-choked.

She got up and moved to the secretary. She opened a drawer and took out a second claw. She walked back toward him, holding it out for him. "I had one made for you, too, in case you ever came back."

Remi took the dark brown curve of nail that had once nearly killed him, and now held a trace of the life that would never be, for a son he would never know. He clenched it tight in his hand. Then he wrapped his arms around her legs, pulling her to him, burying his face in her thighs so she wouldn't see, and he cried.

THEY WERE BOTH exhausted and fell asleep in each other's arms on the couch. Remi had no idea what time it was when he woke. He had no more emotional defenses left. They had all dissolved in the revelations of the past afternoon. As emotional as their reunion had been, he was surprised there were no nightmares to wake him. Instead he felt a heavy sadness, but a peacefulness, too, neither of which he could quite reconcile with the overwhelming urge to make love to her. It was as though all the images and discoveries and pain of the past six hours could be obliterated in the wash of passion. Perhaps it was nature's way of moving forward with the promise of new life, of spilling seed into a fertile womb, of granting a respite for an agitated mind. All he knew was that he had to have her; he had to come as close as a man could get to a woman.

Gently, he woke her.

"Where is your bedroom?"

IT WAS AFTER midnight when, famished, they raided the refrigerator. Sitting at her small table, chicken leg in hand, Remi asked, "How much can you see? The pinprick?"

"No, there's nothing, nothing at all." She wiped her fingers on the paper towel. "Remember the girl who was always late? I lost nearly everything right on schedule," she said with the slightest trace of bitterness.

"You don't seem blind," he said, then regretted it at once.

She smiled appreciatively. "That is such a nice thing to hear. I've worked incredibly hard to get here."

"Wouldn't it have been easier to stay home?"

She frowned. "So let me fill you in on the last three years."

He watched her pour the coffee into the mugs, stopping before it overflowed.

"How did you do that?" he asked, his voice full of awe.

"What?"

"Fill the cup without spilling the coffee?"

"Oh, the sound. It makes a different sound as it nears the top."

"You're blowing me away right now," he said in genuine admiration.

She smiled at the warmth of his praise. "So the last three years…"

"Let me get a sweater on first, you take the coffee to the living room—Can you do that?" he asked, again with a slap of awareness.

"Oh, I'm quite good in the apartment. As long as I use mugs and not cups and saucers." She smiled comfortably.

It was cool in the apartment, cool enough to warrant some

clothes, he noted. He pulled on a cashmere sweater and smiled. She'd like the feel of that. He grabbed the blanket from the bed as he left the room. He sat next to her on the couch. In just a few hours, they had found a way to sit as if they had spent years molding into each other.

"After the baby died," she began as Remi squeezed her hand, "I went into a dark depression. Up until then, I had only focused on my blindness and the baby, how I'd take care of him, what I needed to learn about being blind, and all that. But when there was no baby, my life just seemed empty. I refused to think about you. If you popped into my head, I'd just think about my sweet David instead. Dozens of times a day you tried to get in, but finally, slowly, you gave up and I started to know peace. Daddy and Mother were both wonderful. They were quieter, somehow, deeper. It's hard to explain. In the months I was away, something changed between them. They discovered they liked each other. No, more than liked, they fell in love again, I think. In some ways I was happy for them, but it also left me feeling terribly alone, like I had lost my father, too.

"Of course, Daddy was totally on my side, fueling my anger toward you. But as my anger drifted further away, I was struck with the degree of rancor he continued to hold on my behalf. I wanted him to lighten up. But he just went on and on about how you had betrayed us all."

Remi cleared his throat.

"After a while, even I could see how crazy he was sounding and I found myself defending you."

"I'm glad someone did." He smiled.

"One day, I was reading a quote by George Eliot, a piece about grief."

"How do you do that, read I mean?"

"Oh, on the computer. Everything's voice activated now. And

books on tape. Not Braille. I can feel a few things like elevator floors and room numbers, but I can't read it. But let me tell you the quote. I hope I can say it right. I think I can. Actually, there are two, one that helped me with you and one for little Davy. Okay, so here they both are." She sat straighter and looked ahead as if reciting a difficult passage to a large audience.

"First, the one for you." She cleared her throat. "*She was no longer wrestling with the grief, but could sit down with it as a lasting companion and make it a sharer in her thoughts.*"

"I like it." He paused. "You're lucky. I never got that far."

Deidre reached for his hand and squeezed. "Now for the one by Sascha, the one for our sweet baby.

"*As long as I can I will look at this world for both of us.*
As long as I can I will laugh with the birds,
I will sing with the flowers,
I will pray to the stars, for both of us."

A tear rolled down each cheek before she reached the end.

"That's what saved me. I had to go on. Maybe I couldn't see the world, but I could hear it, I could smell it, I could sing with the flowers. I had to do it for him. Does that make any kind of sense?"

"It makes perfect sense," he said, brushing his thumbs across her cheeks, then kissing the salt gathered on her lips. "Perfect sense."

They hugged for a few minutes in shared grief. So much that could have been. So many mistakes. But could something good come from it? Or was it too late? It seemed there was a possibility. Could they move from this sadness? Wasn't it worth a try, at least?

"What else would you like to know?"

"So tell me about Nanook," he said, nodding toward the wall.

"Who? Oh, the polar bear."

"How'd you manage that?"

"Well, you asked me for a claw and—"

"So you take the whole damn bear?"

Deidre laughed. "It wasn't easy getting just a claw." He tickled her, she screamed, so he made a game of it as she tried to squirm away. At last, she put enough distance between them to be safe.

"They can't sell the bear hide. So how did you do it?"

"They can't sell the claws, either. It took a bit of negotiating, but eventually the counsel of chiefs and I agreed the bear hide was a good trade for a new library building."

He reached for the bear's claw already hanging from the gold chain around his neck and stroked it. From the other end of the couch, he watched her do the same with hers.

"Come over here, you little horse trader."

"No tickling."

"No tickling. I just want to hold you."

She snuggled up under his outstretched arm. Again, it seemed as if she could see.

"Now, what other tall tales do you have for me?"

Deidre tucked the blanket around their feet before starting.

"One day, Bruce, the lawn guy—he called himself a gardener, but he just mowed the lawns—anyway, Bruce got fired. He was pretty angry. He was packing up his stuff in the potting shed when I stumbled in. He caught me—"

"—and accidentally brushed his hand across your breast," he finished.

"How did you know?" She grinned, then wiggled closer. "No. I don't think he's into girls. But that's beside the point. When he saw me, I guess he saw a chance to even the score with Father. He told me then, there in the potting shed, that right after I got home he overheard Father's call to someone asking him to make sure you never came back. Bruce heard 'Embassy' and 'Bangladesh,' but he didn't know much more than that. He said my father was one son of a bitch and he was glad to be leaving."

"So I was supposed to go to Bangladesh."

"I was livid. I confronted Father, but he swore he didn't know anything about you going to Asia. I went to Cassie, and she helped me find someone, a PI, to look for you. Not to bring you back or anything, just to know where you were."

"Oh, a little cyber stalking, was it?" he teased.

"But we couldn't find you."

"No, I was in Moscow."

"Moscow. Hmm," she said. "So at first, I believed him. Then I asked him to find you. I knew he could. He said he would. Then he said you had vanished. The more I thought about it, the more little slips he made, the more convinced I became that the lawn boy had told the truth.

"I went to Mother, and eventually she said enough that I knew it was true. He had lied to me. After everything I'd been through, his deception was unendurable. My father, the one person I thought I could trust above everyone else—oh, God, I thought I would suffocate if I stayed in that house. I had one goal, to get away from him, from the pain, from the memories, from everything.

"I had sold a few articles to the *New York Times*. I'm a writer now," she said, smiling with pride.

"I know. I read some of your stuff. You're good." He kissed her head.

"So I thought maybe I could support myself by writing. I had to get away, and it had to be on my terms. I applied for a full-time job. Years ago, there would have been scads of talented people vying for the same job, but today the newspaper business is a pariah. Everything is done online. And when the *Times* found out I was handicapped I got the edge over the few people who applied."

"And because you are exceptionally talented."

That pleased her.

"So right after that, Cassie and I flew to New York and found this apartment."

"And your father?"

"He was away on business. I was gone before he came back. At first, he was furious. I wouldn't give him my address. I suspect he knows it, though. He can find anyone. But so far he has honored my request to keep out of my life until I'm ready to see him again. I stood up at Cassie's wedding. He was there and we exchanged formal greetings, but beyond that I really haven't much to say to him."

"Dear, dear Deidre," he said, pulling her closer, "you really have lost everyone, haven't you."

"Not Cassie. And now I have Alan for a brother. And you know who else?"

"Who?"

"My mother. Somehow, during that whole summer I was away, she changed, or at least our relationship changed. She has become an ally. She supports me, encourages me. My father still thinks of me as a little girl that he can indulge or protect or control. But Mom seems to know how to help me be the best version of myself. It's almost like they've traded roles. I can't quite figure it out."

"My advice, don't overthink it."

They sat in comfortable silence, sipping coffee, touching gently, and listening to the harmony of the heartbeat they shared.

"Tell me about being blind," he said, lifting her hand to his lips.

"What do you want to know? What I can't do anymore? What I can do? The surprises?"

"Sure. Tell me about the surprises to start."

She snuggled in comfortably, pulling the blanket closer. "I was surprised by the small things. Remember, I had already feared not seeing my baby's face." She paused. "About that, seeing David's face. It really didn't matter in the end. It was the feel of him, the smell of him, his tiny fingers trying to grasp mine. That was enough."

Remi bent down and kissed her.

"But other surprises. Telling time. That was a big one. How many times do we look at a clock or a watch or the sun to know where we stand with the day? Like now, I'm not sure if it's the middle of the night or early morning. There is a church nearby. It chimes the hour, but not at night."

"It's nearly one. So what do you do?" He was quite curious.

"I have a special watch. I can unsnap the bezel and feel the hands. And here in the apartment I have the mantel clock."

She nodded toward the fireplace. He hadn't noticed the subtle chime of the quarter and half hours, but once in the night he thought he heard the long chime of a distant clock.

"During the day, part of my brain just stays tuned. And I know my radio stations. Every day, well, every weekday, I hear the orderly progression of programs so I'm cued in to the time."

"And besides," he teased, "being exactly on time isn't particularly important."

She punched him playfully. "No, no, no. I've changed. You taught me the importance of being punctual."

"You mean I did something right?" He bent to kiss her again.

"A few things."

The kisses were becoming longer.

"What else. Oh, I can't use a smartphone. I've regressed to the old flip phone, but Cassie tells me there used to be a smartphone with an actual keypad, so we're going to check it out. If they make one that has a keypad and is voice activated, I'll probably trade in my flip."

"I'm blown away with how well you're managing."

"I've had time to practice. Inside the apartment, I'm fine. But I still don't do well on the street. And it's impossible to flag down a cab. They won't stop."

"What do you mean, they won't stop?"

"They see someone handicapped and they won't stop."

"They have to. It's the law."

"Yeah, well."

"So turn them in."

"So tell me how the blind girl is supposed to turn in the cab driver that she can't see who won't stop?"

That will change, he decided, but merely said, "I see," then, "Oh, damn. Sorry. God!"

Deidre laughed, then said seriously, "Are you going to be with me?"

Hesitation, that old habit, started to stall his answer, but the passion of their lovemaking quieted the panic. "Yes."

"Then you're going to have to be okay with being with a blind girl."

"Are you okay with being with a sometimes crazy ex-Marine?"

"Are you okay with ignoring the family fortune?"

"Are you okay that I'm old?"

"I'm blind, remember? I can't see your wrinkles. Do you have wrinkles?"

"Gray hair. Lots of gray hair."

She straddled his lap and brushed back his hair, looking for all the world like she could see him.

"Very thoughtful of you to wait until the brown-haired version of you was sealed in my memory before you turned gray." Then, she said, "I smell purple. Why do I smell purple?"

He lifted her off him and got up. He walked to the foyer where the abandoned bouquet lay wilting on the side table. Sheepishly, he brought it back to her and smiled as she buried her face in the fragrance.

"You found lavender," she sighed.

"Found it in some shop on my way here."

"You didn't just *find* it," she said, inhaling the lavender again. "Not in December."

"Sure I did."

She smiled at him, and he could swear she saw him.

"That's like 'climbing a mountain because she's worth it'."

"I might even walk to the next village for her," he said.

"Newark to Harlem—how long would that take?"

Remi groaned. "Are you going to challenge me to do that, too? I will, but—"

She pulled him down to kiss him. "No, my dear gladiator, the lavender is just fine."

"Well if that's all it takes, dear damsel, this gladiator thinks you've earned some serious seducing."

Through her smile, she said, "You're mixing your metaphors again."

He scooped her up, and with her arms around his neck he said, "Glad you're going to be around to improve my grammar, and, by the way, first person singular, present tense, I love you."

* * * * *

NOTES

REMI INSISTED THE author attach Deidre's completed and revised version of her Egyptian article. It was necessary to comply. You, the reader, may have observed how persuasive he can be at times...

Why Travel?

By Deidre Sinclair

Too often, people who don't travel ask of us travelers, "Why travel?" They point out the advantages of modern media, photos, movies, the Internet. Can't more be learned by spending the time researching a place? Certainly it is much easier and cheaper. Have travelers missed the boat, figuratively speaking? Emphatically I shout out, "NO."

Travel is difficult. And sometimes expensive. And sometimes disappointing. Travel has many things in common with living a life. We, those of us who journey, travel for a variety of reasons, and those reasons may change as we grow. First, perhaps we are drawn to the beauty, to the art, to the architecture of civilizations before us. The sumptuous, the extravagant, the workmanship, the creativity is overwhelming. Yes, we could see it in a book. But until we stand before the Basilica San Marco in Venice with the sun glimmering on the golden mosaics, each set at a different angle—because if set smooth it would be impossible to view, like seeing the sun in a mirror—only then can we experience deep within us the genius of the architect and the artists, and the wealth of this city before the discovery of the Americas. Until we stand next to one of the stones of the Great Pyramid, seeing the incredible bulk of just one massive rock, feeling the perspiration run down our back in the incredible heat though it is still early morning, wondering how long our water will last—only then, in the blinding sun bouncing off blinding sand, can we understand that there was a civilization five millennia ago that envisioned and accomplished something so outrageously impossible that we are humbled by their superior determination and abilities. Only when we walk down the main hall of Florence's Academia toward Michelangelo's David do we experience his many other works, each arranged in a progressive state of completion and giving one the feeling of giants struggling to emerge from the marble in which they are caught. For these Titans of stone, Michelangelo was their singular hope of escape. They are sad creatures, only half free, but still, they are half free. It sets the imagination wondering who or what is entrapped in other towers of marble, and who is the next Michelangelo to rescue these poor beings so desperately longing to burst forth.

Or are we all entrapped within ourselves to some extent? And thus a new philosophical idea emerges.

Could I get this sense from a book, from a photo, or from a descriptive passage? Could a reader of this feel what the traveler feels upon stumbling across these struggling giants? No, he or she could not. Because this is what I, the author, feel. Millions of people pass through the gallery annually, and I guarantee they do not all share this experience. Perhaps their eyes are focused exclusively on the David at the end of the hall. Or perhaps they take in things I have totally missed. The engineer studies the transport cart that brought the David into the gallery and wonders how the wood supported the weight and what calculations were needed to ensure its safety. The sculptor looks at the detail of technique, perhaps, envisions how the tools were used, is surprised that we still use the same instruments hundreds of years later—or do we? Each individual brings his or her unique interests or questions or perspective, filters out stimulation that is unintelligible and focuses on that which has specific meaning. How can you trust the author of some journal to bring all the possibilities, unbiased, unfiltered, for you to create your own impression? You cannot. You must make the trip and see with your own life and make your unique application.

So that is probably the first lure of travel. Eventually, if one is fortunate to travel as much as I have, there is a saturation point and one moves on. He begins to look beyond the beauty and the awe-inspiring wonder of the object and toward the broader picture. Travelers eventually become curious about the people, the culture, the underpinnings of the society. How do they make it all work? How do they solve the problem of living? We might discover how efficient or practical something is and wonder how to incorporate it into our society. Then we are stumped, because it won't work in our society the way we have things set up. For example, isn't it nice to live over your shop, have the family nearby to help when things get busy, and have your home nearby when things are slow? You save on gas and time and get to know your neighbors, and there is a greater sense of community and belonging. This is the norm for a small Italian villager. Within the fabric of his own culture, it makes sense. Within corporate America, it can't. But perhaps there is a niche somewhere. Possibly the entrepreneur who is working out of her home? Is it similar? You begin to make comparisons, pros and cons. Learning from the Italians, you take things that might make the American entrepreneur more successful. You twist it and turn it and tweak it and make it American. Your travels now help you become an amateur sociologist or anthropologist. Can you read about it? Yes, but then it's someone else's discovery, not your own. It's the difference between reading the name list of people who are receiving diplomas and receiving one yourself. One takes no effort and has little meaning. The other comes at high cost and is greatly valued.

And that is the final point I'd like to make. Travel is work at the *least, expensive, most likely, and sometimes dangerous either physically or emotionally. In any case there is investment, but only through investment and risk can you experience the thrill and value the outcome in a truly meaningful way. I can read about how someone feels when high on a drug, but in no way do I deceive myself into believing that I can have that same experience, that same understanding, without actually using the drug myself. The comparison holds true for someone who has experienced the death of a child, or the horrors of war, or the fears of the aged. Until we are there in person, the experience is only cerebral. It misses the gut altogether. I am certain that "Saving Private Ryan" had the deepest impact in men who were there at the landing of Normandy. There is another level of response for men who saw battle in Europe. And still a lesser response from men who didn't see battle but lived during the time, and on and on, each response more diluted than the one before until we reach the baby boomer viewer, who thinks he now knows something about this event. But all he knows is what the movie director tried to convey, a reality belonging to someone else, and a reality of mind, not spirit and not soul. Without the investment, everything you know about a place is someone else's diluted reality. I simply have enough knowledge about people to know that they don't see things exactly as I do. They filter and process the stimuli through their particular combination of interests and learning and life experience, and apply their unique brand of reality to produce a biased view, just as I do. Only when it's my interests and my learning and my experience that is doing the filtration can it become my reality, my investment, and my growth. It becomes yet another launching pad for the next experience, more complete, better understood, better prepared. And, one day, in amazement, we realize how much we understand about the world, about people, and, finally, about ourselves.*

ADDITIONAL NOTES

Deidre wanted to get her two cents in, too.
She invites you to view Remi's photos of their travels on:
http://LaFortunePoeticImages.weebly.com

AND ONE FINAL NOTE

Please consider donating
To organizations that provide Companion dogs
To combat veterans suffering from PTSD
And for Service dogs for the visually impaired.
These are remarkable animals that greatly enhance the quality of life
For those lucky enough to have one.
Thank you for your support.

About the Author

WHEN LANA WAS eleven, two things occurred that would impact the rest of her life. First, she decided she wanted to write novels. But what did an 11-year old from the Detroit suburbs have to write about? Second, an ophthalmologist told her that an inherited eye disease could result in permanent blindness at any time. With those two influences she decided on a course of action that would become engrained in her personality: to see, to experience, to remember, and to understand as much of life as she could.

In 1986 with a Masters degree in Social Work she began serving the military community in Vicenza, Italy. Europe was a visual paradise. By accident more than design, she was able to combine three loves: travel, photography, and writing. And so it began… For more about the author and a visual tour of her travels visit LaFortunePoeticImages.weebly.com.

CONNECT WITH LANA LAFORTUNE

Friend me on Facebook:
Lana.LaFortune@facebook.com

Follow the progress of future projects
And enjoy photos of my travels on my Website:
http://LafortunePoeticImages.weebly.com

BOOK CLUB DISCUSSION QUESTIONS

Remi has PTSD. What are his symptoms? Do they change over time?

Deidre attempts to help Remi with his nightmares. What does she do wrong? What does she does she do right?

Four characters have or acquire a major handicap. Discuss how each copes and whether their coping mechanisms are effective?

Was Remi justified in his attack on Jerry? What insights did he acquire about the nature of their relationship as he traveled with Deidre?

How does the relationship between Deidre and her mother change? What contributes to that change?

What subliminal message did Remi miss in the sapphire dream?

Remi and Deidre had a running conversation about God. They came up with more questions than answers. Discuss the Existential notion of the Absurd that basically suggests random things happen to random people at random times, i.e. bad things happen to good people. Could Remi's professed atheism be bravado?

What significance does the title, "The Scent of Color" acquire by the end of the novel? What other smells were highlighted?

Travel to the various countries was the vehicle to carry the story along. Which countries were most challenging or enjoyable for Remi? for Deidre? Where would you like to travel, and why?